Sleepless

VOLUME 2

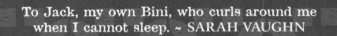

To Jack, my own Bini, who curls around me
when I cannot sleep. ~ SARAH VAUGHN

To Chester Parks, my Helioscope studiomates, and
my family, for the time they spend with me and
the wisdom they share. ~ LEILA DEL DUCA

IMAGE COMICS, INC. Robert Kirkman: Chief Operating Officer ~ Erik Larsen: Chief Financial Officer ~ Todd McFarlane: President ~ Marc Silvestri: Chief Executive Officer ~ Jim Valentino: Vice President ~ Eric Stephenson: Publisher / Chief Creative Officer ~ Corey Hart: Director of Sales ~ Jeff Boison: Director of Publishing Planning & Book Trade Sales Chris Ross: Director of Digital Sales ~ Jeff Stang: Director of Specialty Sales ~ Kat Salazar: Director of PR & Marketing Drew Gill: Art Director ~ Heather Doornink: Production Director ~ Nicole Lapalme: Controller ~ IMAGECOMICS.COM

Sleepless

VOLUME 2

SARAH VAUGHN .... writer

LEILA DEL DUCA .... artist

ALISSA SALLAH .... editor & colors

DERON BENNETT .... letters

GABE FISCHER .... color flats

SHANNA MATUSZAK .... production

CHAPTER SEVEN

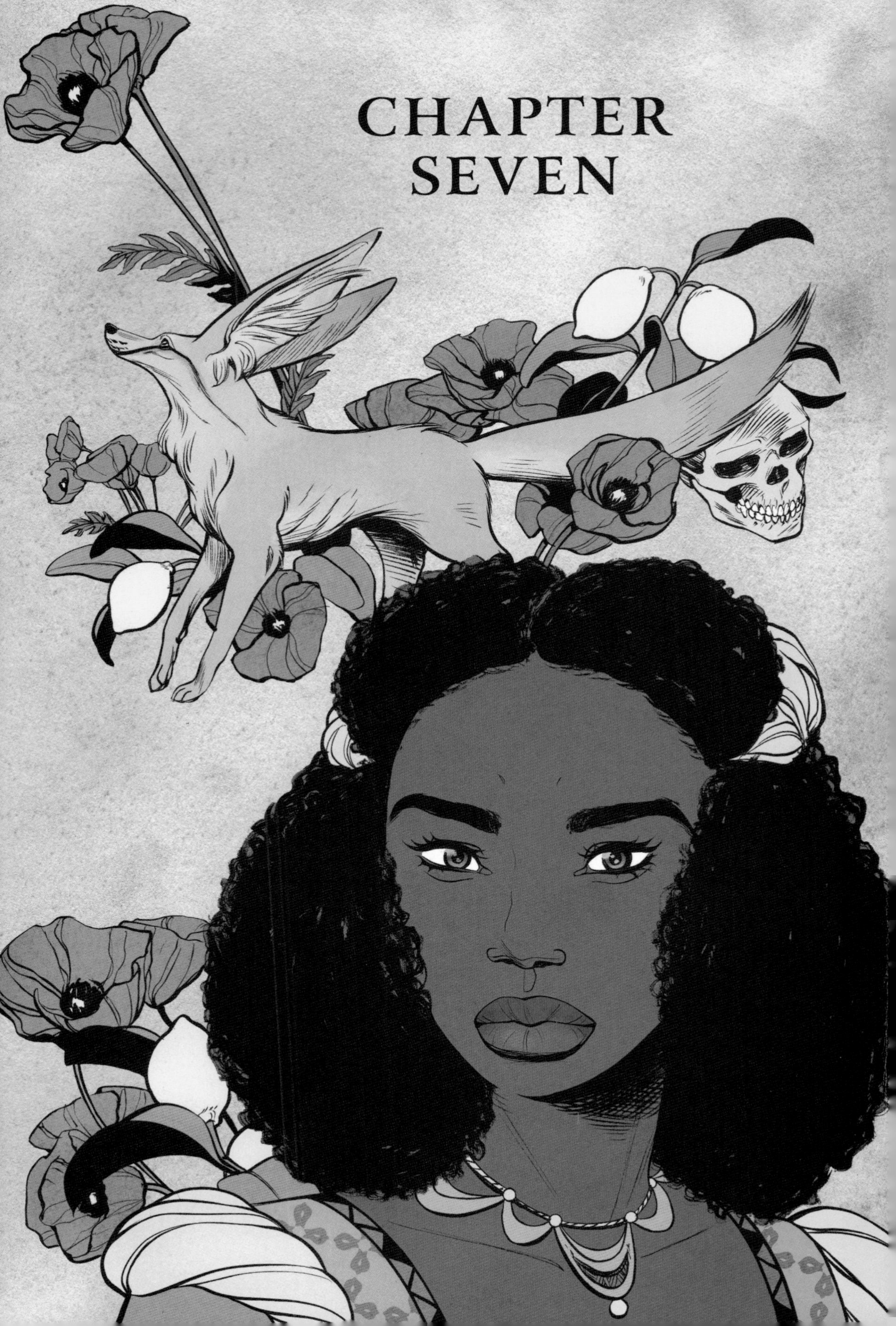

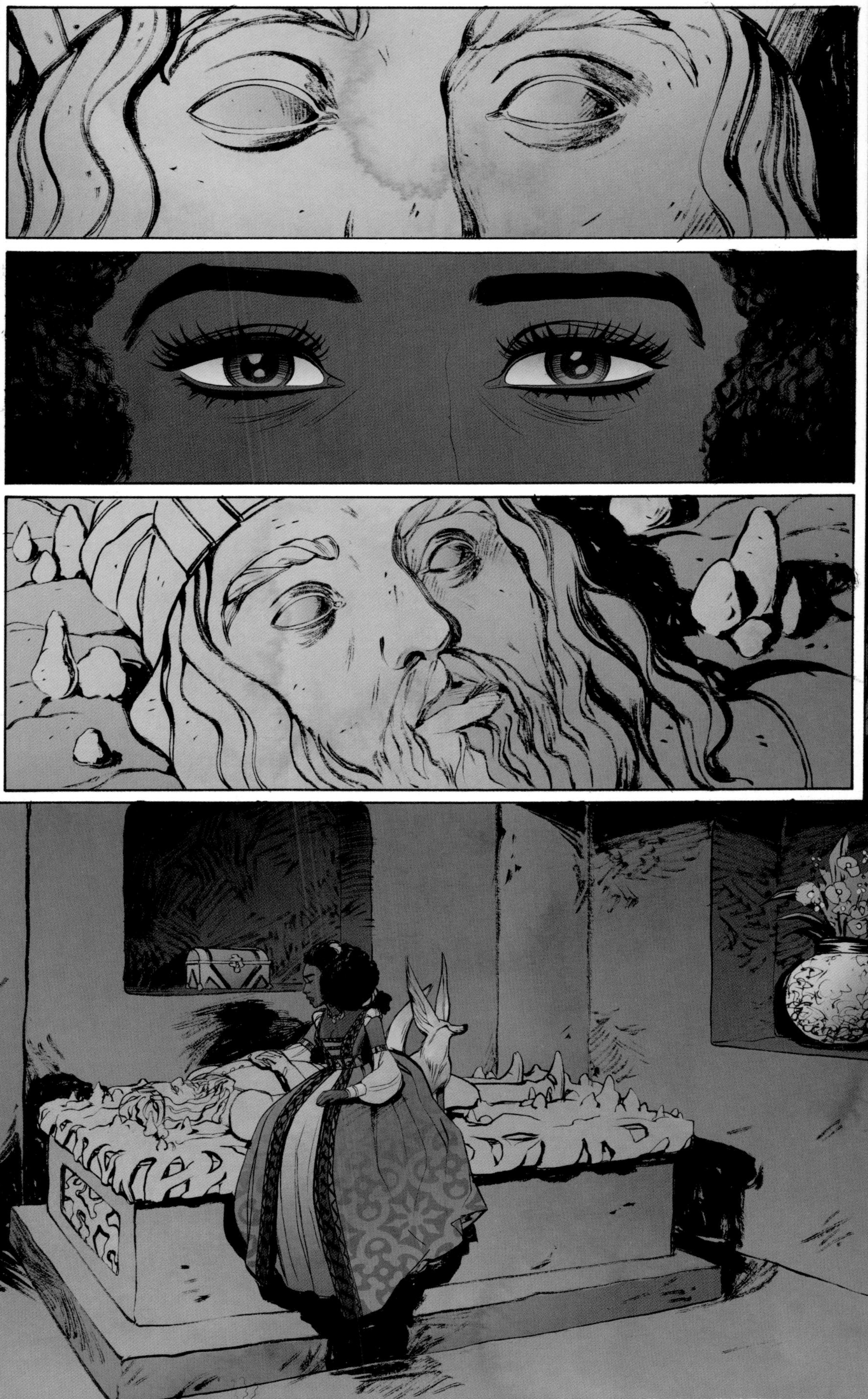

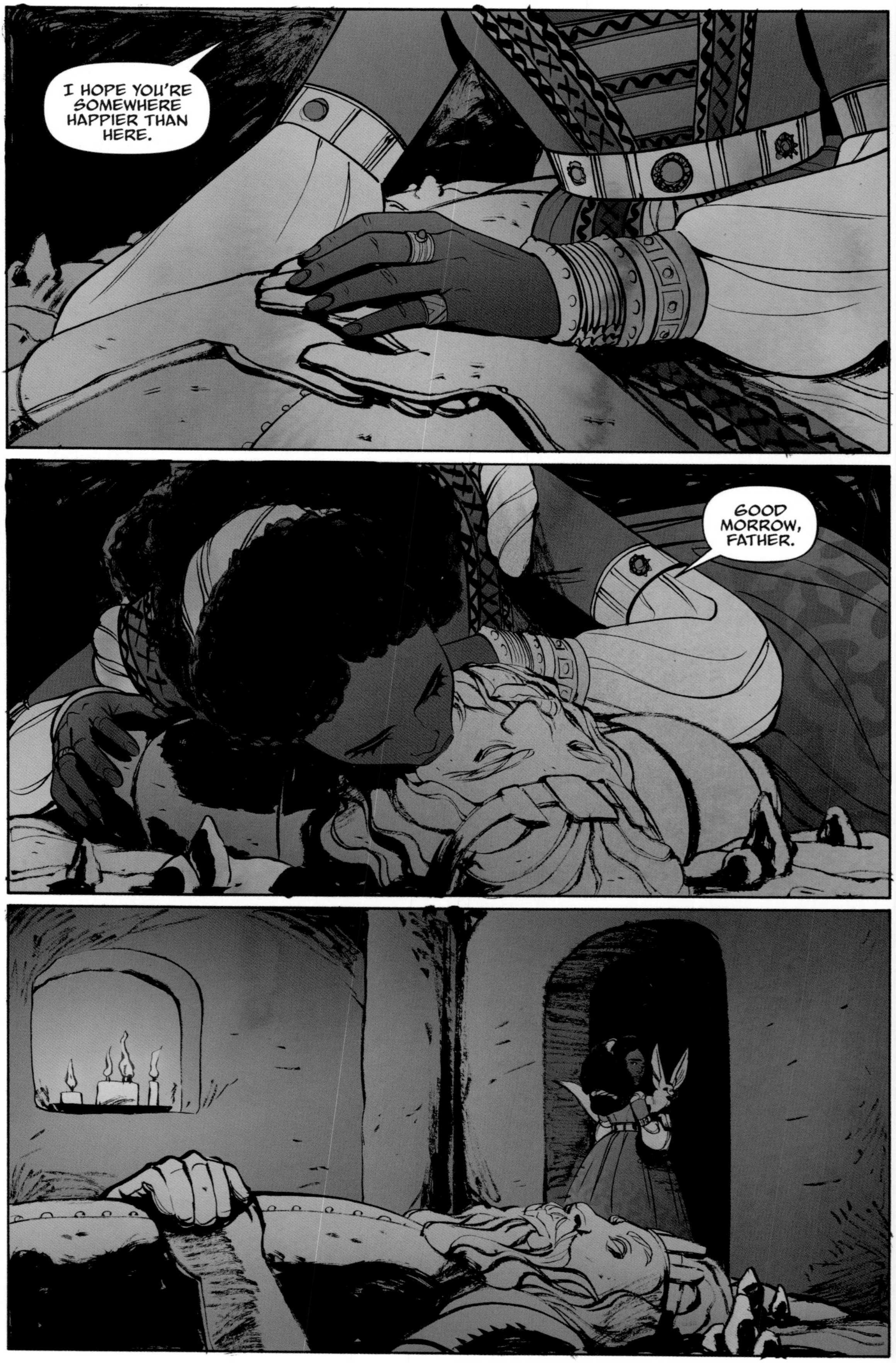

I HOPE YOU'RE SOMEWHERE HAPPIER THAN HERE.
GOOD MORROW, FATHER.

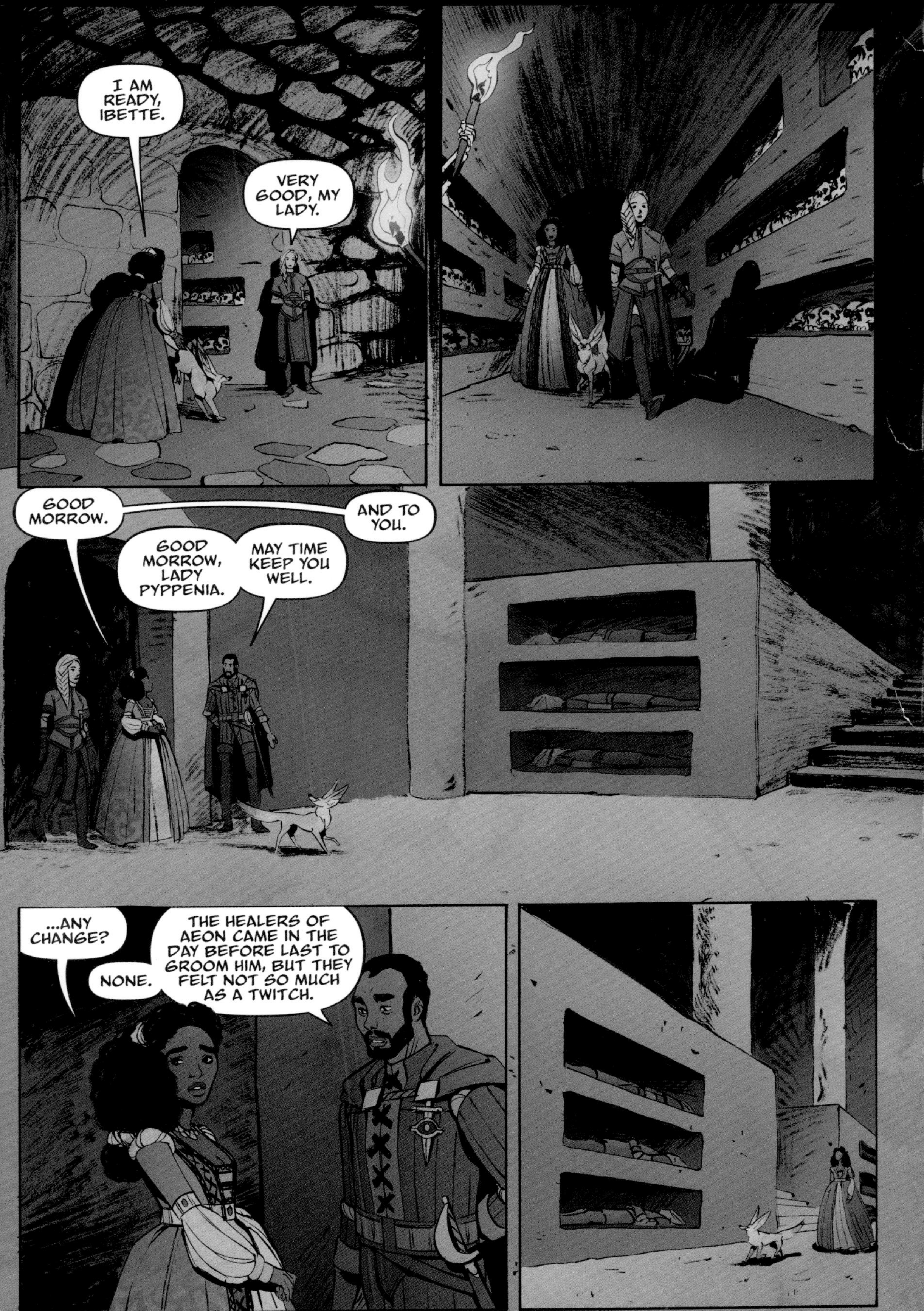
I AM READY, IBETTE.
VERY GOOD, MY LADY.
GOOD MORROW.
AND TO YOU.
GOOD MORROW, LADY PYPPENIA.
MAY TIME KEEP YOU WELL.
...ANY CHANGE?
NONE.
THE HEALERS OF AEON CAME IN THE DAY BEFORE LAST TO GROOM HIM, BUT THEY FELT NOT SO MUCH AS A TWITCH.

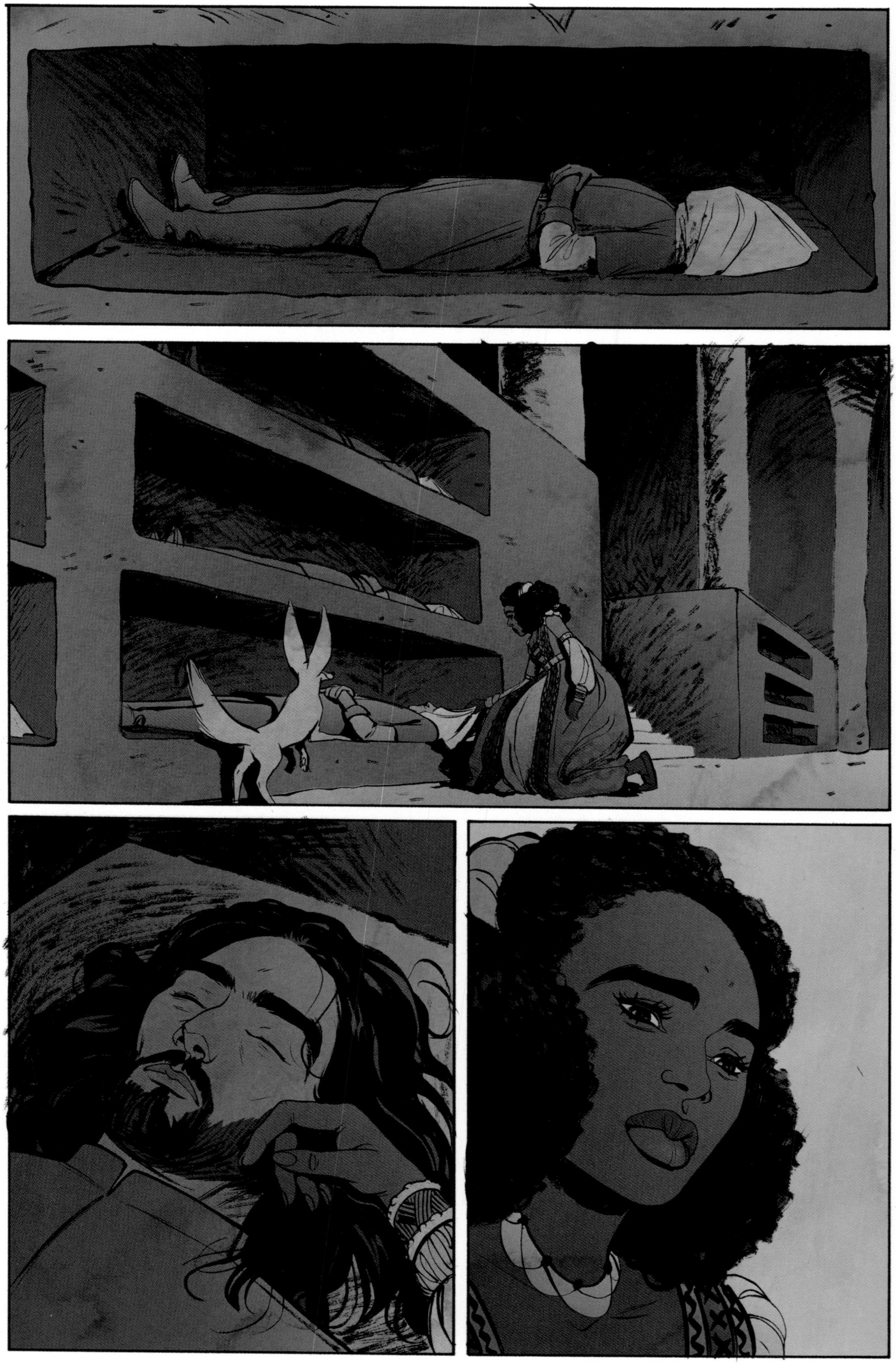

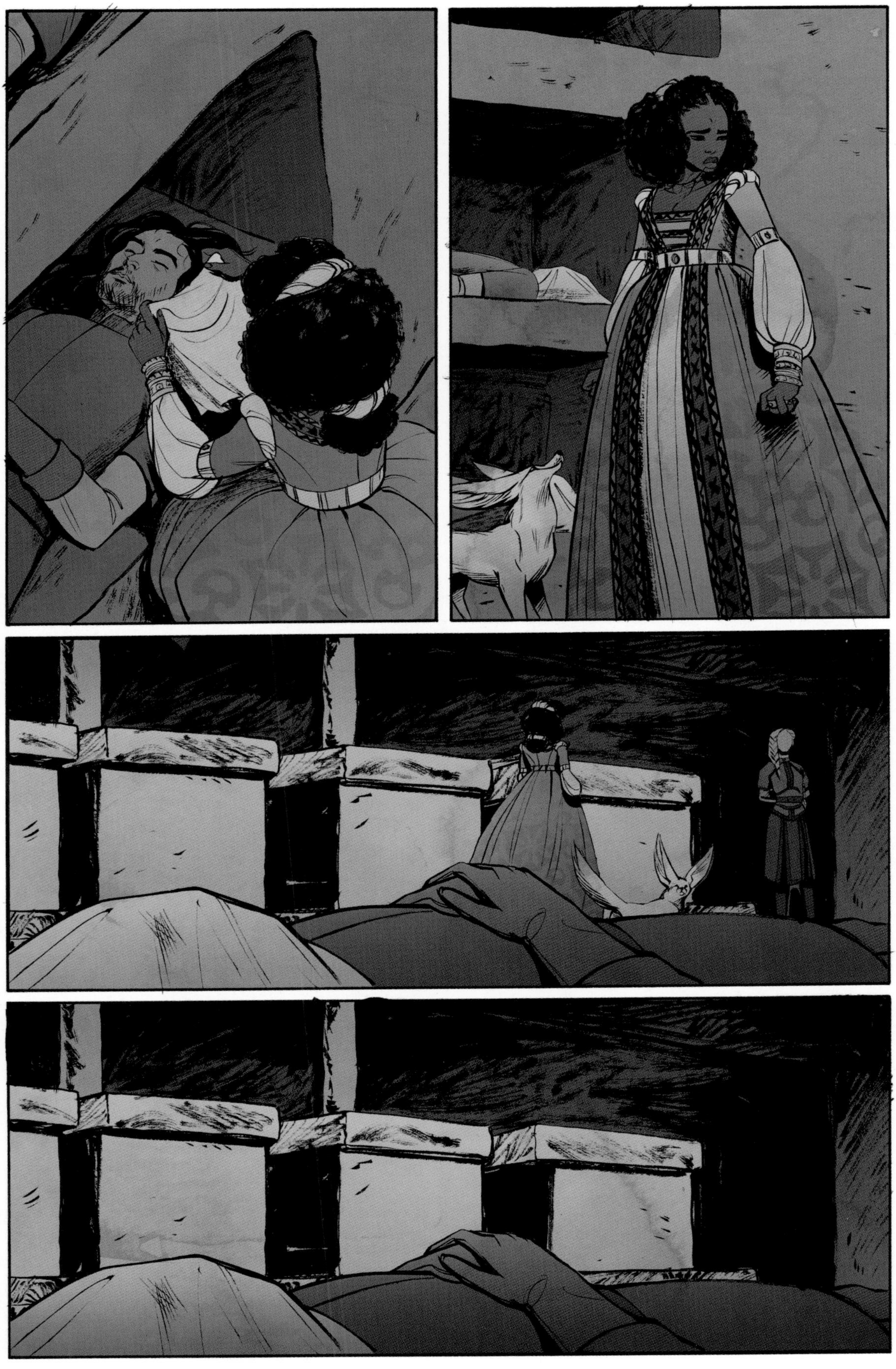

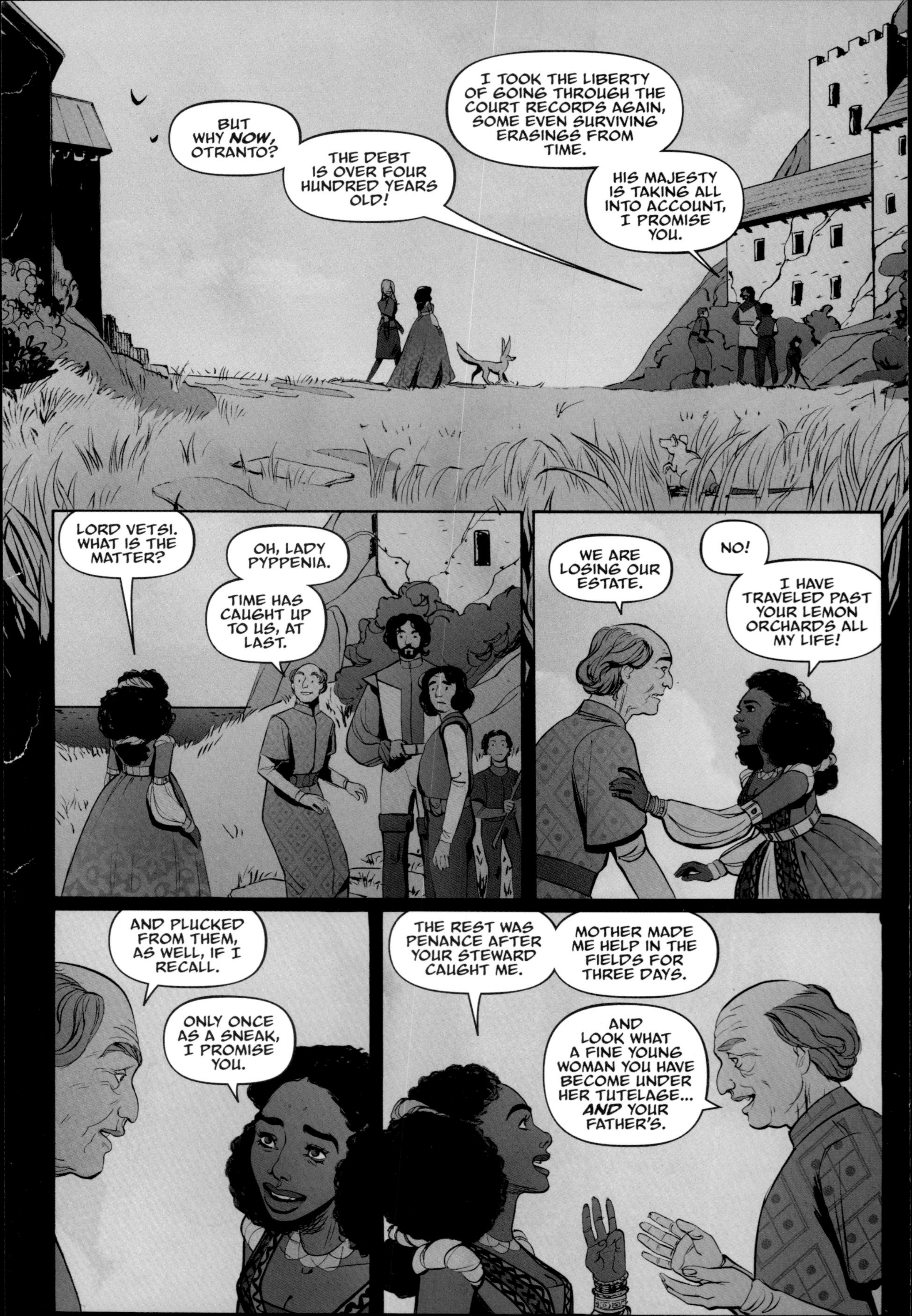
BUT WHY *NOW*, OTRANTO?
THE DEBT IS OVER FOUR HUNDRED YEARS OLD!
I TOOK THE LIBERTY OF GOING THROUGH THE COURT RECORDS AGAIN, SOME EVEN SURVIVING ERASINGS FROM TIME.
HIS MAJESTY IS TAKING ALL INTO ACCOUNT, I PROMISE YOU.
LORD VETSI. WHAT IS THE MATTER?
OH, LADY PYPPENIA.
TIME HAS CAUGHT UP TO US, AT LAST.
WE ARE LOSING OUR ESTATE.
NO!
I HAVE TRAVELED PAST YOUR LEMON ORCHARDS ALL MY LIFE!
AND PLUCKED FROM THEM, AS WELL, IF I RECALL.
ONLY ONCE AS A SNEAK, I PROMISE YOU.
THE REST WAS PENANCE AFTER YOUR STEWARD CAUGHT ME.
MOTHER MADE ME HELP IN THE FIELDS FOR THREE DAYS.
AND LOOK WHAT A FINE YOUNG WOMAN YOU HAVE BECOME UNDER HER TUTELAGE... *AND* YOUR FATHER'S.

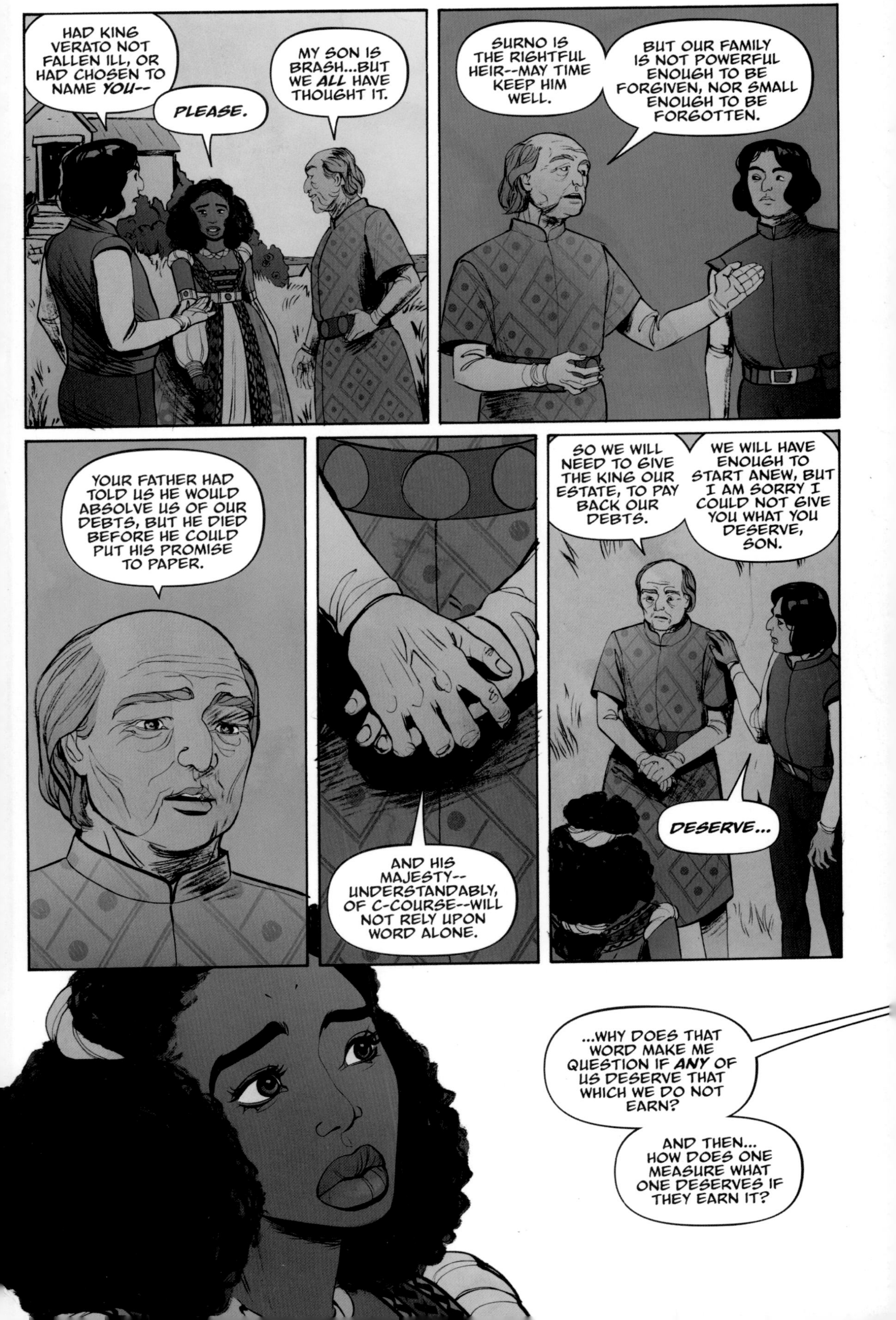
HAD KING VERATO NOT FALLEN ILL, OR HAD CHOSEN TO NAME *YOU*--
PLEASE.
MY SON IS BRASH...BUT WE *ALL* HAVE THOUGHT IT.
SURNO IS THE RIGHTFUL HEIR--MAY TIME KEEP HIM WELL.
BUT OUR FAMILY IS NOT POWERFUL ENOUGH TO BE FORGIVEN, NOR SMALL ENOUGH TO BE FORGOTTEN.
YOUR FATHER HAD TOLD US HE WOULD ABSOLVE US OF OUR DEBTS, BUT HE DIED BEFORE HE COULD PUT HIS PROMISE TO PAPER.
AND HIS MAJESTY--UNDERSTANDABLY, OF C-COURSE--WILL NOT RELY UPON WORD ALONE.
SO WE WILL NEED TO GIVE THE KING OUR ESTATE, TO PAY BACK OUR DEBTS.
WE WILL HAVE ENOUGH TO START ANEW, BUT I AM SORRY I COULD NOT GIVE YOU WHAT YOU DESERVE, SON.
DESERVE...
...WHY DOES THAT WORD MAKE ME QUESTION IF *ANY* OF US DESERVE THAT WHICH WE DO NOT EARN?
AND THEN... HOW DOES ONE MEASURE WHAT ONE DESERVES IF THEY EARN IT?

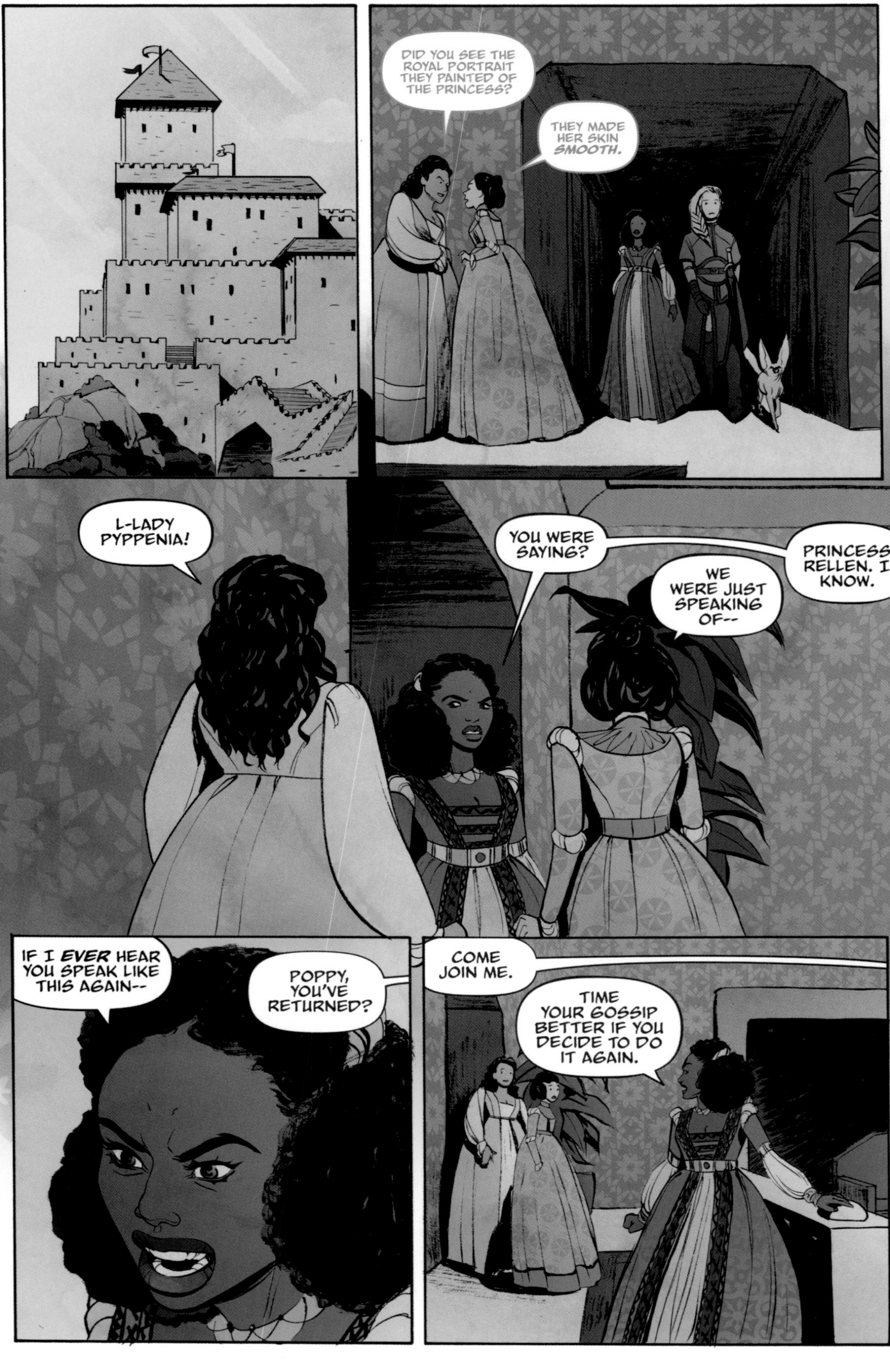
DID YOU SEE THE ROYAL PORTRAIT THEY PAINTED OF THE PRINCESS?
THEY MADE HER SKIN *SMOOTH.*
L-LADY PYPPENIA!
YOU WERE SAYING?
WE WERE JUST SPEAKING OF--
PRINCESS RELLEN. I KNOW.
IF I *EVER* HEAR YOU SPEAK LIKE THIS AGAIN--
POPPY, YOU'VE RETURNED?
COME JOIN ME.
TIME YOUR GOSSIP BETTER IF YOU DECIDE TO DO IT AGAIN.

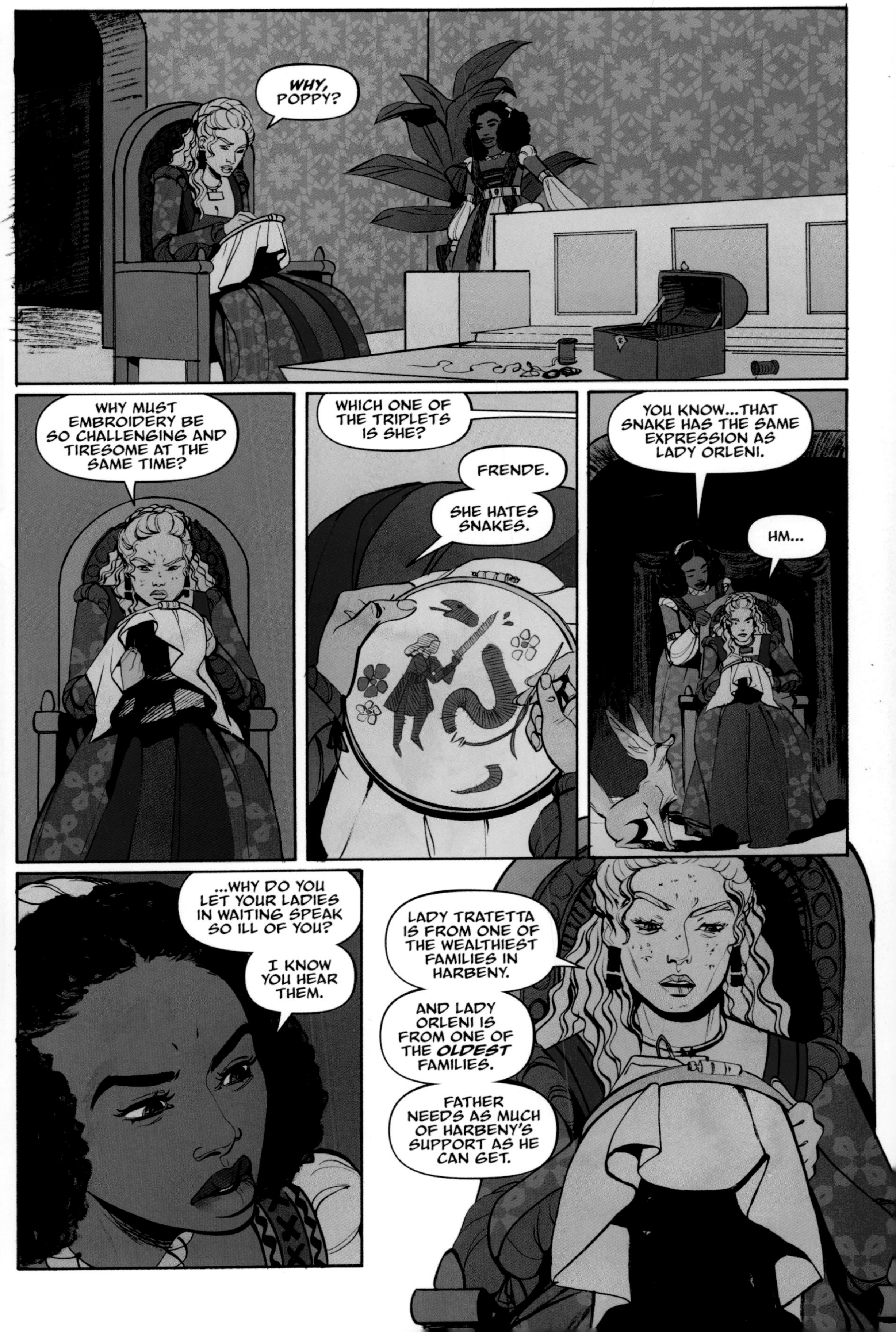
WHY, POPPY?
WHY MUST EMBROIDERY BE SO CHALLENGING AND TIRESOME AT THE SAME TIME?
WHICH ONE OF THE TRIPLETS IS SHE?
FRENDE.
SHE HATES SNAKES.
YOU KNOW...THAT SNAKE HAS THE SAME EXPRESSION AS LADY ORLENI.
HM...
...WHY DO YOU LET YOUR LADIES IN WAITING SPEAK SO ILL OF YOU?
I KNOW YOU HEAR THEM.
LADY TRATETTA IS FROM ONE OF THE WEALTHIEST FAMILIES IN HARBENY.
AND LADY ORLENI IS FROM ONE OF THE OLDEST FAMILIES.
FATHER NEEDS AS MUCH OF HARBENY'S SUPPORT AS HE CAN GET.

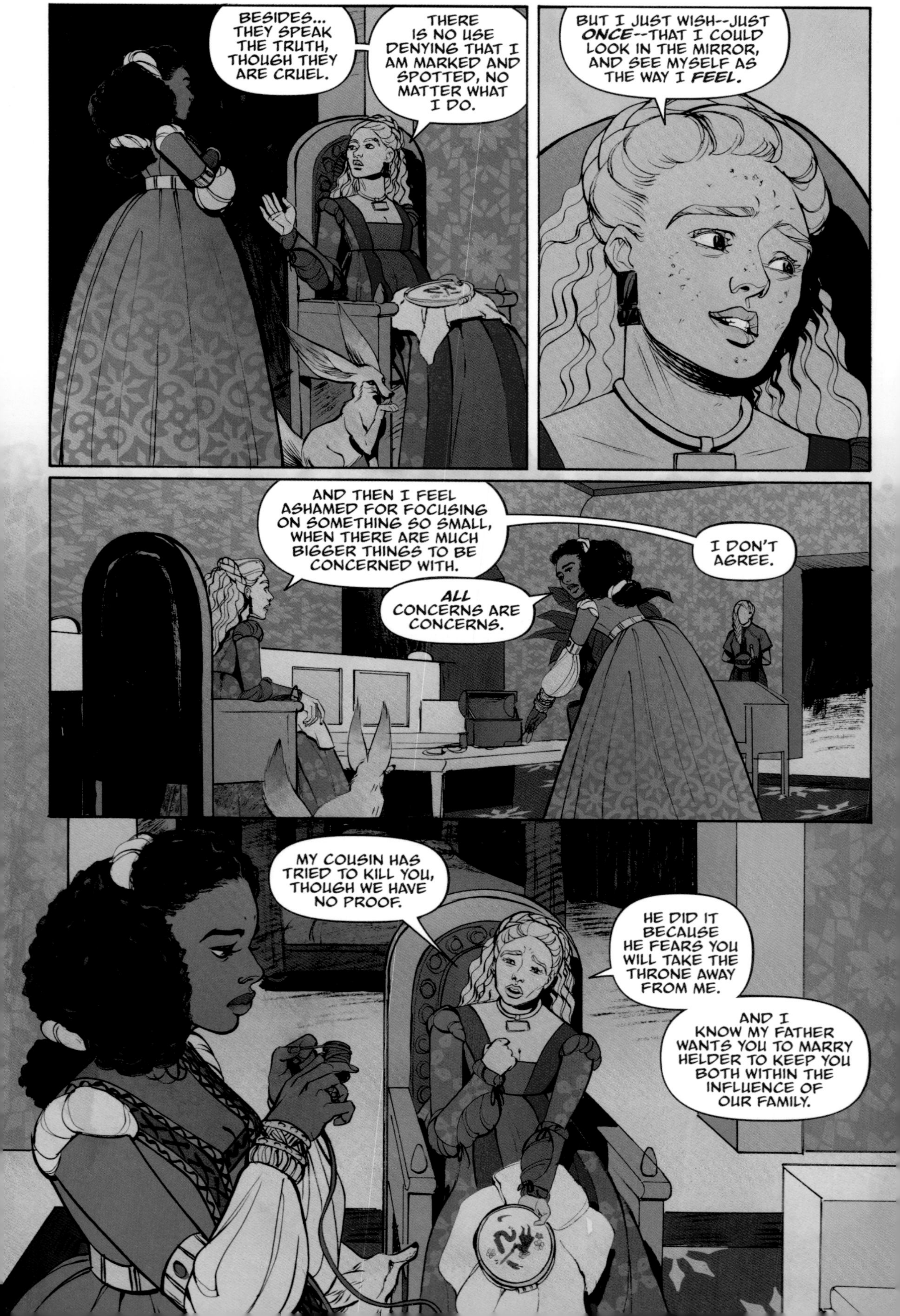
BESIDES... THEY SPEAK THE TRUTH, THOUGH THEY ARE CRUEL.
THERE IS NO USE DENYING THAT I AM MARKED AND SPOTTED, NO MATTER WHAT I DO.
BUT I JUST WISH--JUST *ONCE*--THAT I COULD LOOK IN THE MIRROR, AND SEE MYSELF AS THE WAY I *FEEL.*
AND THEN I FEEL ASHAMED FOR FOCUSING ON SOMETHING SO SMALL, WHEN THERE ARE MUCH BIGGER THINGS TO BE CONCERNED WITH.
I DON'T AGREE.
ALL CONCERNS ARE CONCERNS.
MY COUSIN HAS TRIED TO KILL YOU, THOUGH WE HAVE NO PROOF.
HE DID IT BECAUSE HE FEARS YOU WILL TAKE THE THRONE AWAY FROM ME.
AND I KNOW MY FATHER WANTS YOU TO MARRY HELDER TO KEEP YOU BOTH WITHIN THE INFLUENCE OF OUR FAMILY.

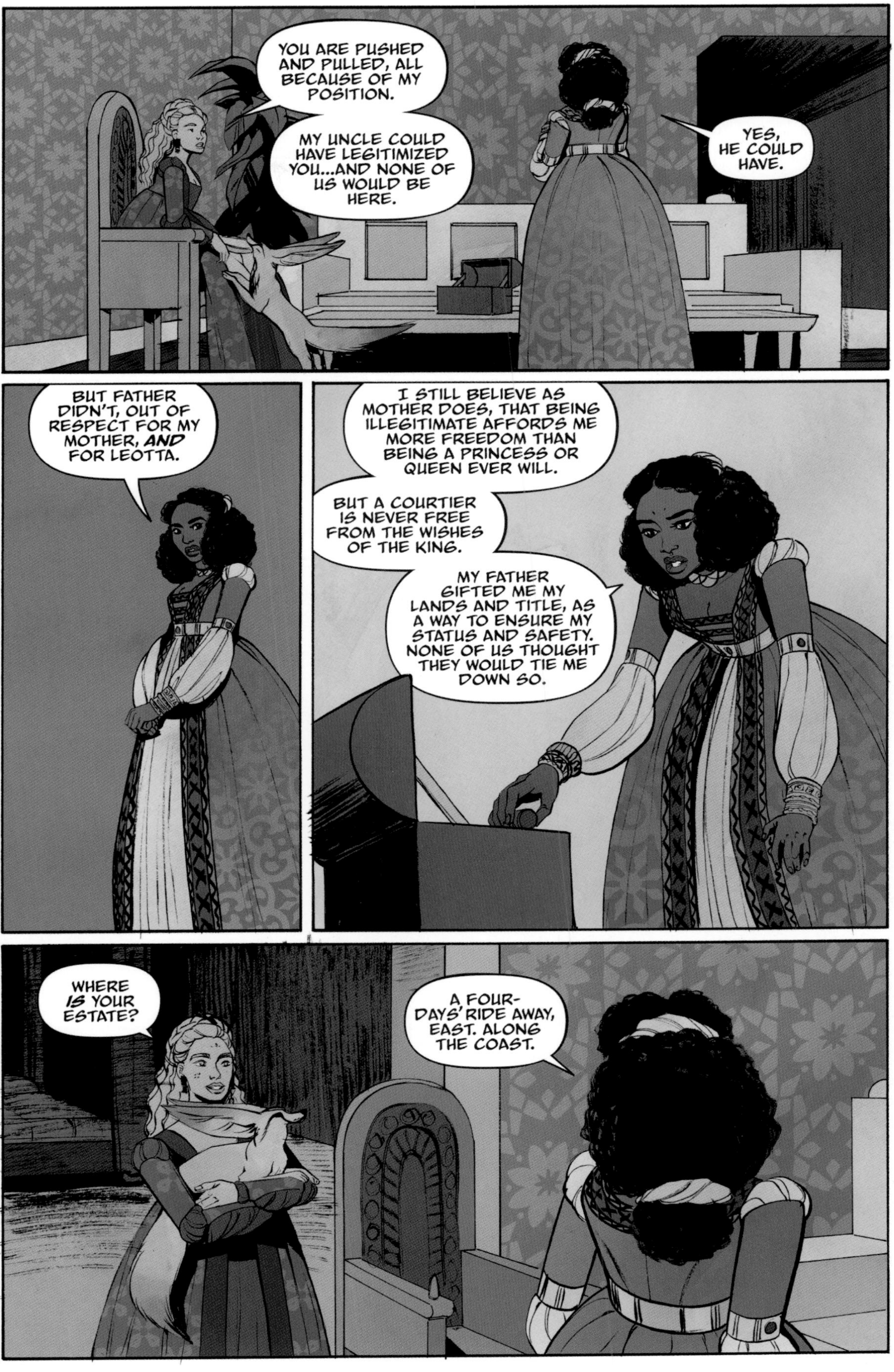
YOU ARE PUSHED AND PULLED, ALL BECAUSE OF MY POSITION.
MY UNCLE COULD HAVE LEGITIMIZED YOU...AND NONE OF US WOULD BE HERE.
YES, HE COULD HAVE.
BUT FATHER DIDN'T, OUT OF RESPECT FOR MY MOTHER, *AND* FOR LEOTTA.
I STILL BELIEVE AS MOTHER DOES, THAT BEING ILLEGITIMATE AFFORDS ME MORE FREEDOM THAN BEING A PRINCESS OR QUEEN EVER WILL.
BUT A COURTIER IS NEVER FREE FROM THE WISHES OF THE KING.
MY FATHER GIFTED ME MY LANDS AND TITLE, AS A WAY TO ENSURE MY STATUS AND SAFETY. NONE OF US THOUGHT THEY WOULD TIE ME DOWN SO.
WHERE *IS* YOUR ESTATE?
A FOUR-DAYS' RIDE AWAY, EAST. ALONG THE COAST.

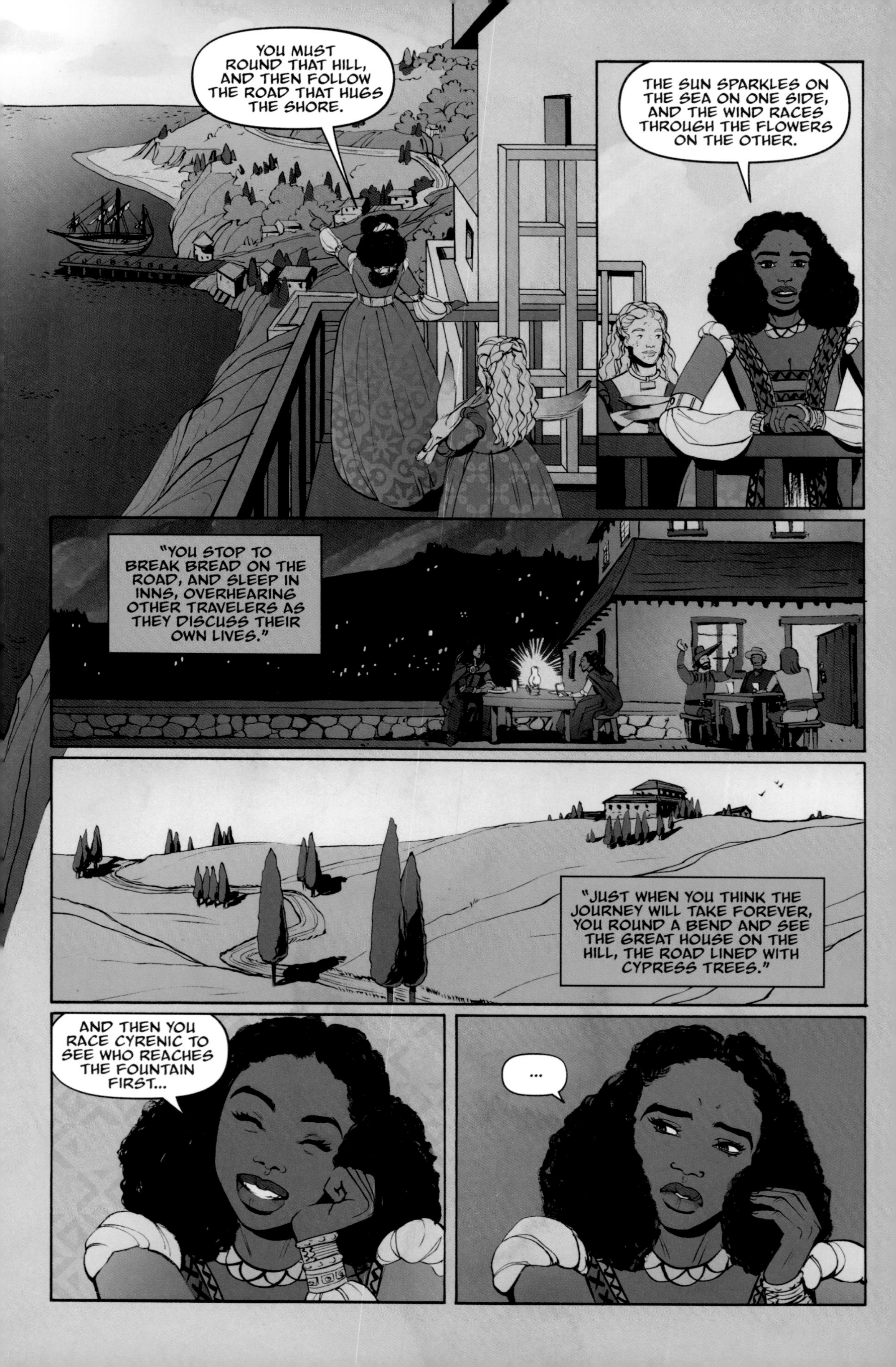

YOU MUST ROUND THAT HILL, AND THEN FOLLOW THE ROAD THAT HUGS THE SHORE.
THE SUN SPARKLES ON THE SEA ON ONE SIDE, AND THE WIND RACES THROUGH THE FLOWERS ON THE OTHER.
"YOU STOP TO BREAK BREAD ON THE ROAD, AND SLEEP IN INNS, OVERHEARING OTHER TRAVELERS AS THEY DISCUSS THEIR OWN LIVES."
"JUST WHEN YOU THINK THE JOURNEY WILL TAKE FOREVER, YOU ROUND A BEND AND SEE THE GREAT HOUSE ON THE HILL, THE ROAD LINED WITH CYPRESS TREES."
AND THEN YOU RACE CYRENIC TO SEE WHO REACHES THE FOUNTAIN FIRST...
...

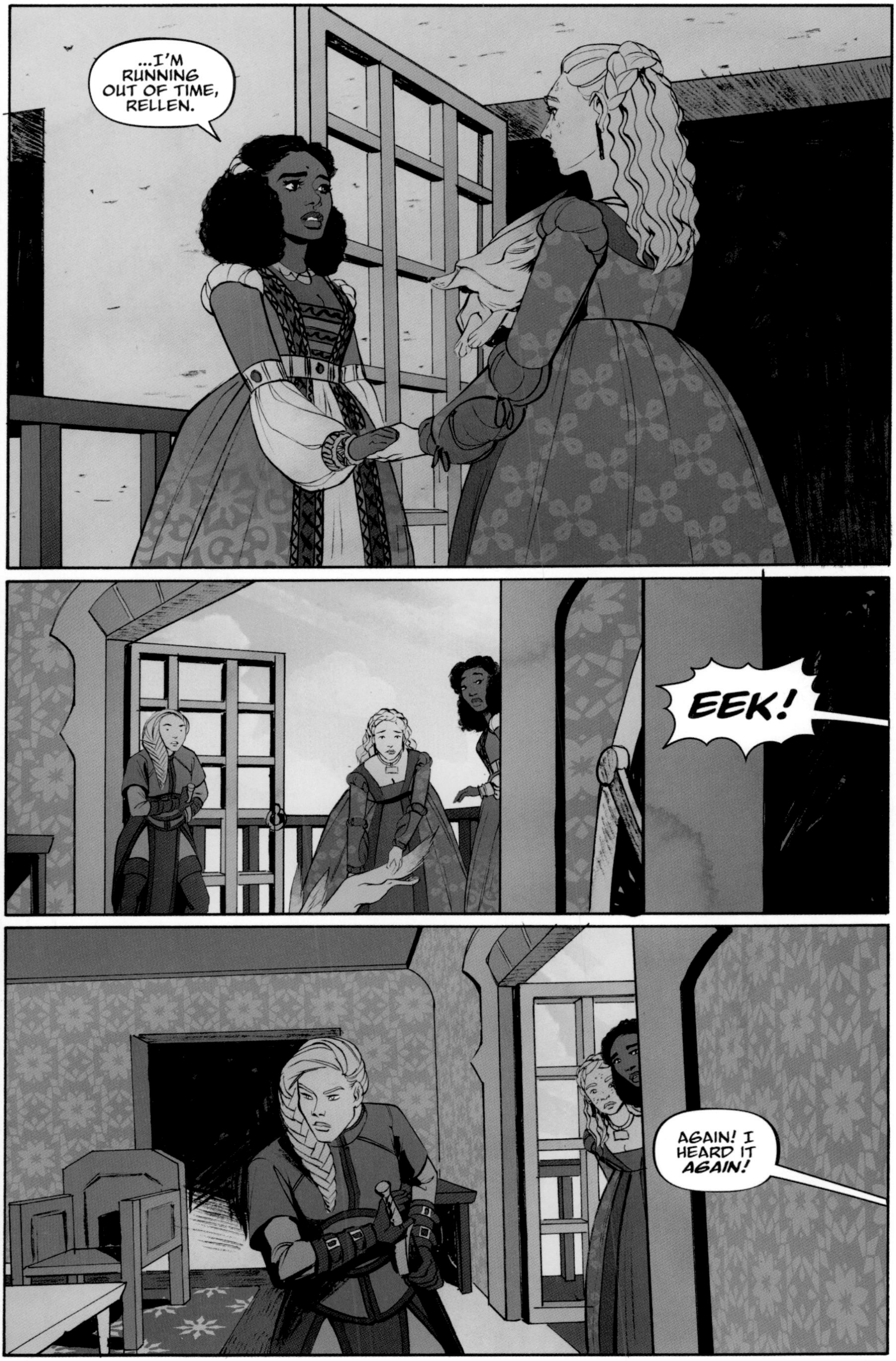
...I'M RUNNING OUT OF TIME, RELLEN.
EEK!
AGAIN! I HEARD IT *AGAIN!*

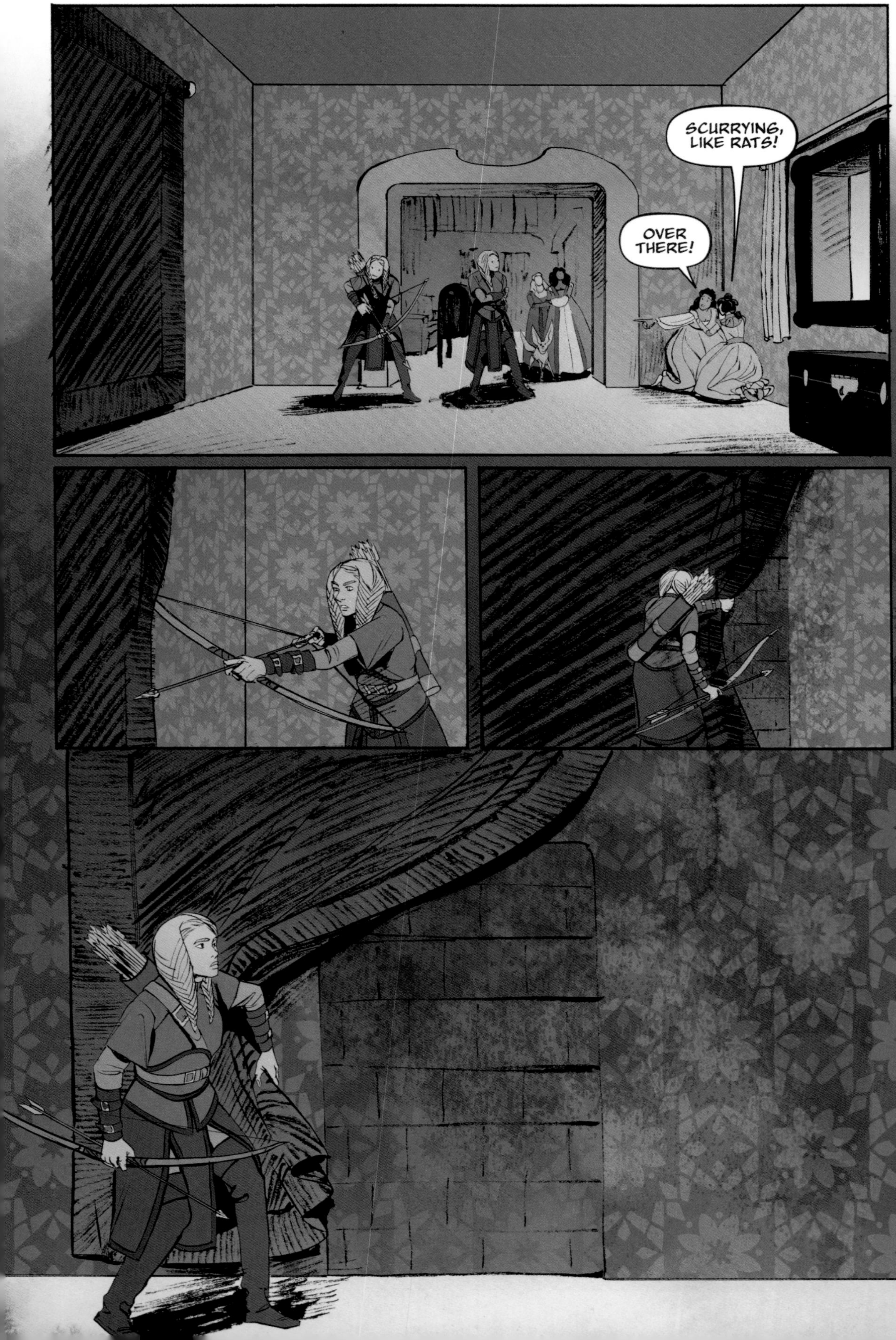
SCURRYING, LIKE RATS!
OVER THERE!

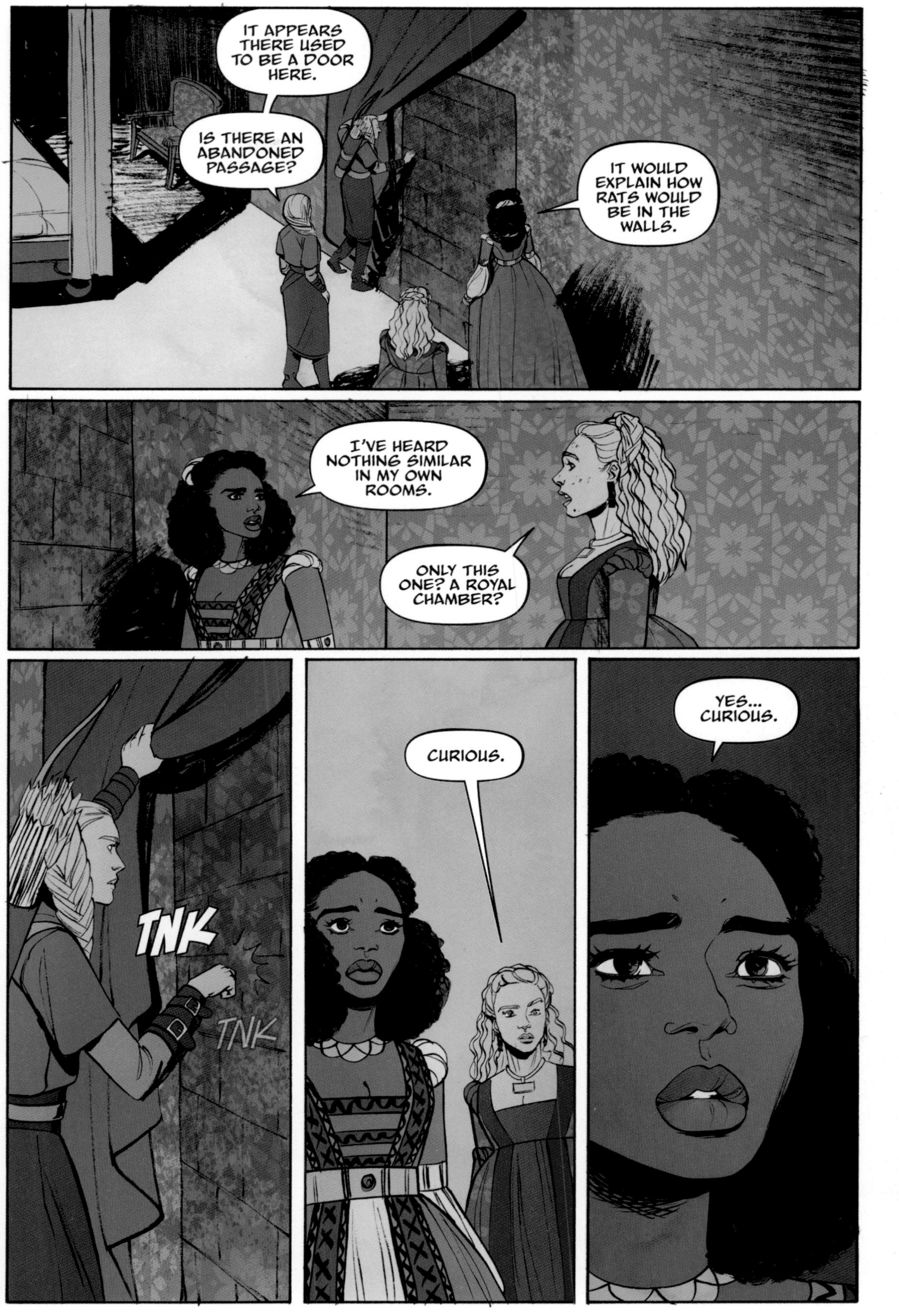
IT APPEARS THERE USED TO BE A DOOR HERE.
IS THERE AN ABANDONED PASSAGE?
IT WOULD EXPLAIN HOW RATS WOULD BE IN THE WALLS.
I'VE HEARD NOTHING SIMILAR IN MY OWN ROOMS.
ONLY THIS ONE? A ROYAL CHAMBER?
TNK
TNK
CURIOUS.
YES... CURIOUS.

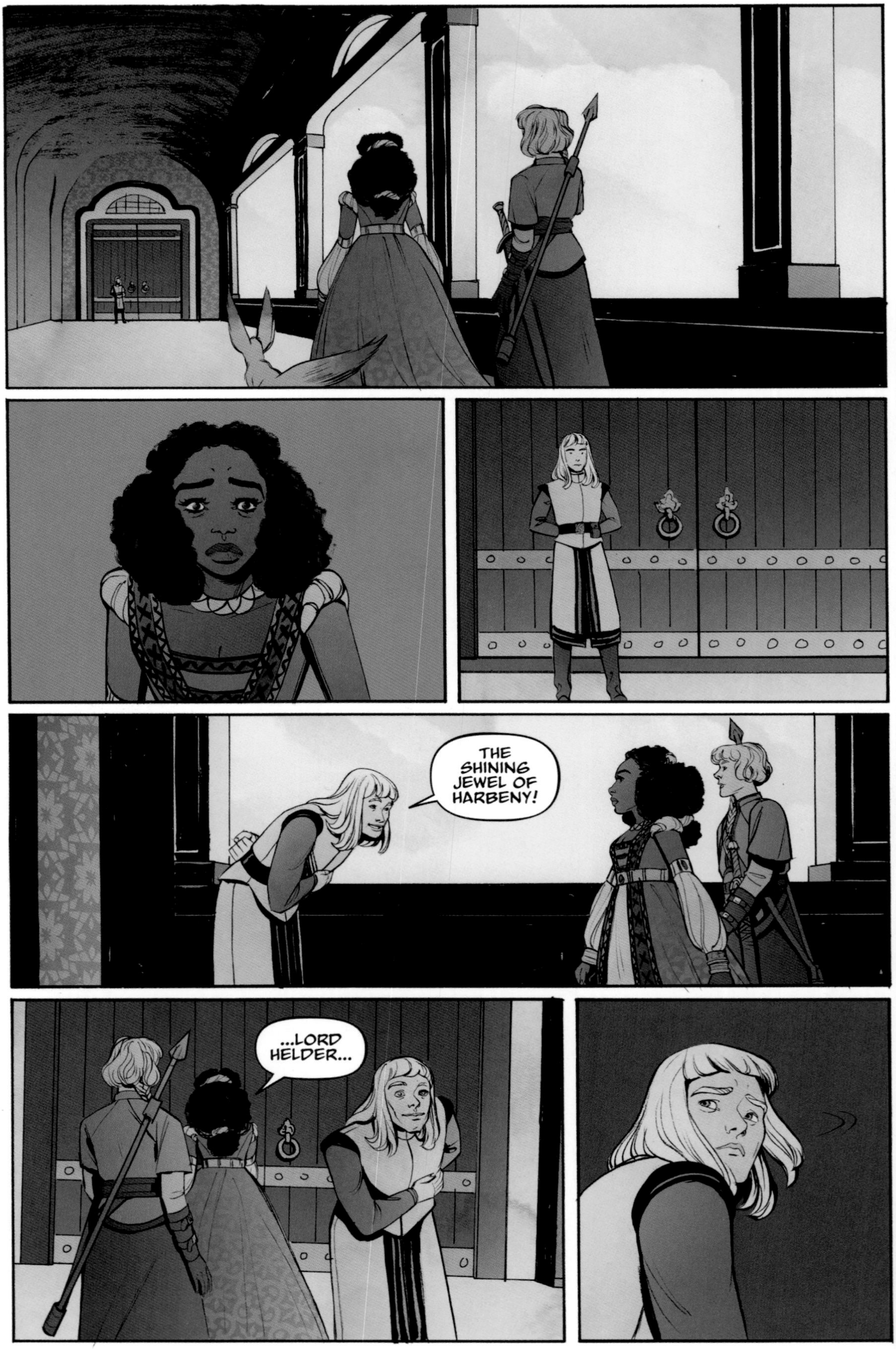
THE SHINING JEWEL OF HARBENY!
...LORD HELDER...

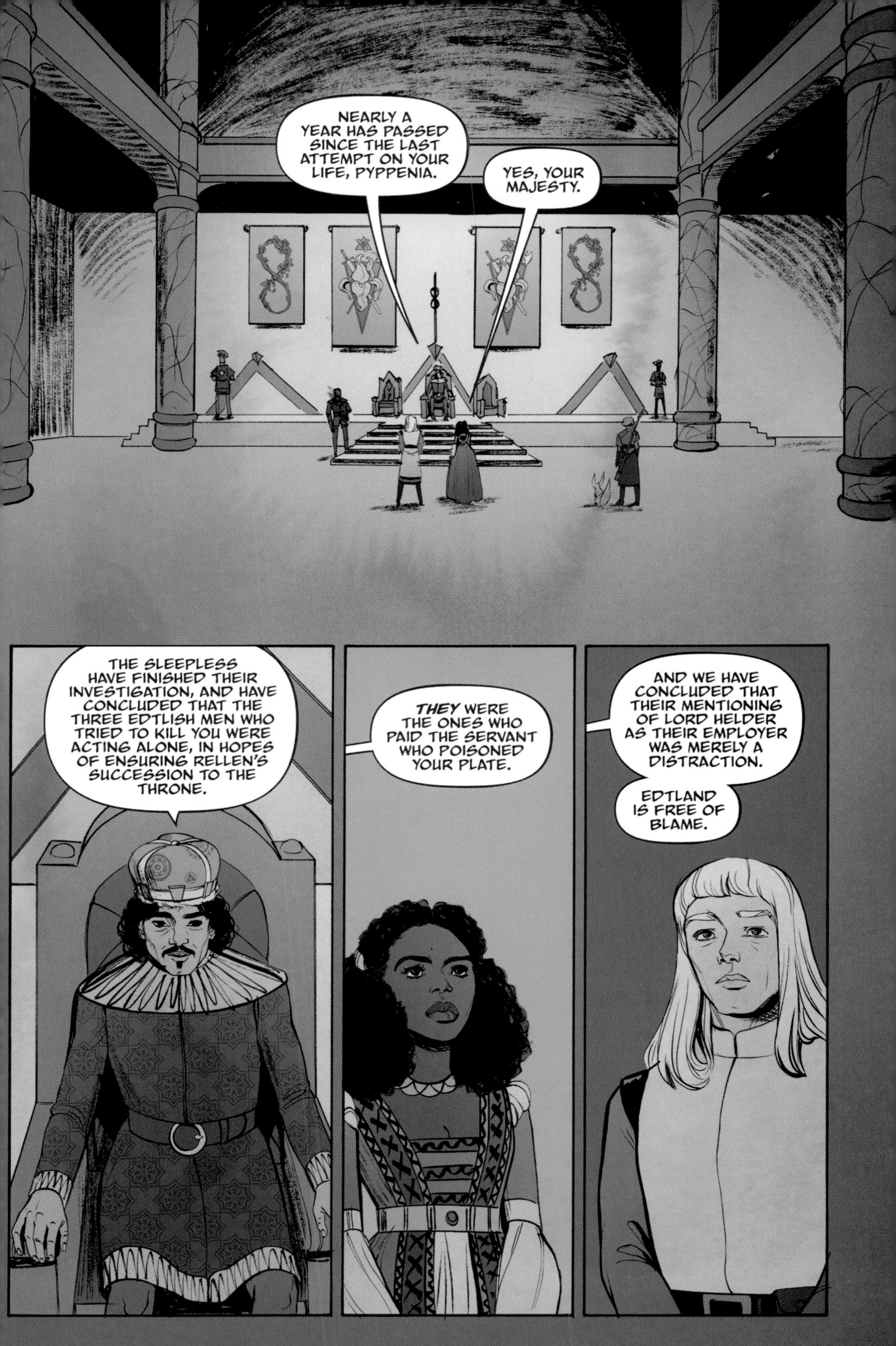
NEARLY A YEAR HAS PASSED SINCE THE LAST ATTEMPT ON YOUR LIFE, PYPPENIA.
YES, YOUR MAJESTY.
THE SLEEPLESS HAVE FINISHED THEIR INVESTIGATION, AND HAVE CONCLUDED THAT THE THREE EDTLISH MEN WHO TRIED TO KILL YOU WERE ACTING ALONE, IN HOPES OF ENSURING RELLEN'S SUCCESSION TO THE THRONE.
THEY WERE THE ONES WHO PAID THE SERVANT WHO POISONED YOUR PLATE.
AND WE HAVE CONCLUDED THAT THEIR MENTIONING OF LORD HELDER AS THEIR EMPLOYER WAS MERELY A DISTRACTION.
EDTLAND IS FREE OF BLAME.

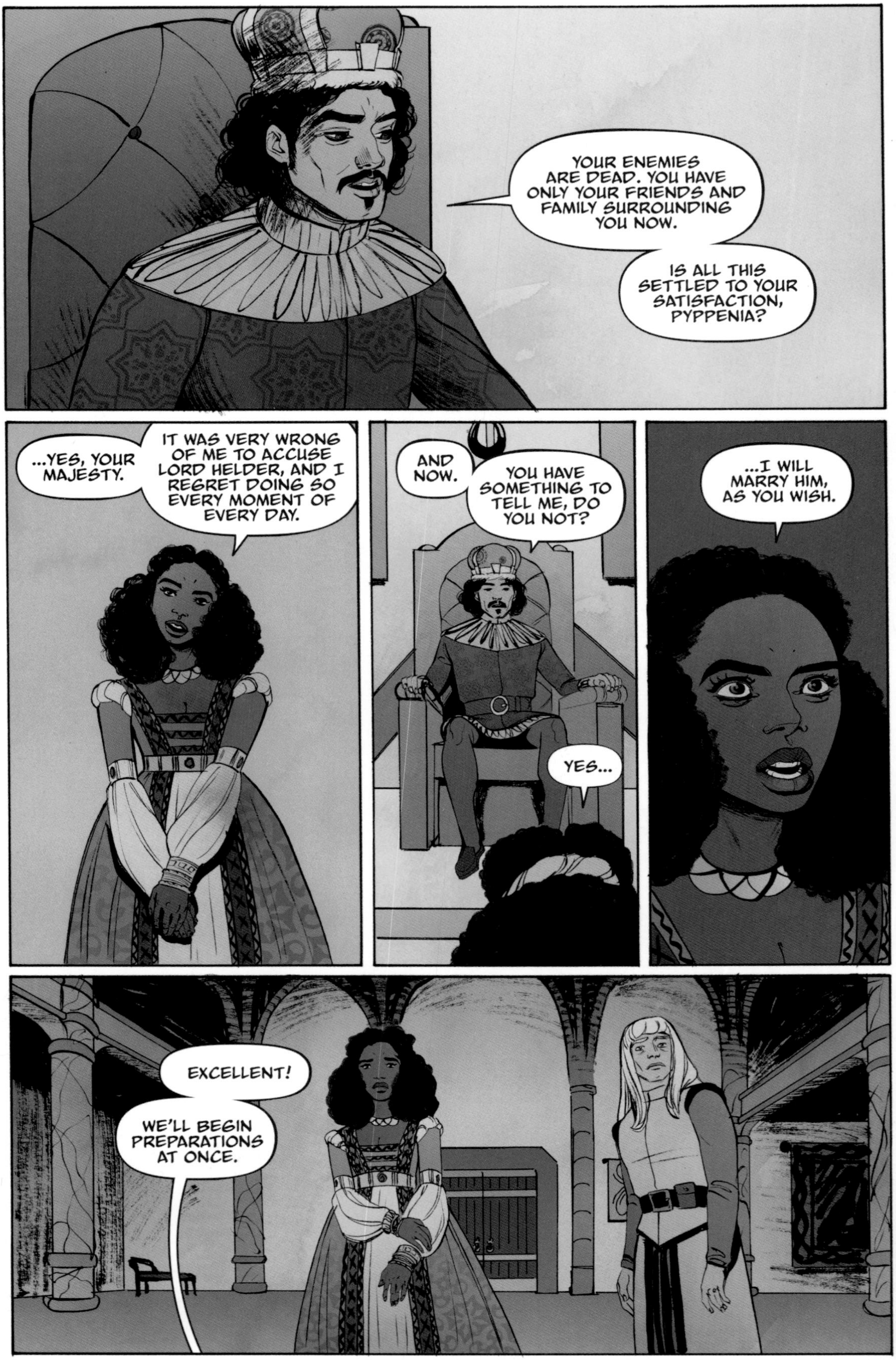
YOUR ENEMIES ARE DEAD. YOU HAVE ONLY YOUR FRIENDS AND FAMILY SURROUNDING YOU NOW.
IS ALL THIS SETTLED TO YOUR SATISFACTION, PYPPENIA?
...YES, YOUR MAJESTY.
IT WAS VERY WRONG OF ME TO ACCUSE LORD HELDER, AND I REGRET DOING SO EVERY MOMENT OF EVERY DAY.
AND NOW.
YOU HAVE SOMETHING TO TELL ME, DO YOU NOT?
YES...
...I WILL MARRY HIM, AS YOU WISH.
EXCELLENT!
WE'LL BEGIN PREPARATIONS AT ONCE.

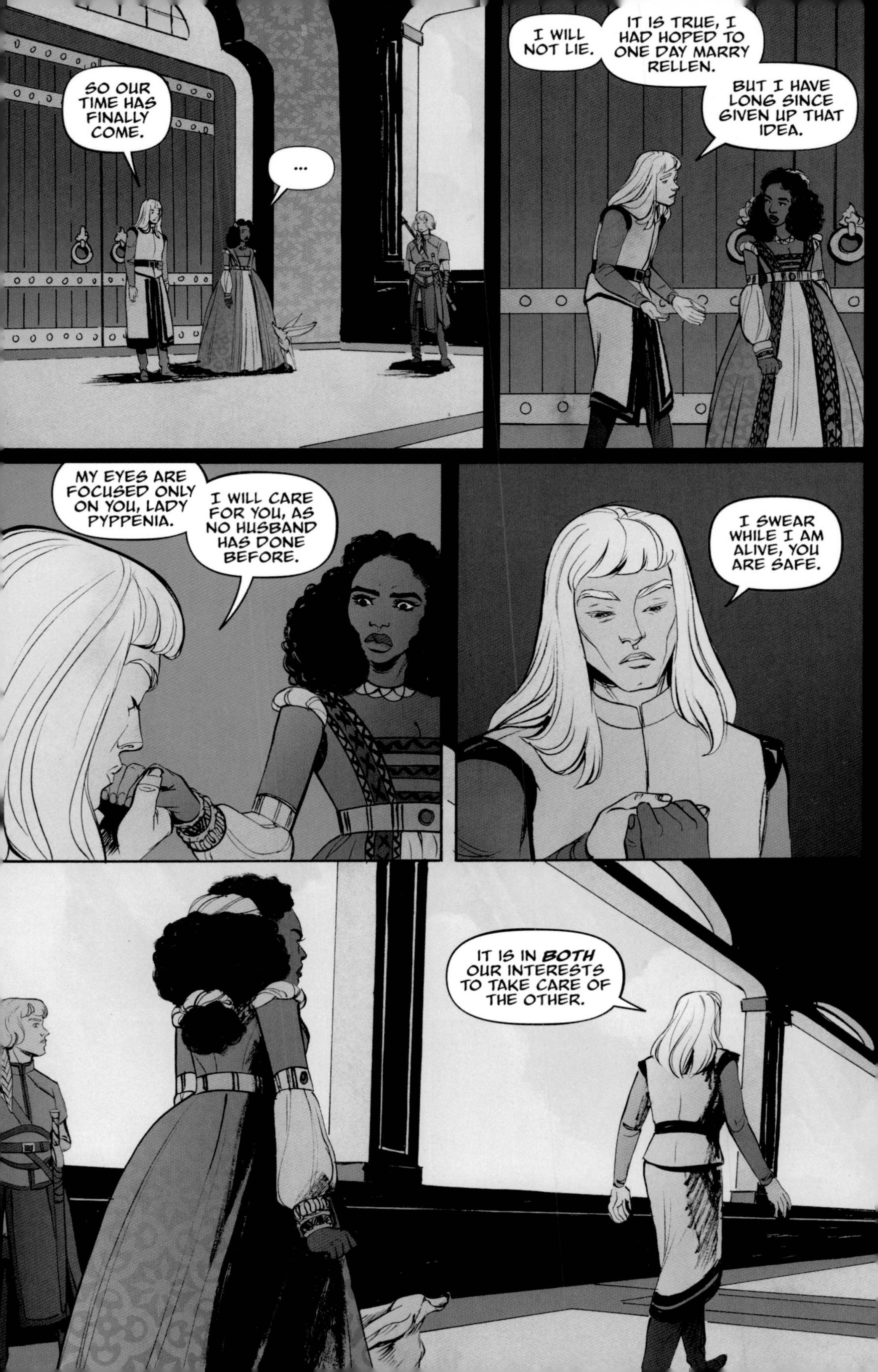
SO OUR TIME HAS FINALLY COME.
...
I WILL NOT LIE.
IT IS TRUE, I HAD HOPED TO ONE DAY MARRY RELLEN.
BUT I HAVE LONG SINCE GIVEN UP THAT IDEA.
MY EYES ARE FOCUSED ONLY ON YOU, LADY PYPPENIA.
I WILL CARE FOR YOU, AS NO HUSBAND HAS DONE BEFORE.
I SWEAR WHILE I AM ALIVE, YOU ARE SAFE.
IT IS IN *BOTH* OUR INTERESTS TO TAKE CARE OF THE OTHER.

GOOD NIGHT, MY LADY.

GOOD NIGHT, MYRA.

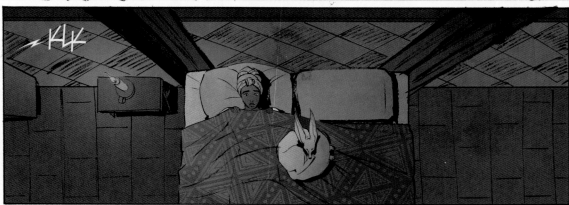

KLK

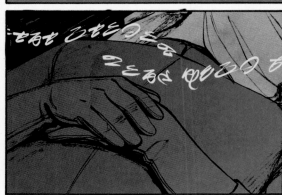

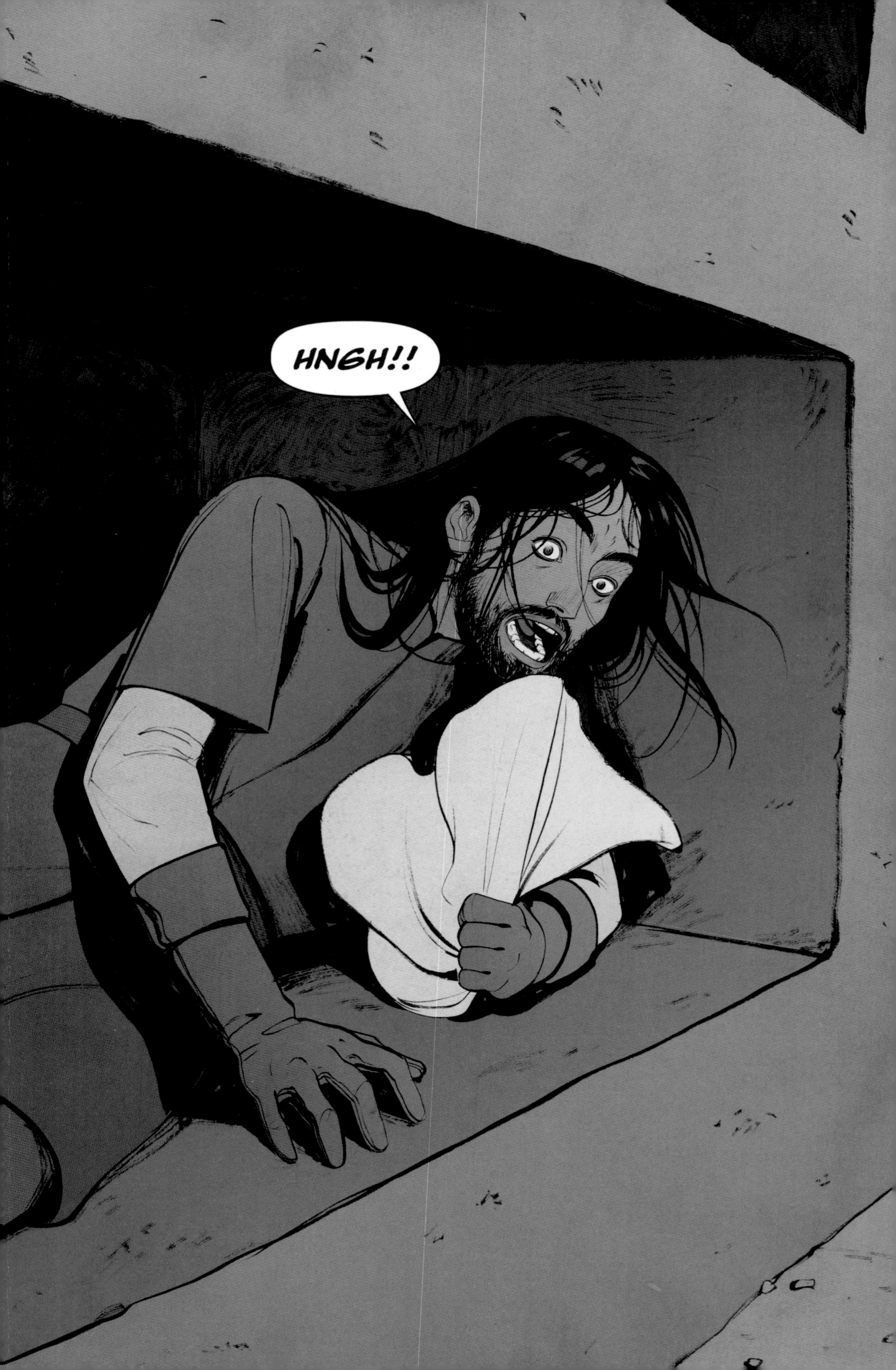
HNGH!!

CHAPTER EIGHT

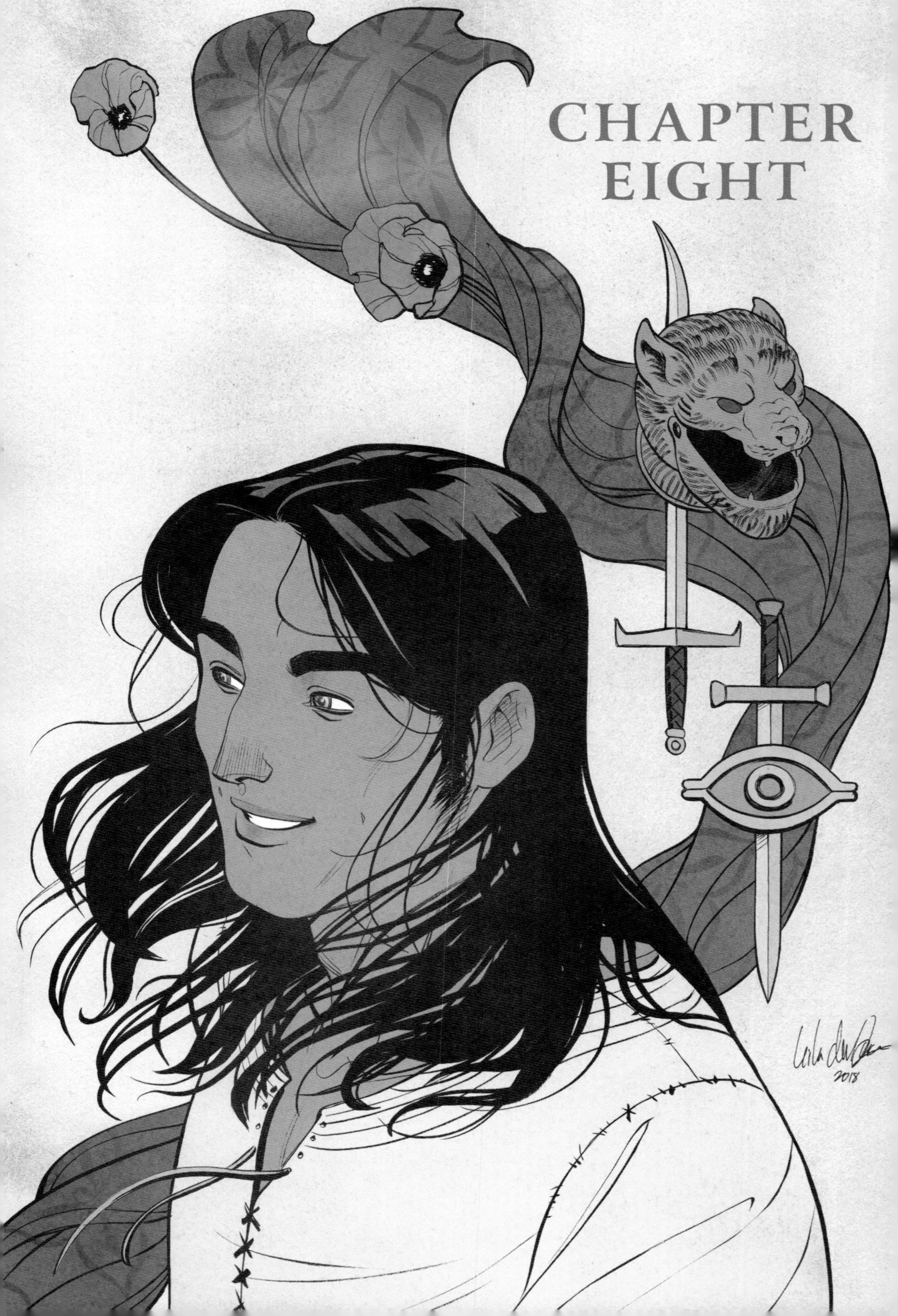

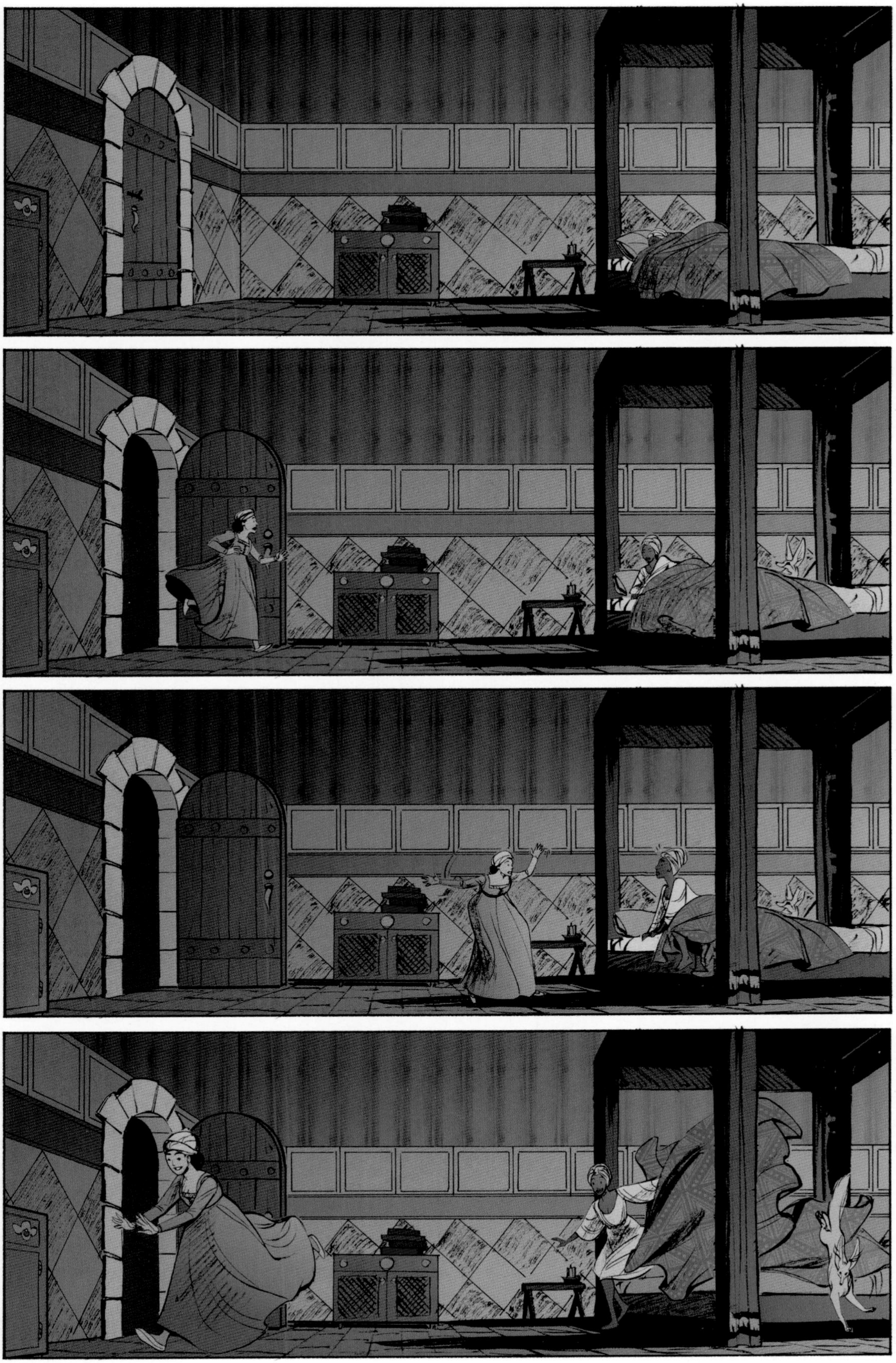

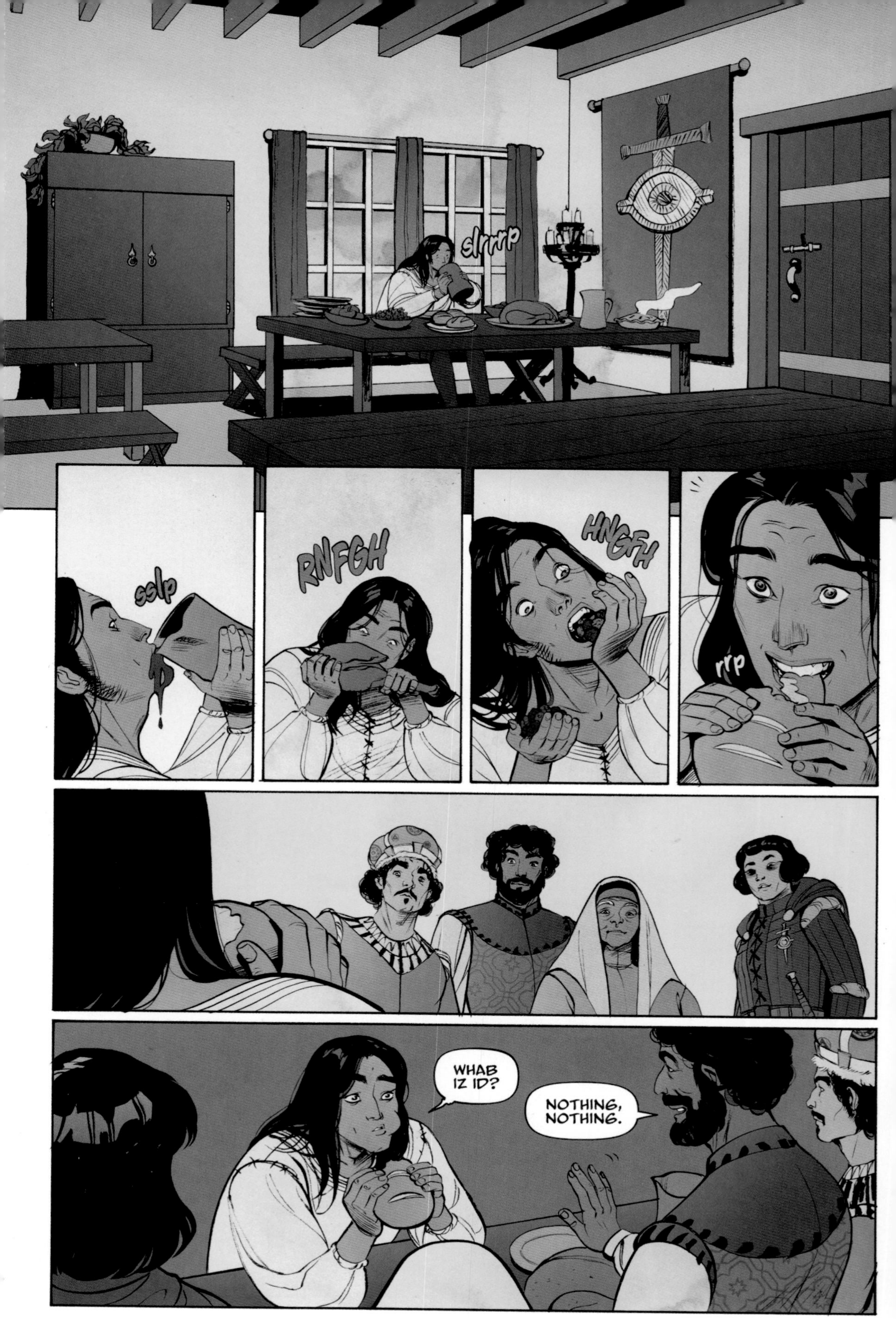
slrrrp
sslp
RNFGH
HNGFH
rrp
WHAB IZ ID?
NOTHING, NOTHING.

STILL THIRSTY?

MM.

I CAN'T--I CAN'T SEEM TO SATE MYSELF.

TIME IS CATCHING UP TO YOU.

YOU HAVE BEEN ASLEEP FOR MONTHS, ANYONE UNDER NATURAL CIRCUMSTANCES WOULD HAVE DIED LONG AGO.

I'M SURE IT WILL RIGHT ITSELF SHORTLY.

MM.

BUT TAKE CARE!

AT LEAST CHEW BEFORE YOU SWALLOW!

SlrrrP

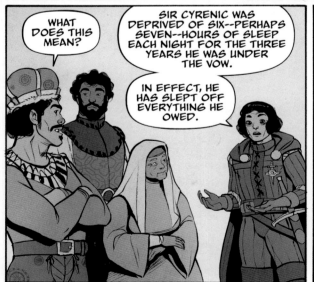

WHAT DOES THIS MEAN?

SIR CYRENIC WAS DEPRIVED OF SIX--PERHAPS SEVEN--HOURS OF SLEEP EACH NIGHT FOR THE THREE YEARS HE WAS UNDER THE VOW.

IN EFFECT, HE HAS SLEPT OFF EVERYTHING HE OWED.

WILL HE START FRESH NOW?

HE IS OUR BEST KNIGHT IN THE KINGDOM.

ONLY TIME CAN TELL.

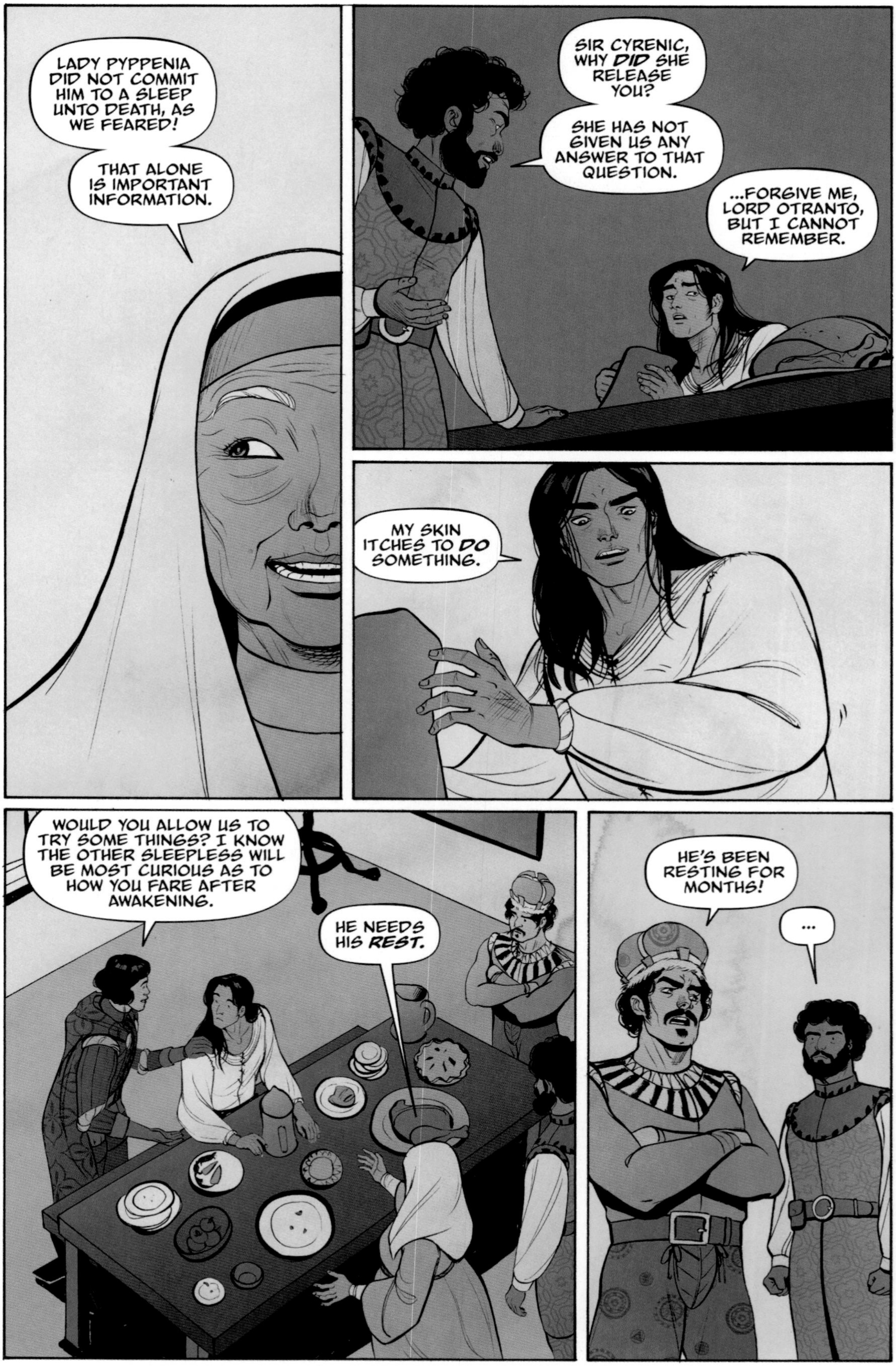
LADY PYPPENIA DID NOT COMMIT HIM TO A SLEEP UNTO DEATH, AS WE FEARED!
THAT ALONE IS IMPORTANT INFORMATION.
SIR CYRENIC, WHY *DID* SHE RELEASE YOU?
SHE HAS NOT GIVEN US ANY ANSWER TO THAT QUESTION.
...FORGIVE ME, LORD OTRANTO, BUT I CANNOT REMEMBER.
MY SKIN ITCHES TO *DO* SOMETHING.
WOULD YOU ALLOW US TO TRY SOME THINGS? I KNOW THE OTHER SLEEPLESS WILL BE MOST CURIOUS AS TO HOW YOU FARE AFTER AWAKENING.
HE NEEDS HIS ***REST.***
HE'S BEEN RESTING FOR MONTHS!
...

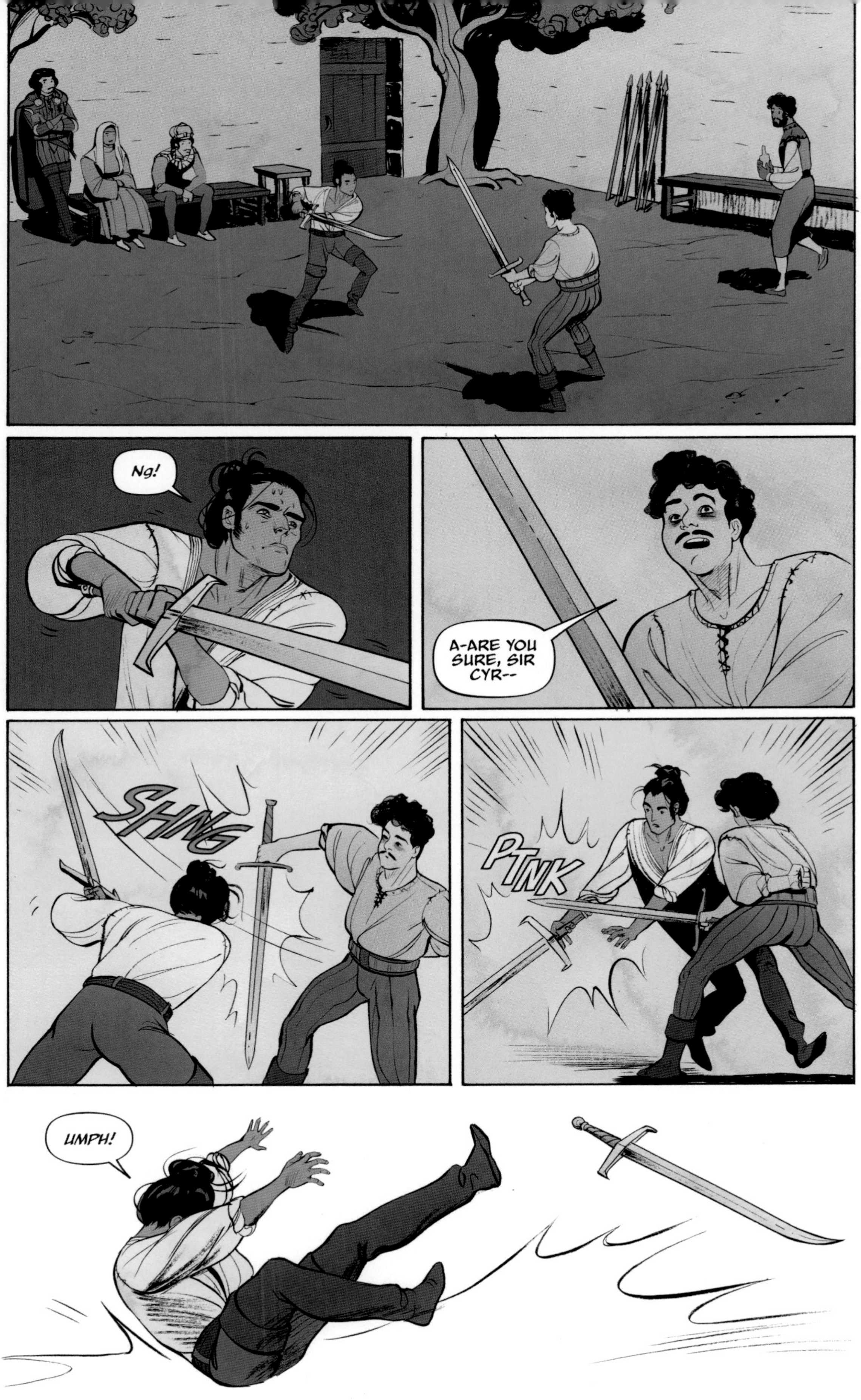
Ng!
A-ARE YOU SURE, SIR CYR--
SHNG
PTNK
UMPH!

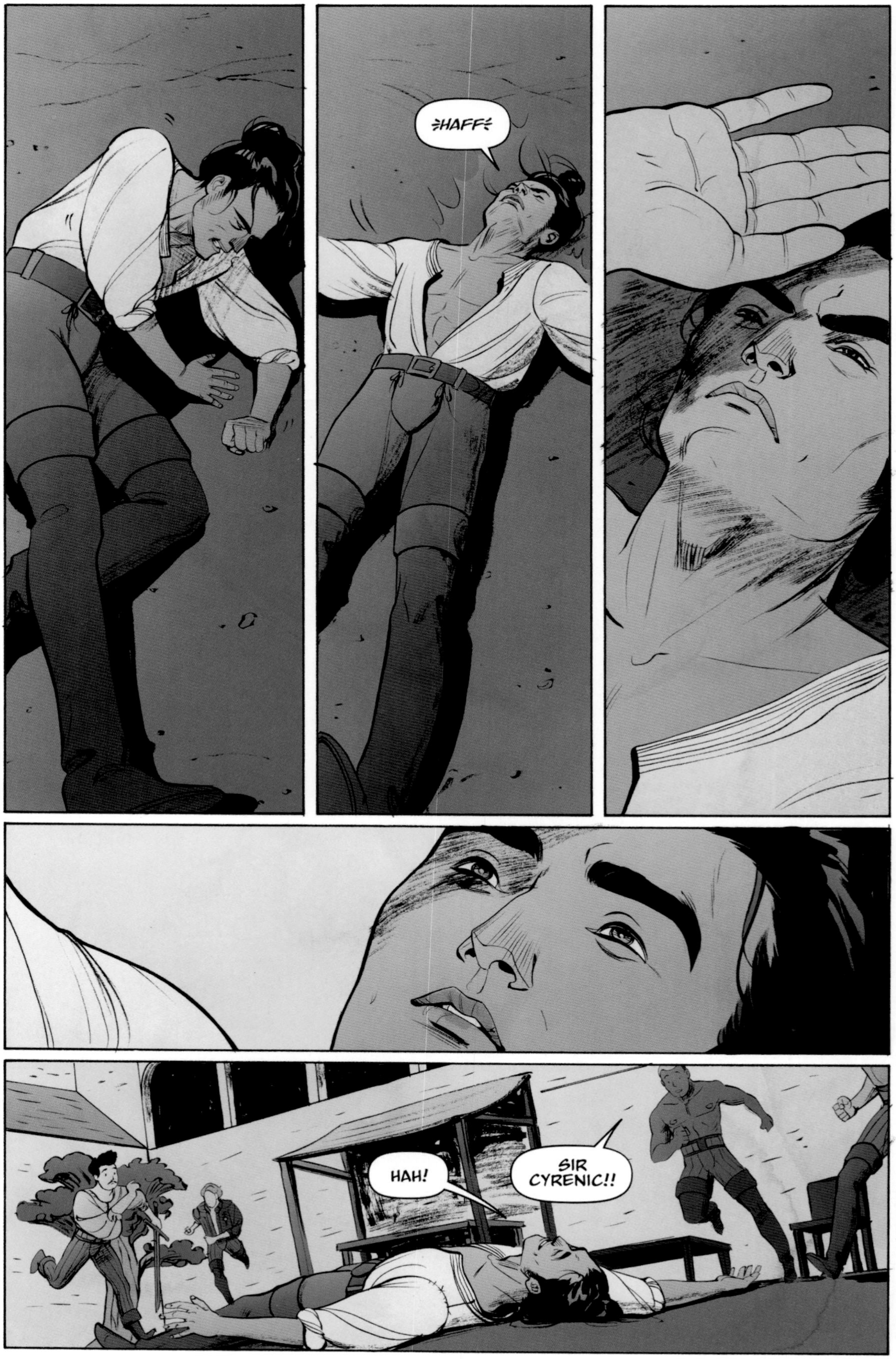
HAFF
HAH!
SIR CYRENIC!!

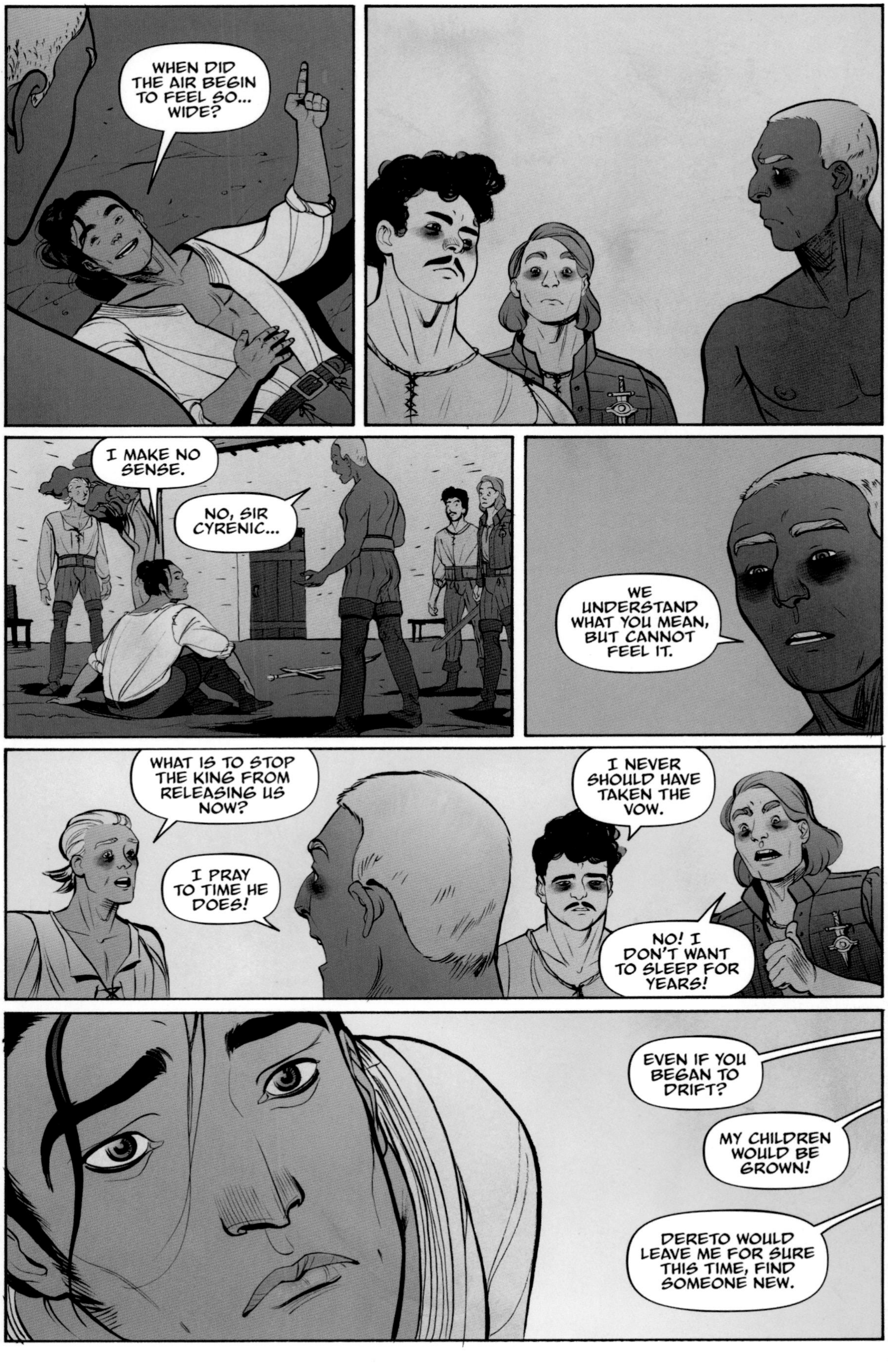
WHEN DID THE AIR BEGIN TO FEEL SO... WIDE?
I MAKE NO SENSE.
NO, SIR CYRENIC...
WE UNDERSTAND WHAT YOU MEAN, BUT CANNOT FEEL IT.
WHAT IS TO STOP THE KING FROM RELEASING US NOW?
I PRAY TO TIME HE DOES!
I NEVER SHOULD HAVE TAKEN THE VOW.
NO! I DON'T WANT TO SLEEP FOR YEARS!
EVEN IF YOU BEGAN TO DRIFT?
MY CHILDREN WOULD BE GROWN!
DERETO WOULD LEAVE ME FOR SURE THIS TIME, FIND SOMEONE NEW.

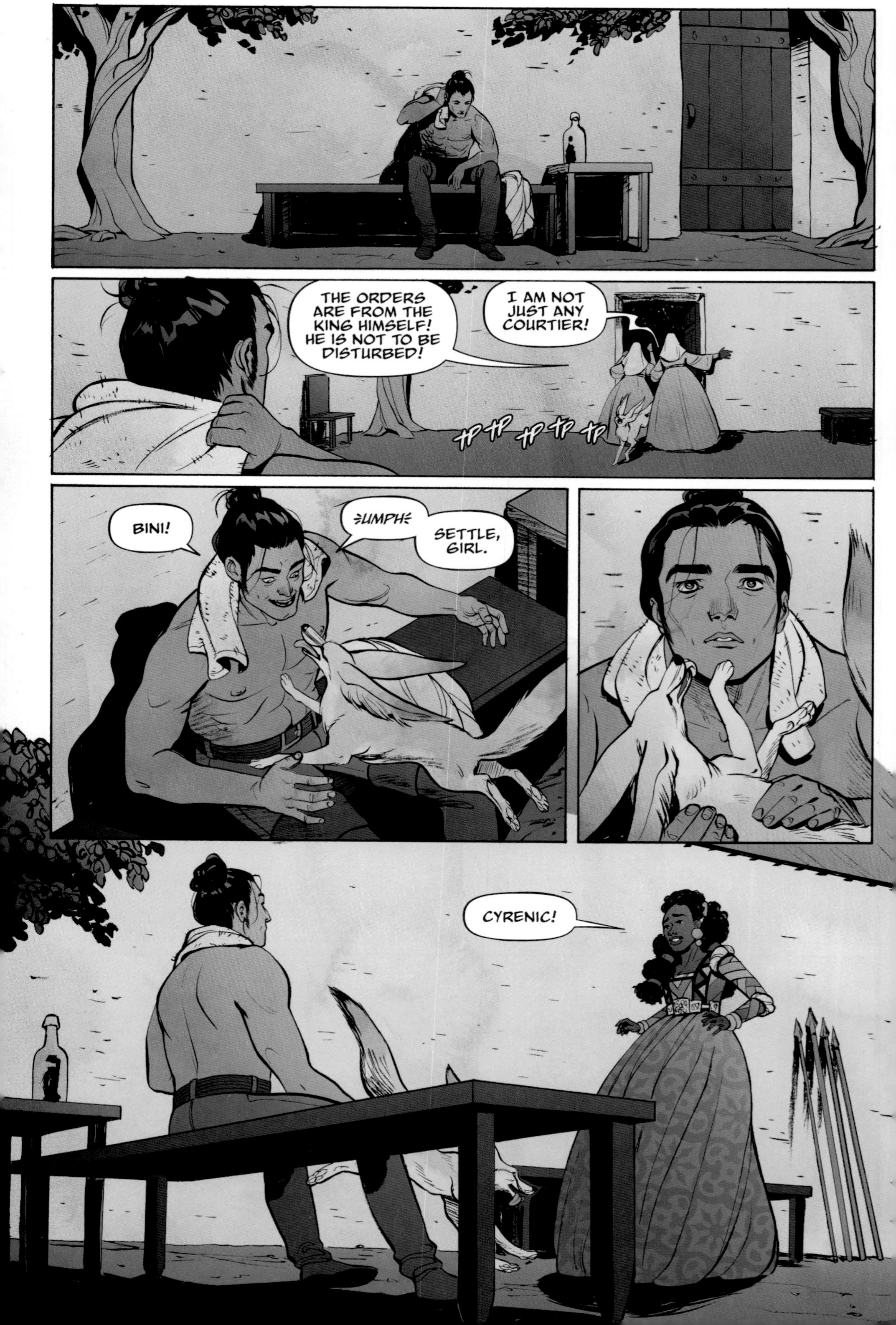
THE ORDERS ARE FROM THE KING HIMSELF! HE IS NOT TO BE DISTURBED!
I AM NOT JUST ANY COURTIER!
TP TP TP TP TP
BINI!
UMPH
SETTLE, GIRL.
CYRENIC!

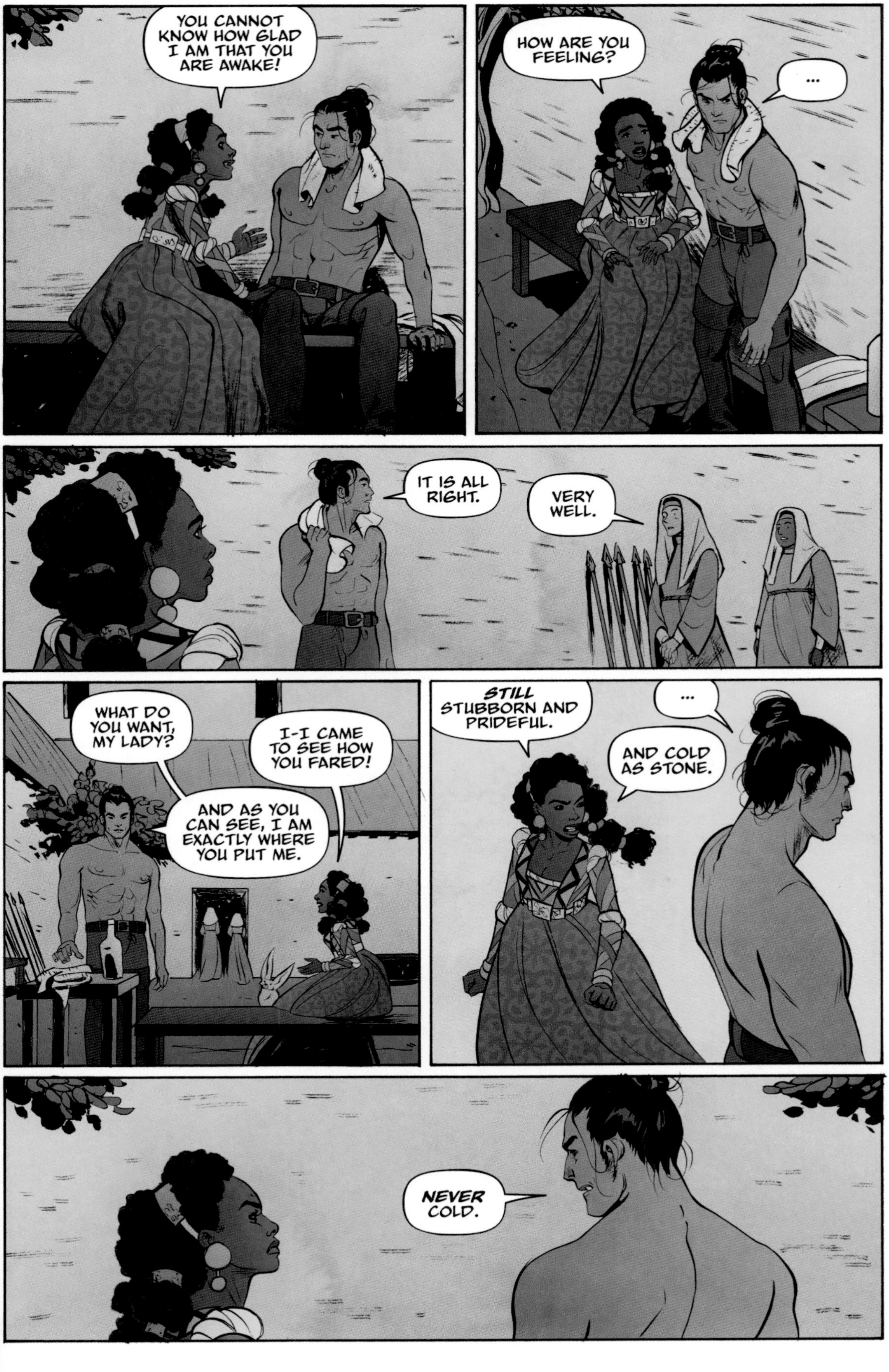
YOU CANNOT KNOW HOW GLAD I AM THAT YOU ARE AWAKE!
HOW ARE YOU FEELING?
...
IT IS ALL RIGHT.
VERY WELL.
WHAT DO YOU WANT, MY LADY?
I-I CAME TO SEE HOW YOU FARED!
AND AS YOU CAN SEE, I AM EXACTLY WHERE YOU PUT ME.
STILL STUBBORN AND PRIDEFUL.
...
AND COLD AS STONE.
NEVER COLD.

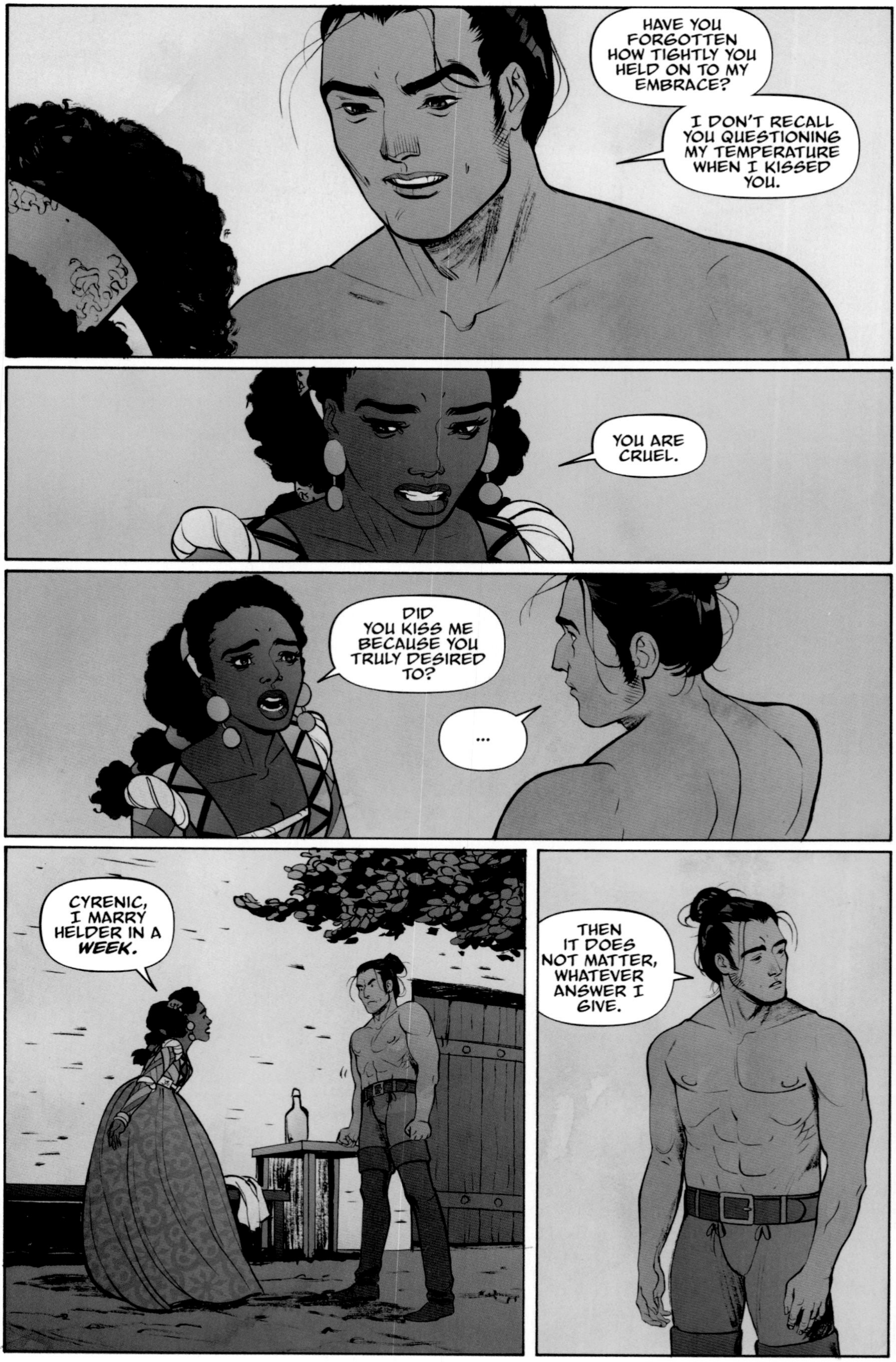
HAVE YOU FORGOTTEN HOW TIGHTLY YOU HELD ON TO MY EMBRACE?
I DON'T RECALL YOU QUESTIONING MY TEMPERATURE WHEN I KISSED YOU.
YOU ARE CRUEL.
DID YOU KISS ME BECAUSE YOU TRULY DESIRED TO?
...
CYRENIC, I MARRY HELDER IN A *WEEK.*
THEN IT DOES NOT MATTER, WHATEVER ANSWER I GIVE.

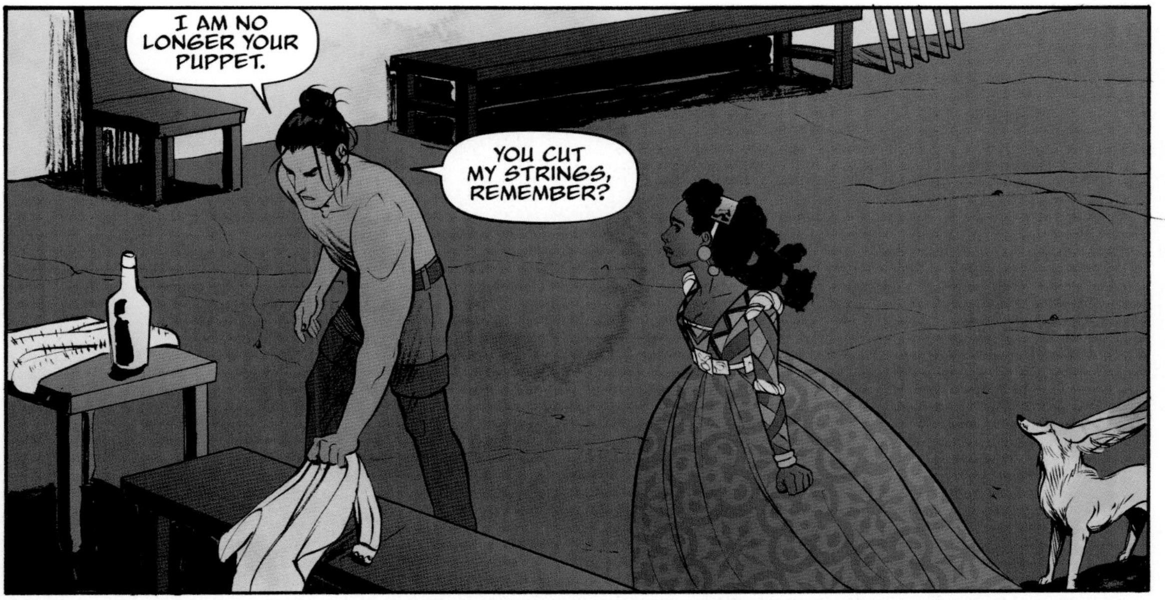
I AM NO LONGER YOUR PUPPET.
YOU CUT MY STRINGS, REMEMBER?
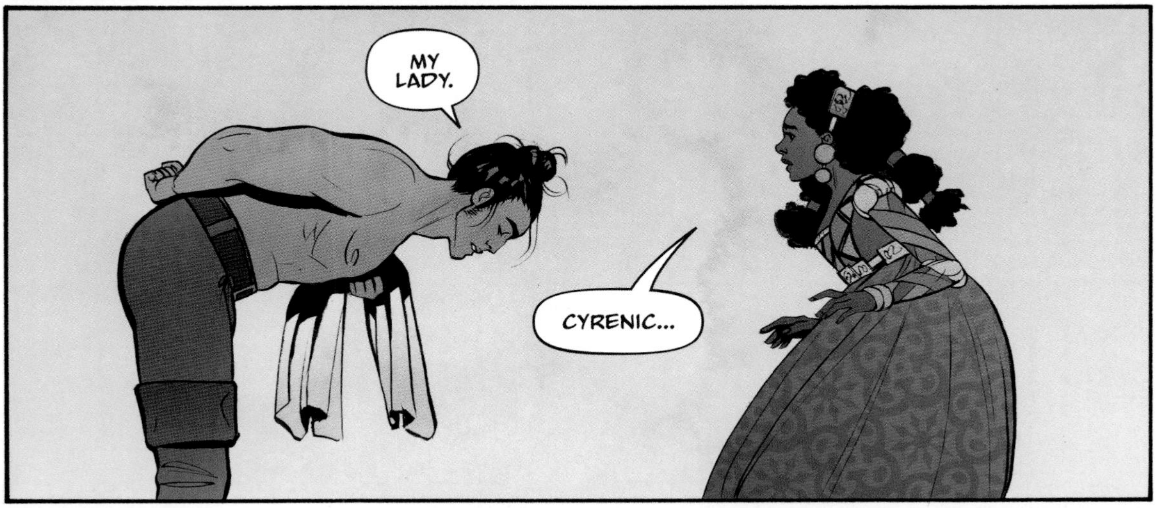
MY LADY.
CYRENIC...
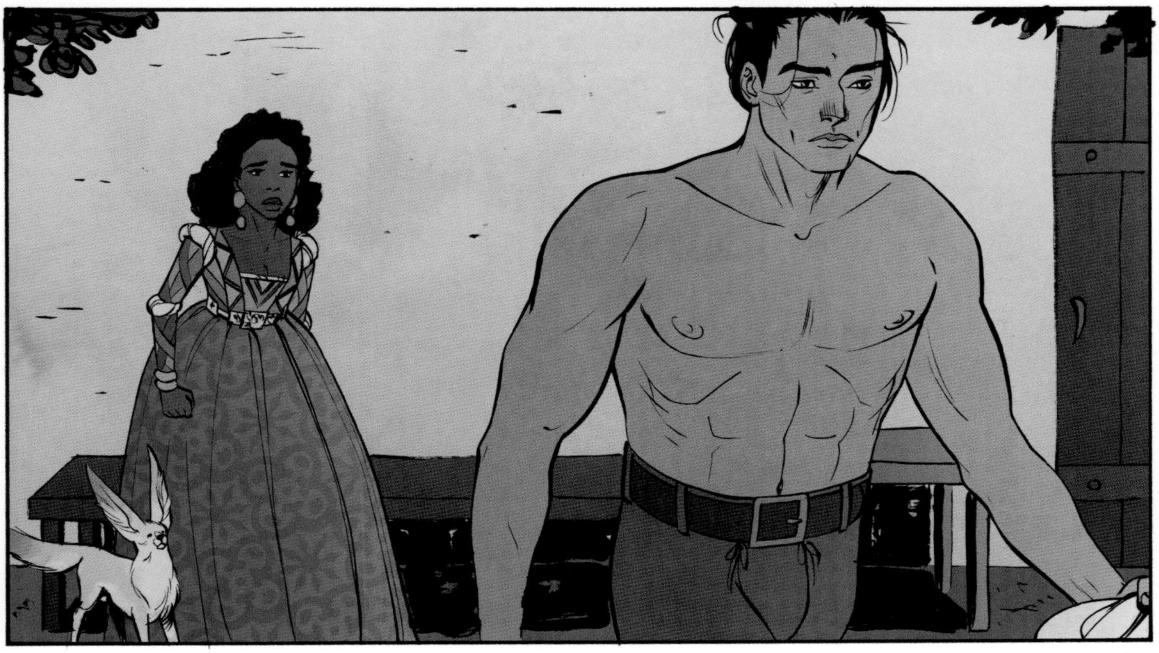

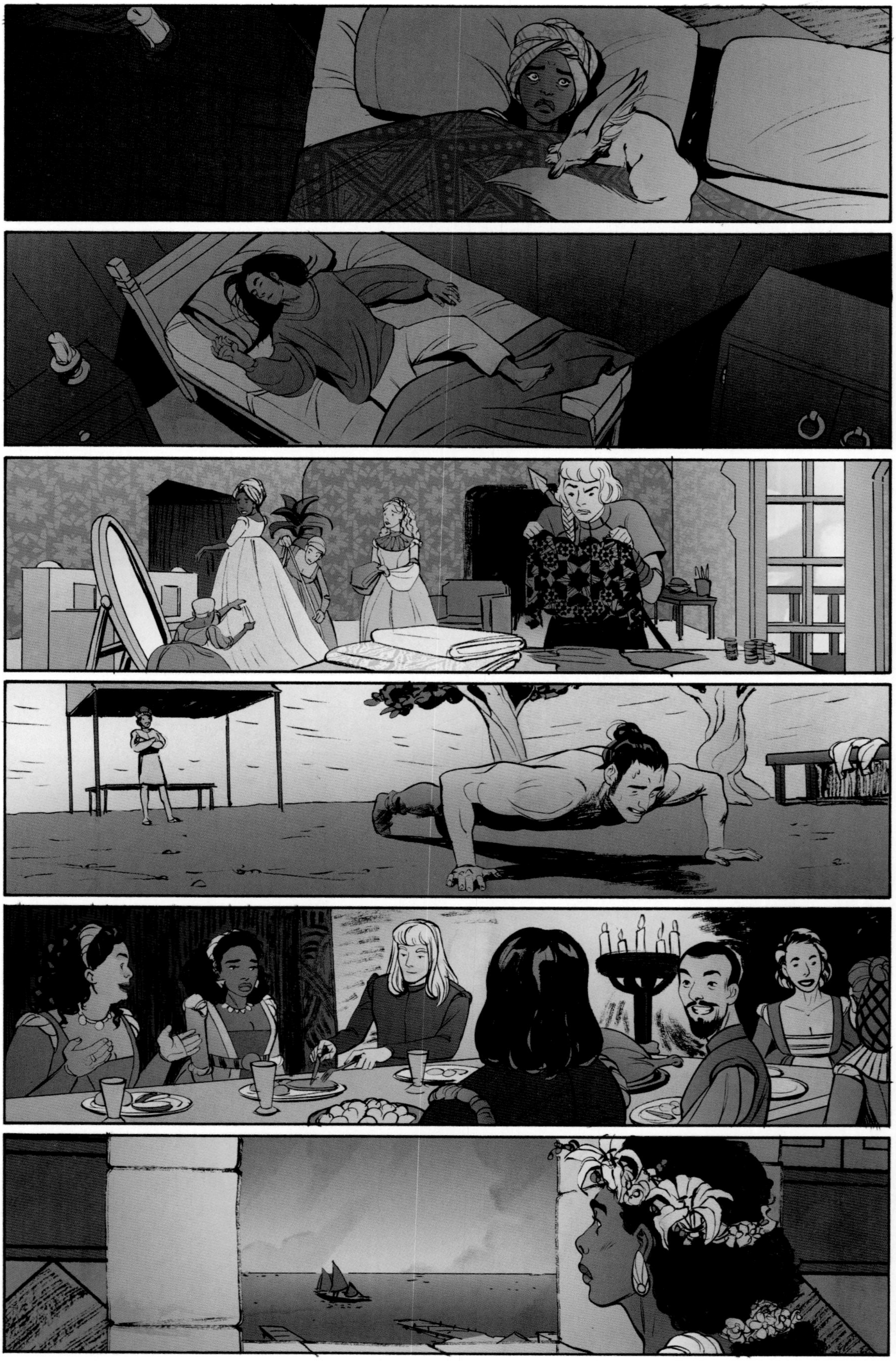

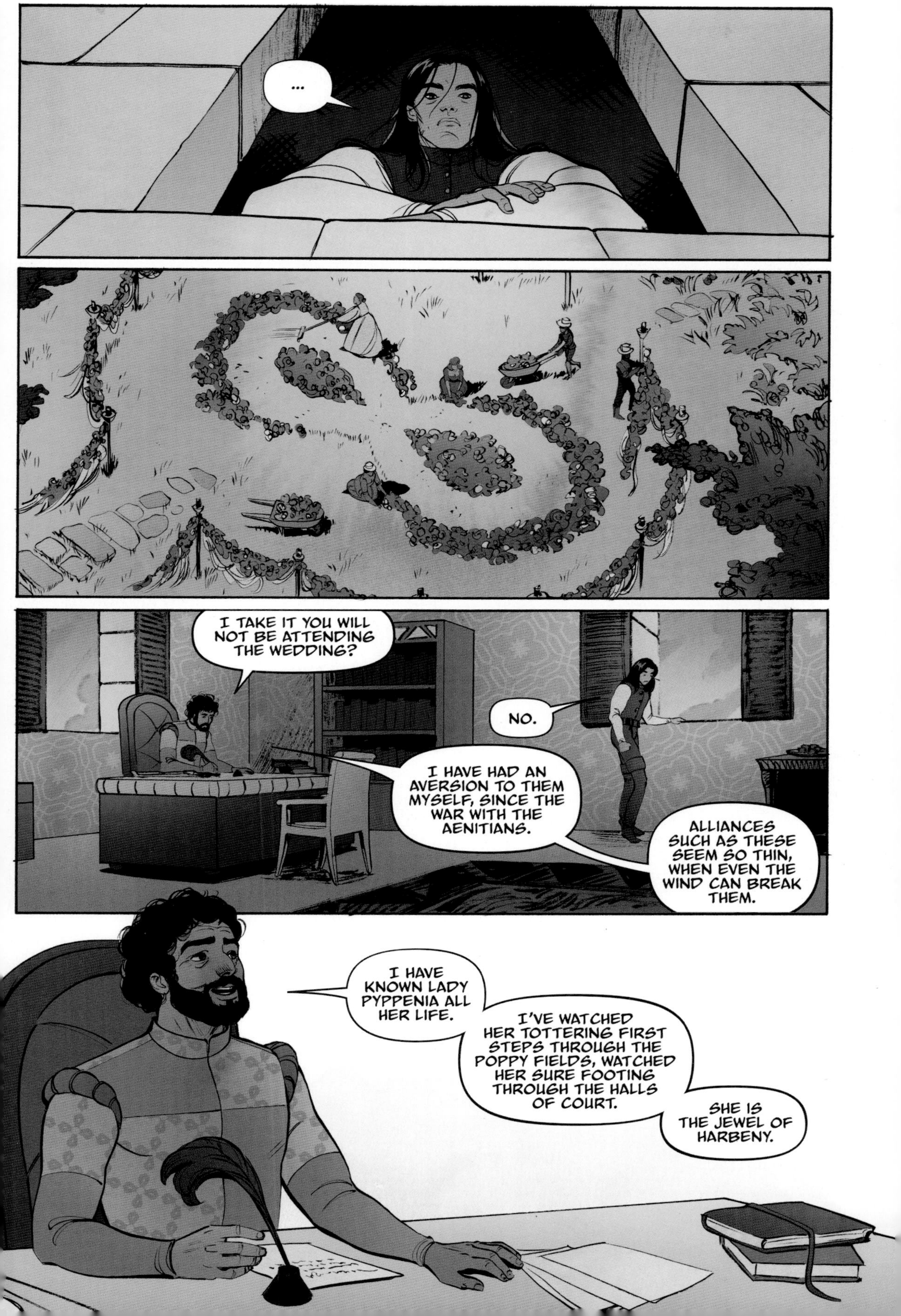
...
I TAKE IT YOU WILL NOT BE ATTENDING THE WEDDING?
NO.
I HAVE HAD AN AVERSION TO THEM MYSELF, SINCE THE WAR WITH THE AENITIANS.
ALLIANCES SUCH AS THESE SEEM SO THIN, WHEN EVEN THE WIND CAN BREAK THEM.
I HAVE KNOWN LADY PYPPENIA ALL HER LIFE.
I'VE WATCHED HER TOTTERING FIRST STEPS THROUGH THE POPPY FIELDS, WATCHED HER SURE FOOTING THROUGH THE HALLS OF COURT.
SHE IS THE JEWEL OF HARBENY.

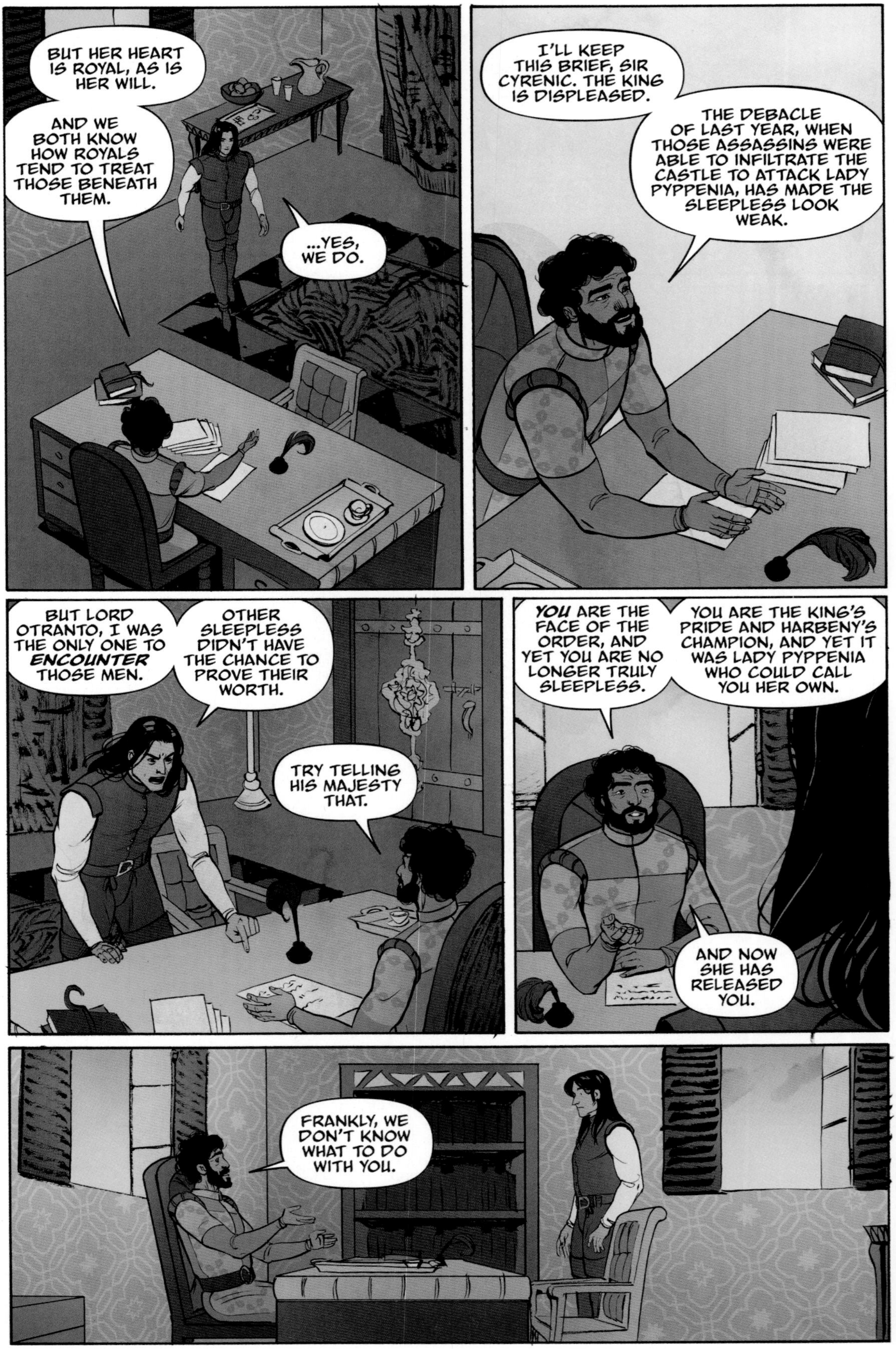
BUT HER HEART IS ROYAL, AS IS HER WILL.
AND WE BOTH KNOW HOW ROYALS TEND TO TREAT THOSE BENEATH THEM.
...YES, WE DO.
I'LL KEEP THIS BRIEF, SIR CYRENIC. THE KING IS DISPLEASED.
THE DEBACLE OF LAST YEAR, WHEN THOSE ASSASSINS WERE ABLE TO INFILTRATE THE CASTLE TO ATTACK LADY PYPPENIA, HAS MADE THE SLEEPLESS LOOK WEAK.
BUT LORD OTRANTO, I WAS THE ONLY ONE TO *ENCOUNTER* THOSE MEN.
OTHER SLEEPLESS DIDN'T HAVE THE CHANCE TO PROVE THEIR WORTH.
TRY TELLING HIS MAJESTY THAT.
YOU ARE THE FACE OF THE ORDER, AND YET YOU ARE NO LONGER TRULY SLEEPLESS.
YOU ARE THE KING'S PRIDE AND HARBENY'S CHAMPION, AND YET IT WAS LADY PYPPENIA WHO COULD CALL YOU HER OWN.
AND NOW SHE HAS RELEASED YOU.
FRANKLY, WE DON'T KNOW WHAT TO DO WITH YOU.

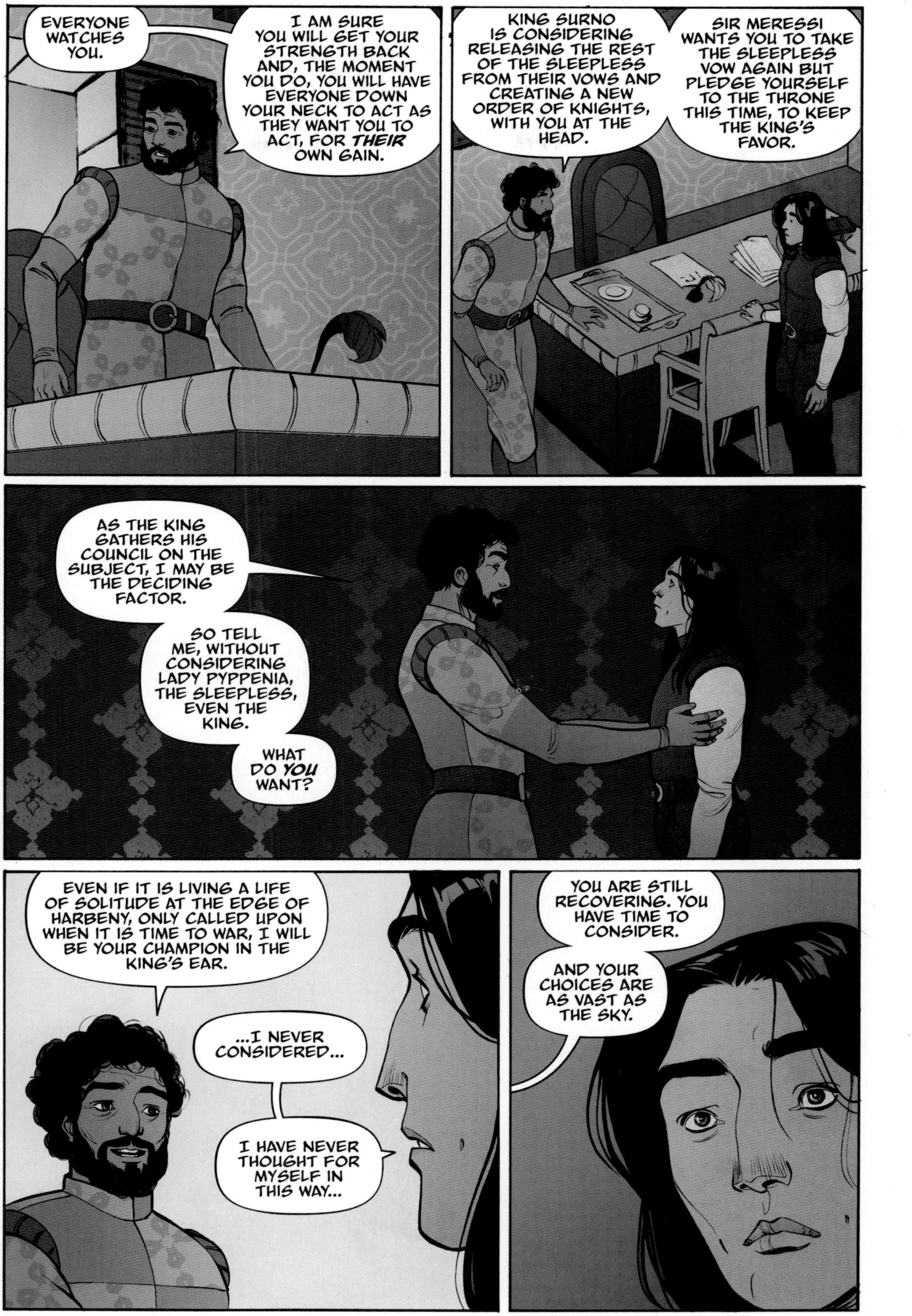
EVERYONE WATCHES YOU.
I AM SURE YOU WILL GET YOUR STRENGTH BACK AND, THE MOMENT YOU DO, YOU WILL HAVE EVERYONE DOWN YOUR NECK TO ACT AS THEY WANT YOU TO ACT, FOR *THEIR* OWN GAIN.
KING SURNO IS CONSIDERING RELEASING THE REST OF THE SLEEPLESS FROM THEIR VOWS AND CREATING A NEW ORDER OF KNIGHTS, WITH YOU AT THE HEAD.
SIR MERESSI WANTS YOU TO TAKE THE SLEEPLESS VOW AGAIN BUT PLEDGE YOURSELF TO THE THRONE THIS TIME, TO KEEP THE KING'S FAVOR.
AS THE KING GATHERS HIS COUNCIL ON THE SUBJECT, I MAY BE THE DECIDING FACTOR.
SO TELL ME, WITHOUT CONSIDERING LADY PYPPENIA, THE SLEEPLESS, EVEN THE KING.
WHAT DO *YOU* WANT?
EVEN IF IT IS LIVING A LIFE OF SOLITUDE AT THE EDGE OF HARBENY, ONLY CALLED UPON WHEN IT IS TIME TO WAR, I WILL BE YOUR CHAMPION IN THE KING'S EAR.
...I NEVER CONSIDERED...
I HAVE NEVER THOUGHT FOR MYSELF IN THIS WAY...
YOU ARE STILL RECOVERING. YOU HAVE TIME TO CONSIDER.
AND YOUR CHOICES ARE AS VAST AS THE SKY.

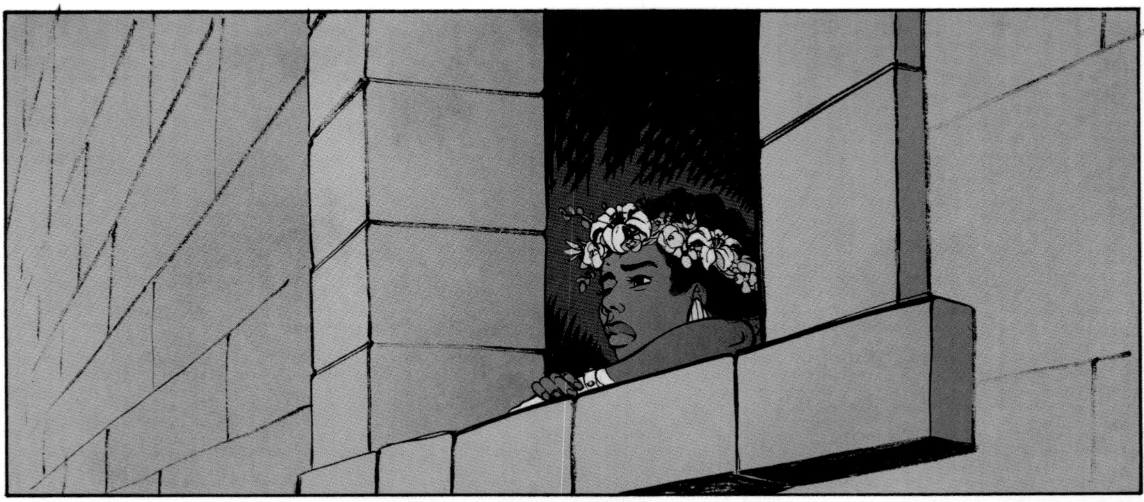

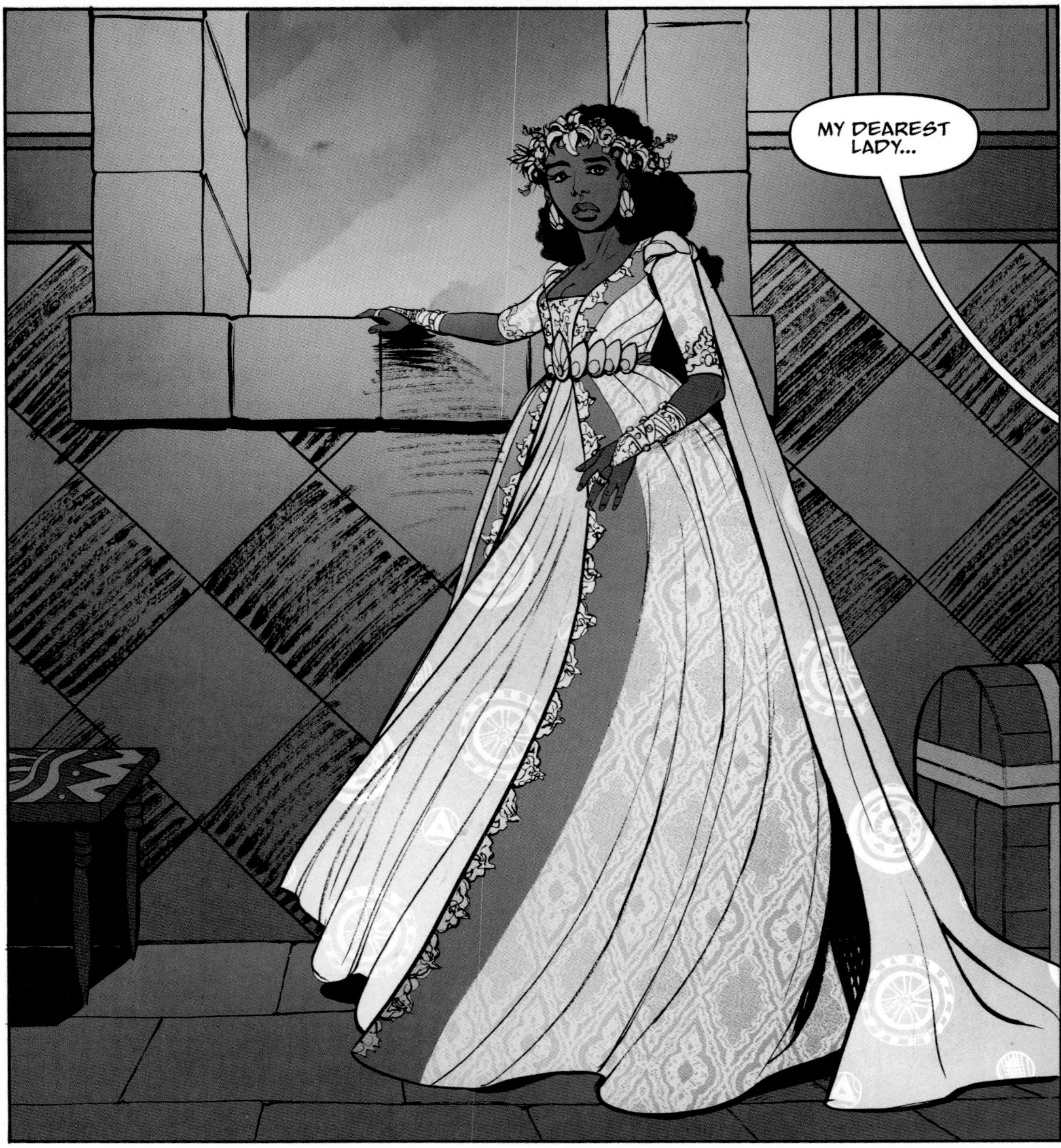
MY DEAREST LADY...

YOU SHINE AS BRIGHT AS THE STARS.

WE COME WITH A GIFT FROM YOUR MOTHER, ARRIVED JUST THIS HOUR.

CHILD, I TREMBLE MORE THAN YOU.

WHEN I READ THE STARS THAT FATEFUL NIGHT...

I DO NOT LIKE THIS.

MY QUEEN CAN HAVE NO OPINION ON THE MATTER.

BUT I DO NOT LIKE THIS.

BUT ENOUGH. I AM HERE ON A MISSION.

ON BEHALF OF LADY AMENA...

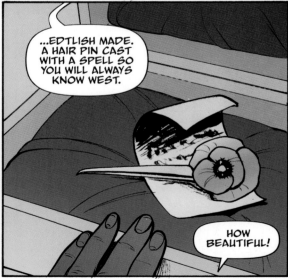

...EDTLISH MADE. A HAIR PIN CAST WITH A SPELL SO YOU WILL ALWAYS KNOW WEST.

HOW BEAUTIFUL!

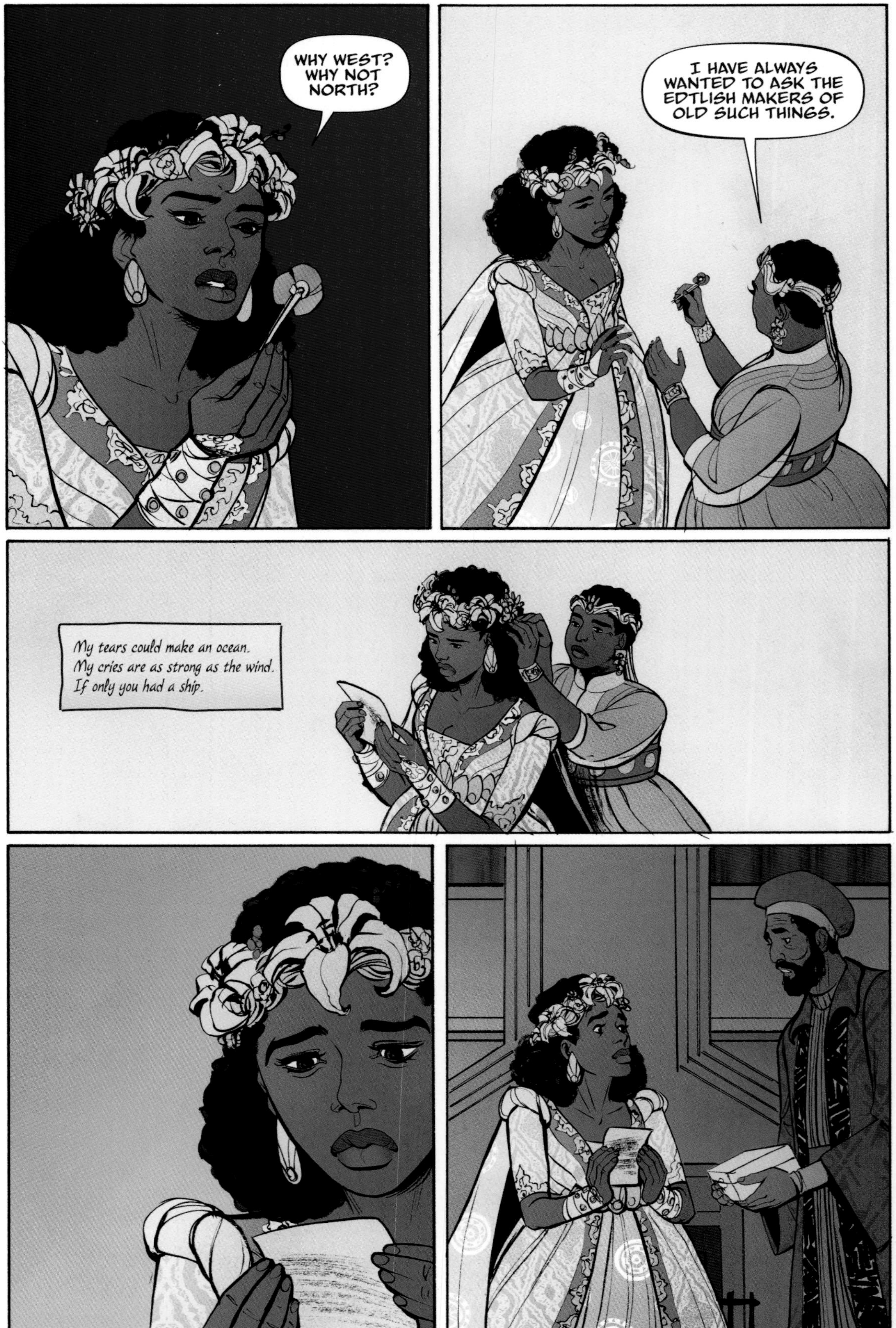
WHY WEST? WHY NOT NORTH?
I HAVE ALWAYS WANTED TO ASK THE EDTLISH MAKERS OF OLD SUCH THINGS.
My tears could make an ocean.
My cries are as strong as the wind.
If only you had a ship.

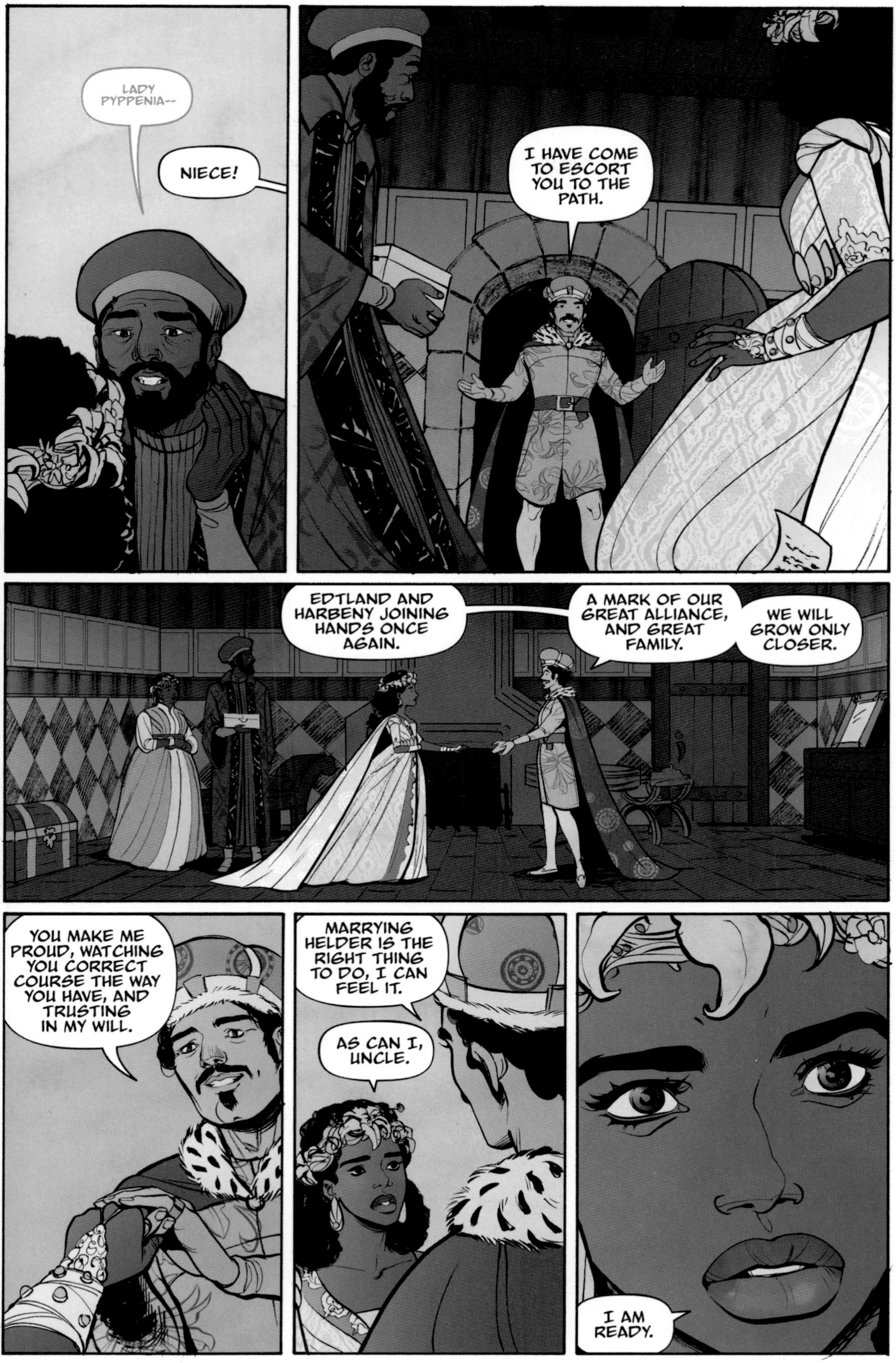
LADY PYPPENIA--
NIECE!
I HAVE COME TO ESCORT YOU TO THE PATH.
EDTLAND AND HARBENY JOINING HANDS ONCE AGAIN.
A MARK OF OUR GREAT ALLIANCE, AND GREAT FAMILY.
WE WILL GROW ONLY CLOSER.
YOU MAKE ME PROUD, WATCHING YOU CORRECT COURSE THE WAY YOU HAVE, AND TRUSTING IN MY WILL.
MARRYING HELDER IS THE RIGHT THING TO DO, I CAN FEEL IT.
AS CAN I, UNCLE.
I AM READY.

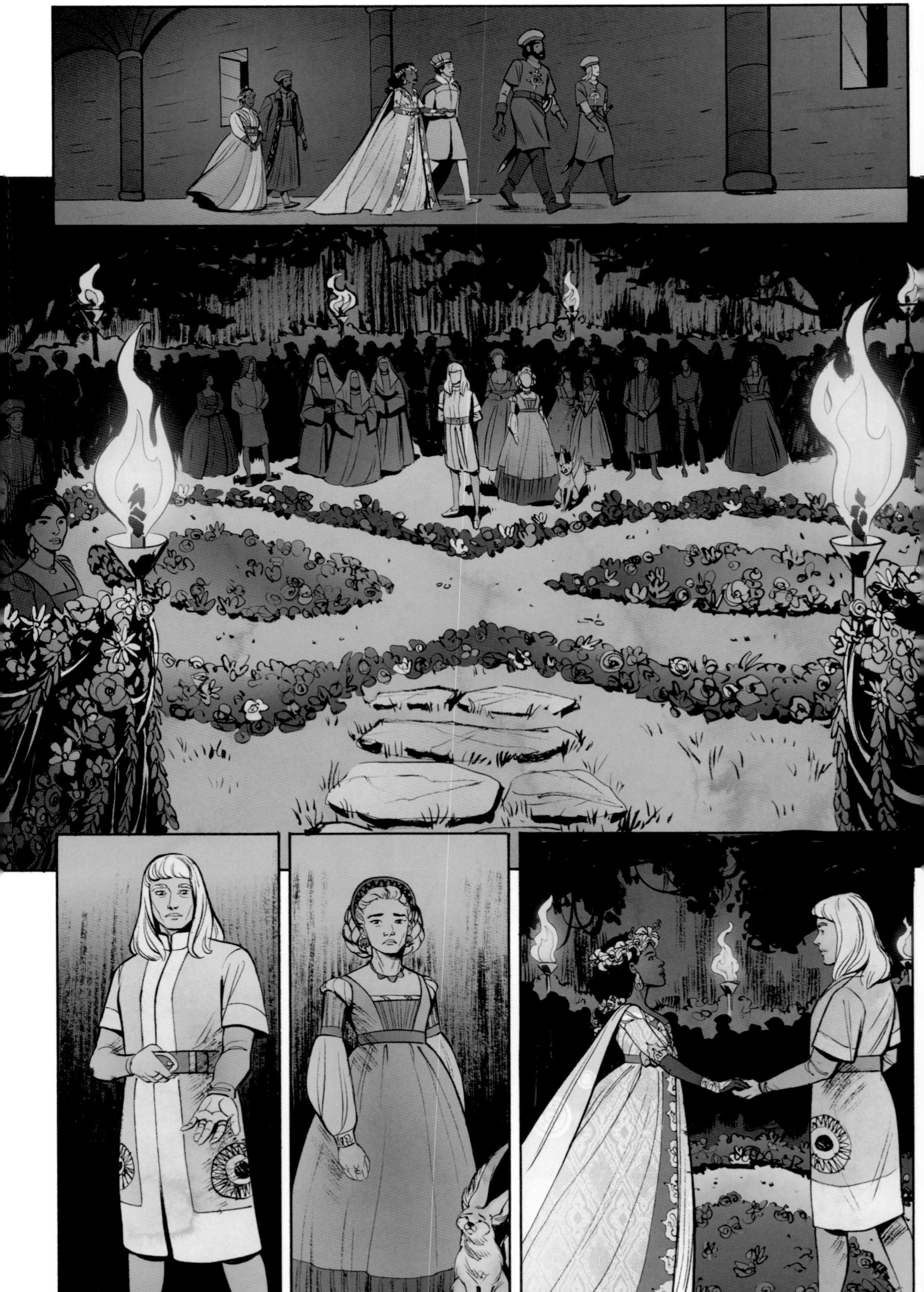

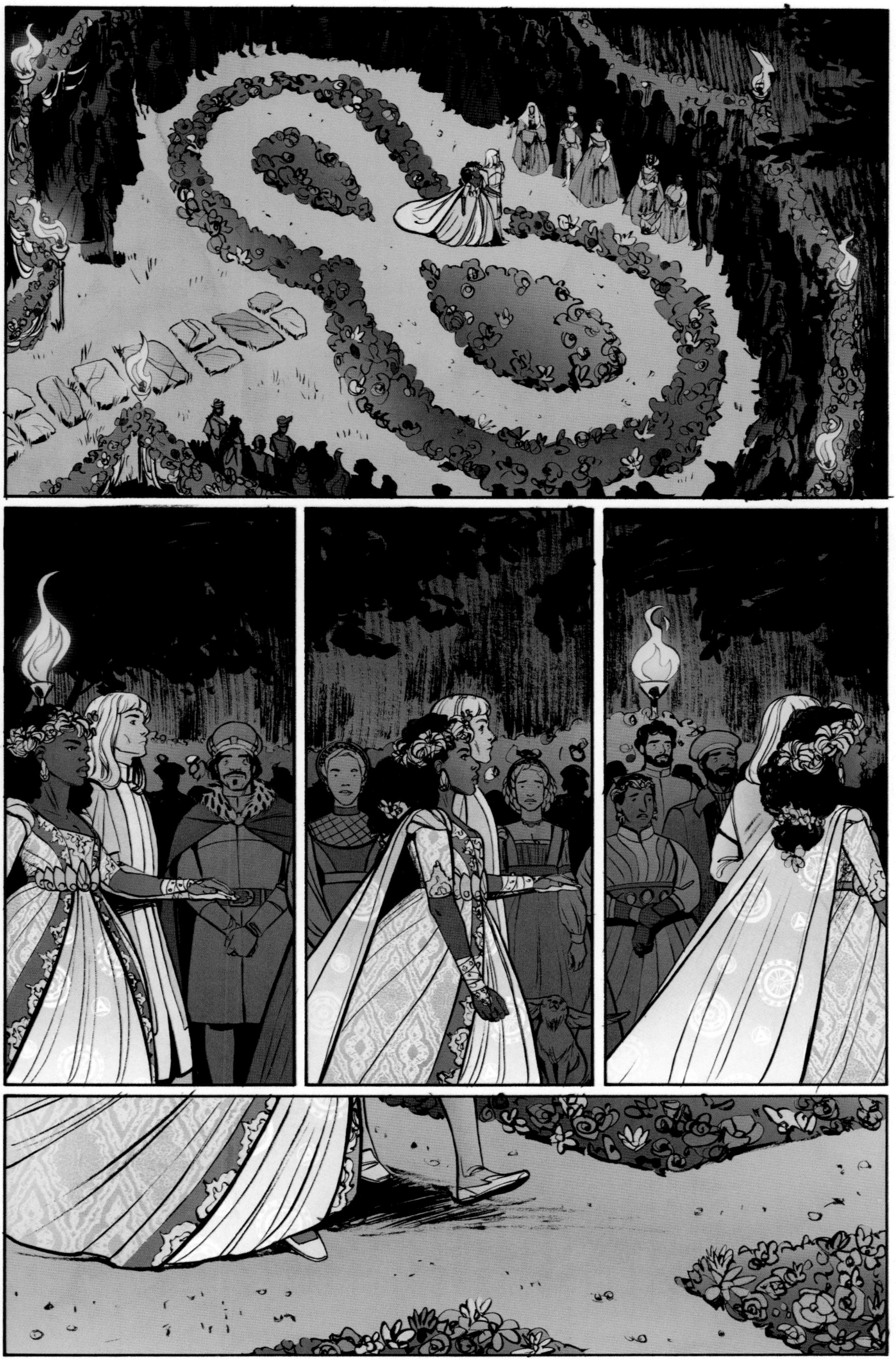

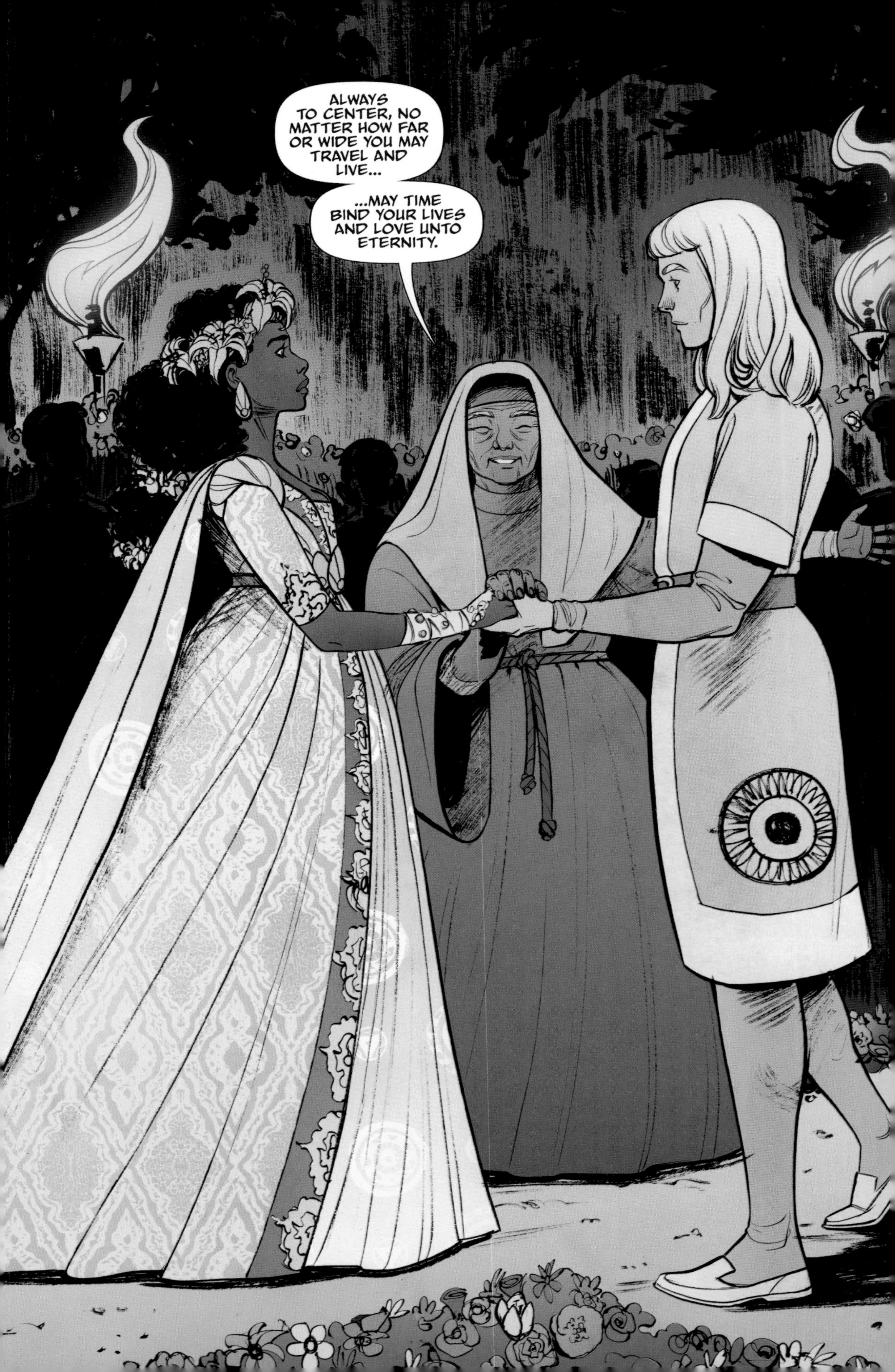
ALWAYS TO CENTER, NO MATTER HOW FAR OR WIDE YOU MAY TRAVEL AND LIVE...
...MAY TIME BIND YOUR LIVES AND LOVE UNTO ETERNITY.

CHAPTER NINE

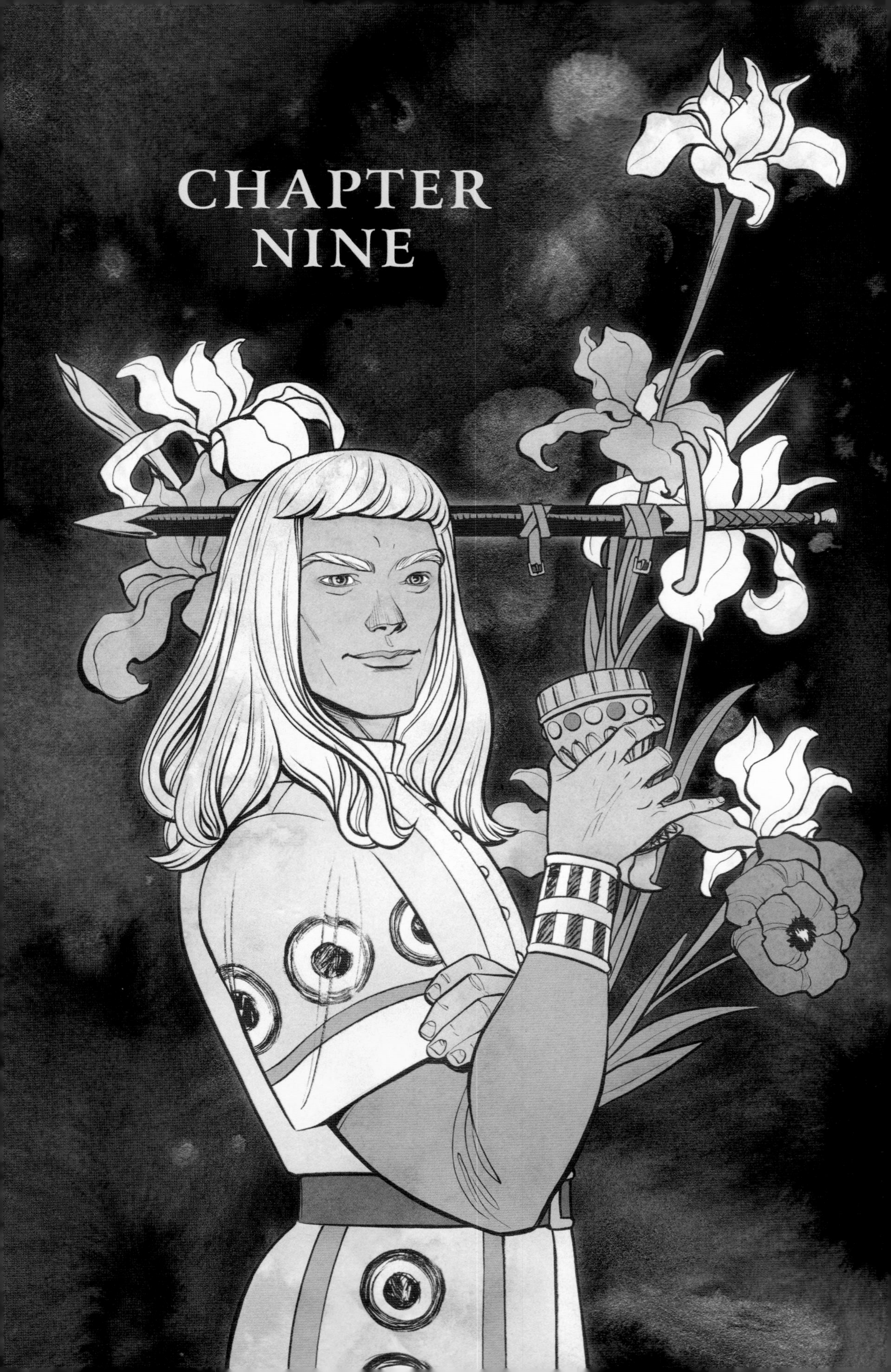

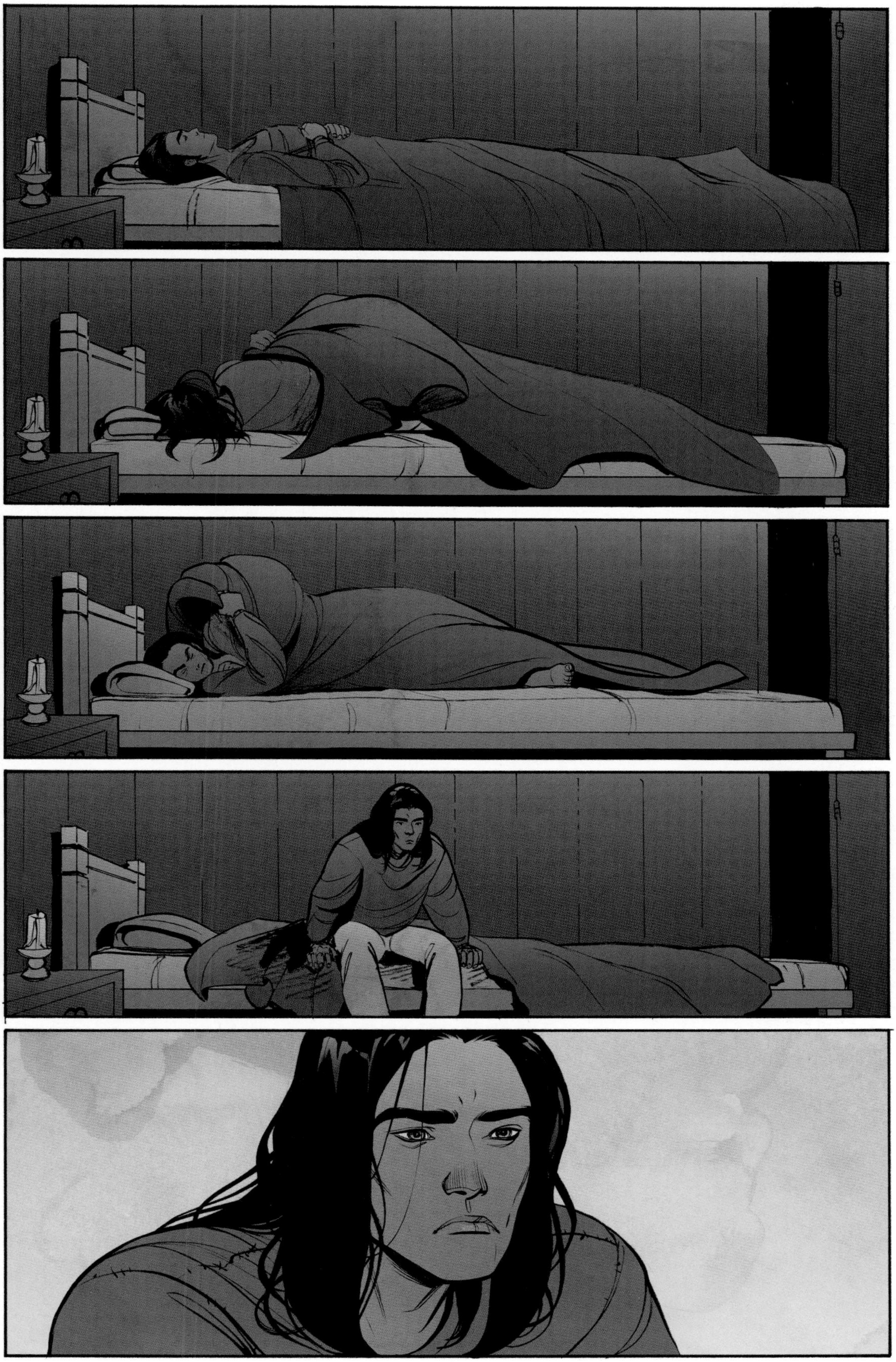

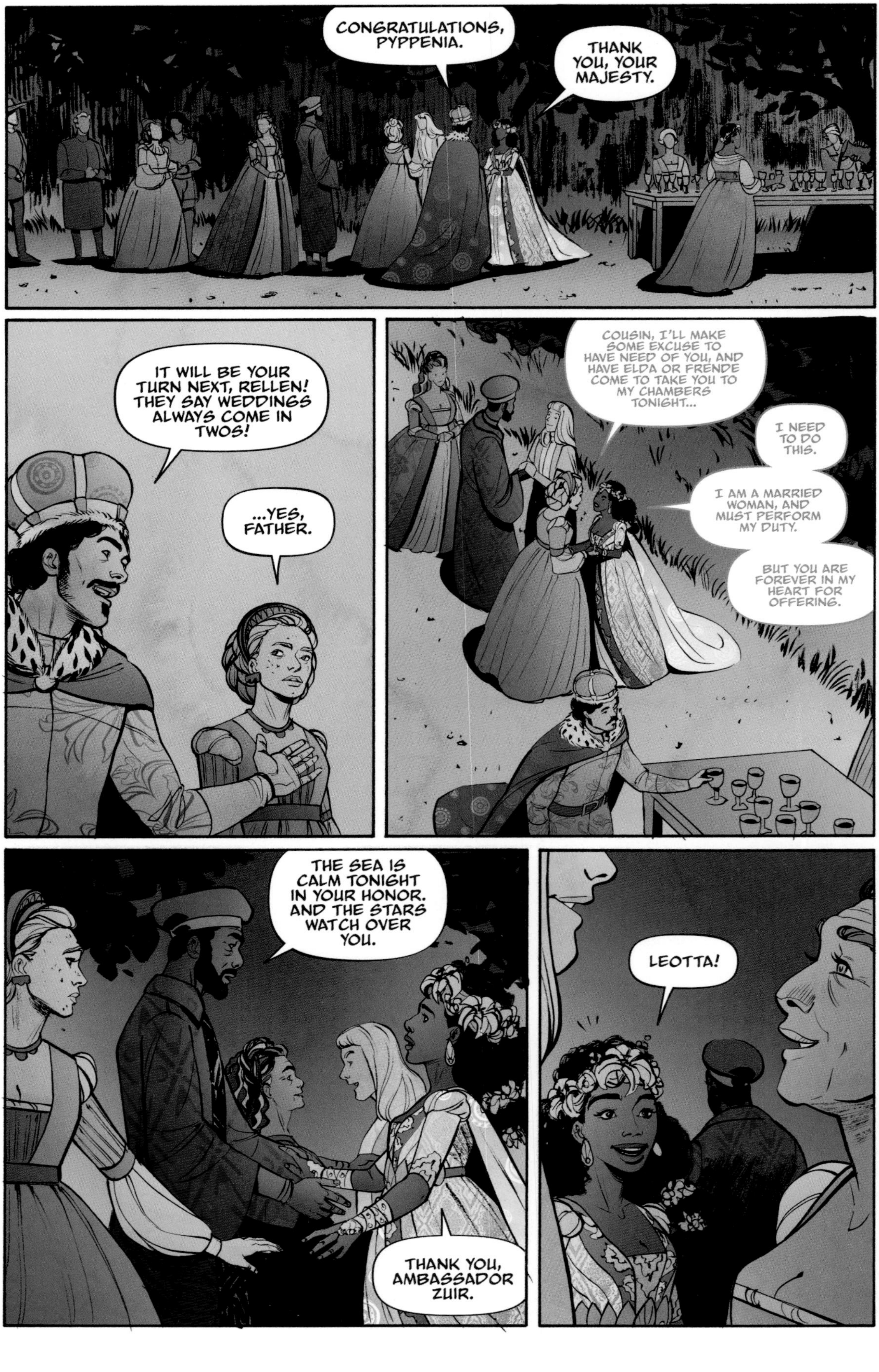
CONGRATULATIONS, PYPPENIA.
THANK YOU, YOUR MAJESTY.
IT WILL BE YOUR TURN NEXT, RELLEN! THEY SAY WEDDINGS ALWAYS COME IN TWOS!
...YES, FATHER.
COUSIN, I'LL MAKE SOME EXCUSE TO HAVE NEED OF YOU, AND HAVE ELDA OR FRENDE COME TO TAKE YOU TO MY CHAMBERS TONIGHT...
I NEED TO DO THIS.
I AM A MARRIED WOMAN, AND MUST PERFORM MY DUTY.
BUT YOU ARE FOREVER IN MY HEART FOR OFFERING.
THE SEA IS CALM TONIGHT IN YOUR HONOR. AND THE STARS WATCH OVER YOU.
THANK YOU, AMBASSADOR ZUIR.
LEOTTA!

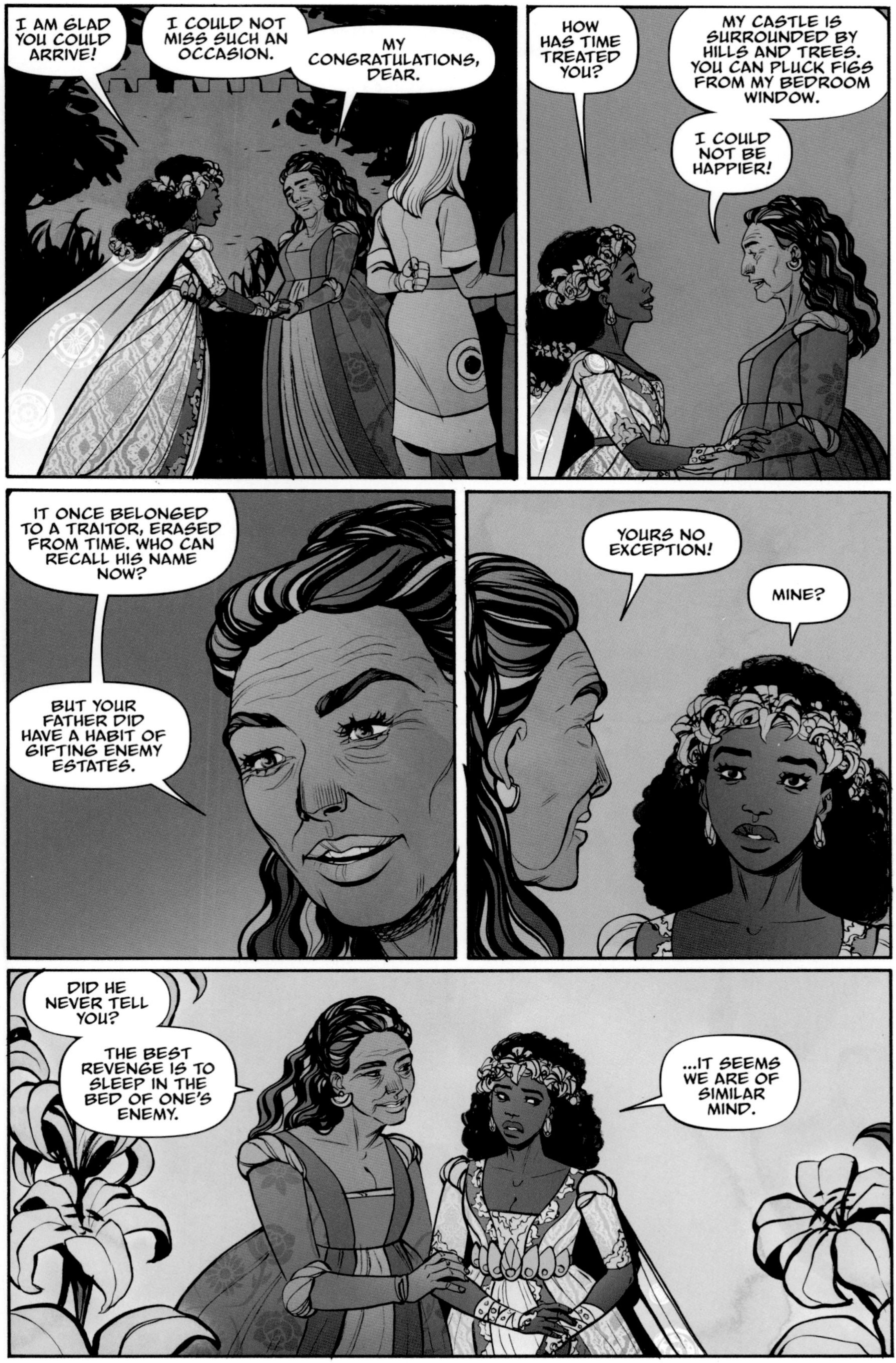
I AM GLAD YOU COULD ARRIVE!
I COULD NOT MISS SUCH AN OCCASION.
MY CONGRATULATIONS, DEAR.
HOW HAS TIME TREATED YOU?
MY CASTLE IS SURROUNDED BY HILLS AND TREES. YOU CAN PLUCK FIGS FROM MY BEDROOM WINDOW.
I COULD NOT BE HAPPIER!
IT ONCE BELONGED TO A TRAITOR, ERASED FROM TIME. WHO CAN RECALL HIS NAME NOW?
BUT YOUR FATHER DID HAVE A HABIT OF GIFTING ENEMY ESTATES.
YOURS NO EXCEPTION!
MINE?
DID HE NEVER TELL YOU?
THE BEST REVENGE IS TO SLEEP IN THE BED OF ONE'S ENEMY.
...IT SEEMS WE ARE OF SIMILAR MIND.

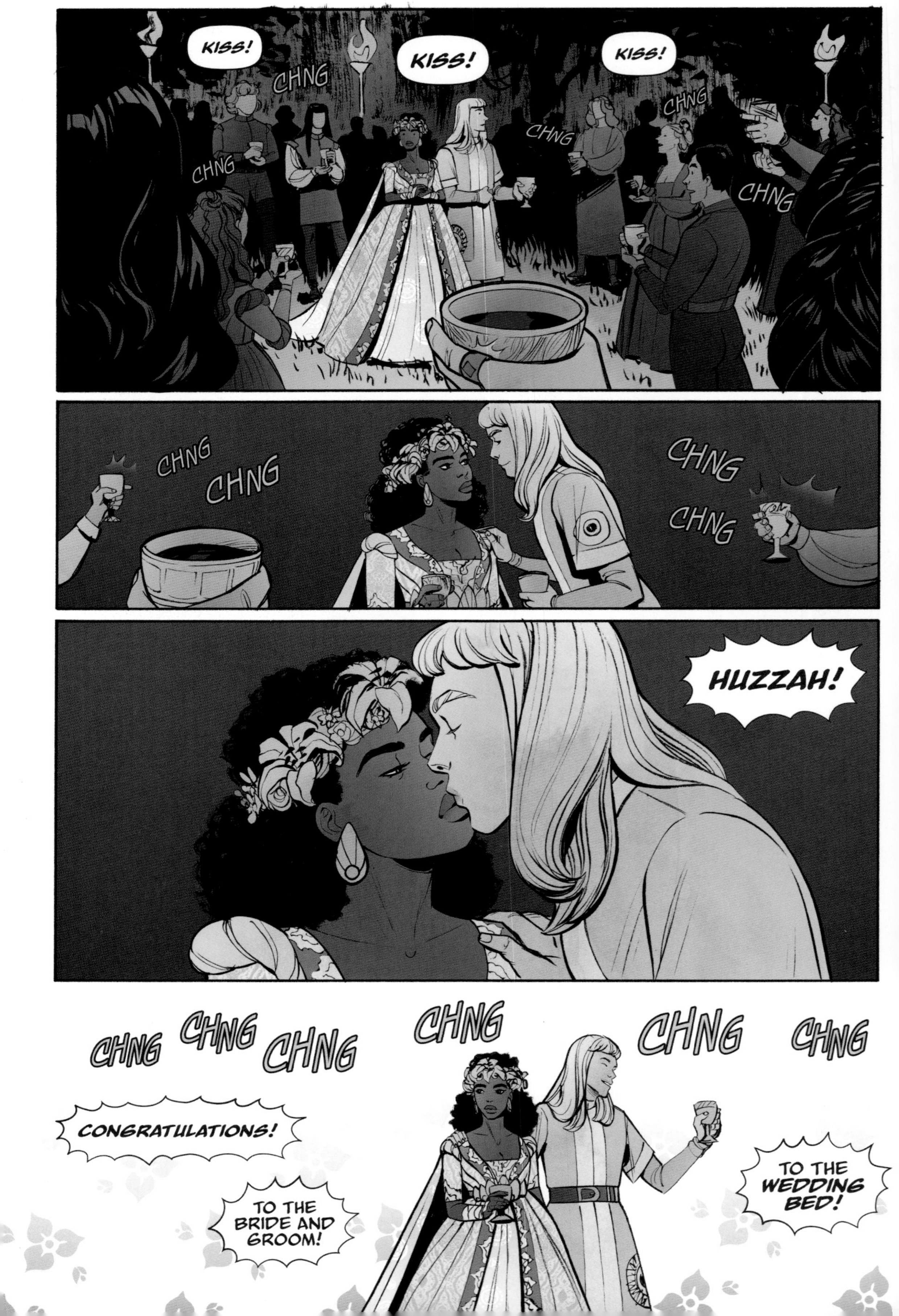
KISS!
KISS!
KISS!
CHNG
CHNG
CHNG
CHNG
CHNG
CHNG
CHNG
CHNG
CHNG
HUZZAH!
CHNG
CHNG
CHNG
CHNG
CHNG
CHNG
CONGRATULATIONS!
TO THE BRIDE AND GROOM!
TO THE WEDDING BED!

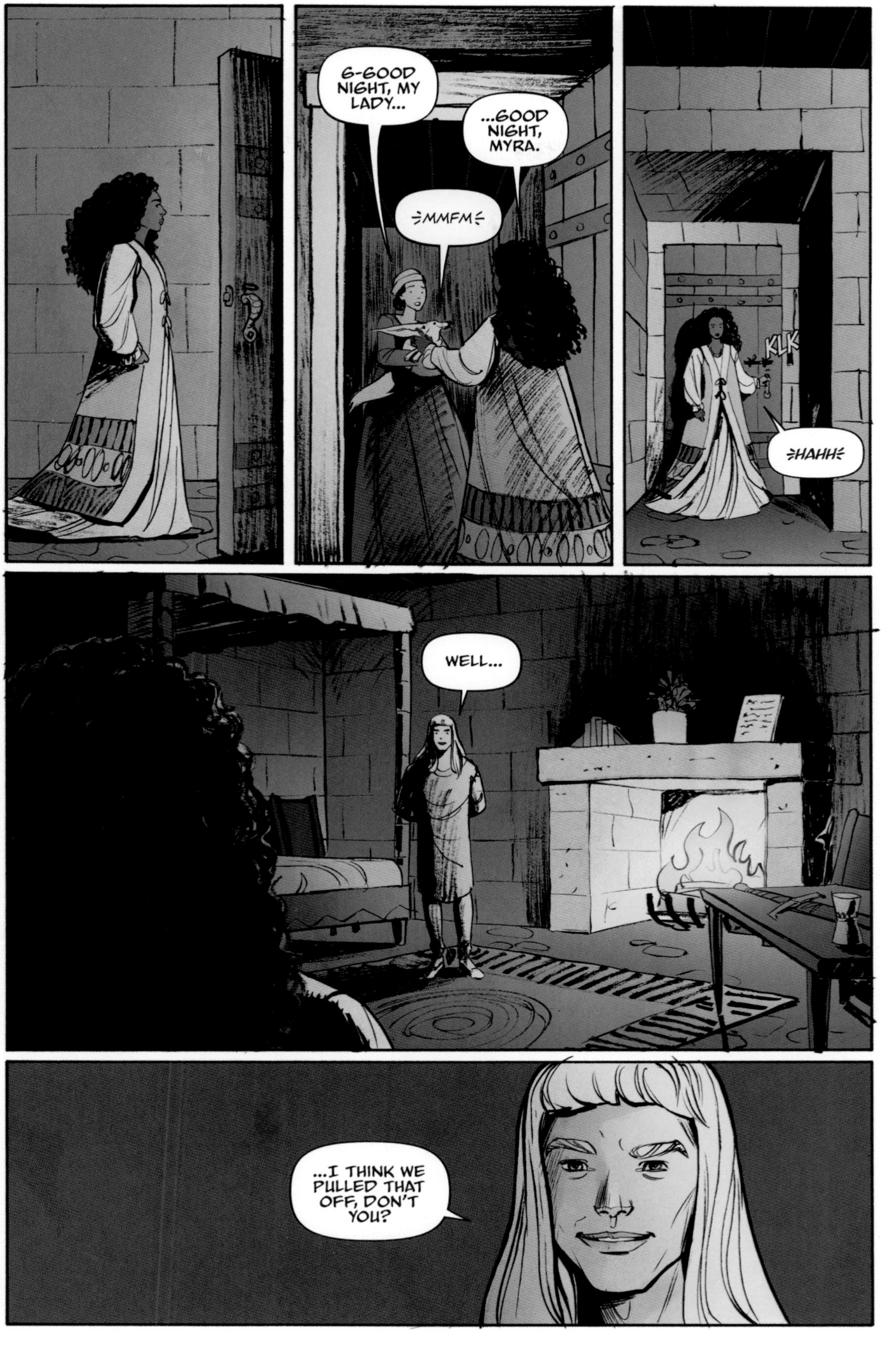
G-GOOD NIGHT, MY LADY...
...GOOD NIGHT, MYRA.
MMFM
KLK
HAHH
WELL...
...I THINK WE PULLED THAT OFF, DON'T YOU?

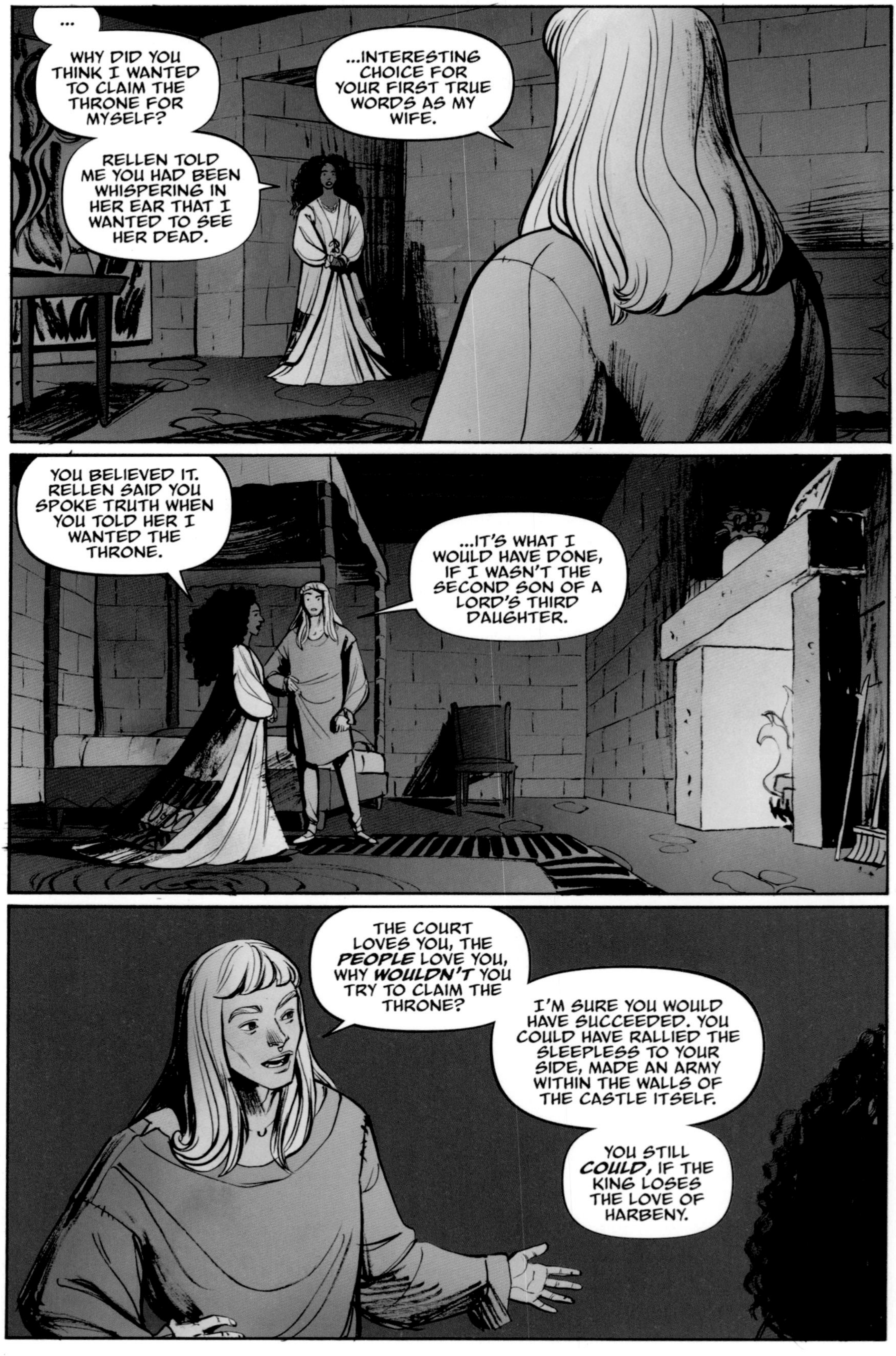
...
WHY DID YOU THINK I WANTED TO CLAIM THE THRONE FOR MYSELF?
RELLEN TOLD ME YOU HAD BEEN WHISPERING IN HER EAR THAT I WANTED TO SEE HER DEAD.
...INTERESTING CHOICE FOR YOUR FIRST TRUE WORDS AS MY WIFE.
YOU BELIEVED IT. RELLEN SAID YOU SPOKE TRUTH WHEN YOU TOLD HER I WANTED THE THRONE.
...IT'S WHAT I WOULD HAVE DONE, IF I WASN'T THE SECOND SON OF A LORD'S THIRD DAUGHTER.
THE COURT LOVES YOU, THE *PEOPLE* LOVE YOU, WHY *WOULDN'T* YOU TRY TO CLAIM THE THRONE?
I'M SURE YOU WOULD HAVE SUCCEEDED. YOU COULD HAVE RALLIED THE SLEEPLESS TO YOUR SIDE, MADE AN ARMY WITHIN THE WALLS OF THE CASTLE ITSELF.
YOU STILL *COULD,* IF THE KING LOSES THE LOVE OF HARBENY.

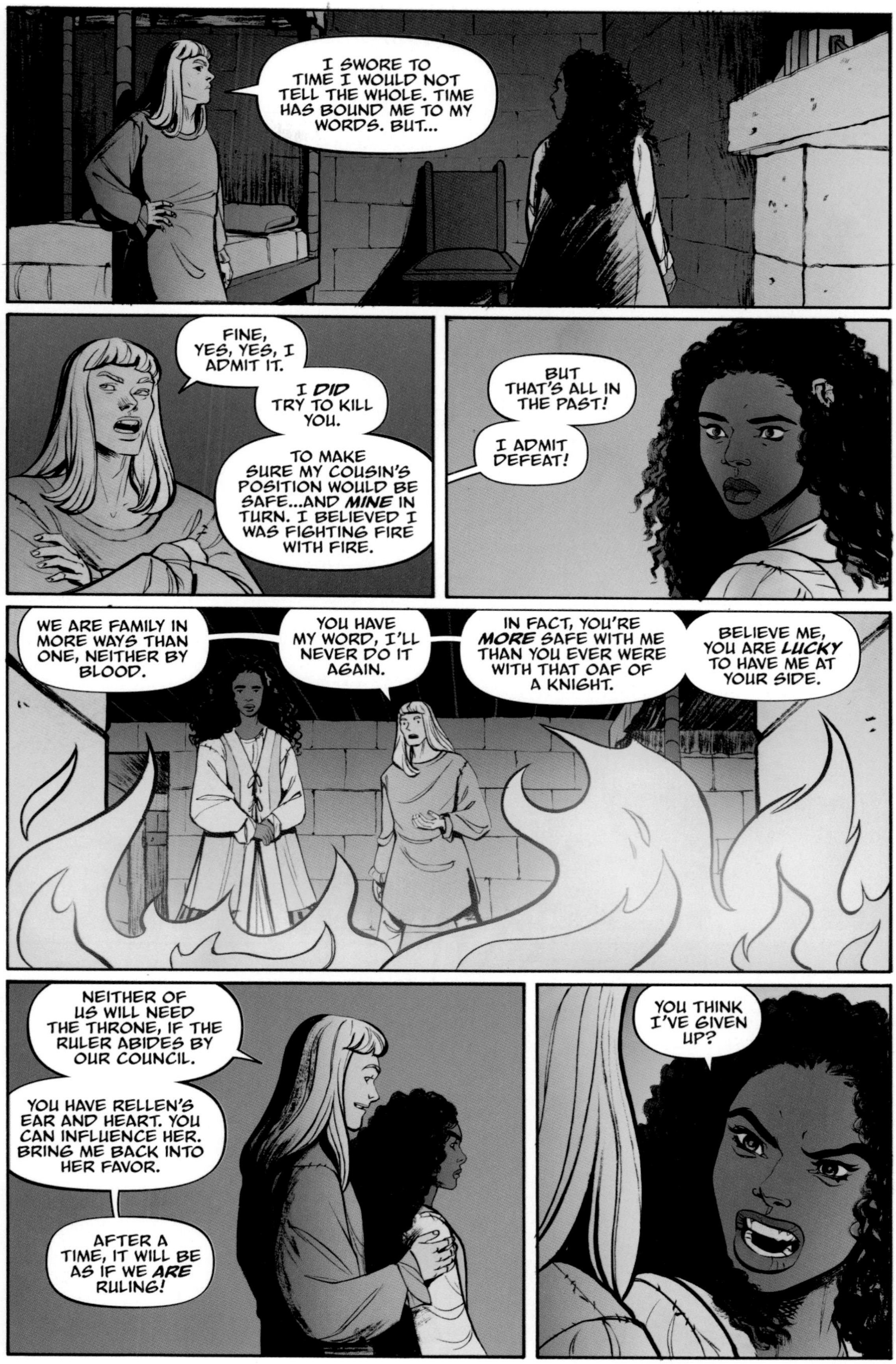
I SWORE TO TIME I WOULD NOT TELL THE WHOLE. TIME HAS BOUND ME TO MY WORDS. BUT...
FINE, YES, YES, I ADMIT IT.
I *DID* TRY TO KILL YOU.
TO MAKE SURE MY COUSIN'S POSITION WOULD BE SAFE...AND *MINE* IN TURN. I BELIEVED I WAS FIGHTING FIRE WITH FIRE.
BUT THAT'S ALL IN THE PAST!
I ADMIT DEFEAT!
WE ARE FAMILY IN MORE WAYS THAN ONE, NEITHER BY BLOOD.
YOU HAVE MY WORD, I'LL NEVER DO IT AGAIN.
IN FACT, YOU'RE *MORE* SAFE WITH ME THAN YOU EVER WERE WITH THAT OAF OF A KNIGHT.
BELIEVE ME, YOU ARE *LUCKY* TO HAVE ME AT YOUR SIDE.
NEITHER OF US WILL NEED THE THRONE, IF THE RULER ABIDES BY OUR COUNCIL.
YOU HAVE RELLEN'S EAR AND HEART. YOU CAN INFLUENCE HER. BRING ME BACK INTO HER FAVOR.
AFTER A TIME, IT WILL BE AS IF WE *ARE* RULING!
YOU THINK I'VE GIVEN UP?

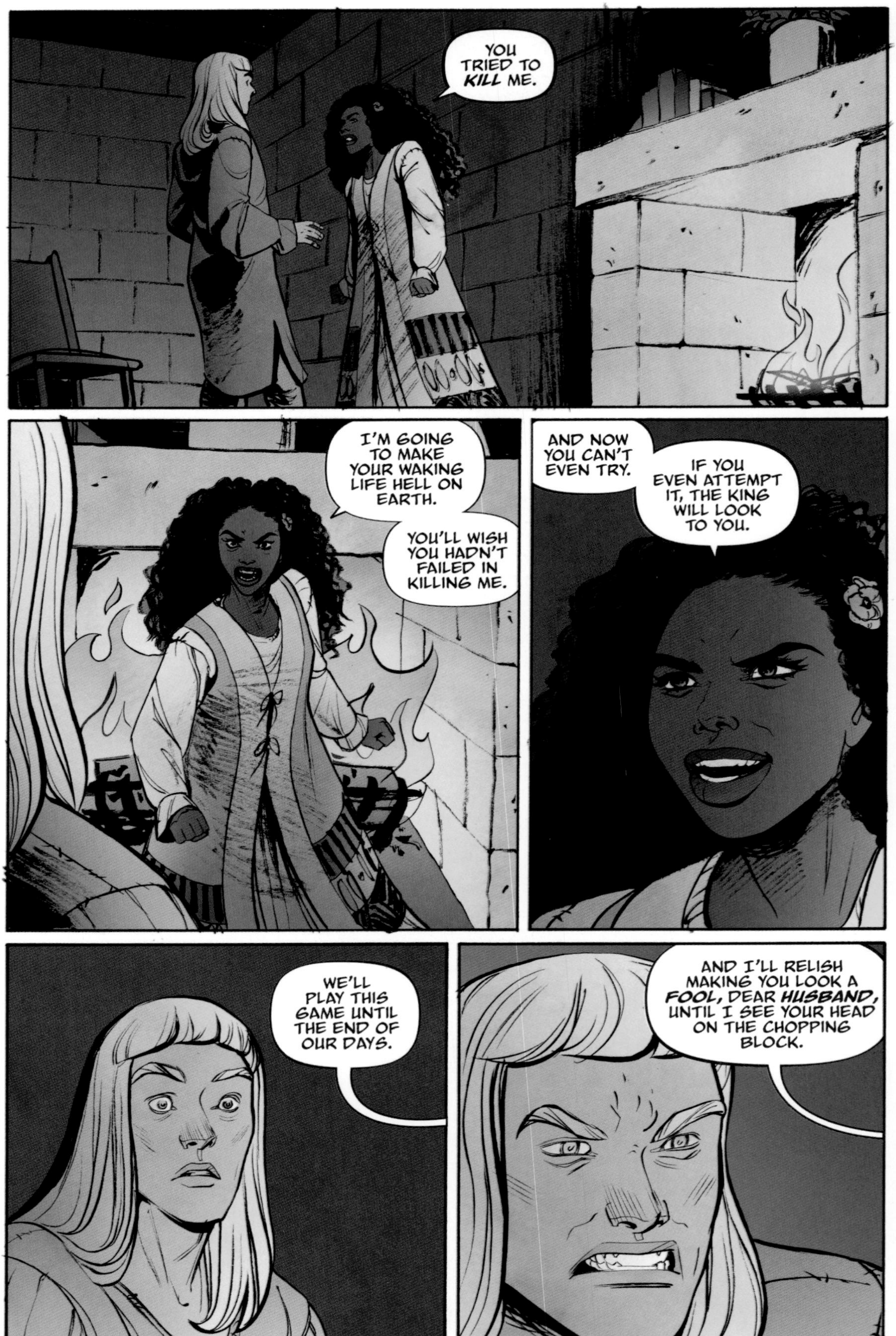

YOU TRIED TO **KILL** ME.
I'M GOING TO MAKE YOUR WAKING LIFE HELL ON EARTH.
YOU'LL WISH YOU HADN'T FAILED IN KILLING ME.
AND NOW YOU CAN'T EVEN TRY.
IF YOU EVEN ATTEMPT IT, THE KING WILL LOOK TO YOU.
WE'LL PLAY THIS GAME UNTIL THE END OF OUR DAYS.
AND I'LL RELISH MAKING YOU LOOK A **FOOL**, DEAR **HUSBAND**, UNTIL I SEE YOUR HEAD ON THE CHOPPING BLOCK.

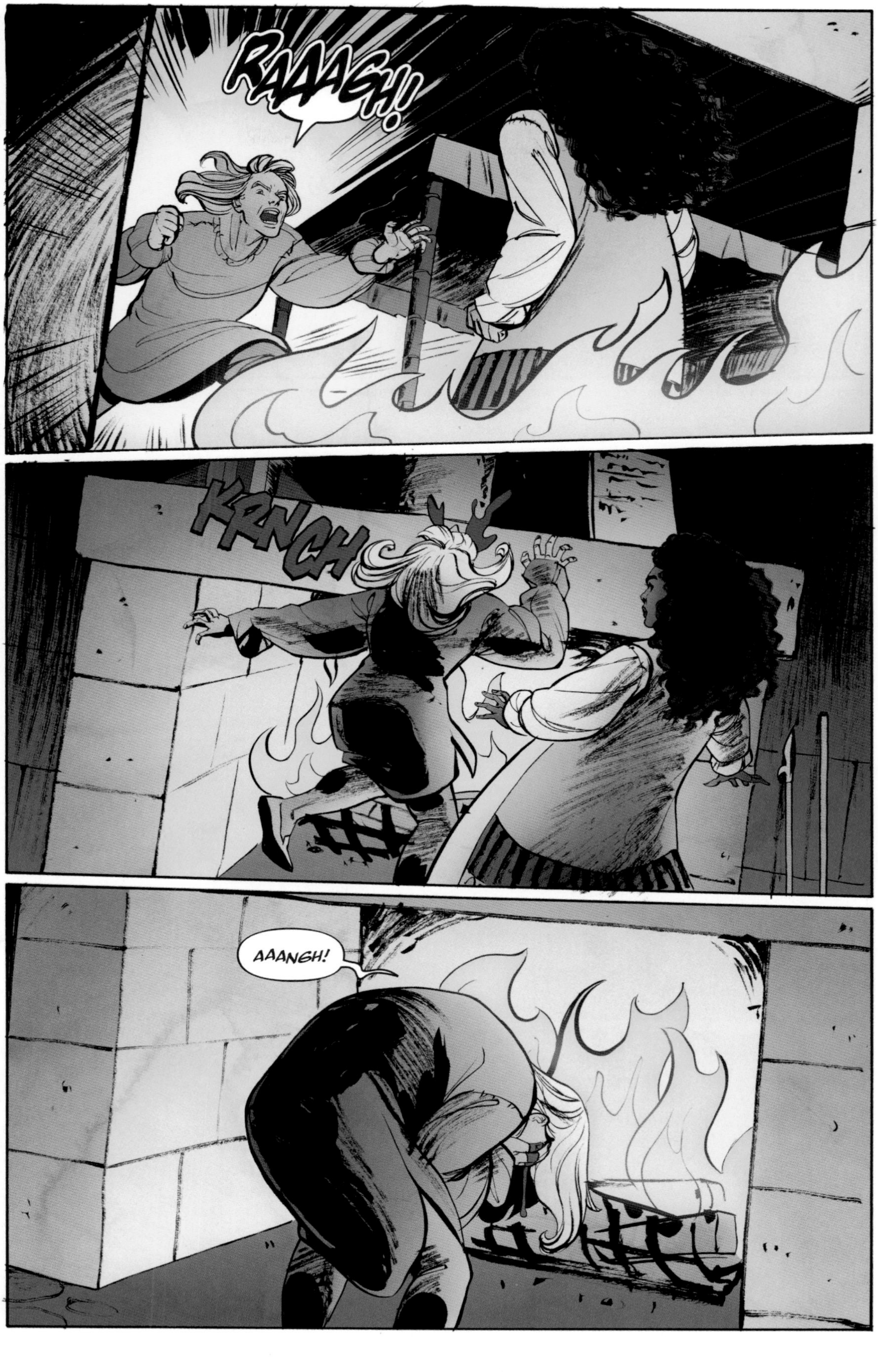
RAAAGH!
KRNCH
AAANGH!

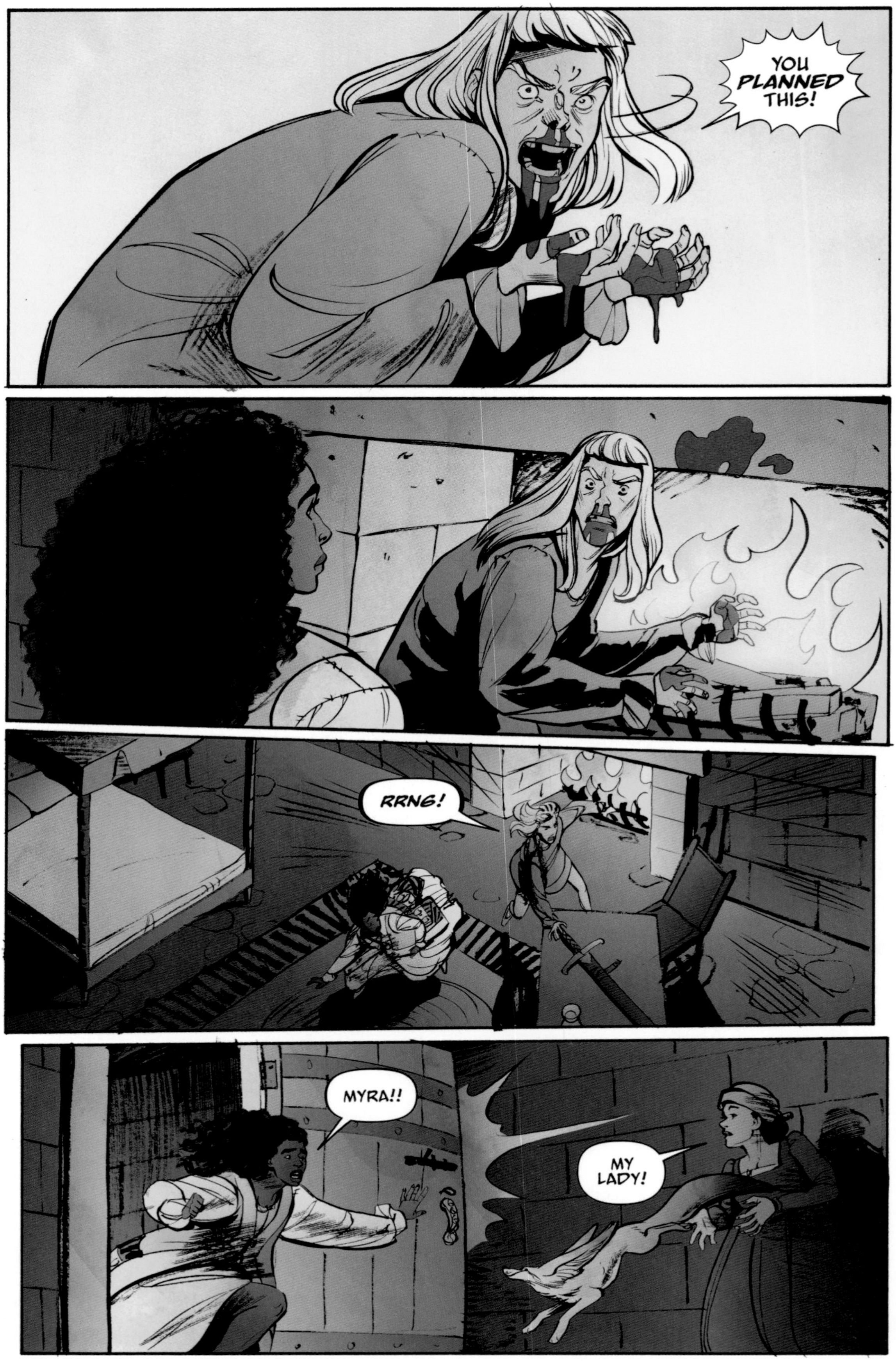
YOU PLANNED THIS!
RRNG!
MYRA!!
MY LADY!

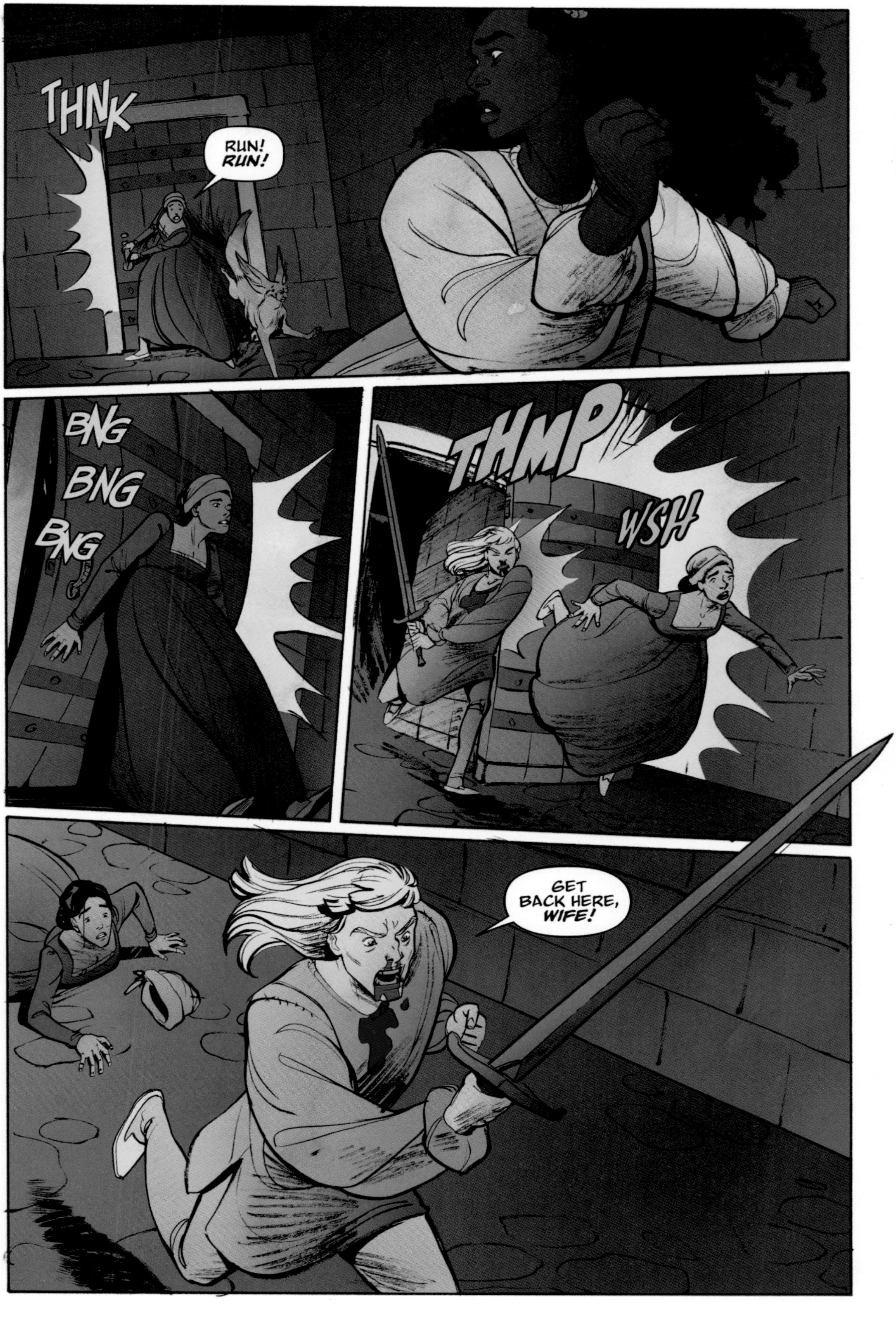
THNK
RUN! RUN!
BNG
BNG
BNG
THMP
WSH
GET BACK HERE, WIFE!

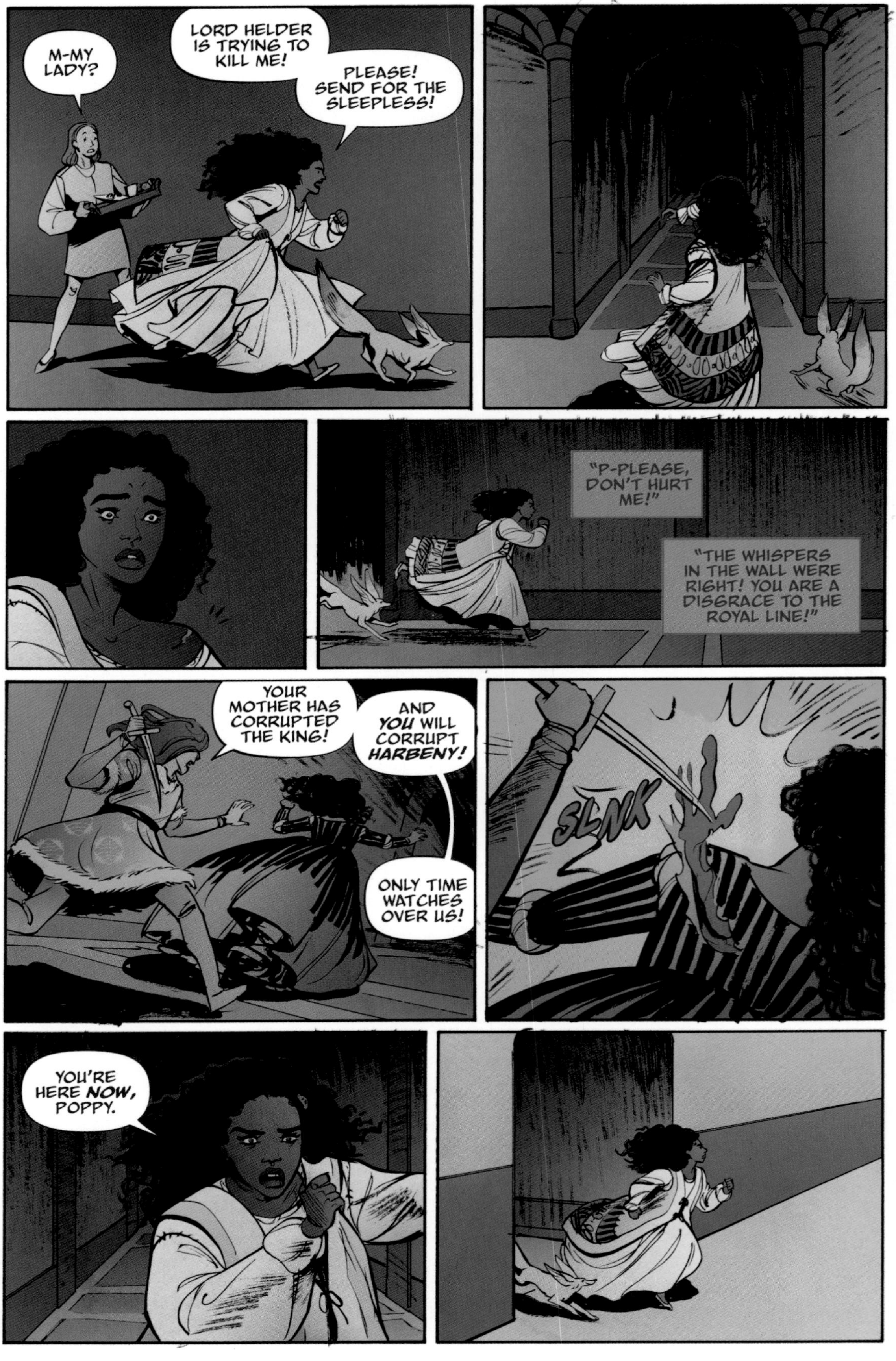
M-MY LADY?
LORD HELDER IS TRYING TO KILL ME!
PLEASE! SEND FOR THE SLEEPLESS!
"P-PLEASE, DON'T HURT ME!"
"THE WHISPERS IN THE WALL WERE RIGHT! YOU ARE A DISGRACE TO THE ROYAL LINE!"
YOUR MOTHER HAS CORRUPTED THE KING!
AND YOU WILL CORRUPT HARBENY!
ONLY TIME WATCHES OVER US!
SLNK
YOU'RE HERE NOW, POPPY.

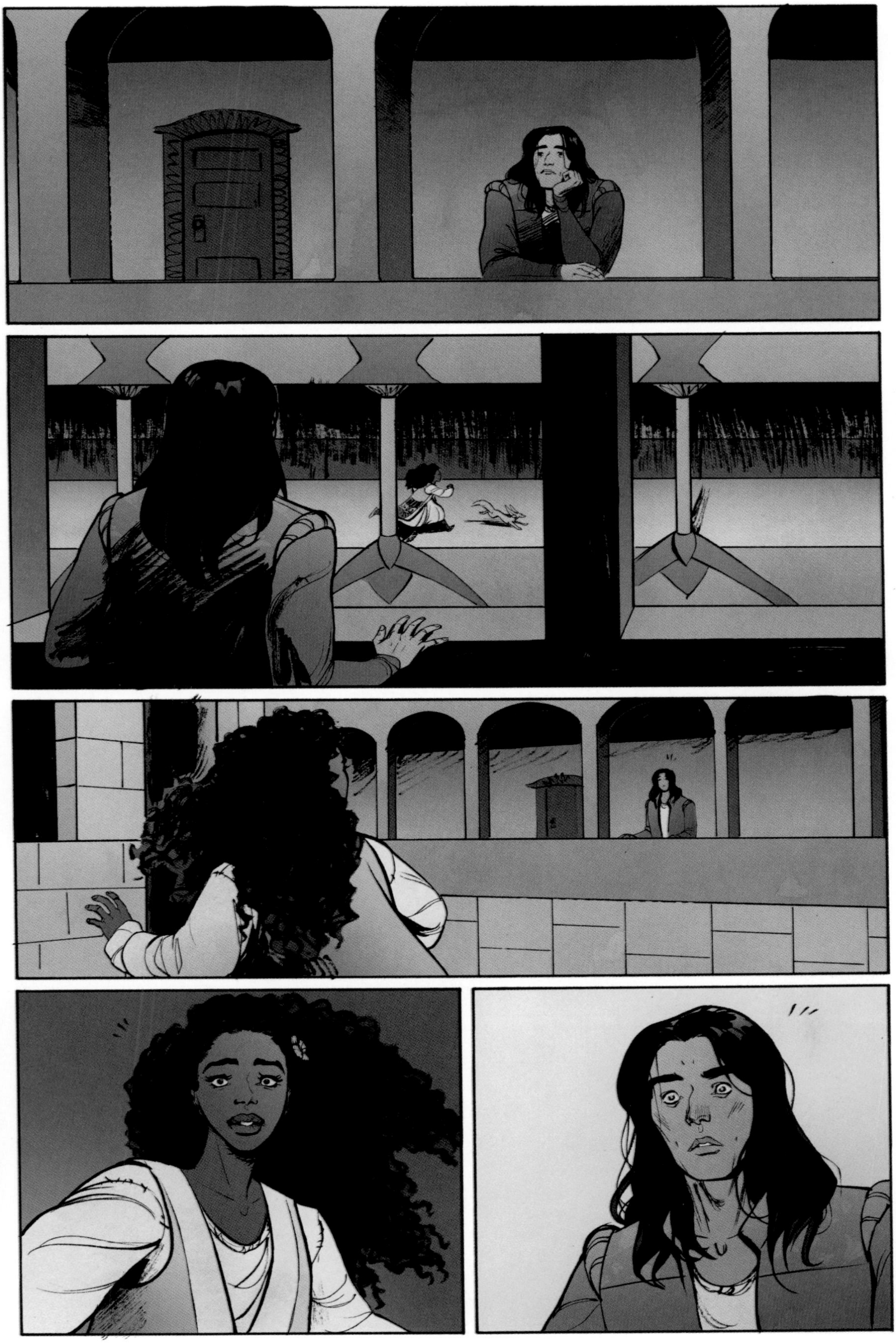

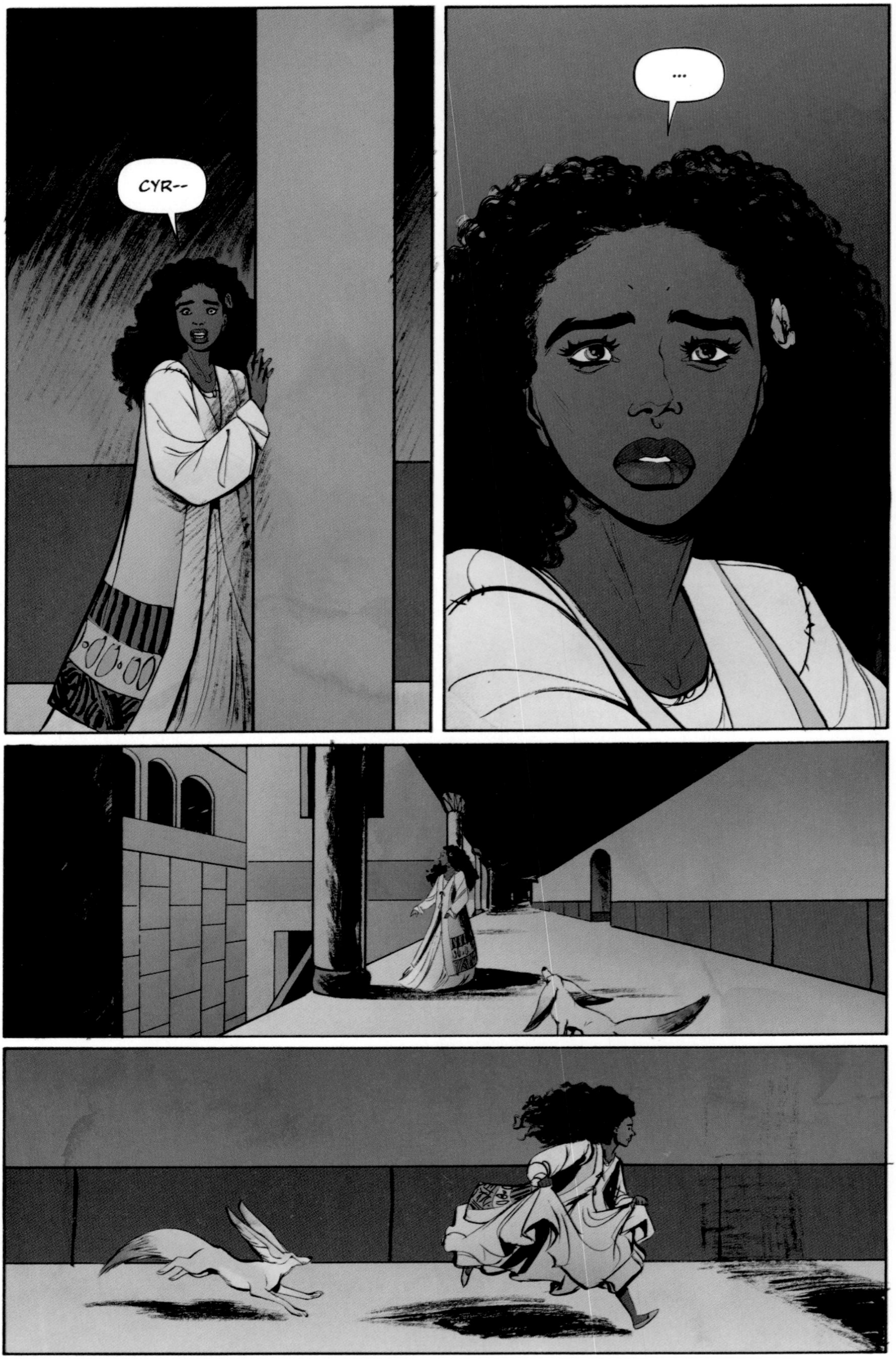
CYR--
...

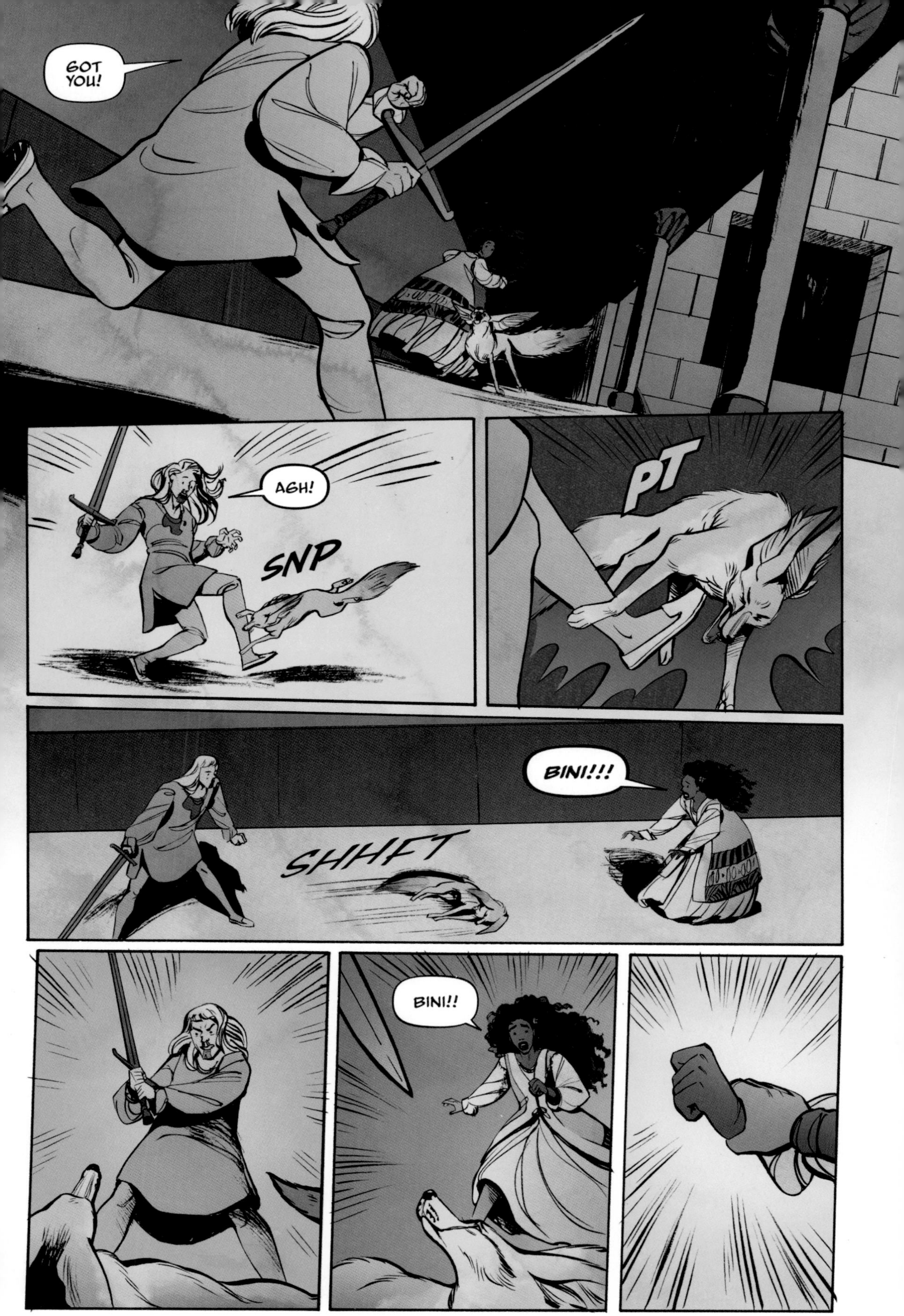
GOT YOU!
AGH!
SNP
PT
BINI!!!
SHHFT
BINI!!

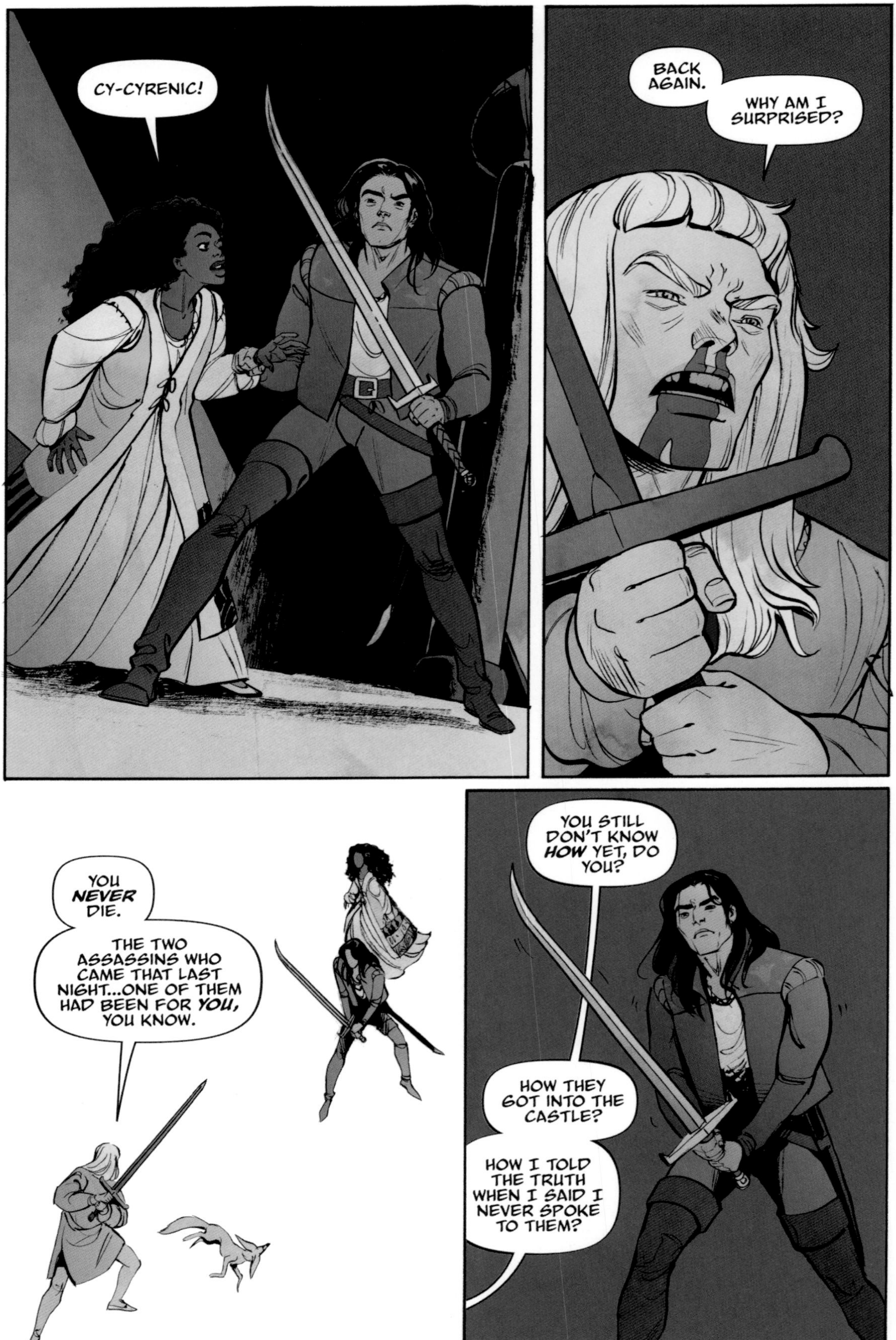
CY-CYRENIC!
BACK AGAIN.
WHY AM I SURPRISED?
YOU *NEVER* DIE.
THE TWO ASSASSINS WHO CAME THAT LAST NIGHT...ONE OF THEM HAD BEEN FOR *YOU,* YOU KNOW.
YOU STILL DON'T KNOW *HOW* YET, DO YOU?
HOW THEY GOT INTO THE CASTLE?
HOW I TOLD THE TRUTH WHEN I SAID I NEVER SPOKE TO THEM?

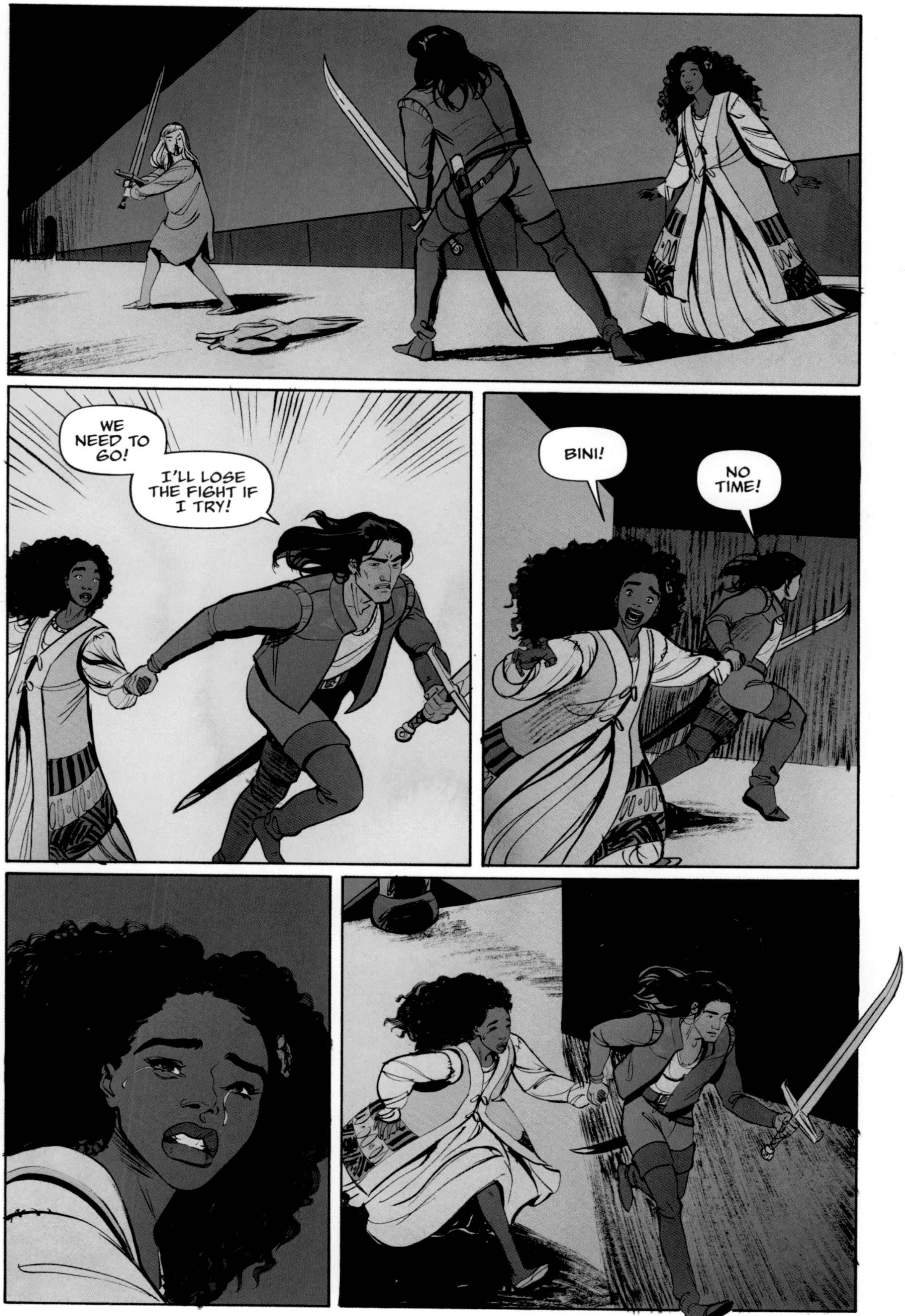
WE NEED TO GO!
I'LL LOSE THE FIGHT IF I TRY!
BINI!
NO TIME!

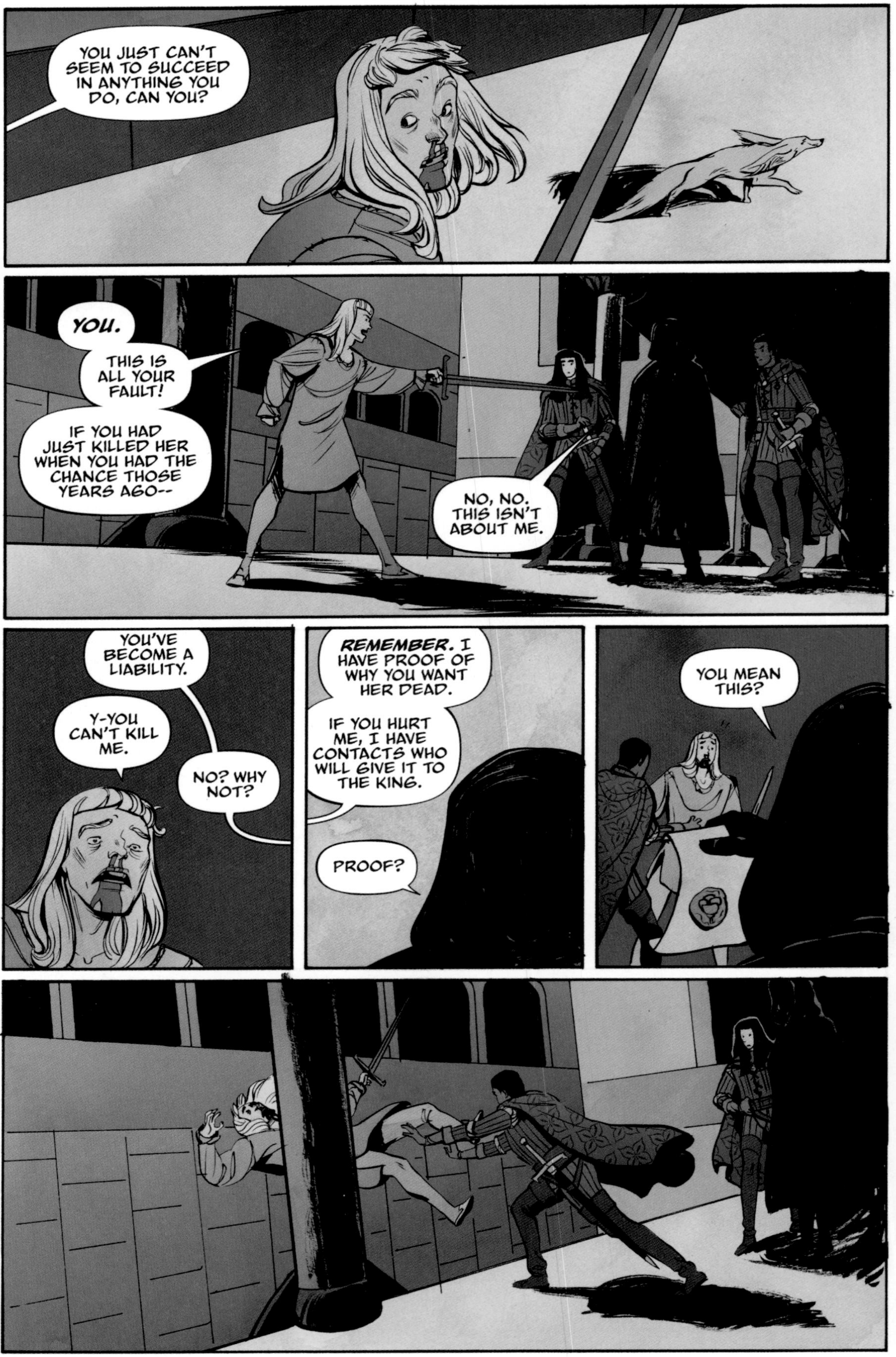
YOU JUST CAN'T SEEM TO SUCCEED IN ANYTHING YOU DO, CAN YOU?
YOU.
THIS IS ALL YOUR FAULT!
IF YOU HAD JUST KILLED HER WHEN YOU HAD THE CHANCE THOSE YEARS AGO--
NO, NO. THIS ISN'T ABOUT ME.
YOU'VE BECOME A LIABILITY.
Y-YOU CAN'T KILL ME.
NO? WHY NOT?
REMEMBER. I HAVE PROOF OF WHY YOU WANT HER DEAD.
IF YOU HURT ME, I HAVE CONTACTS WHO WILL GIVE IT TO THE KING.
PROOF?
YOU MEAN THIS?

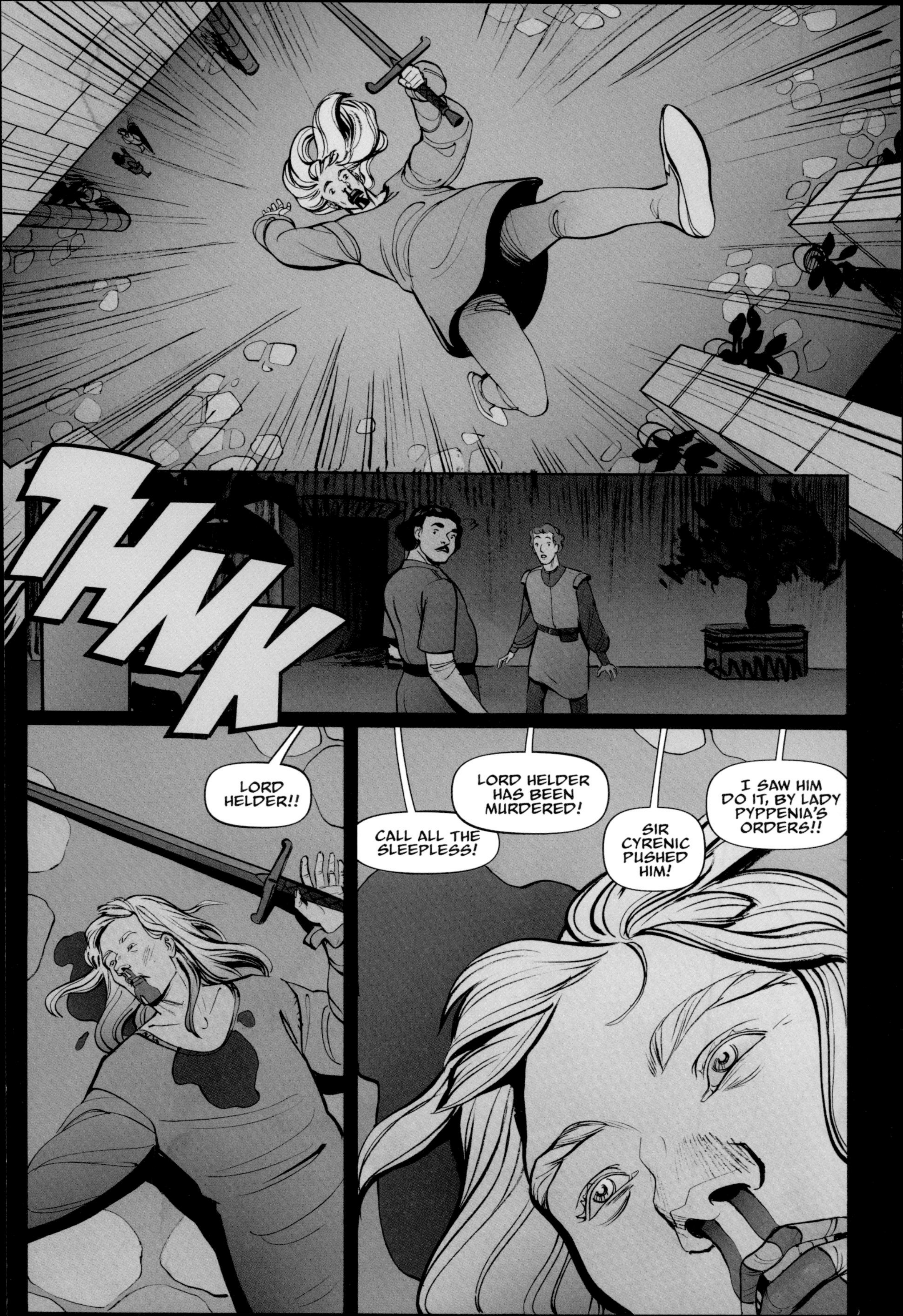
THNK
LORD HELDER!!
LORD HELDER HAS BEEN MURDERED!
CALL ALL THE SLEEPLESS!
SIR CYRENIC PUSHED HIM!
I SAW HIM DO IT, BY LADY PYPPENIA'S ORDERS!!

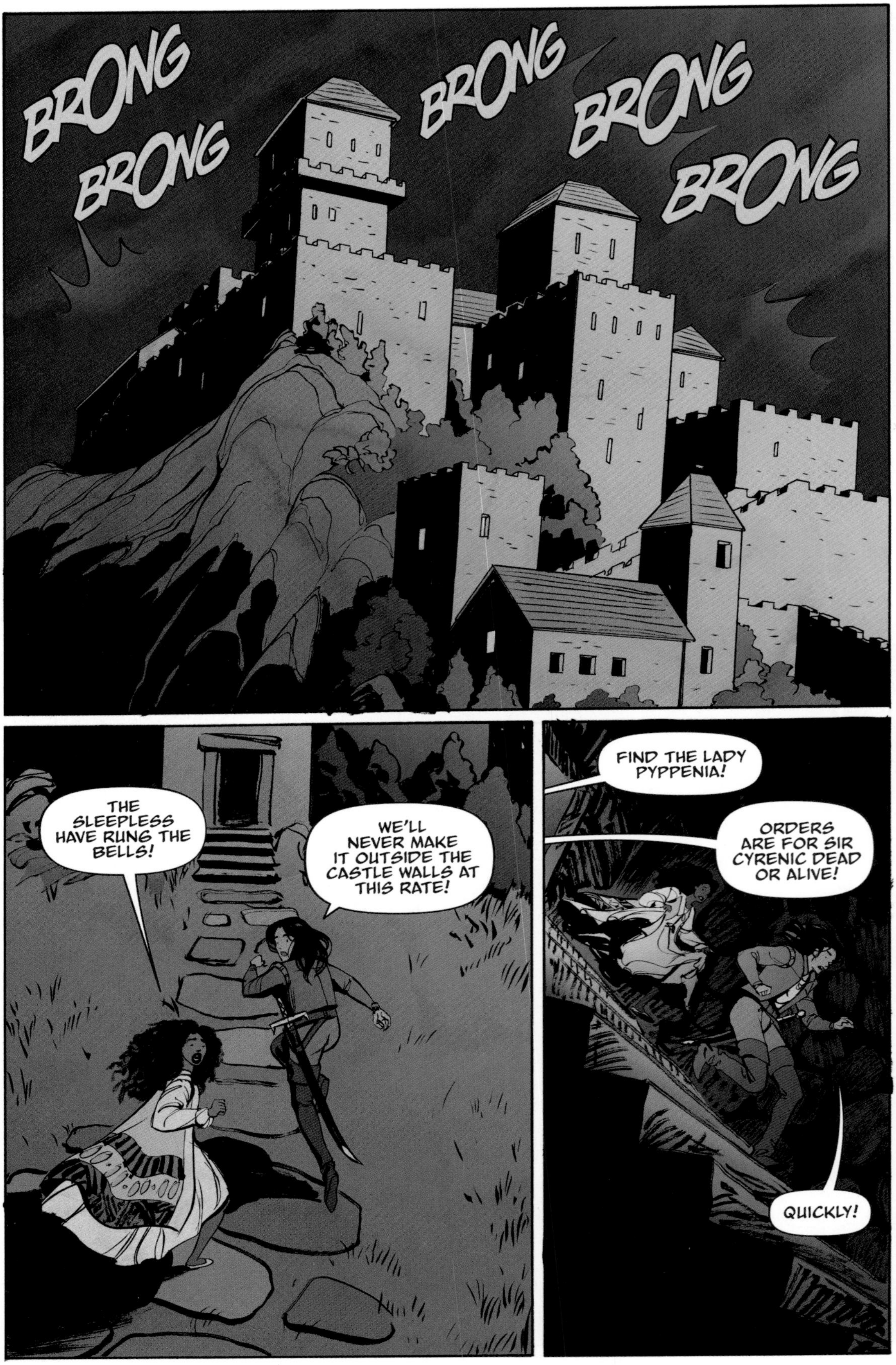
BRONG
BRONG
BRONG
BRONG
BRONG
THE SLEEPLESS HAVE RUNG THE BELLS!
WE'LL NEVER MAKE IT OUTSIDE THE CASTLE WALLS AT THIS RATE!
FIND THE LADY PYPPENIA!
ORDERS ARE FOR SIR CYRENIC DEAD OR ALIVE!
QUICKLY!

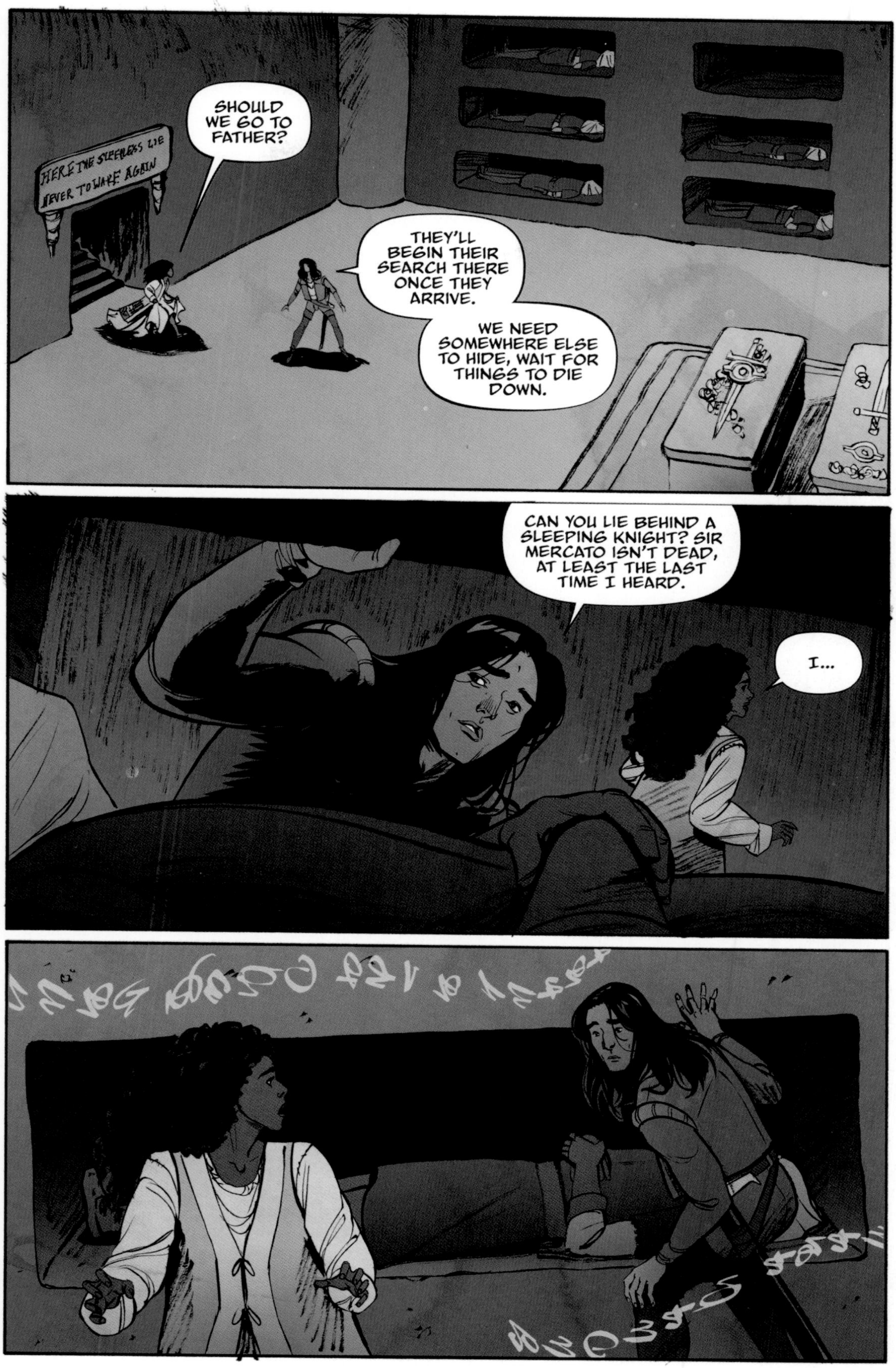
HERE THE SLEEPLESS LIE NEVER TO WAKE AGAIN
SHOULD WE GO TO FATHER?
THEY'LL BEGIN THEIR SEARCH THERE ONCE THEY ARRIVE.
WE NEED SOMEWHERE ELSE TO HIDE, WAIT FOR THINGS TO DIE DOWN.
CAN YOU LIE BEHIND A SLEEPING KNIGHT? SIR MERCATO ISN'T DEAD, AT LEAST THE LAST TIME I HEARD.
I...

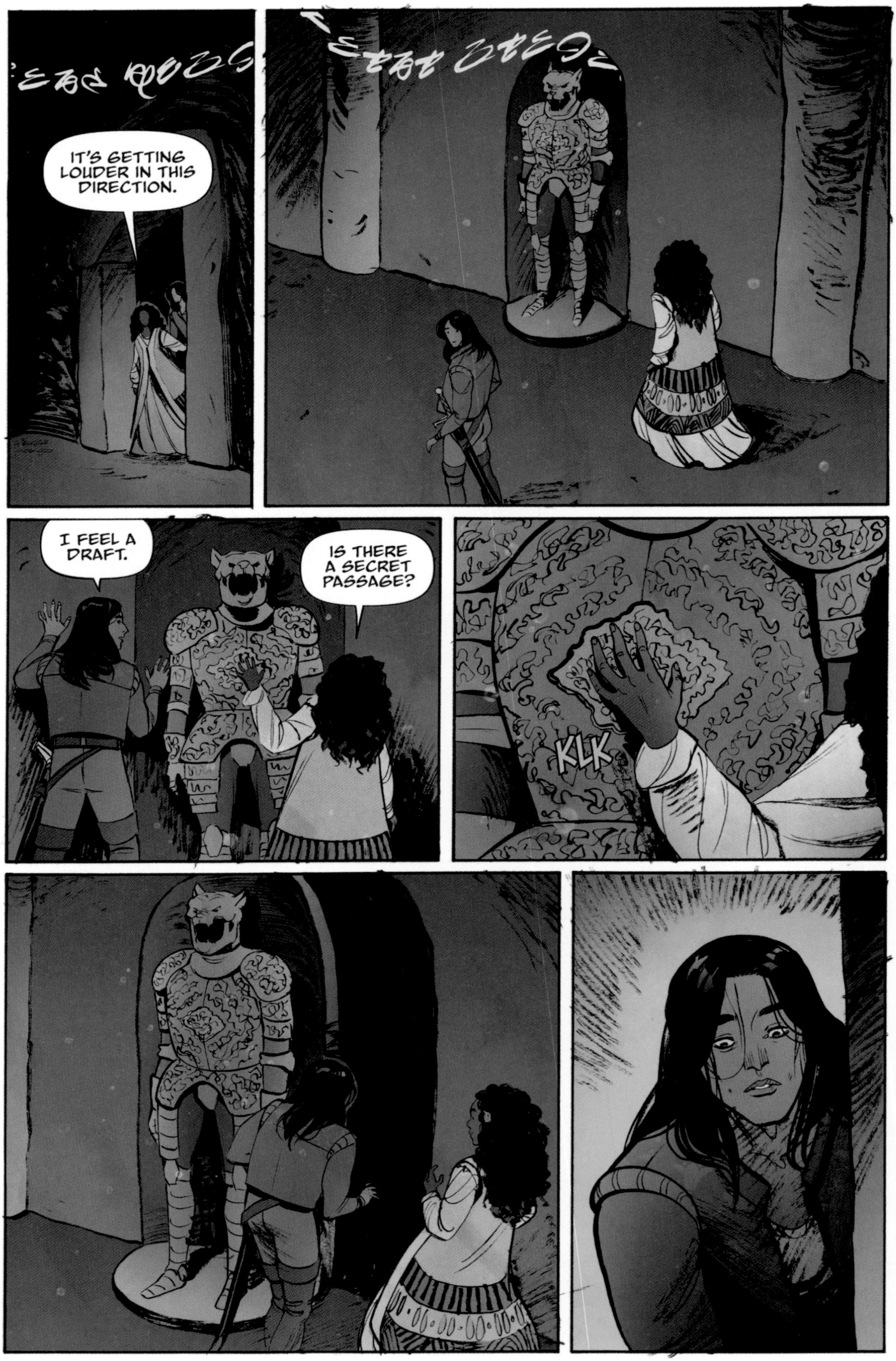
IT'S GETTING LOUDER IN THIS DIRECTION.
I FEEL A DRAFT.
IS THERE A SECRET PASSAGE?
KLK

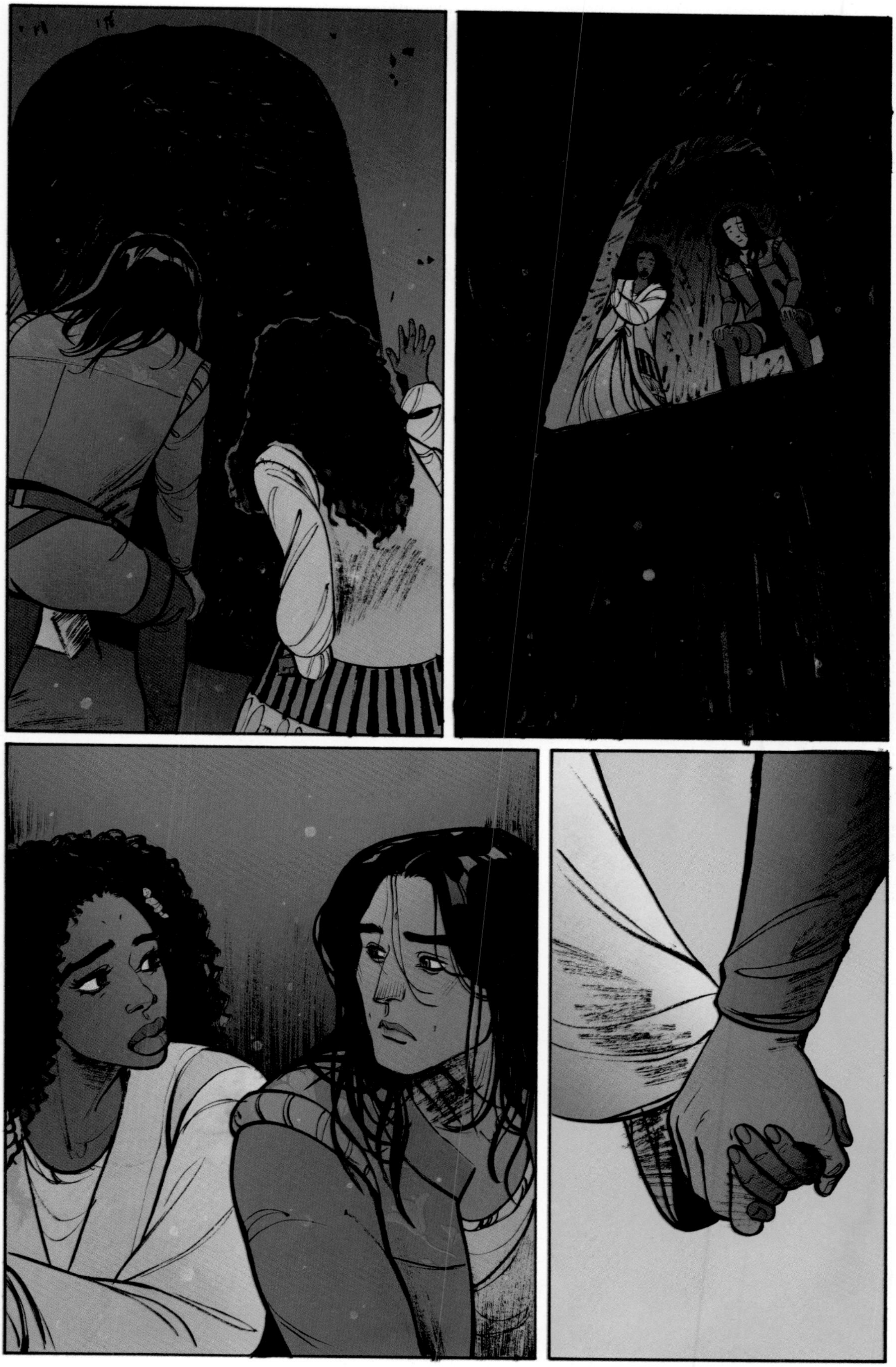

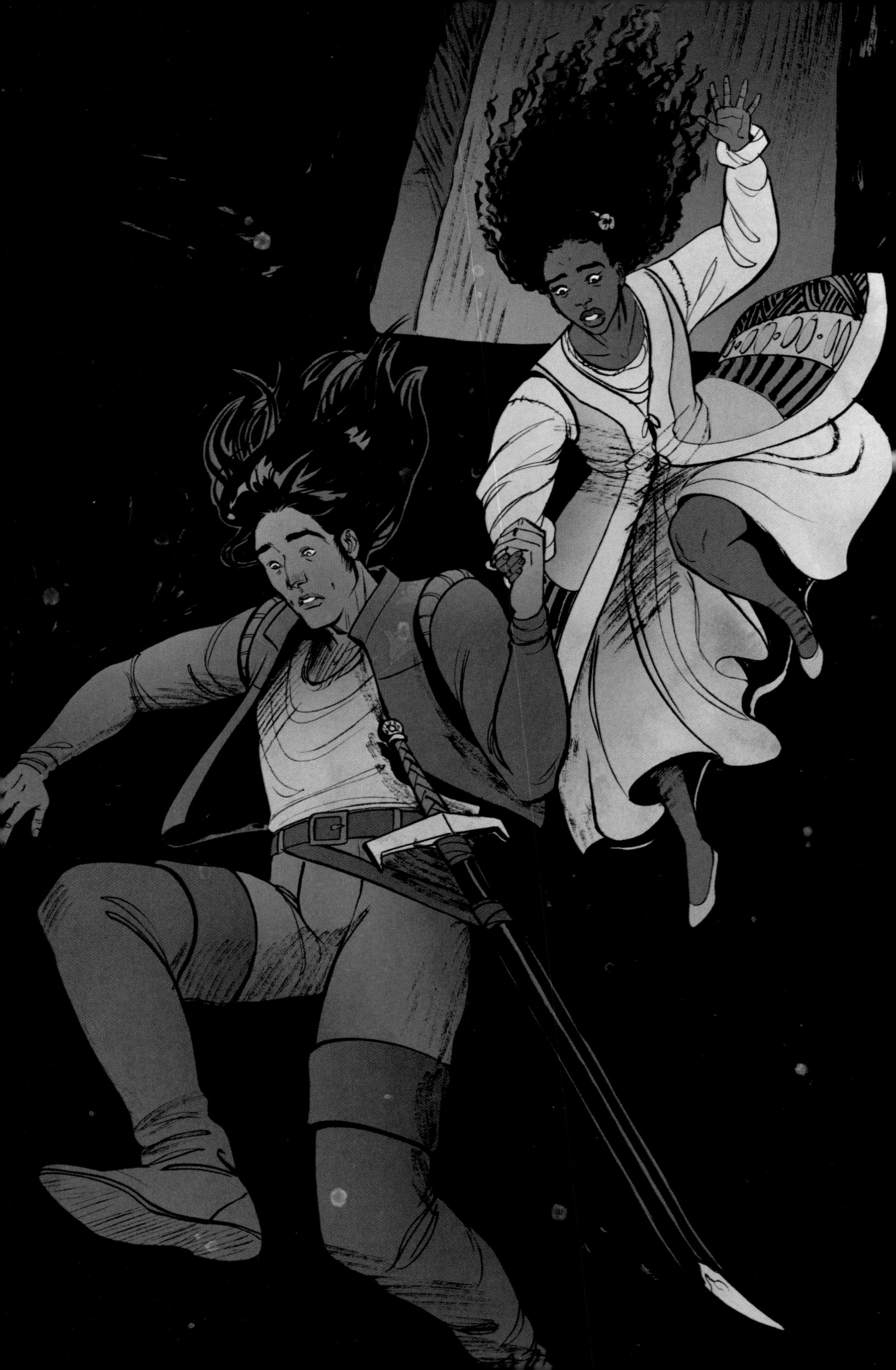

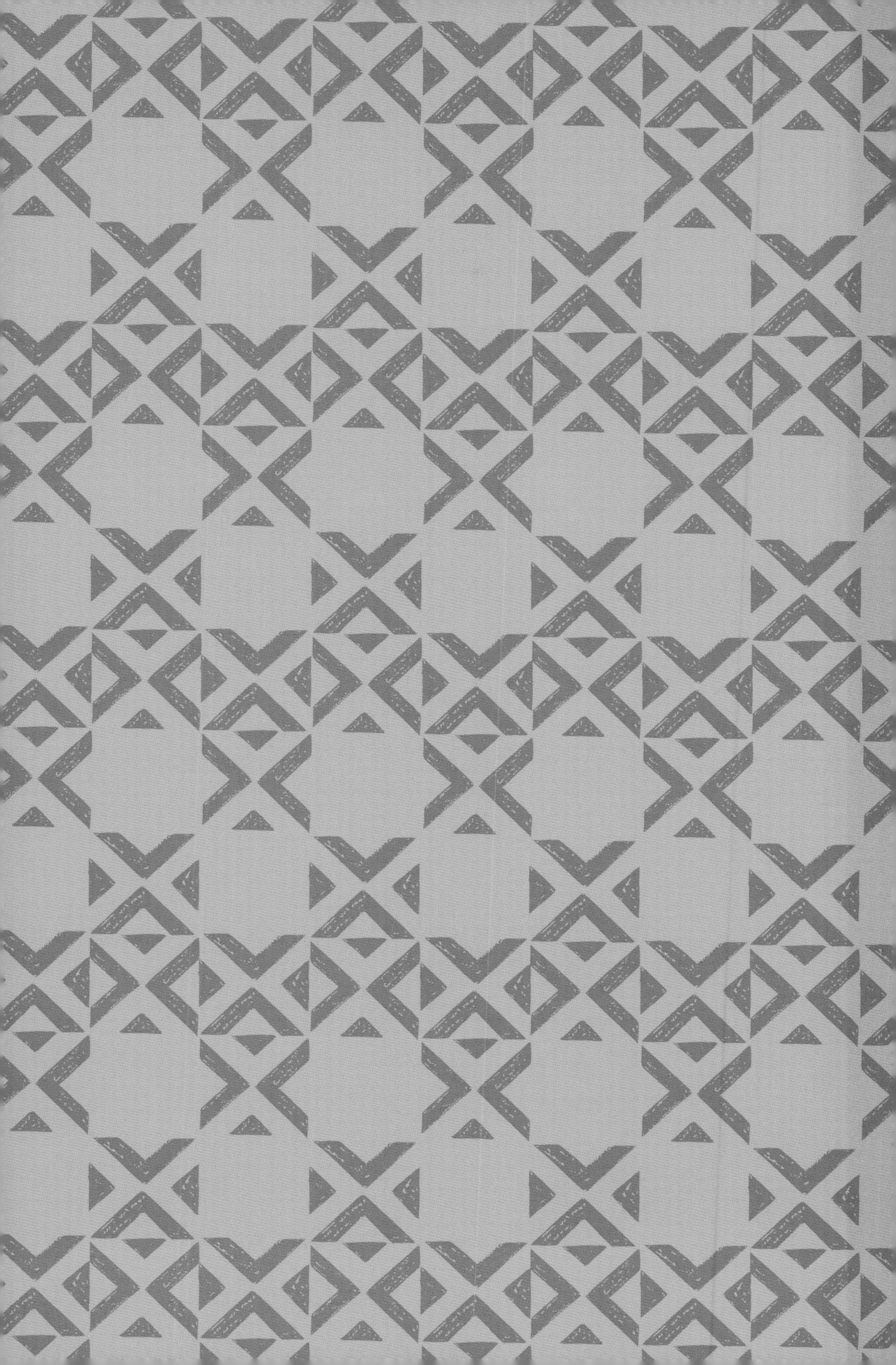

CHAPTER TEN

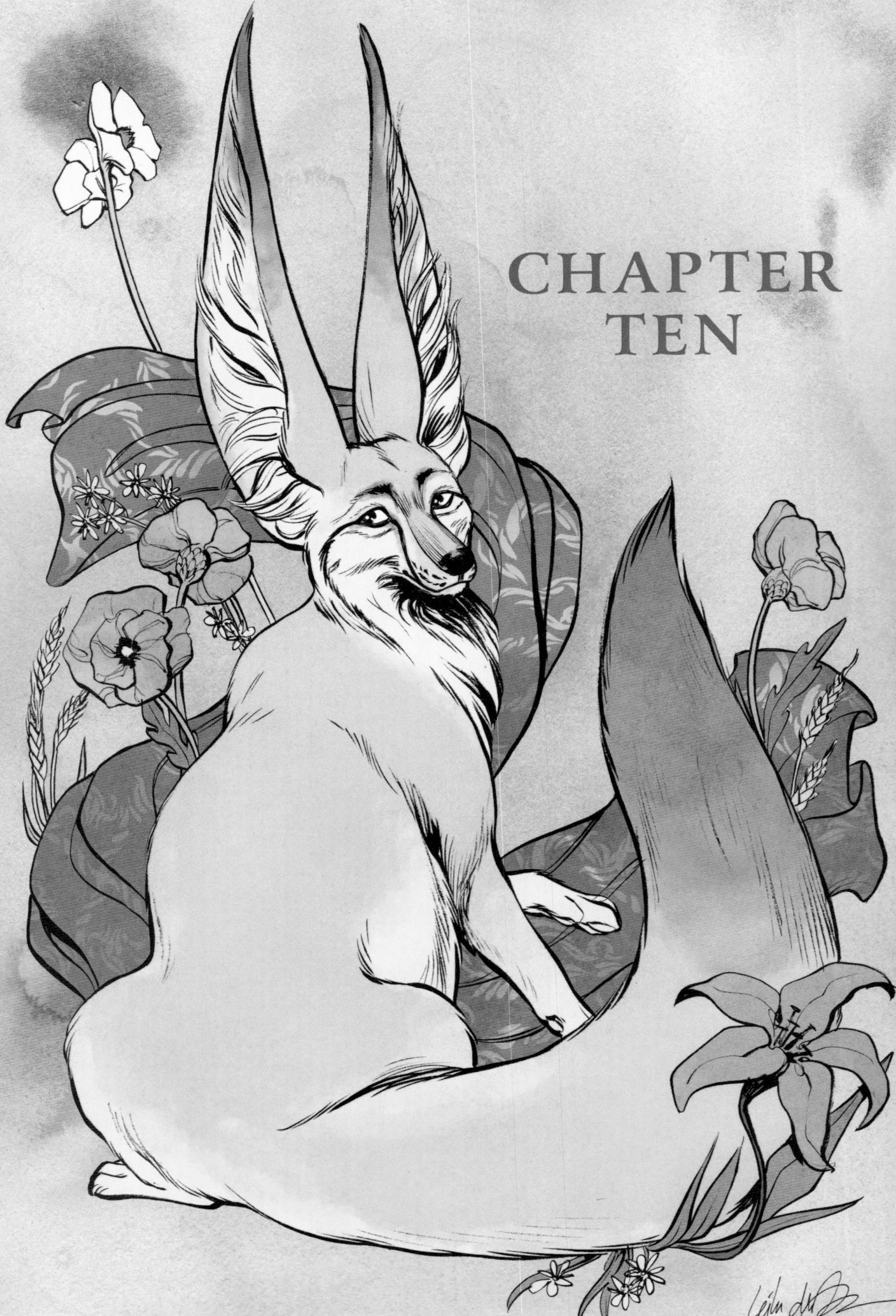

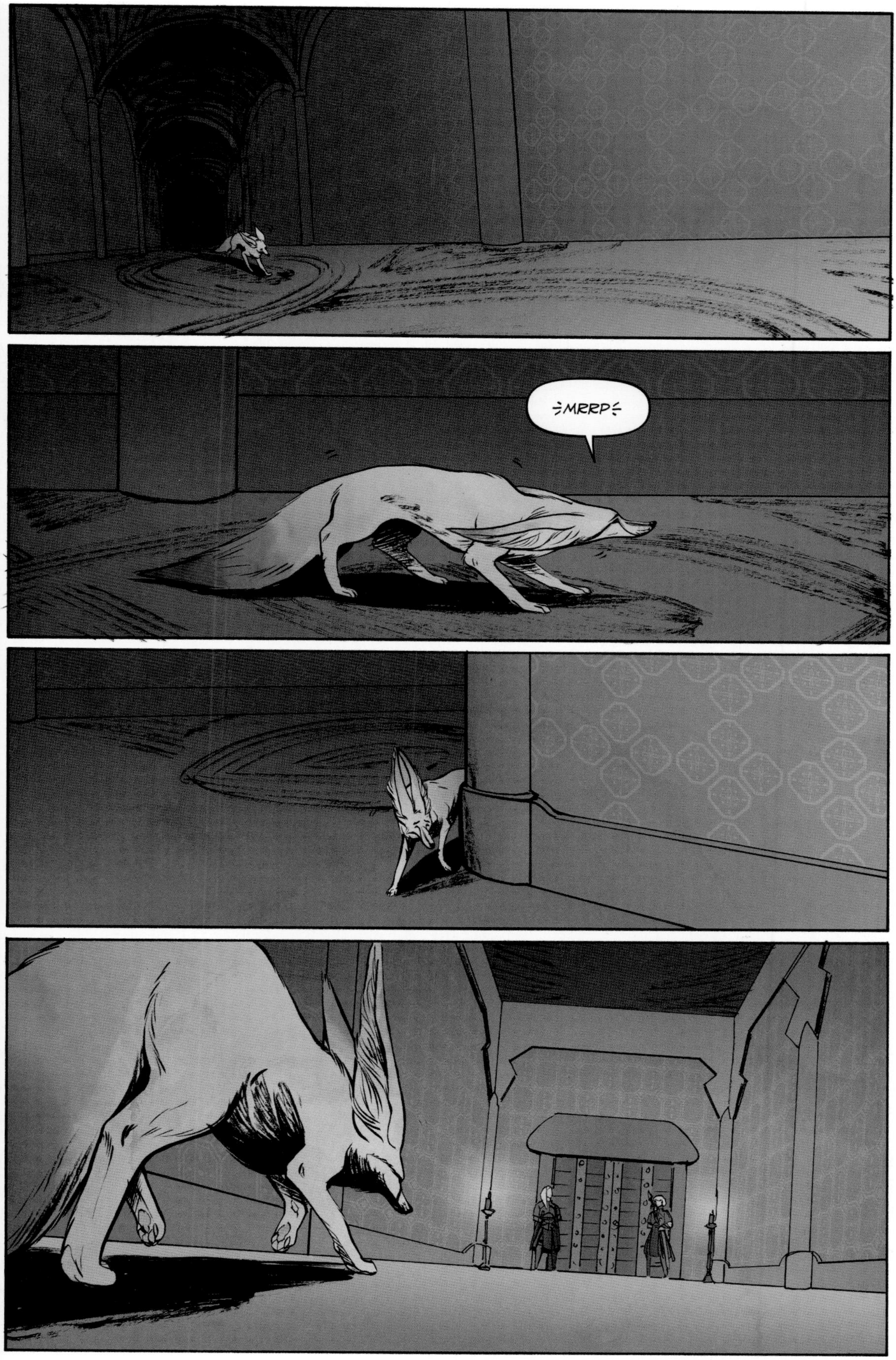
MRRP

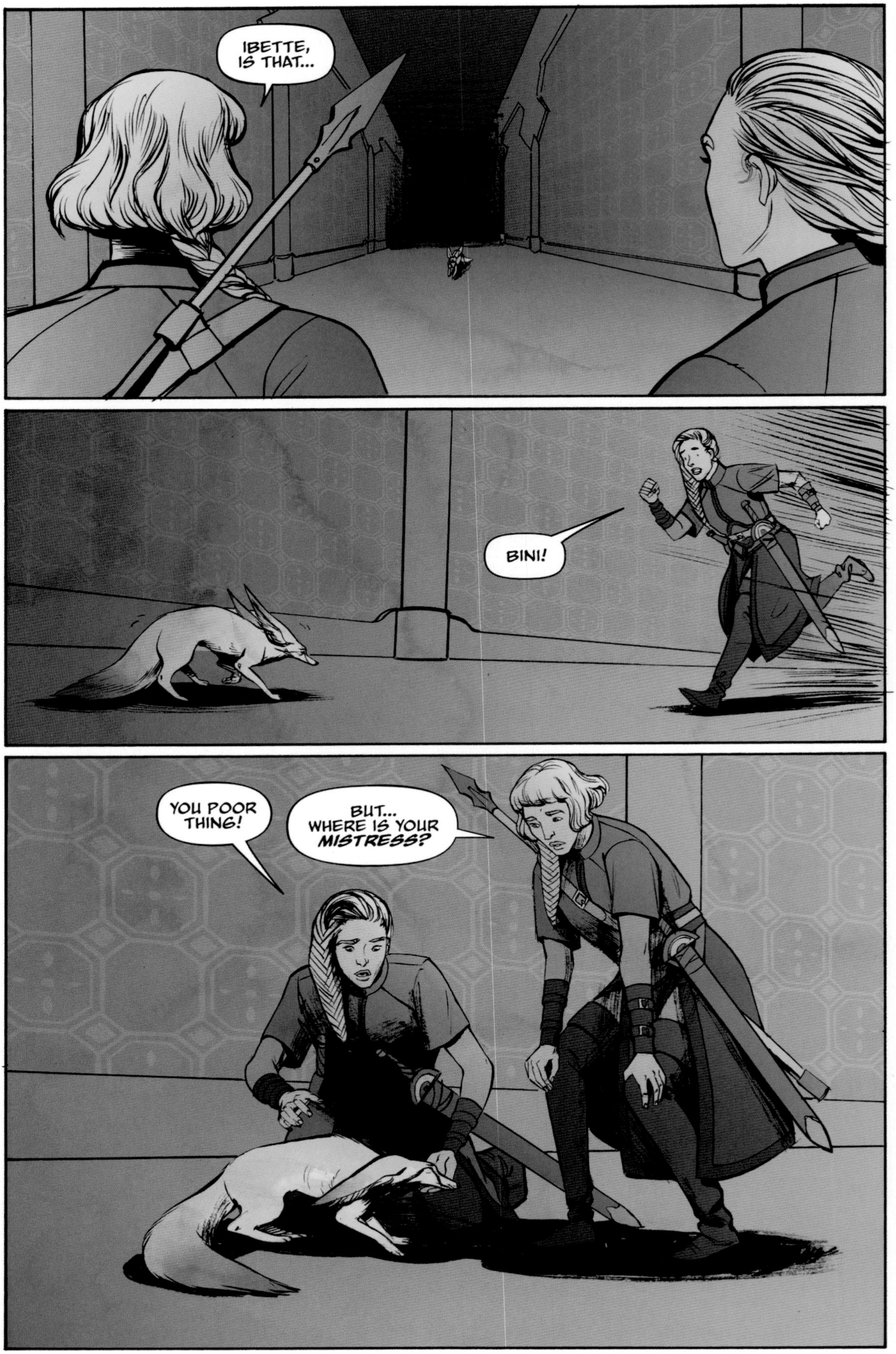
IBETTE, IS THAT...
BINI!
YOU POOR THING!
BUT... WHERE IS YOUR *MISTRESS?*

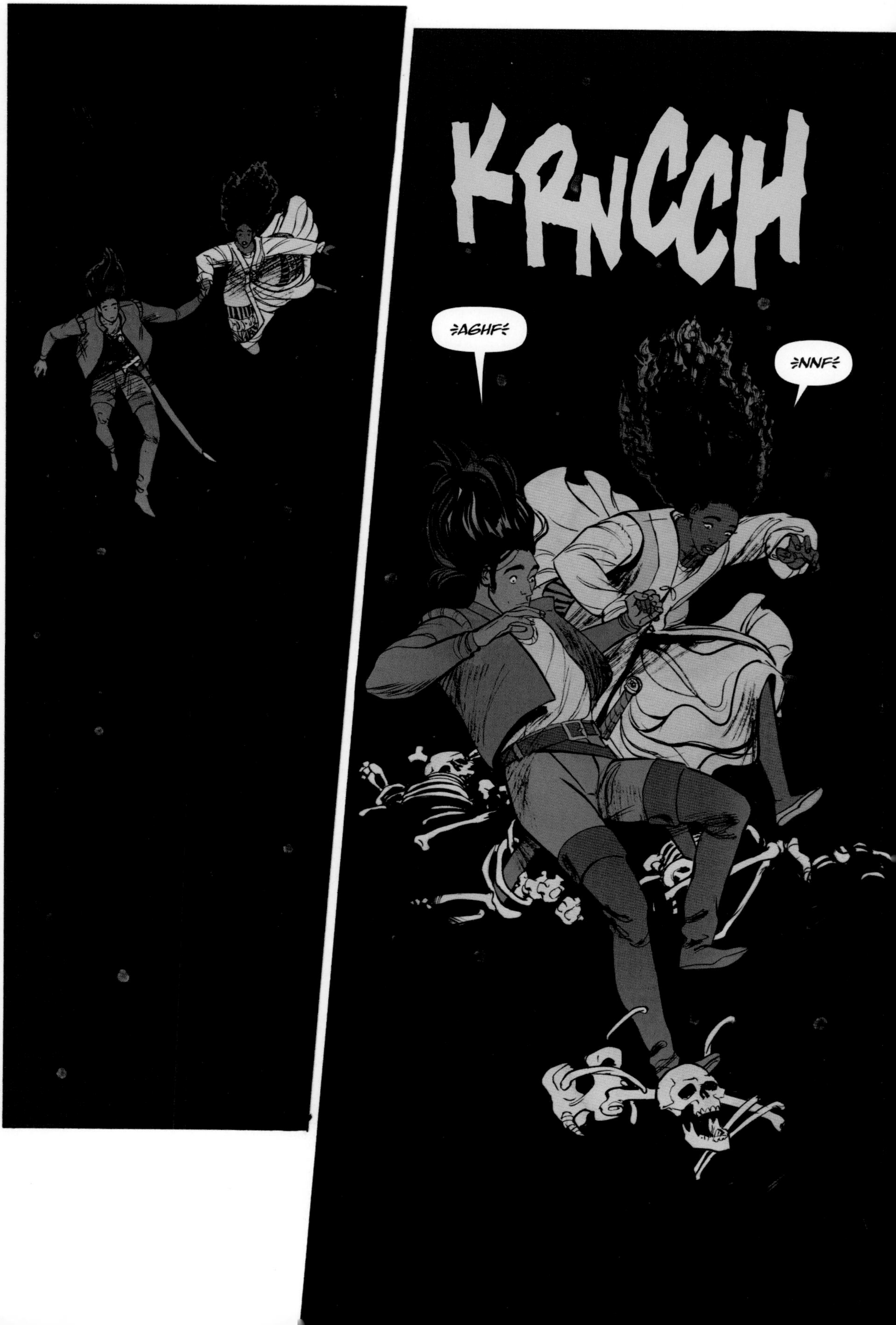
KRNCCH
AGHF
NNF

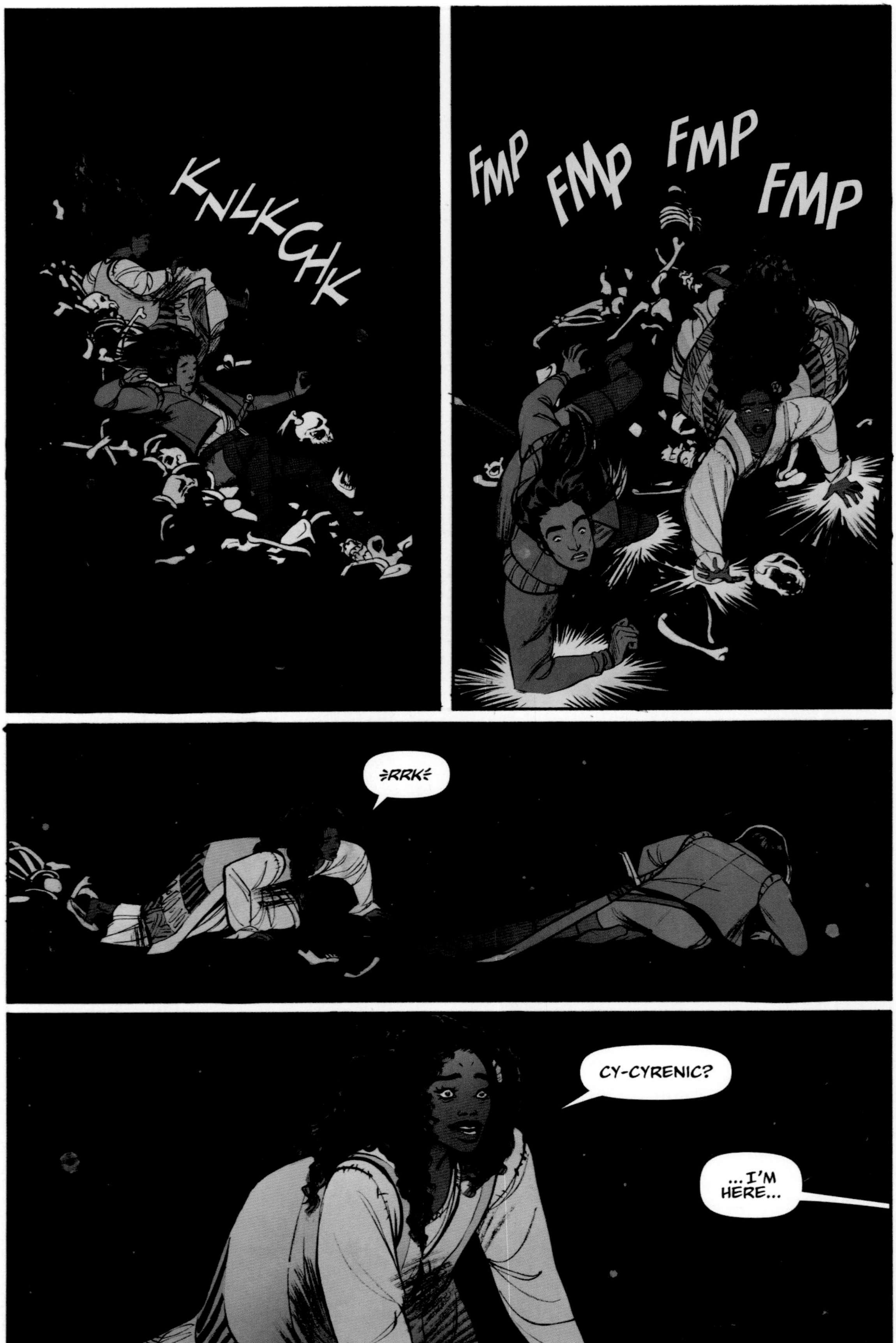
KNLKCHK
FMP FMP FMP FMP
RRK
CY-CYRENIC?
...I'M HERE...

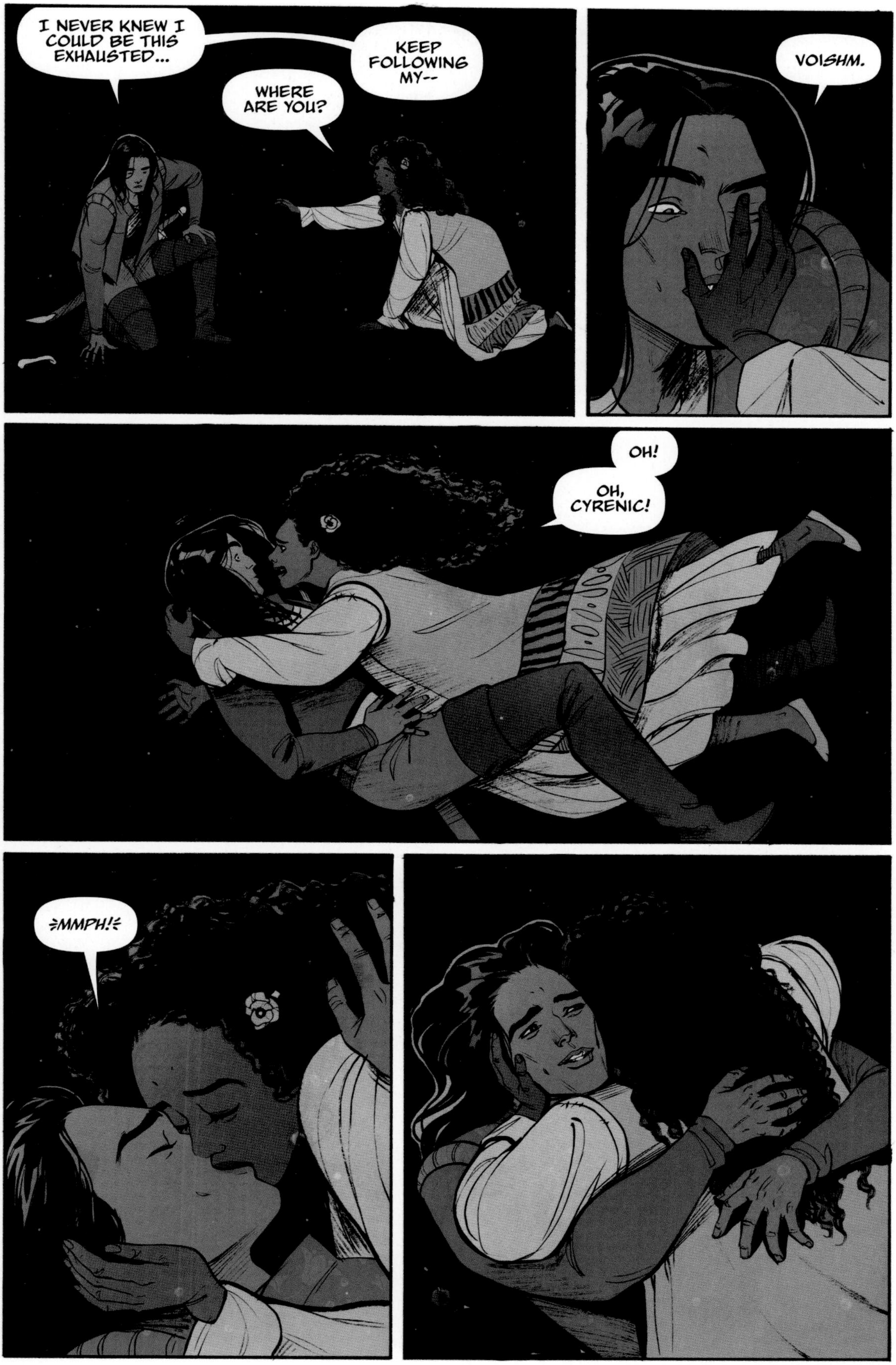
I NEVER KNEW I COULD BE THIS EXHAUSTED...
KEEP FOLLOWING MY--
WHERE ARE YOU?
VOISHM.
OH!
OH, CYRENIC!
MMPH!

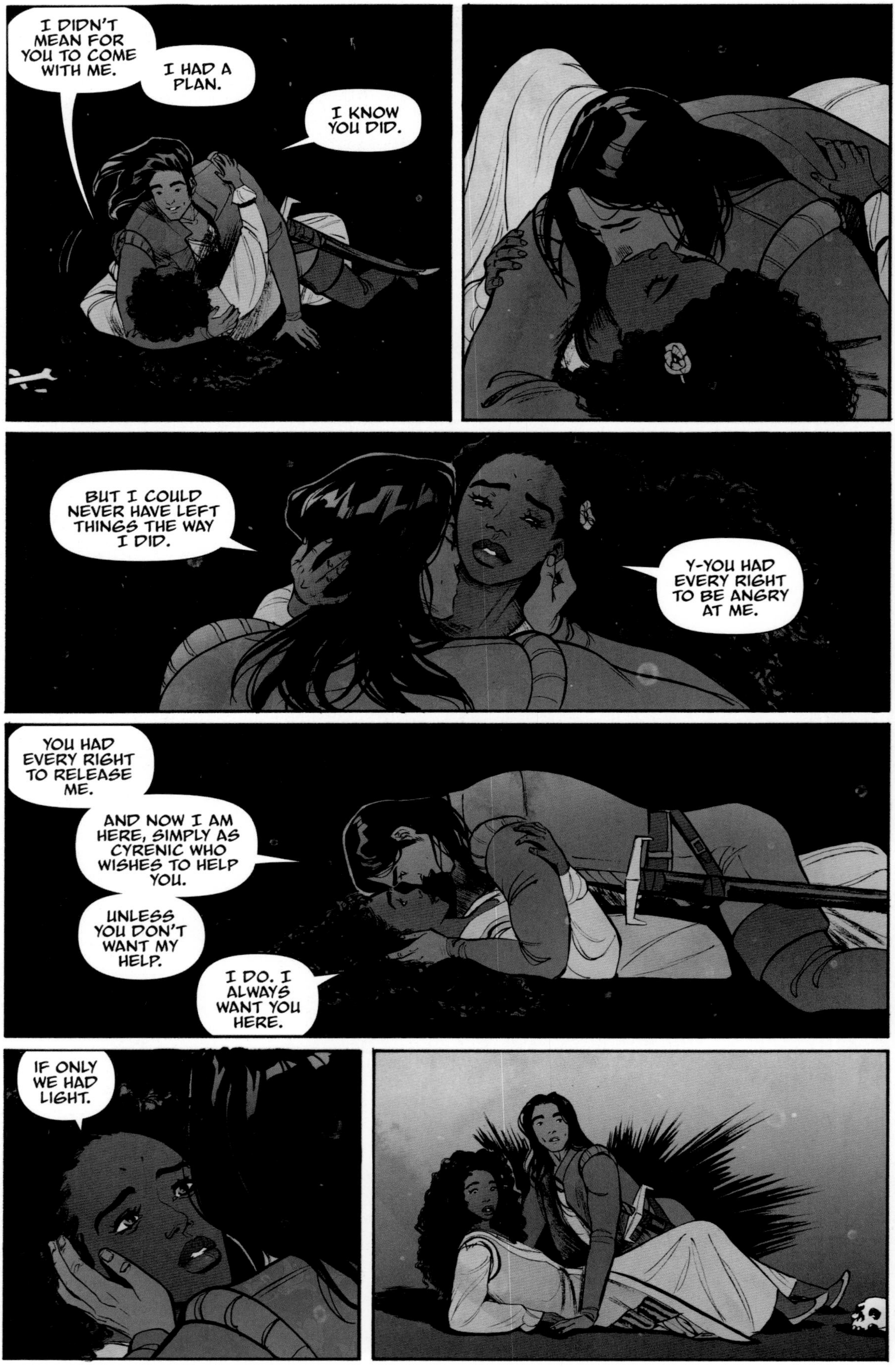
I DIDN'T MEAN FOR YOU TO COME WITH ME.
I HAD A PLAN.
I KNOW YOU DID.
BUT I COULD NEVER HAVE LEFT THINGS THE WAY I DID.
Y-YOU HAD EVERY RIGHT TO BE ANGRY AT ME.
YOU HAD EVERY RIGHT TO RELEASE ME.
AND NOW I AM HERE, SIMPLY AS CYRENIC WHO WISHES TO HELP YOU.
UNLESS YOU DON'T WANT MY HELP.
I DO. I ALWAYS WANT YOU HERE.
IF ONLY WE HAD LIGHT.

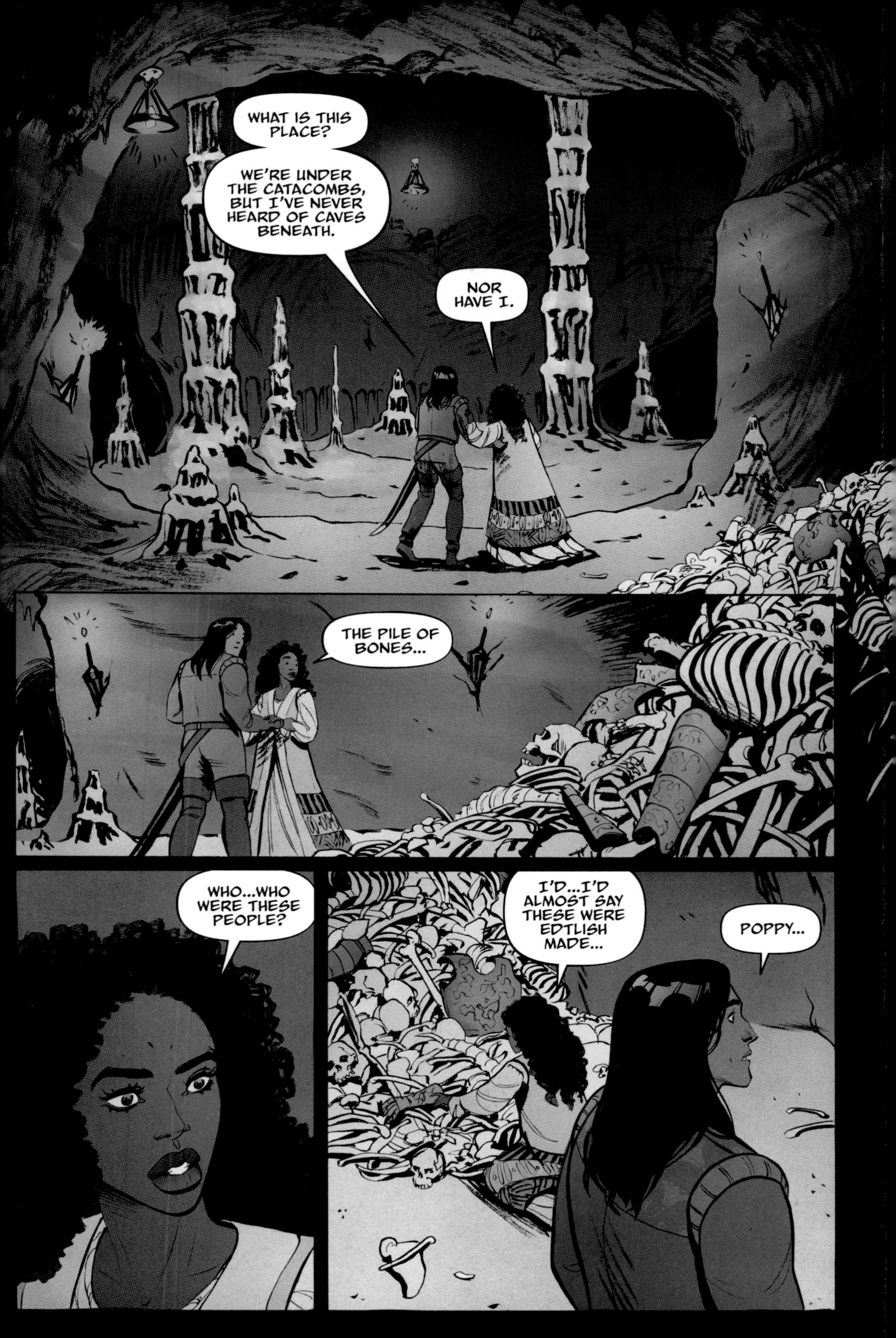
WHAT IS THIS PLACE?
WE'RE UNDER THE CATACOMBS, BUT I'VE NEVER HEARD OF CAVES BENEATH.
NOR HAVE I.
THE PILE OF BONES...
WHO...WHO WERE THESE PEOPLE?
I'D...I'D ALMOST SAY THESE WERE EDTLISH MADE...
POPPY...

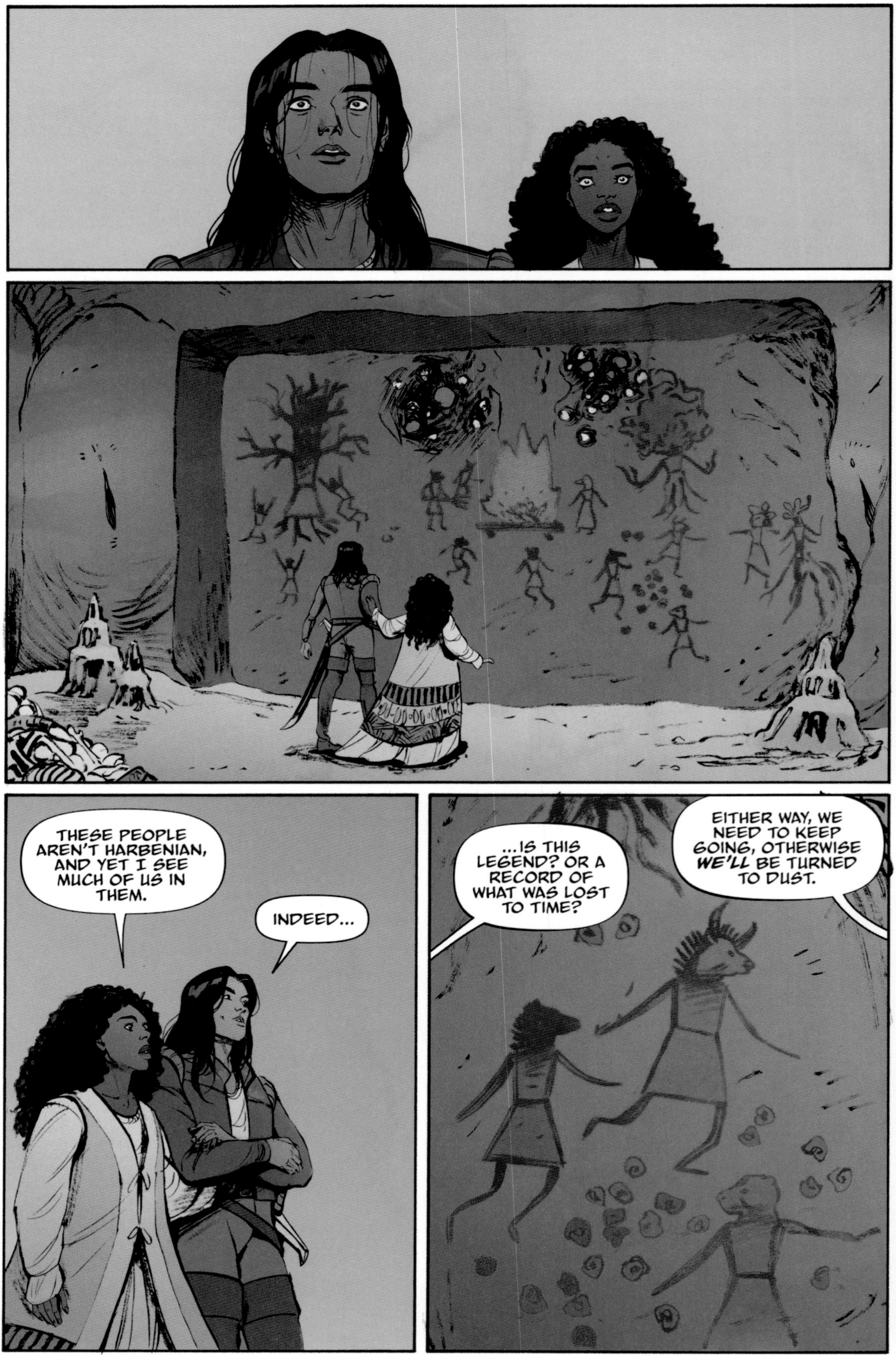
THESE PEOPLE AREN'T HARBENIAN, AND YET I SEE MUCH OF US IN THEM.
INDEED...
...IS THIS LEGEND? OR A RECORD OF WHAT WAS LOST TO TIME?
EITHER WAY, WE NEED TO KEEP GOING, OTHERWISE WE'LL BE TURNED TO DUST.

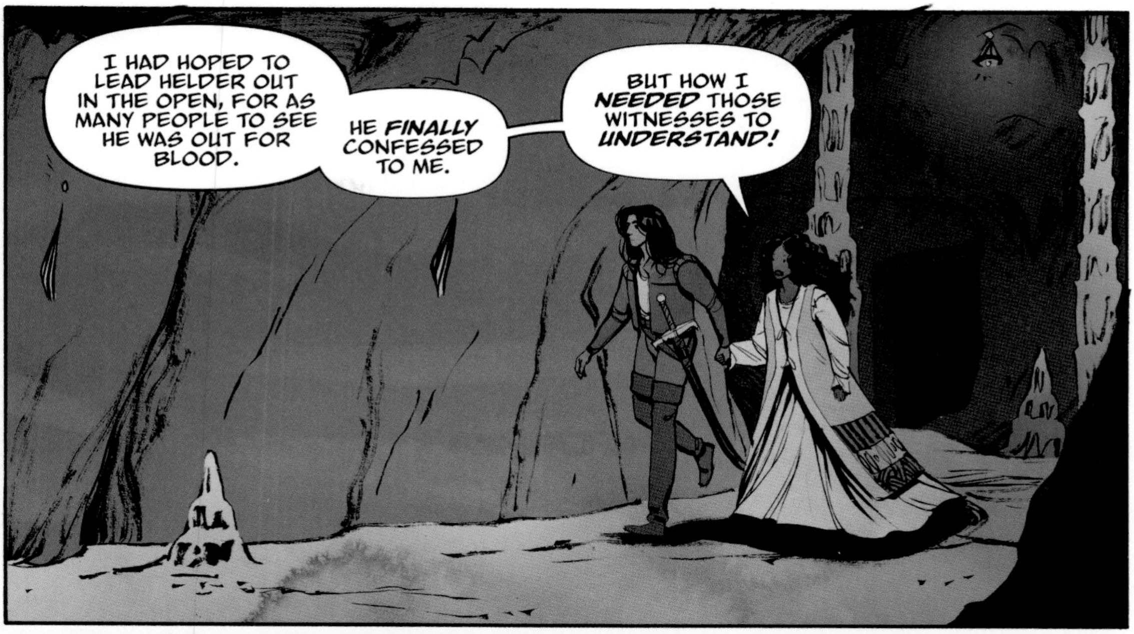
I HAD HOPED TO LEAD HELDER OUT IN THE OPEN, FOR AS MANY PEOPLE TO SEE HE WAS OUT FOR BLOOD.
HE *FINALLY* CONFESSED TO ME.
BUT HOW I ***NEEDED*** THOSE WITNESSES TO ***UNDERSTAND!***

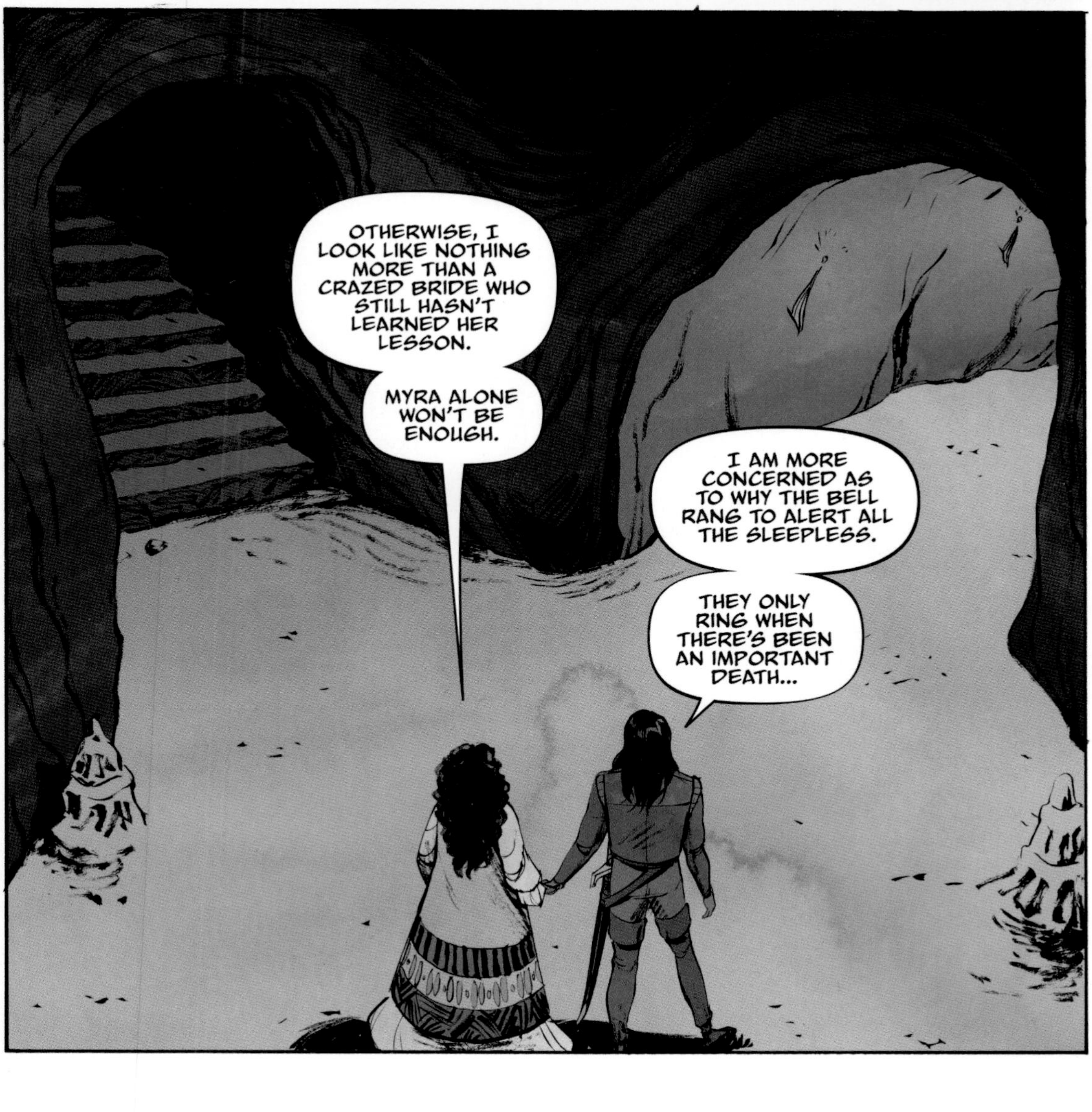
OTHERWISE, I LOOK LIKE NOTHING MORE THAN A CRAZED BRIDE WHO STILL HASN'T LEARNED HER LESSON.
MYRA ALONE WON'T BE ENOUGH.
I AM MORE CONCERNED AS TO WHY THE BELL RANG TO ALERT ALL THE SLEEPLESS.
THEY ONLY RING WHEN THERE'S BEEN AN IMPORTANT DEATH...

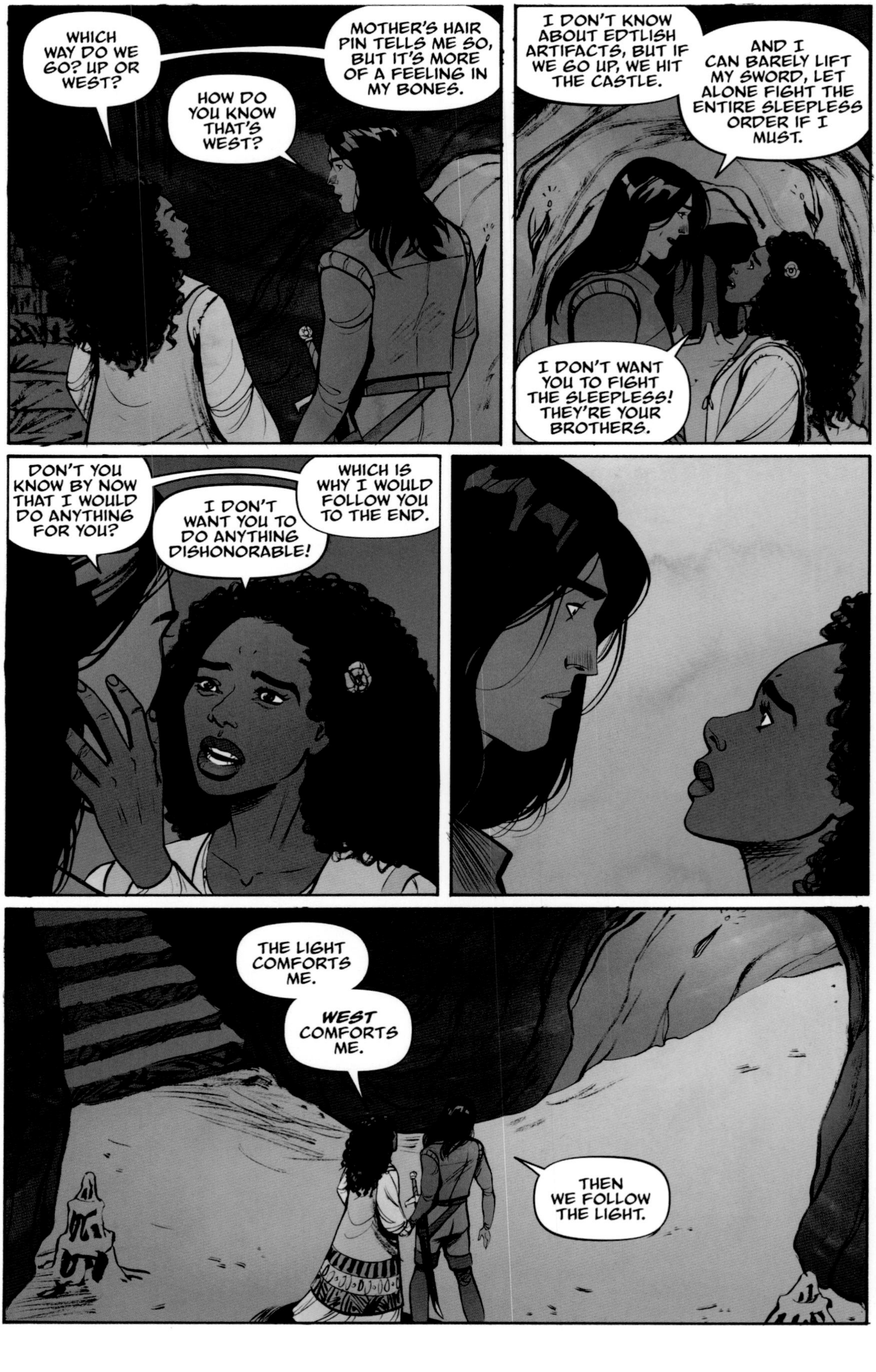
WHICH WAY DO WE GO? UP OR WEST?
HOW DO YOU KNOW THAT'S WEST?
MOTHER'S HAIR PIN TELLS ME SO, BUT IT'S MORE OF A FEELING IN MY BONES.
I DON'T KNOW ABOUT EDTLISH ARTIFACTS, BUT IF WE GO UP, WE HIT THE CASTLE.
AND I CAN BARELY LIFT MY SWORD, LET ALONE FIGHT THE ENTIRE SLEEPLESS ORDER IF I MUST.
I DON'T WANT YOU TO FIGHT THE SLEEPLESS! THEY'RE YOUR BROTHERS.
DON'T YOU KNOW BY NOW THAT I WOULD DO ANYTHING FOR YOU?
I DON'T WANT YOU TO DO ANYTHING DISHONORABLE!
WHICH IS WHY I WOULD FOLLOW YOU TO THE END.
THE LIGHT COMFORTS ME.
WEST COMFORTS ME.
THEN WE FOLLOW THE LIGHT.

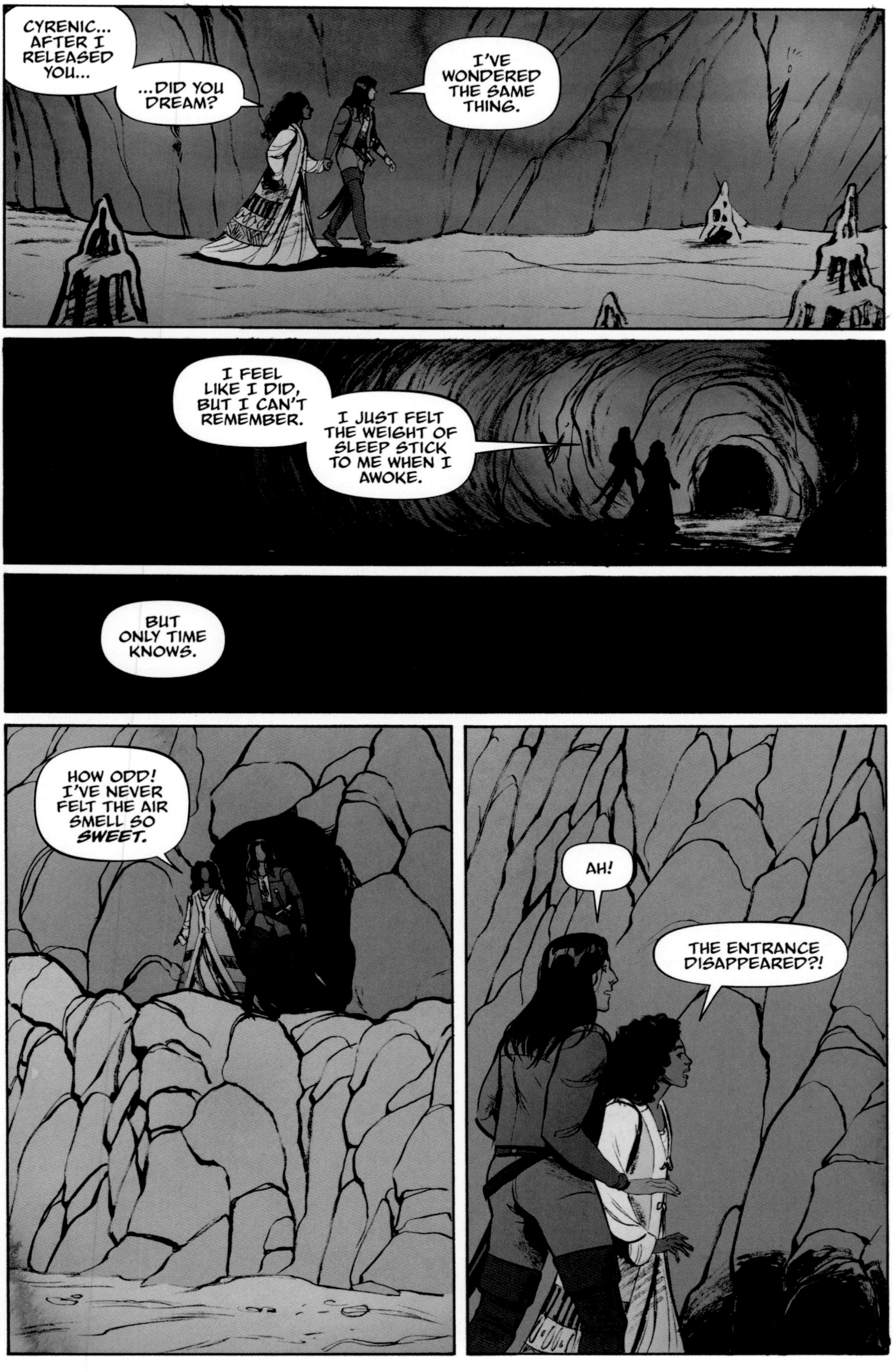
CYRENIC... AFTER I RELEASED YOU...
...DID YOU DREAM?
I'VE WONDERED THE SAME THING.
I FEEL LIKE I DID, BUT I CAN'T REMEMBER.
I JUST FELT THE WEIGHT OF SLEEP STICK TO ME WHEN I AWOKE.
BUT ONLY TIME KNOWS.
HOW ODD! I'VE NEVER FELT THE AIR SMELL SO SWEET.
AH!
THE ENTRANCE DISAPPEARED?!

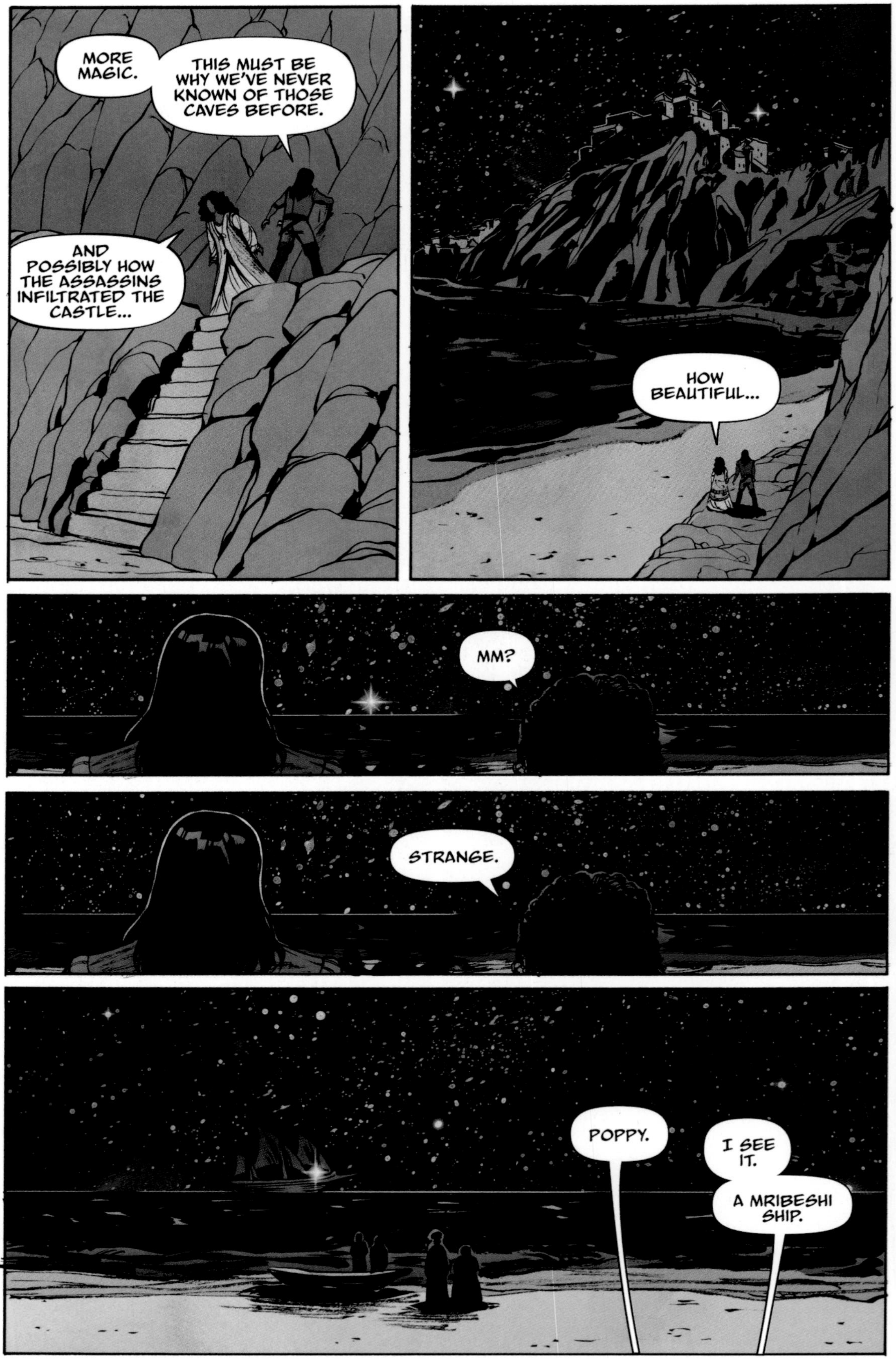
MORE MAGIC.
THIS MUST BE WHY WE'VE NEVER KNOWN OF THOSE CAVES BEFORE.
AND POSSIBLY HOW THE ASSASSINS INFILTRATED THE CASTLE...
HOW BEAUTIFUL...
MM?
STRANGE.
POPPY.
I SEE IT.
A MRIBESHI SHIP.

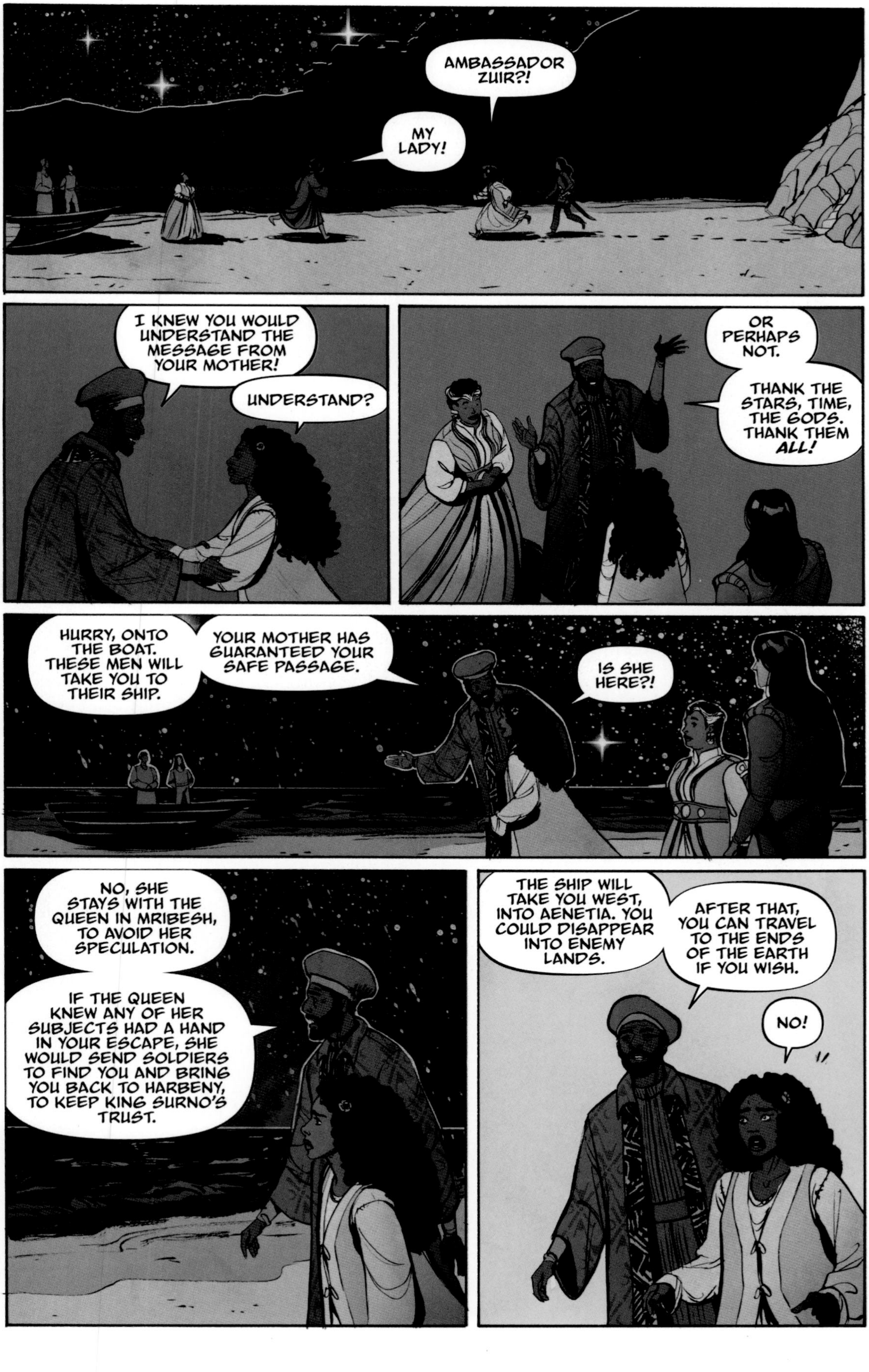
AMBASSADOR ZUIR?!
MY LADY!
I KNEW YOU WOULD UNDERSTAND THE MESSAGE FROM YOUR MOTHER!
UNDERSTAND?
OR PERHAPS NOT.
THANK THE STARS, TIME, THE GODS. THANK THEM ALL!
HURRY, ONTO THE BOAT. THESE MEN WILL TAKE YOU TO THEIR SHIP.
YOUR MOTHER HAS GUARANTEED YOUR SAFE PASSAGE.
IS SHE HERE?!
NO, SHE STAYS WITH THE QUEEN IN MRIBESH, TO AVOID HER SPECULATION.
IF THE QUEEN KNEW ANY OF HER SUBJECTS HAD A HAND IN YOUR ESCAPE, SHE WOULD SEND SOLDIERS TO FIND YOU AND BRING YOU BACK TO HARBENY, TO KEEP KING SURNO'S TRUST.
THE SHIP WILL TAKE YOU WEST, INTO AENETIA. YOU COULD DISAPPEAR INTO ENEMY LANDS.
AFTER THAT, YOU CAN TRAVEL TO THE ENDS OF THE EARTH IF YOU WISH.
NO!

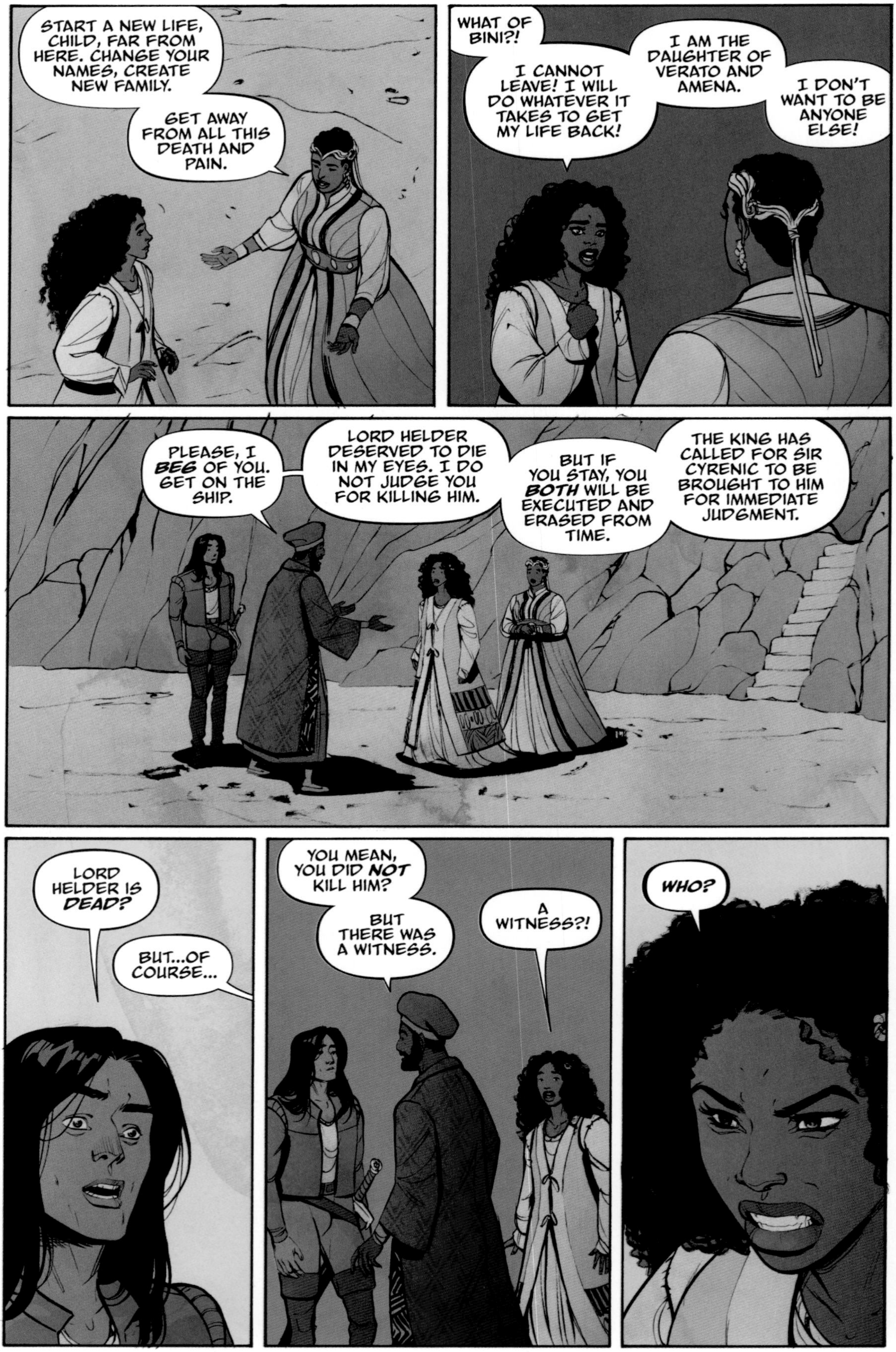
START A NEW LIFE, CHILD, FAR FROM HERE. CHANGE YOUR NAMES, CREATE NEW FAMILY.
GET AWAY FROM ALL THIS DEATH AND PAIN.
WHAT OF BINI?!
I CANNOT LEAVE! I WILL DO WHATEVER IT TAKES TO GET MY LIFE BACK!
I AM THE DAUGHTER OF VERATO AND AMENA.
I DON'T WANT TO BE ANYONE ELSE!
PLEASE, I *BEG* OF YOU. GET ON THE SHIP.
LORD HELDER DESERVED TO DIE IN MY EYES. I DO NOT JUDGE YOU FOR KILLING HIM.
BUT IF YOU STAY, YOU *BOTH* WILL BE EXECUTED AND ERASED FROM TIME.
THE KING HAS CALLED FOR SIR CYRENIC TO BE BROUGHT TO HIM FOR IMMEDIATE JUDGMENT.
LORD HELDER IS *DEAD?*
BUT...OF COURSE...
YOU MEAN, YOU DID *NOT* KILL HIM?
BUT THERE WAS A WITNESS.
A WITNESS?!
WHO?

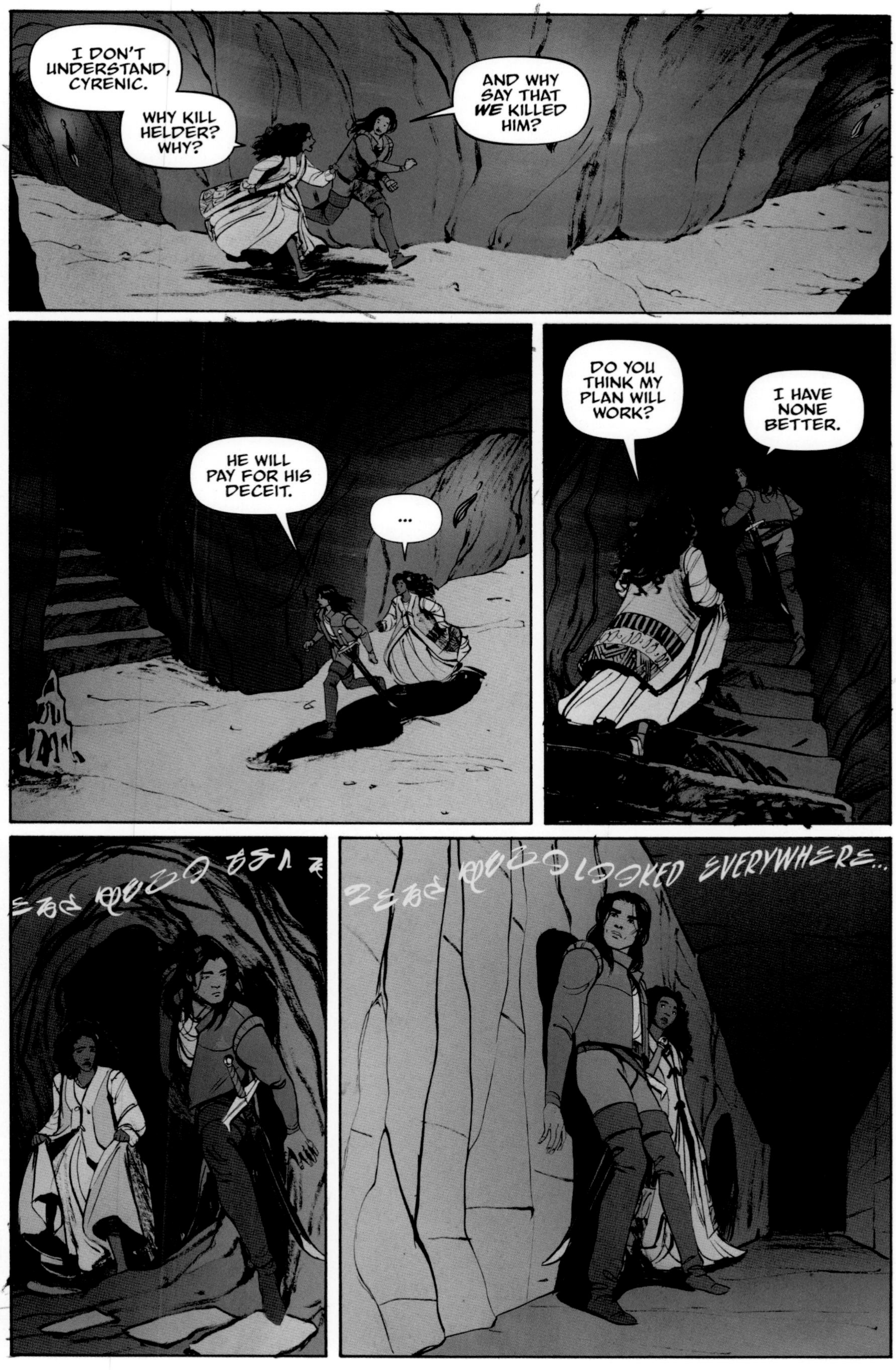
I DON'T UNDERSTAND, CYRENIC.
WHY KILL HELDER? WHY?
AND WHY SAY THAT *WE* KILLED HIM?
HE WILL PAY FOR HIS DECEIT.
...
DO YOU THINK MY PLAN WILL WORK?
I HAVE NONE BETTER.
LOOKED EVERYWHERE...

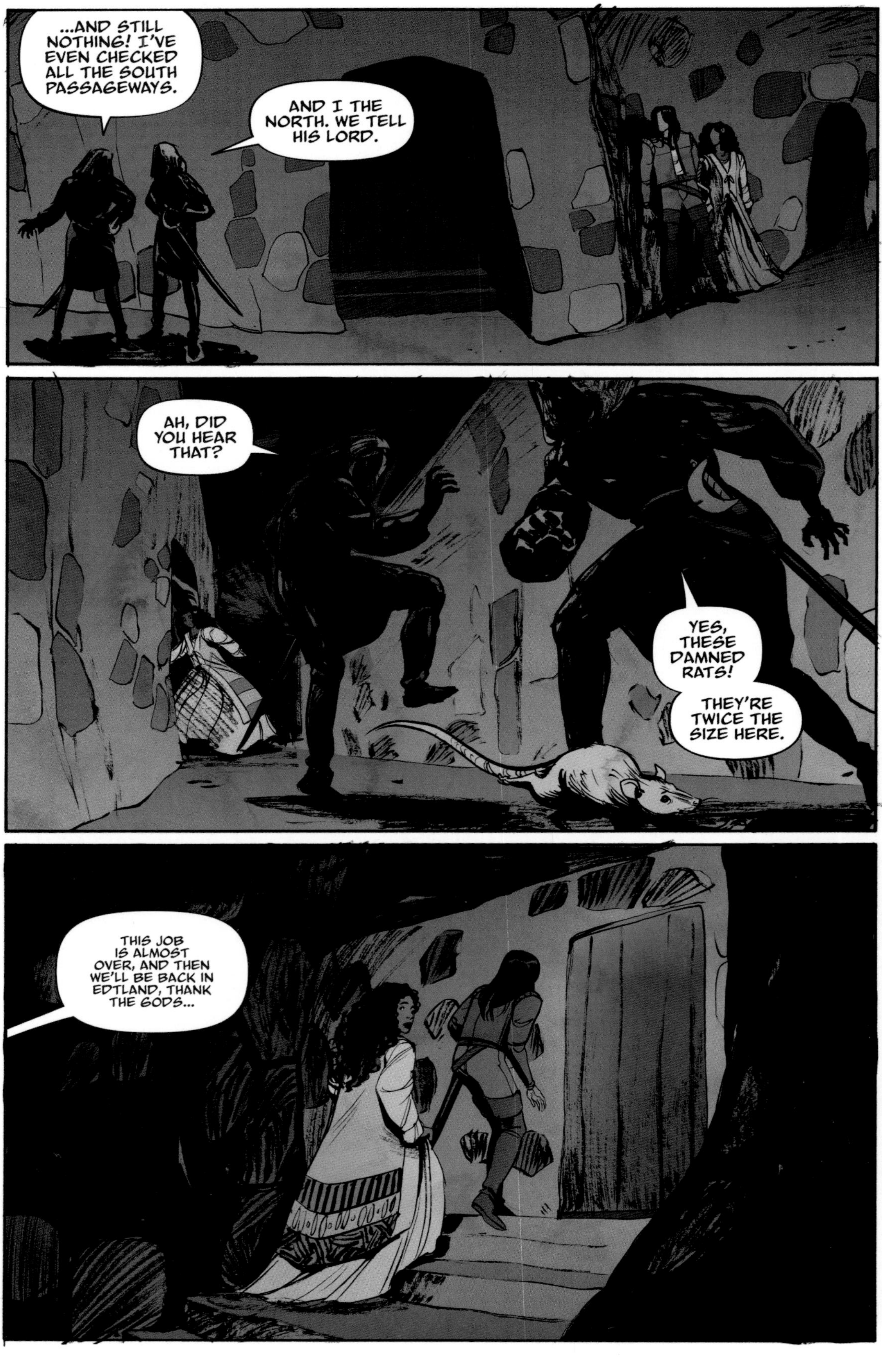
...AND STILL NOTHING! I'VE EVEN CHECKED ALL THE SOUTH PASSAGEWAYS.
AND I THE NORTH. WE TELL HIS LORD.
AH, DID YOU HEAR THAT?
YES, THESE DAMNED RATS!
THEY'RE TWICE THE SIZE HERE.
THIS JOB IS ALMOST OVER, AND THEN WE'LL BE BACK IN EDTLAND, THANK THE GODS...

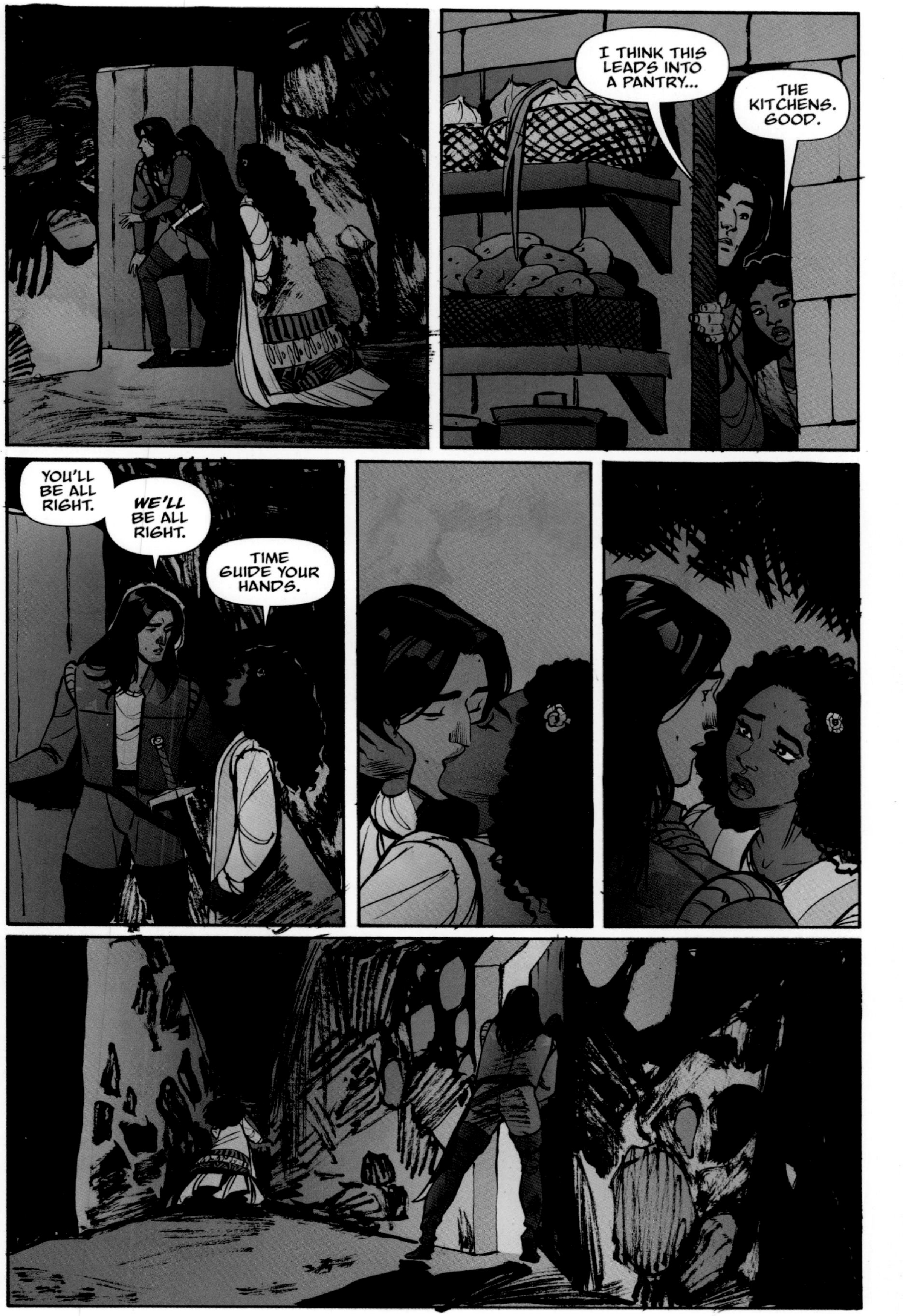
I THINK THIS LEADS INTO A PANTRY...
THE KITCHENS. GOOD.
YOU'LL BE ALL RIGHT.
WE'LL BE ALL RIGHT.
TIME GUIDE YOUR HANDS.

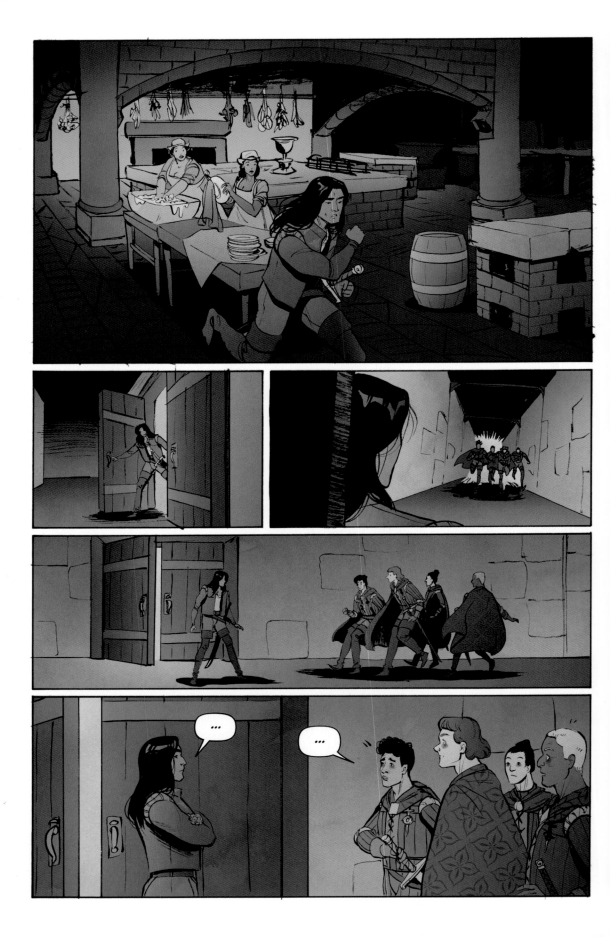

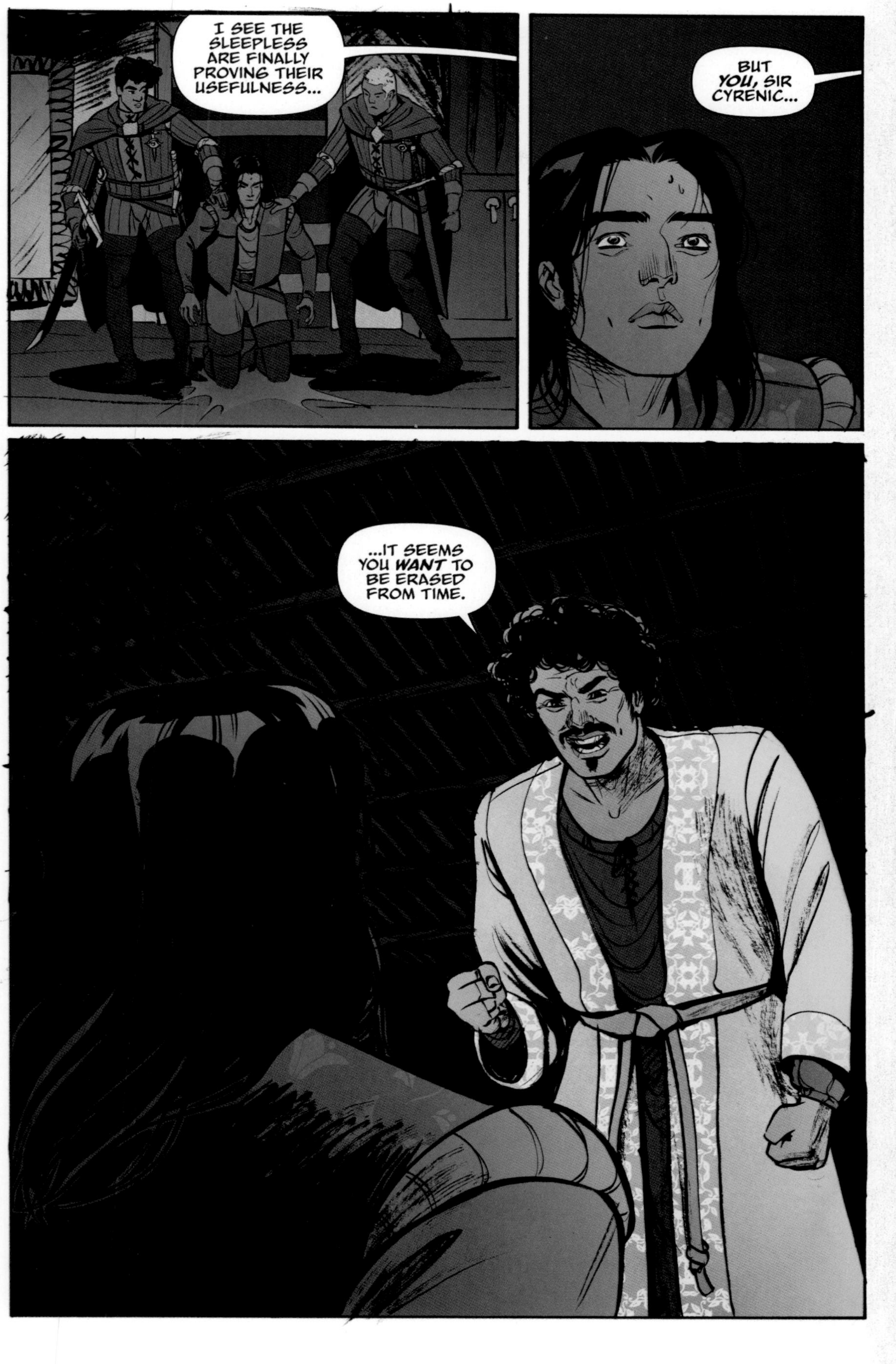
I SEE THE SLEEPLESS ARE FINALLY PROVING THEIR USEFULNESS...
BUT *YOU*, SIR CYRENIC...
...IT SEEMS YOU *WANT* TO BE ERASED FROM TIME.

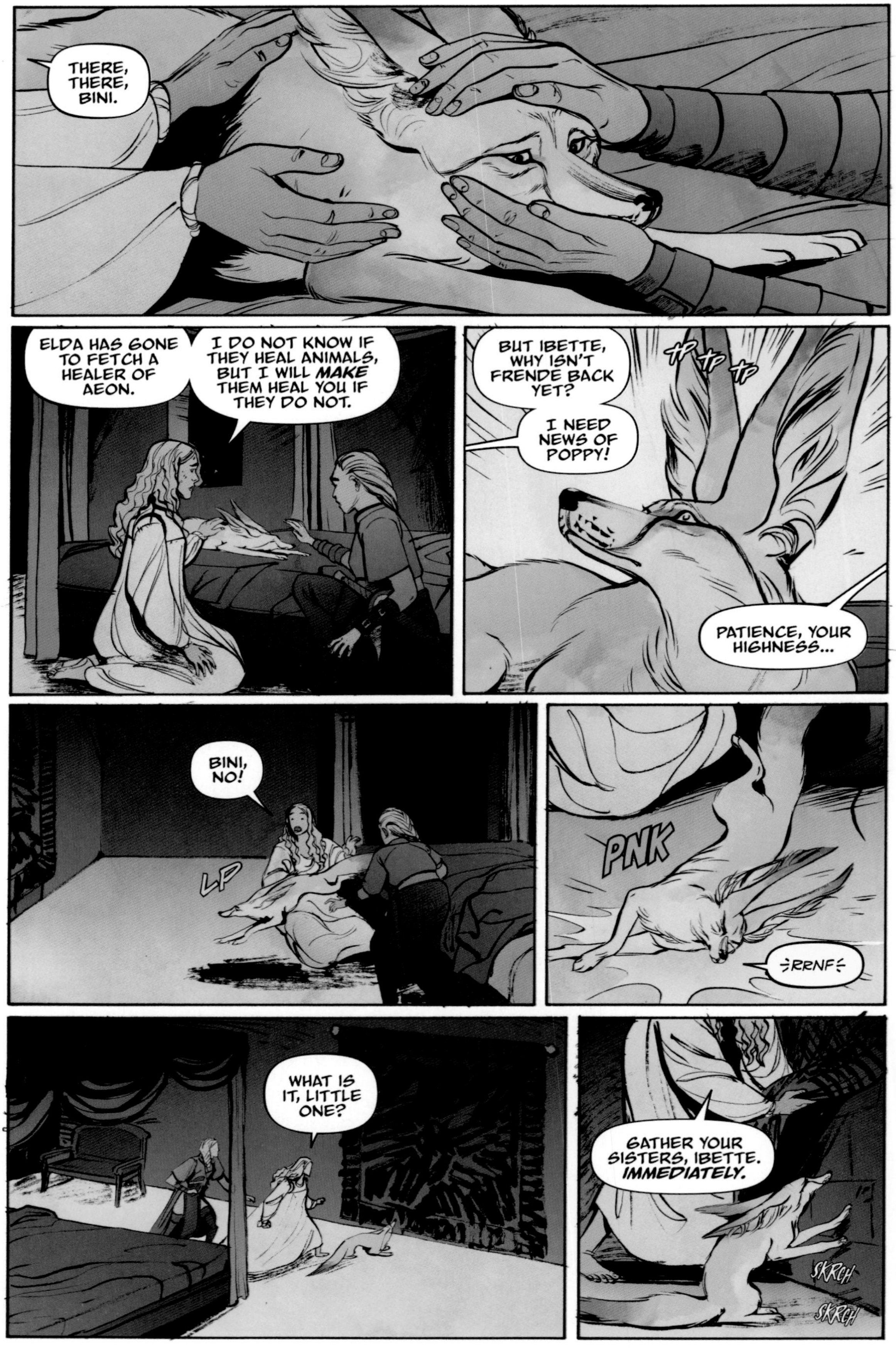
THERE, THERE, BINI.
ELDA HAS GONE TO FETCH A HEALER OF AEON.
I DO NOT KNOW IF THEY HEAL ANIMALS, BUT I WILL *MAKE* THEM HEAL YOU IF THEY DO NOT.
BUT IBETTE, WHY ISN'T FRENDE BACK YET?
I NEED NEWS OF POPPY!
TP TP TP
PATIENCE, YOUR HIGHNESS...
BINI, NO!
LP
PNK
RRNF
WHAT IS IT, LITTLE ONE?
GATHER YOUR SISTERS, IBETTE. *IMMEDIATELY.*
SKRCH
SKRCH

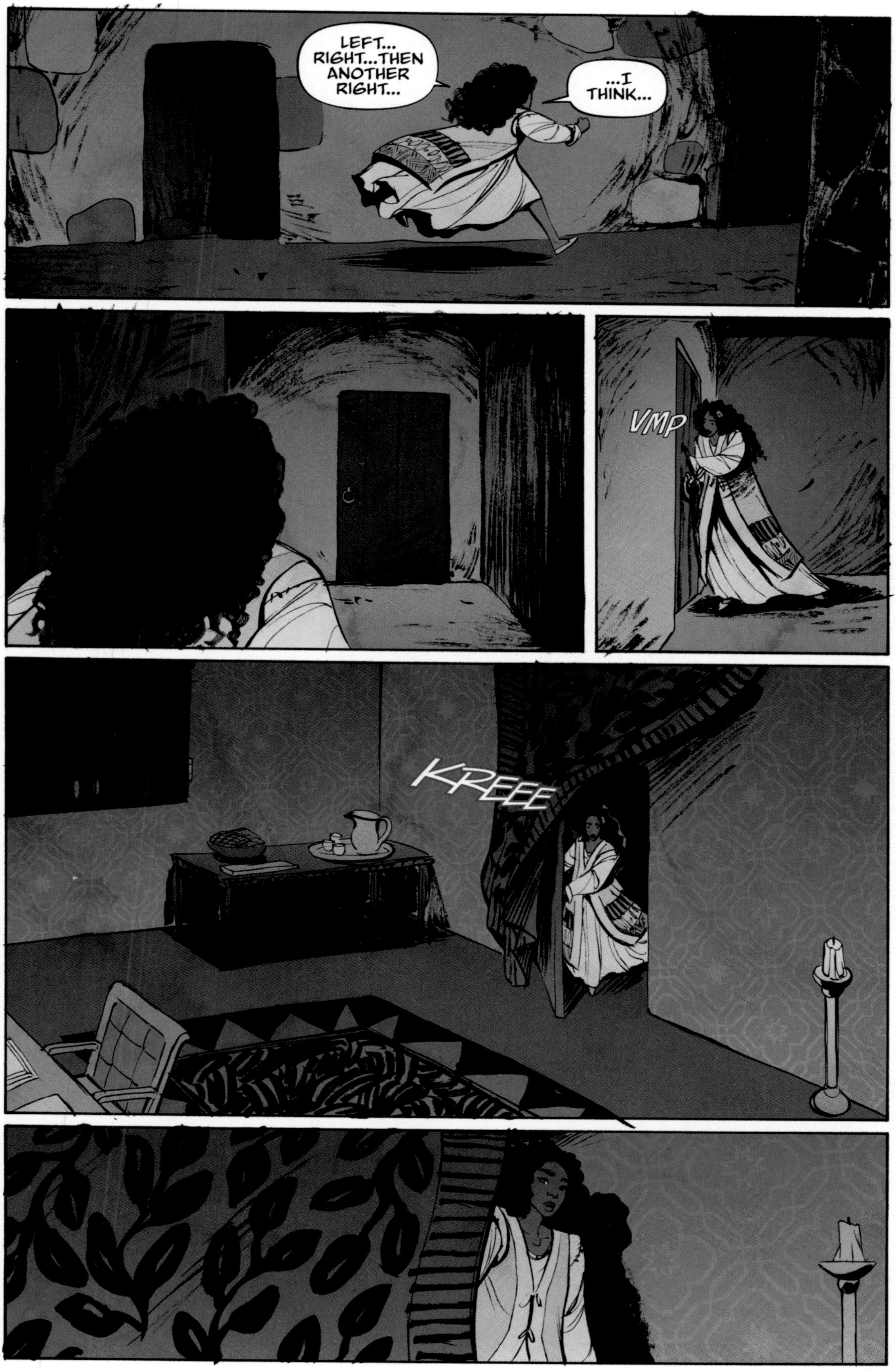
LEFT... RIGHT...THEN ANOTHER RIGHT...
...I THINK...
VMP
KREEE

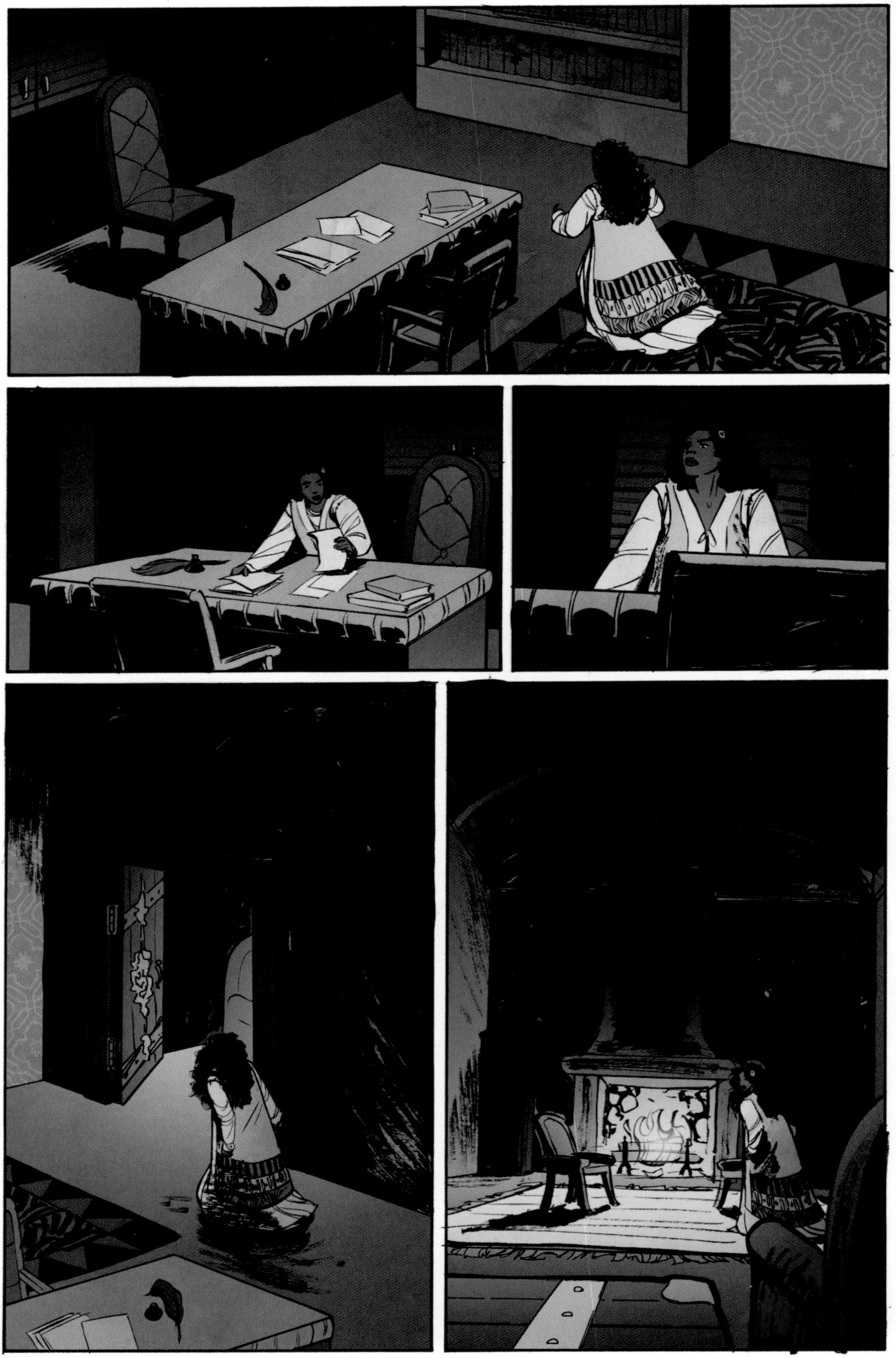

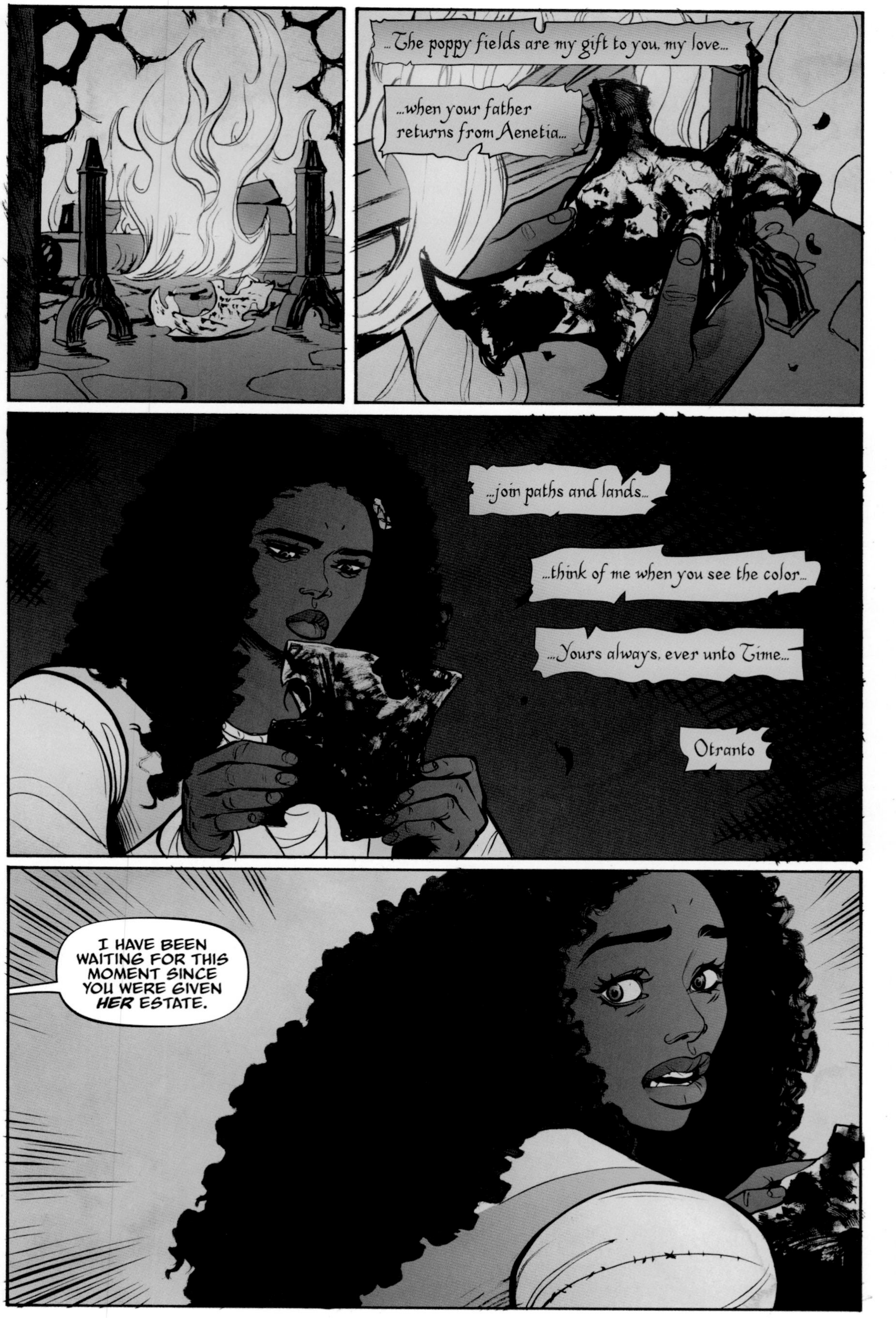
...The poppy fields are my gift to you, my love...
...when your father returns from Aenetia...
...join paths and lands...
...think of me when you see the color...
...Yours always, ever unto Time...
Otranto
I HAVE BEEN WAITING FOR THIS MOMENT SINCE YOU WERE GIVEN HER ESTATE.

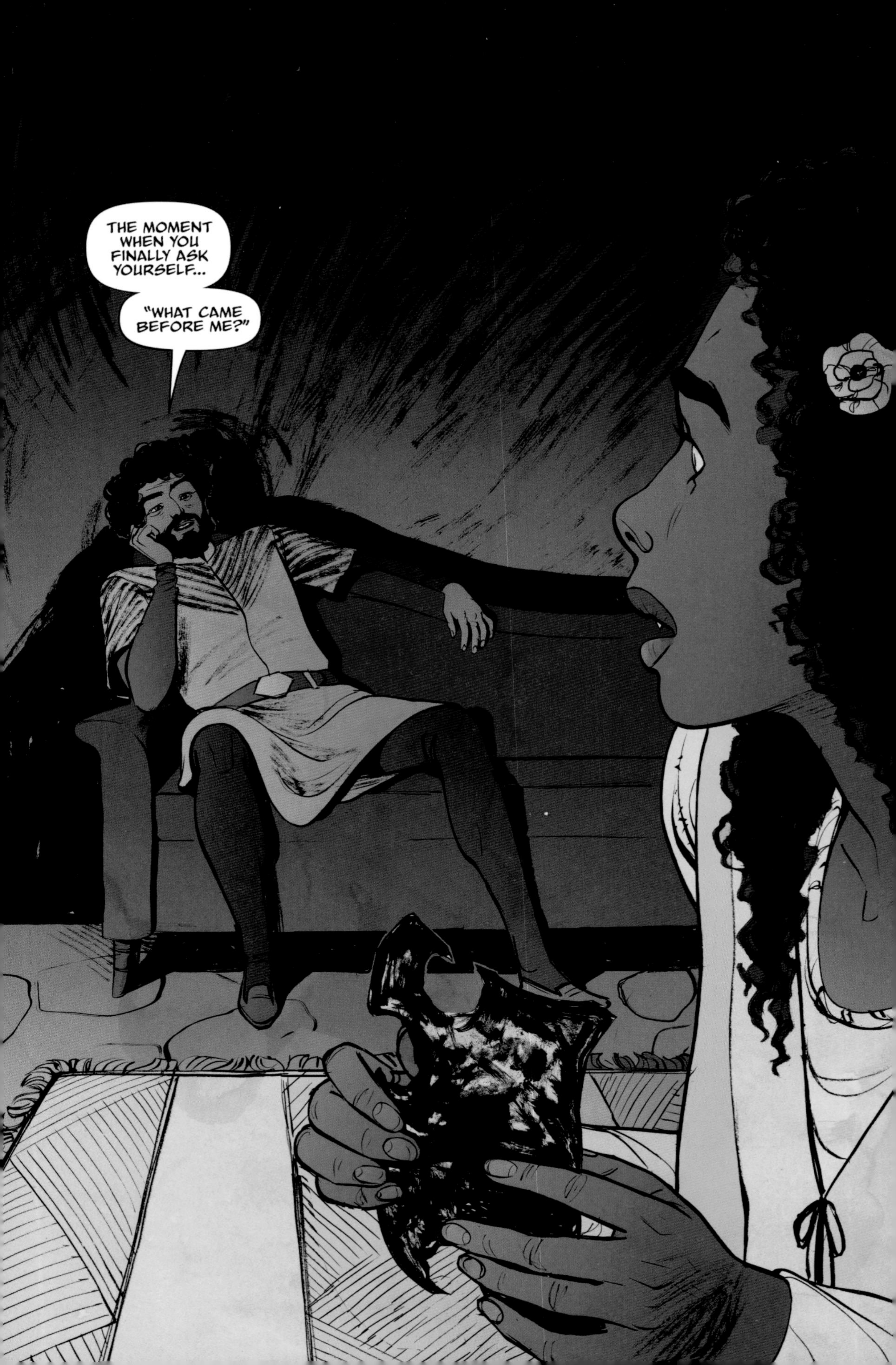
THE MOMENT WHEN YOU FINALLY ASK YOURSELF...
"WHAT CAME BEFORE ME?"

CHAPTER ELEVEN

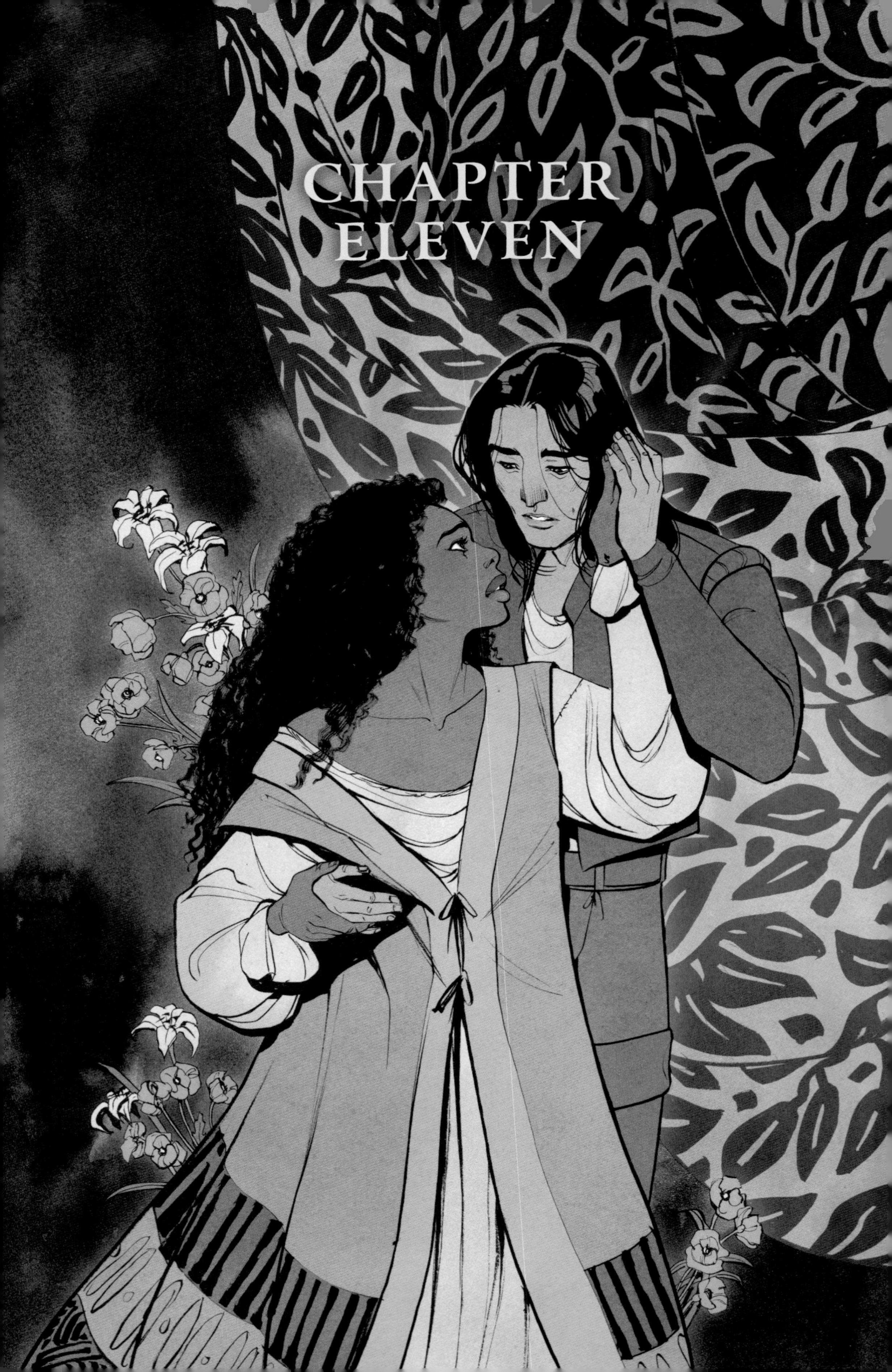

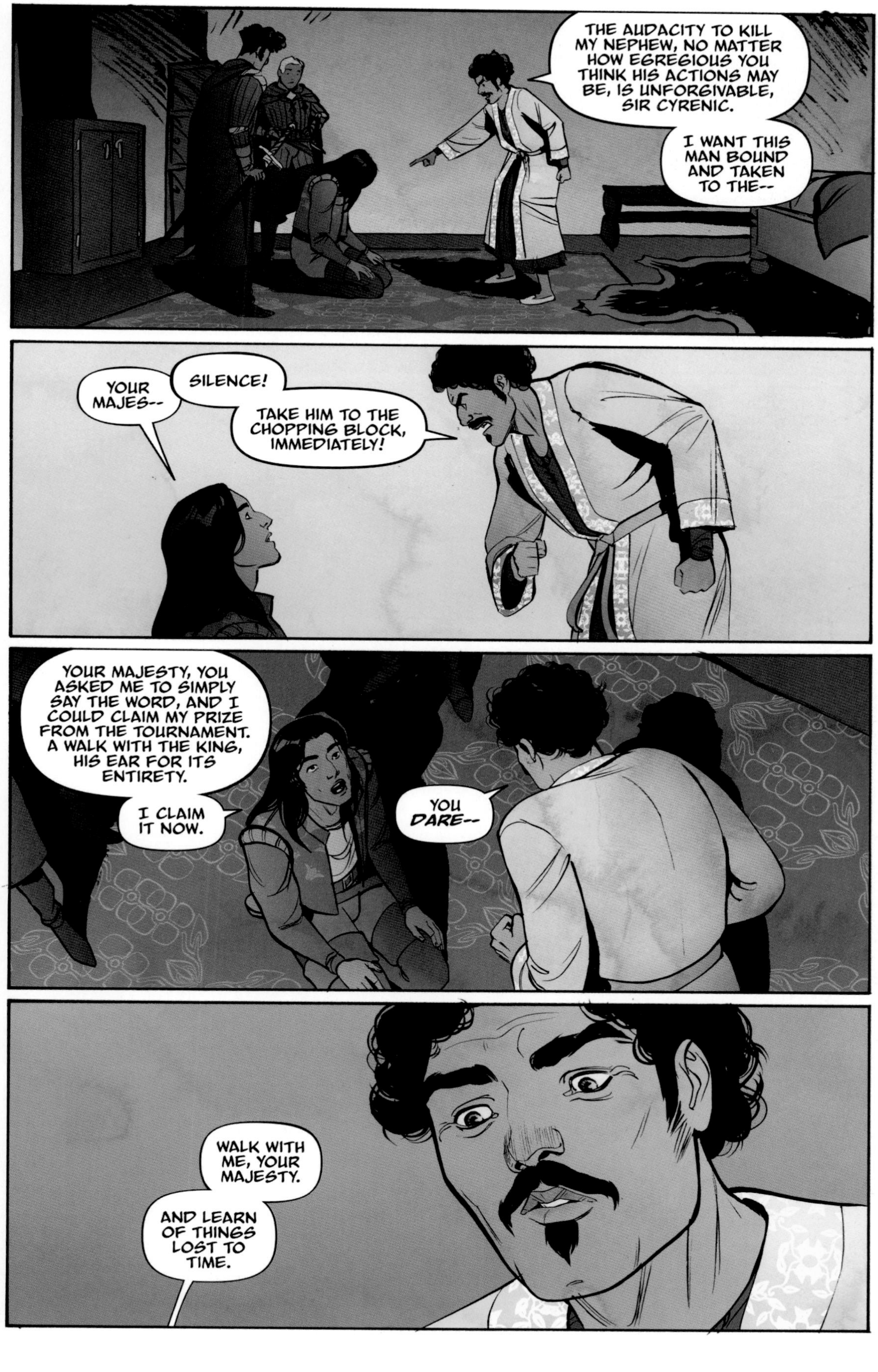
THE AUDACITY TO KILL MY NEPHEW, NO MATTER HOW EGREGIOUS YOU THINK HIS ACTIONS MAY BE, IS UNFORGIVABLE, SIR CYRENIC.
I WANT THIS MAN BOUND AND TAKEN TO THE--
YOUR MAJES--
SILENCE!
TAKE HIM TO THE CHOPPING BLOCK, IMMEDIATELY!
YOUR MAJESTY, YOU ASKED ME TO SIMPLY SAY THE WORD, AND I COULD CLAIM MY PRIZE FROM THE TOURNAMENT. A WALK WITH THE KING, HIS EAR FOR ITS ENTIRETY.
I CLAIM IT NOW.
YOU *DARE*--
WALK WITH ME, YOUR MAJESTY.
AND LEARN OF THINGS LOST TO TIME.

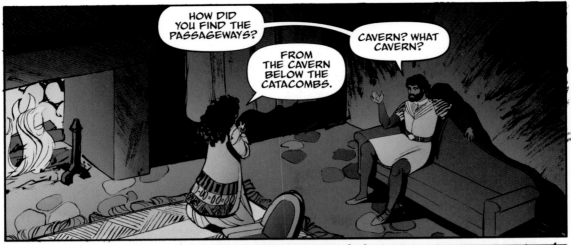

HOW DID YOU FIND THE PASSAGEWAYS?

FROM THE CAVERN BELOW THE CATACOMBS.

CAVERN? WHAT CAVERN?

I THOUGHT *YOU* WOULD KNOW MORE THAN I.

TIME HAS A WAY OF SWALLOWING UP KNOWLEDGE. LIKE FIRE TO PAPER, SUCH AS THE LETTER IN YOUR HAND.

DID YOU NEVER STOP TO THINK HOW YOU RECEIVED YOUR ESTATE?

FATHER GAVE IT TO ME, TO GIVE ME STATUS, TO PROTECT ME!

BUT DID HE NEVER TELL YOU WHO OWNED IT BEFORE?

...NO...

BUT LEOTTA TOLD ME IT WAS AN *ENEMY'S* ESTATE.

AH, YES, OF COURSE IT WAS.

ANYONE WHO DOES NOT AGREE WITH A KING IS AN ENEMY.

AND MY INTENDED HAD THE MISFORTUNE OF BEING IN A TIME OF WAR, AND FROM A FAMILY WITH TIES TO AENITIA.

"MANY IN THE FAMILY DIDN'T WANT THE WAR TO BEGIN WITH, OR DIDN'T WANT TO CHOOSE SIDES."

"SOME EVEN SIDED WITH AENITIA, WITH PROMISE THEY WOULD BE ABSOLVED OF THEIR DEBTS SHOULD AENITIA CONQUER HARBENY."

"HE EXECUTED THE TRAITORS, STRIPPING THEM OF THEIR LANDS AND TITLES, ERASING THE LINEAGE FROM TIME.

"MY INTENDED WAS ACCUSED OF TREASON WHEN SHE VOICED HER ALARM AT THE STATE OF HER CIRCUMSTANCES."

"SHE MADE ME ABANDON HER, IN FEAR THAT HER MISFORTUNE WOULD BEFALL ME."

"AND THEN SHE MET HER END BY VERATO'S JUDGMENT."

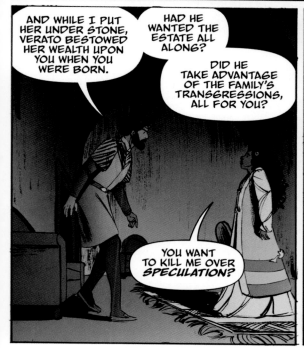

AND WHILE I PUT HER UNDER STONE, VERATO BESTOWED HER WEALTH UPON YOU WHEN YOU WERE BORN.

HAD HE WANTED THE ESTATE ALL ALONG?

DID HE TAKE ADVANTAGE OF THE FAMILY'S TRANSGRESSIONS, ALL FOR YOU?

YOU WANT TO KILL ME OVER *SPECULATION?*

AND YET I HEAR THE HESITANCY IN YOUR VOICE.

BECAUSE YOU KNOW HE WAS CAPABLE OF IT. JUST AS YOUR UNCLE IS CAPABLE. BECAUSE THEY WERE MOLDED BY THEIR FATHER, AND HIS FATHER BEFORE HIM.

AND *YOU* SHARE THE SAME BLOOD AND THE SAME UPBRINGING.

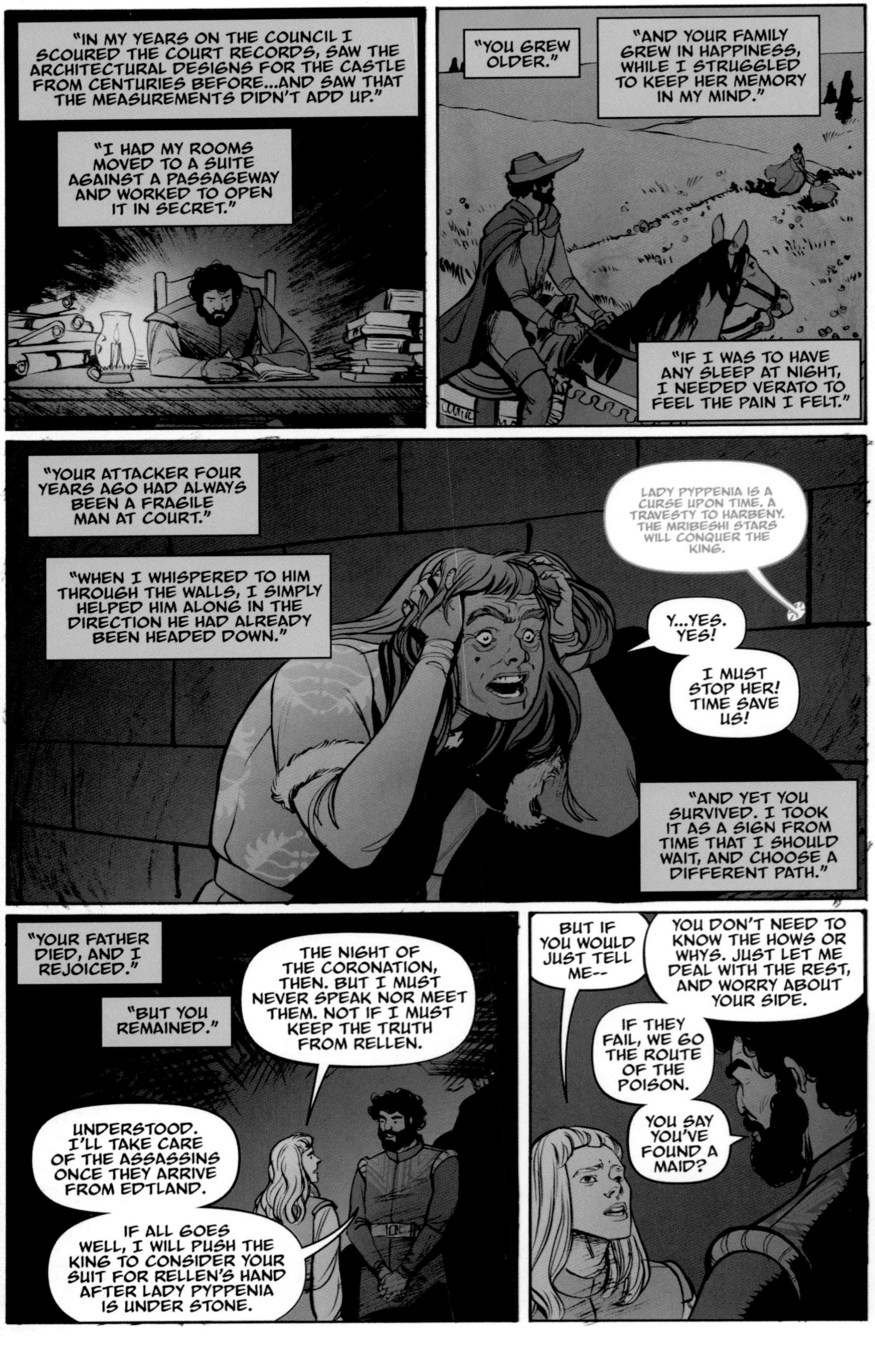
"IN MY YEARS ON THE COUNCIL I SCOURED THE COURT RECORDS, SAW THE ARCHITECTURAL DESIGNS FOR THE CASTLE FROM CENTURIES BEFORE...AND SAW THAT THE MEASUREMENTS DIDN'T ADD UP."
"I HAD MY ROOMS MOVED TO A SUITE AGAINST A PASSAGEWAY AND WORKED TO OPEN IT IN SECRET."
"YOU GREW OLDER."
"AND YOUR FAMILY GREW IN HAPPINESS, WHILE I STRUGGLED TO KEEP HER MEMORY IN MY MIND."
"IF I WAS TO HAVE ANY SLEEP AT NIGHT, I NEEDED VERATO TO FEEL THE PAIN I FELT."
"YOUR ATTACKER FOUR YEARS AGO HAD ALWAYS BEEN A FRAGILE MAN AT COURT."
"WHEN I WHISPERED TO HIM THROUGH THE WALLS, I SIMPLY HELPED HIM ALONG IN THE DIRECTION HE HAD ALREADY BEEN HEADED DOWN."
LADY PYPPENIA IS A CURSE UPON TIME. A TRAVESTY TO HARBENY. THE MRIBESHI STARS WILL CONQUER THE KING.
Y...YES. YES!
I MUST STOP HER! TIME SAVE US!
"AND YET YOU SURVIVED. I TOOK IT AS A SIGN FROM TIME THAT I SHOULD WAIT, AND CHOOSE A DIFFERENT PATH."
"YOUR FATHER DIED, AND I REJOICED."
"BUT YOU REMAINED."
THE NIGHT OF THE CORONATION, THEN. BUT I MUST NEVER SPEAK NOR MEET THEM. NOT IF I MUST KEEP THE TRUTH FROM RELLEN.
UNDERSTOOD. I'LL TAKE CARE OF THE ASSASSINS ONCE THEY ARRIVE FROM EDTLAND.
IF ALL GOES WELL, I WILL PUSH THE KING TO CONSIDER YOUR SUIT FOR RELLEN'S HAND AFTER LADY PYPPENIA IS UNDER STONE.
BUT IF YOU WOULD JUST TELL ME--
YOU DON'T NEED TO KNOW THE HOWS OR WHYS. JUST LET ME DEAL WITH THE REST, AND WORRY ABOUT YOUR SIDE.
IF THEY FAIL, WE GO THE ROUTE OF THE POISON.
YOU SAY YOU'VE FOUND A MAID?

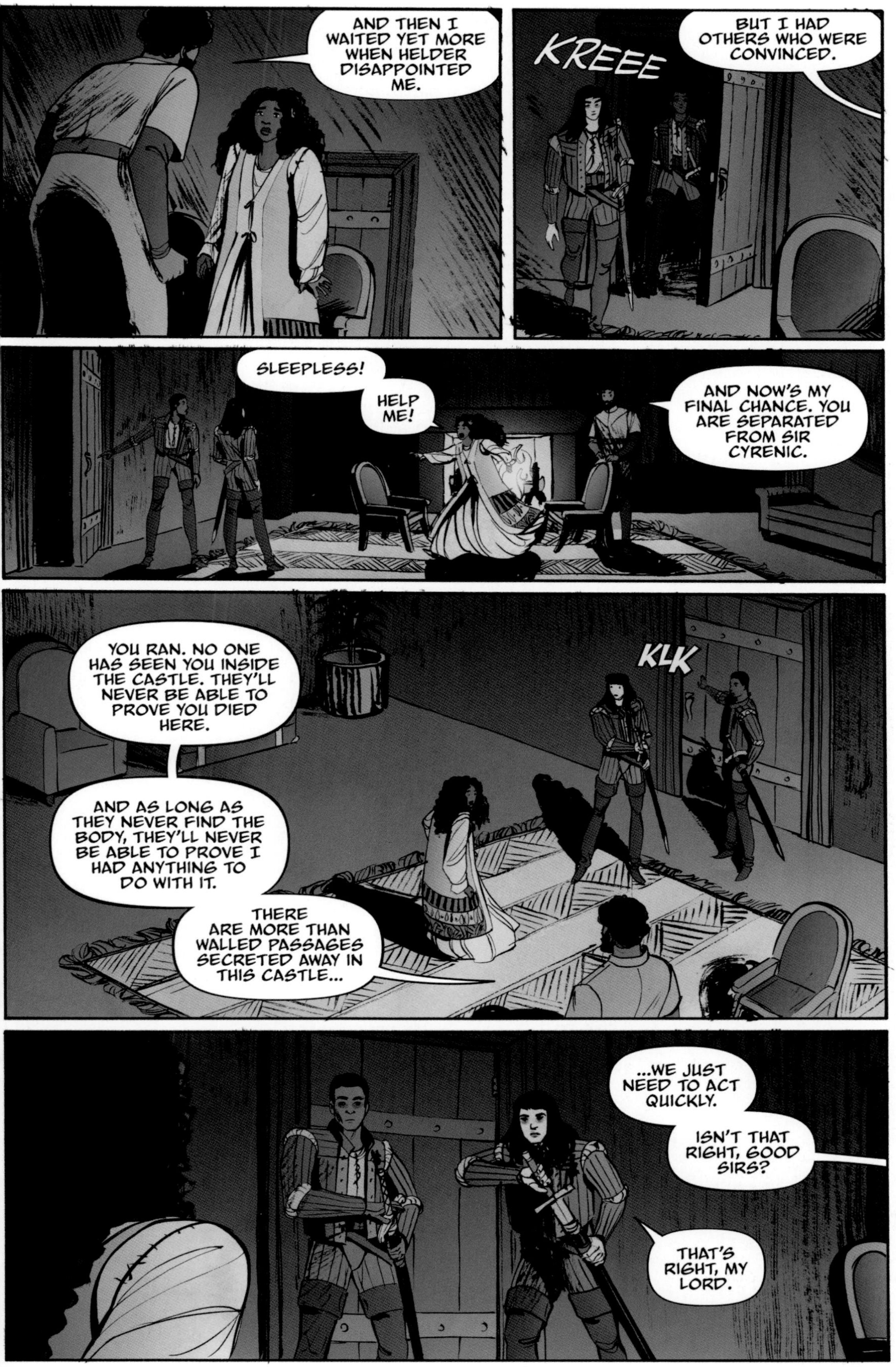
AND THEN I WAITED YET MORE WHEN HELDER DISAPPOINTED ME.
KREEE
BUT I HAD OTHERS WHO WERE CONVINCED.
SLEEPLESS!
HELP ME!
AND NOW'S MY FINAL CHANCE. YOU ARE SEPARATED FROM SIR CYRENIC.
YOU RAN. NO ONE HAS SEEN YOU INSIDE THE CASTLE. THEY'LL NEVER BE ABLE TO PROVE YOU DIED HERE.
KLK
AND AS LONG AS THEY NEVER FIND THE BODY, THEY'LL NEVER BE ABLE TO PROVE I HAD ANYTHING TO DO WITH IT.
THERE ARE MORE THAN WALLED PASSAGES SECRETED AWAY IN THIS CASTLE...
...WE JUST NEED TO ACT QUICKLY.
ISN'T THAT RIGHT, GOOD SIRS?
THAT'S RIGHT, MY LORD.

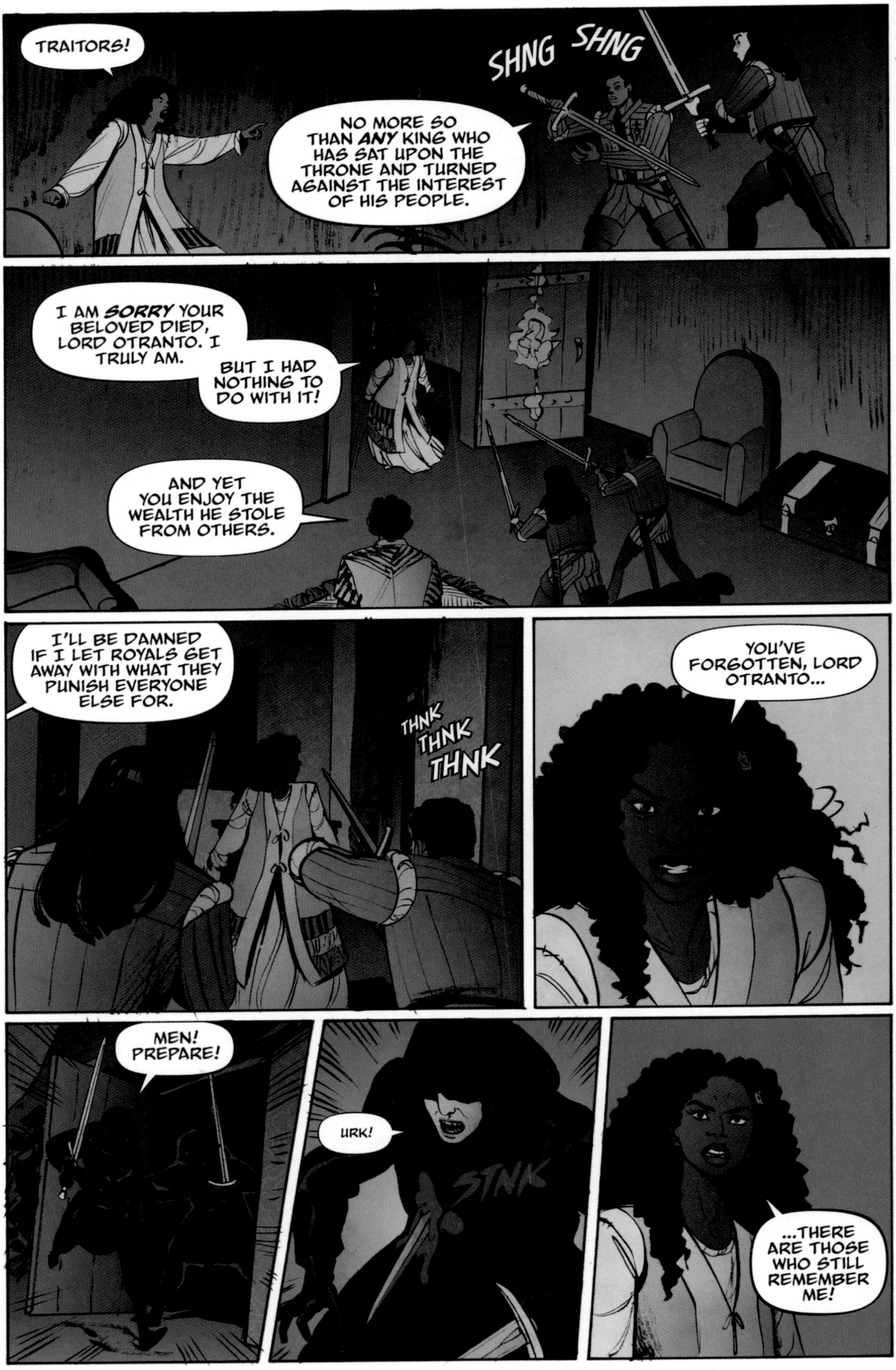
TRAITORS!
SHNG SHNG
NO MORE SO THAN ANY KING WHO HAS SAT UPON THE THRONE AND TURNED AGAINST THE INTEREST OF HIS PEOPLE.
I AM SORRY YOUR BELOVED DIED, LORD OTRANTO. I TRULY AM.
BUT I HAD NOTHING TO DO WITH IT!
AND YET YOU ENJOY THE WEALTH HE STOLE FROM OTHERS.
I'LL BE DAMNED IF I LET ROYALS GET AWAY WITH WHAT THEY PUNISH EVERYONE ELSE FOR.
THNK THNK THNK
YOU'VE FORGOTTEN, LORD OTRANTO...
MEN! PREPARE!
URK!
STNK
...THERE ARE THOSE WHO STILL REMEMBER ME!

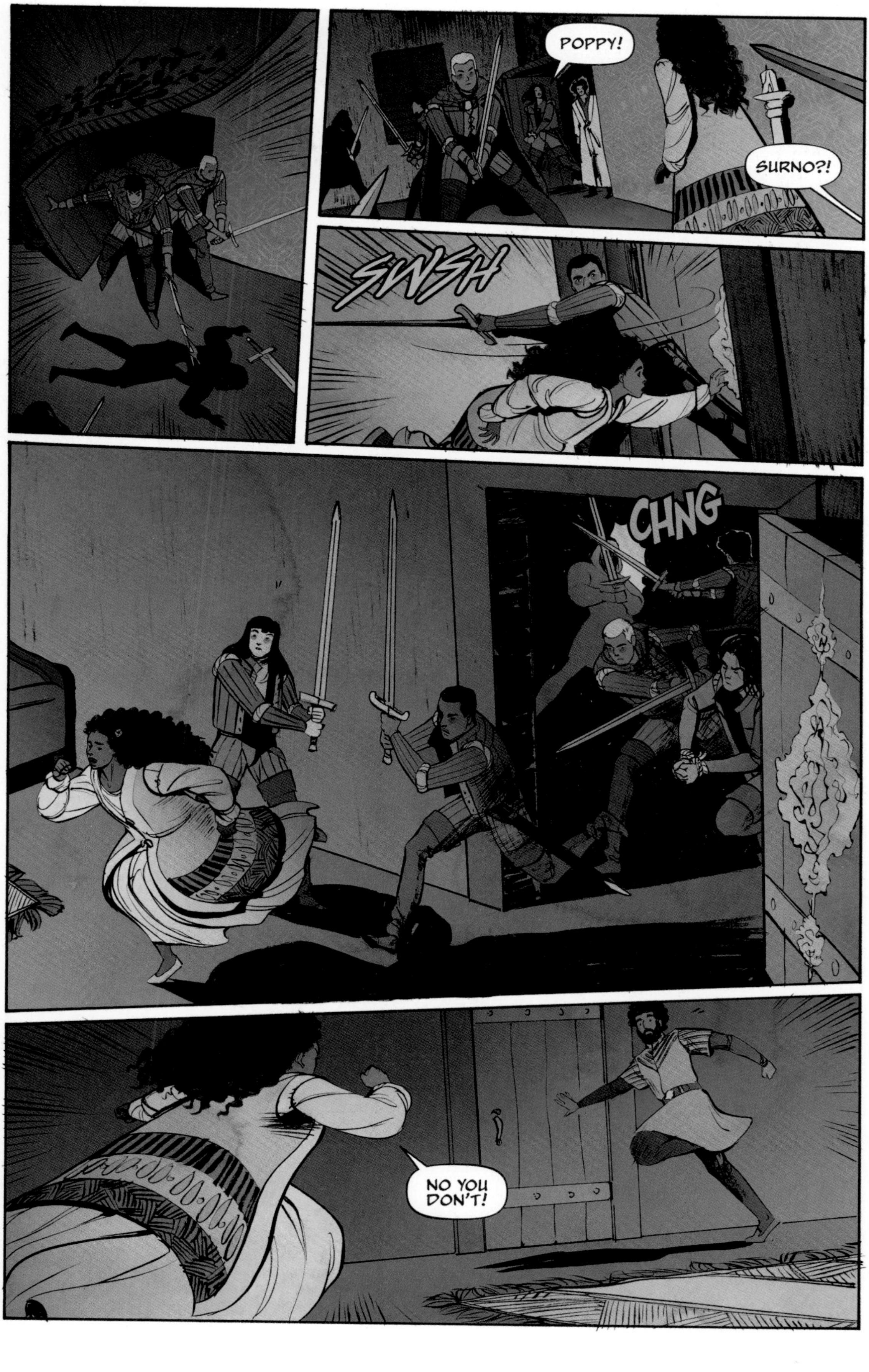
POPPY!
SURNO?!
SWISH
CHNG
NO YOU DON'T!

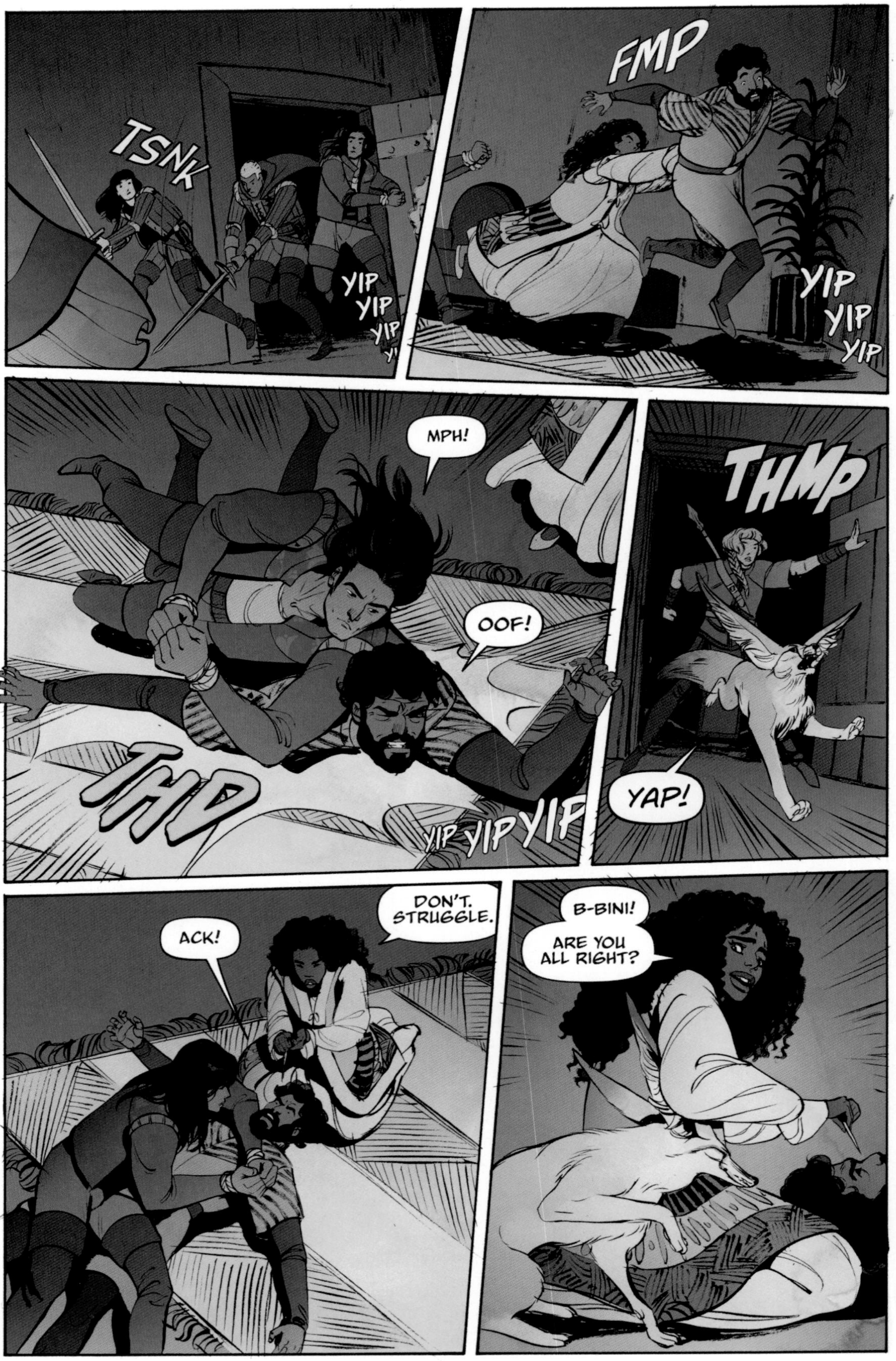
TSNk
YIP
YIP
YIP
FMP
YIP
YIP
YIP
MPH!
OOF!
THD
YIP YIP YIP
THMP
YAP!
ACK!
DON'T. STRUGGLE.
B-BINI!
ARE YOU ALL RIGHT?

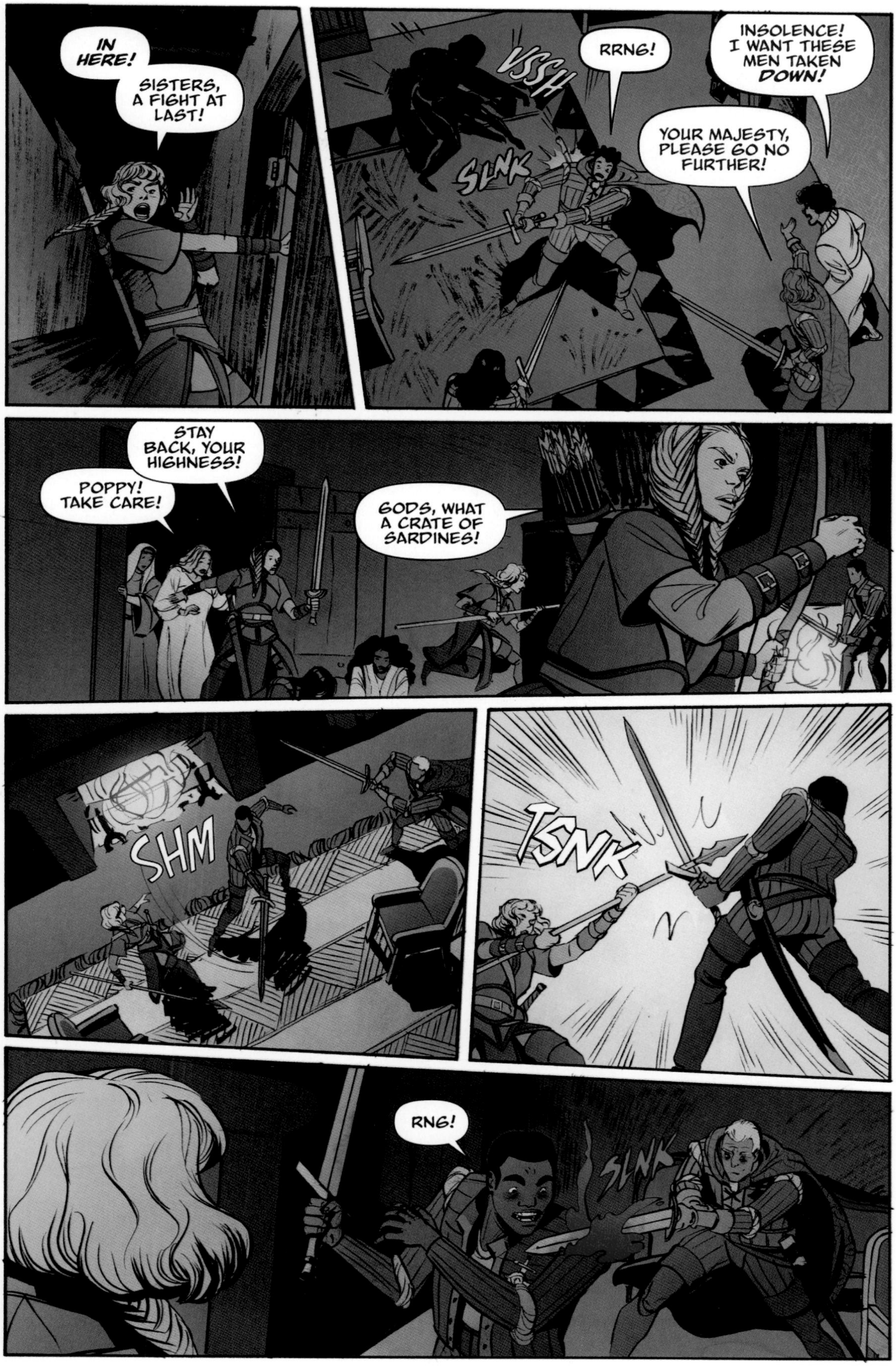
IN HERE!
SISTERS, A FIGHT AT LAST!
VSSH
SLNK
RRNG!
INSOLENCE! I WANT THESE MEN TAKEN DOWN!
YOUR MAJESTY, PLEASE GO NO FURTHER!
STAY BACK, YOUR HIGHNESS!
POPPY! TAKE CARE!
GODS, WHAT A CRATE OF SARDINES!
SHM
TSNK
RNG!
SLNK

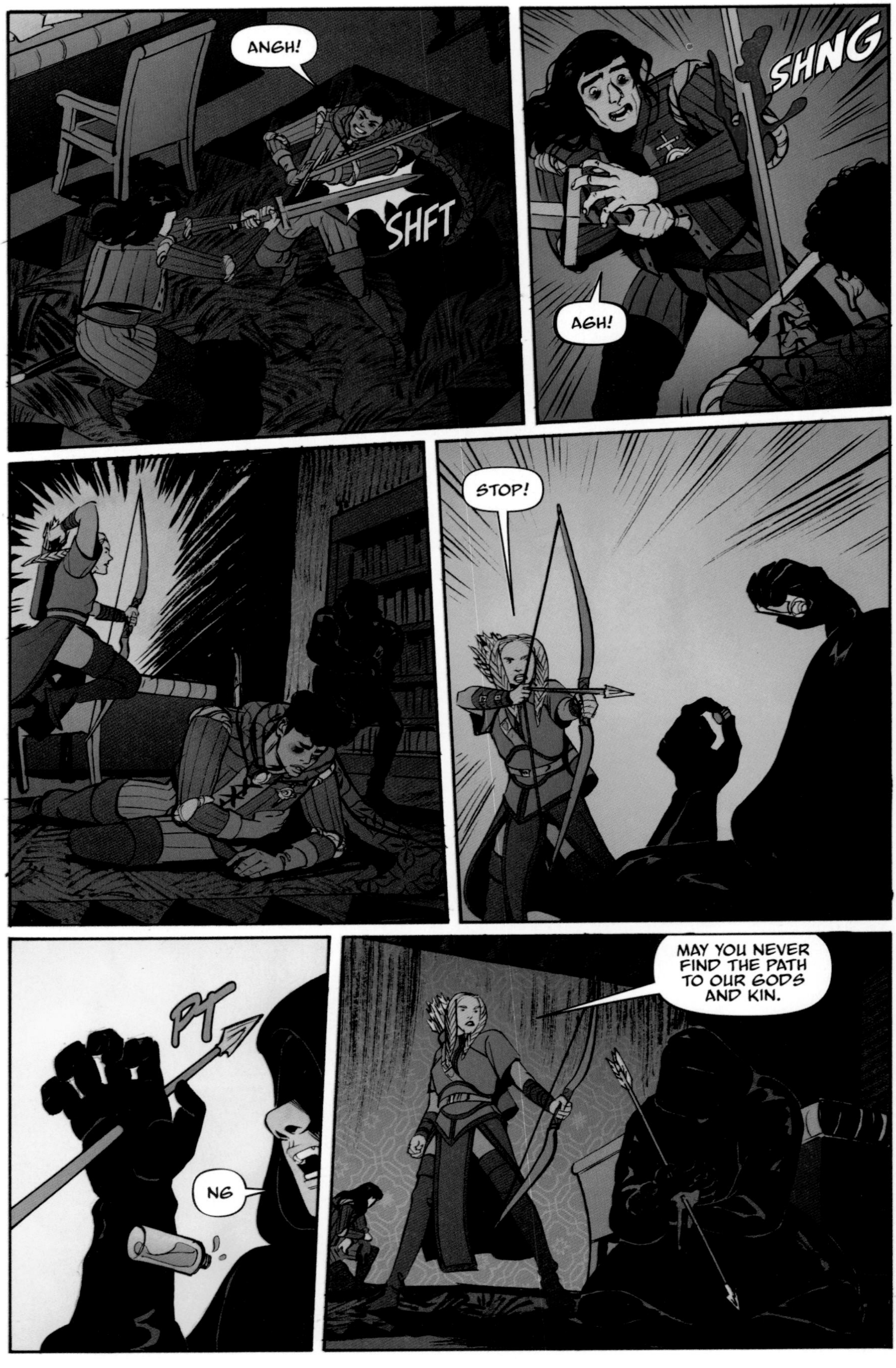
ANGH!
SHFT
SHNG
AGH!
STOP!
PT
NG
MAY YOU NEVER FIND THE PATH TO OUR GODS AND KIN.

ANGH!

YOU DRAG OUR NAME THROUGH THE MUD! FOR WHAT?

OUR NAME HAS BEEN IN THE MUD FOR YEARS ALREADY!

WHY DO YOU THINK IT WAS SO EASY FOR THE ASSASSINS TO SLIP THROUGH THE HALLWAYS OF THE CASTLE?

IT WAS BECAUSE WE *LET* THEM.

THE USELESS SLEEPLESS.

OF *COURSE* WE ARE, WHEN WE ARE GIVEN NOTHING TO DO BUT STAND ALL DAY.

I GAVE UP MY LIFE FOR THE CROWN! AND *YOUR MAJESTY* TALKS OF RELEASING ME AS IF YOU WERE GOING TO FLICK A FLY OFF YOUR SLEEVE!

WHY SHOULD I BE LOYAL TO THE THRONE IF THE MAN WHO SITS ON IT TREATS ME AS IF I AM NOTHING?

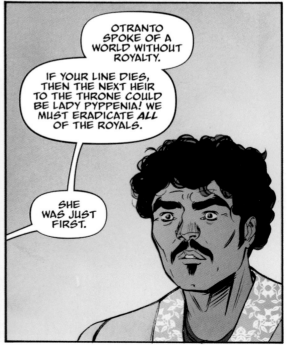

OTRANTO SPOKE OF A WORLD WITHOUT ROYALTY.

IF YOUR LINE DIES, THEN THE NEXT HEIR TO THE THRONE COULD BE LADY PYPPENIA! WE MUST ERADICATE *ALL* OF THE ROYALS.

SHE WAS JUST FIRST.

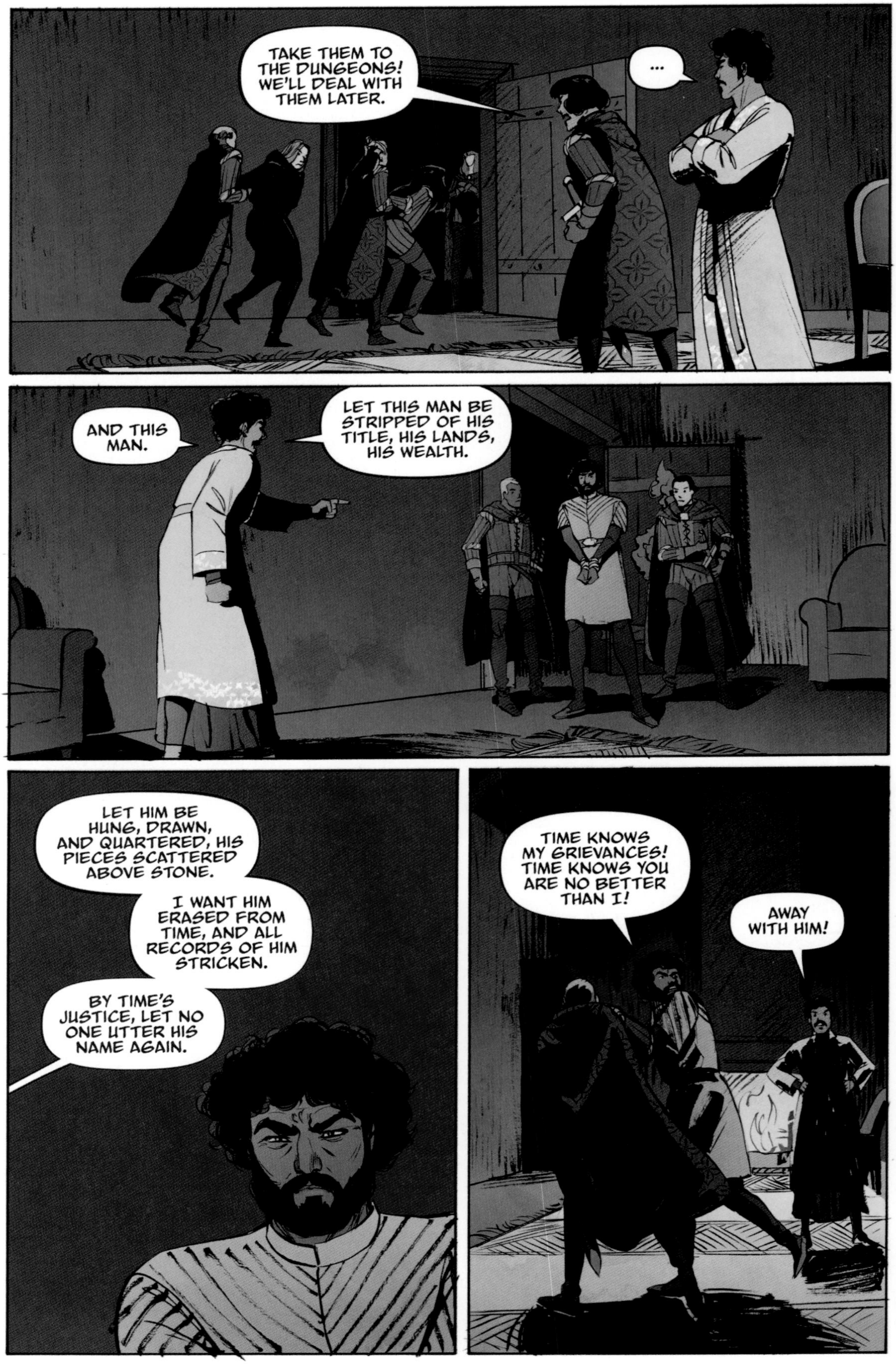
TAKE THEM TO THE DUNGEONS! WE'LL DEAL WITH THEM LATER.
...
AND THIS MAN.
LET THIS MAN BE STRIPPED OF HIS TITLE, HIS LANDS, HIS WEALTH.
LET HIM BE HUNG, DRAWN, AND QUARTERED, HIS PIECES SCATTERED ABOVE STONE.
I WANT HIM ERASED FROM TIME, AND ALL RECORDS OF HIM STRICKEN.
BY TIME'S JUSTICE, LET NO ONE UTTER HIS NAME AGAIN.
TIME KNOWS MY GRIEVANCES! TIME KNOWS YOU ARE NO BETTER THAN I!
AWAY WITH HIM!

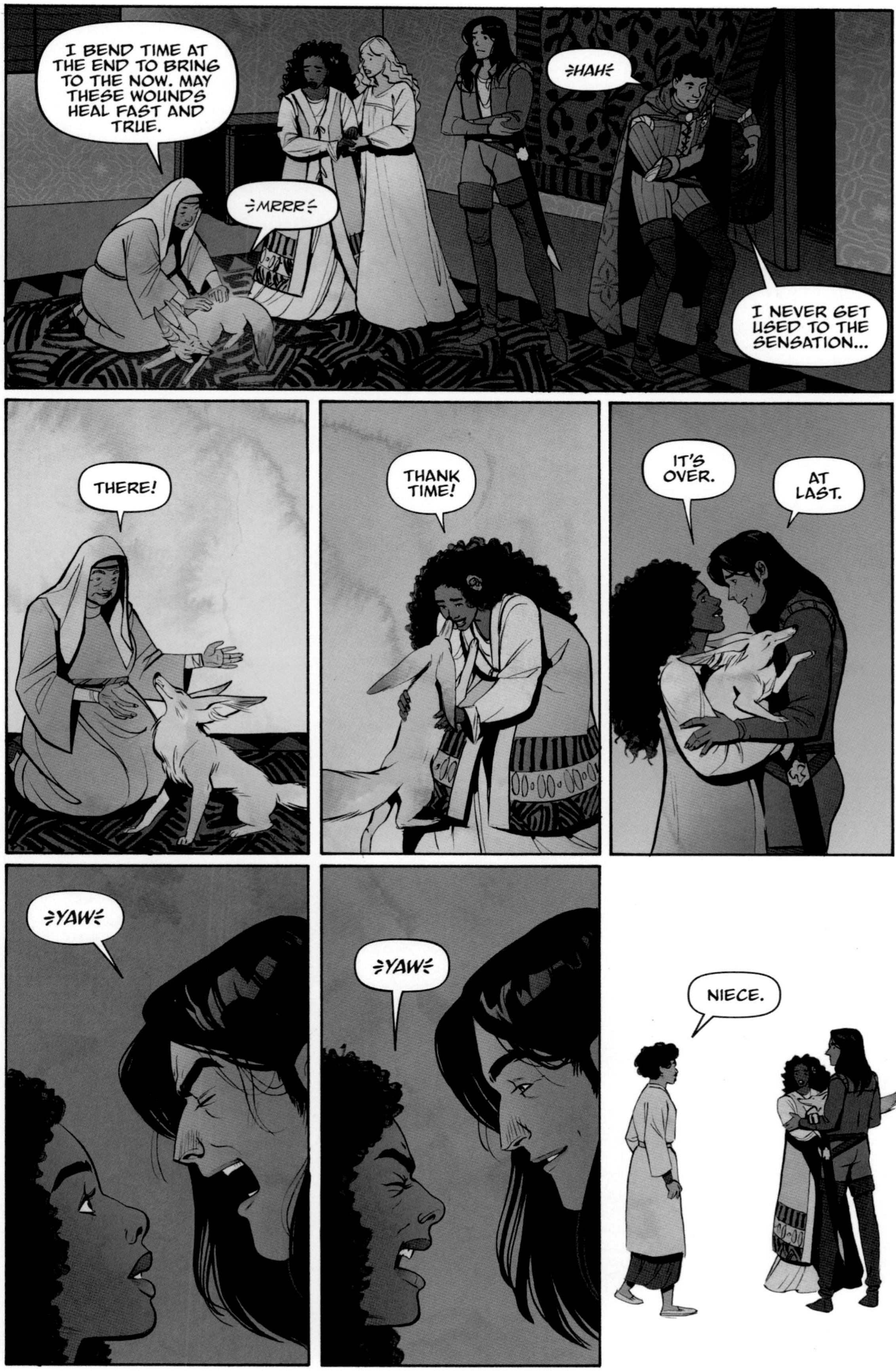

I BEND TIME AT THE END TO BRING TO THE NOW. MAY THESE WOUNDS HEAL FAST AND TRUE.
=MRRR=
=HAH=
I NEVER GET USED TO THE SENSATION...
THERE!
THANK TIME!
IT'S OVER.
AT LAST.
=YAW=
=YAW=
NIECE.

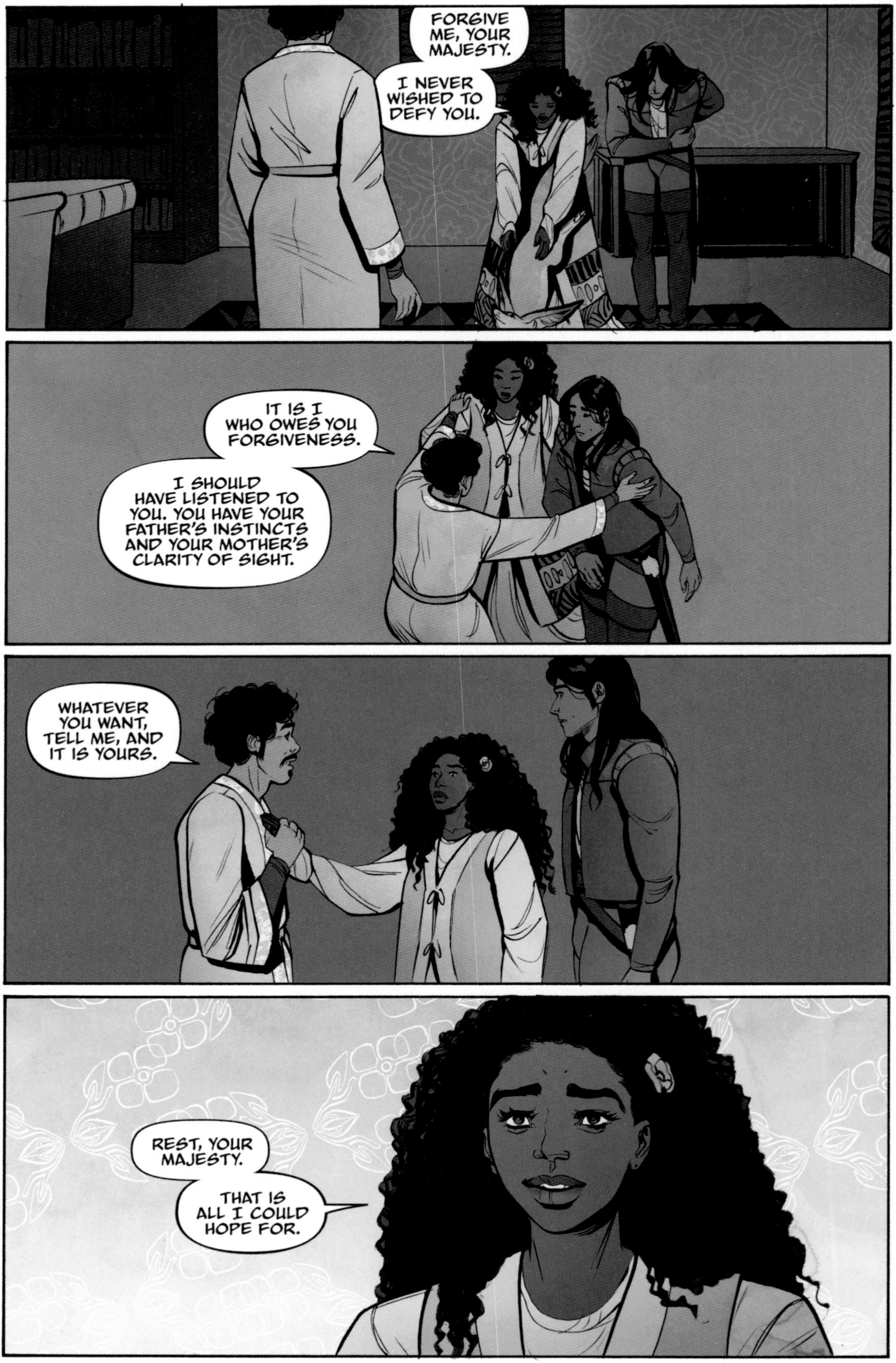
FORGIVE ME, YOUR MAJESTY.
I NEVER WISHED TO DEFY YOU.
IT IS I WHO OWES YOU FORGIVENESS.
I SHOULD HAVE LISTENED TO YOU. YOU HAVE YOUR FATHER'S INSTINCTS AND YOUR MOTHER'S CLARITY OF SIGHT.
WHATEVER YOU WANT, TELL ME, AND IT IS YOURS.
REST, YOUR MAJESTY.
THAT IS ALL I COULD HOPE FOR.

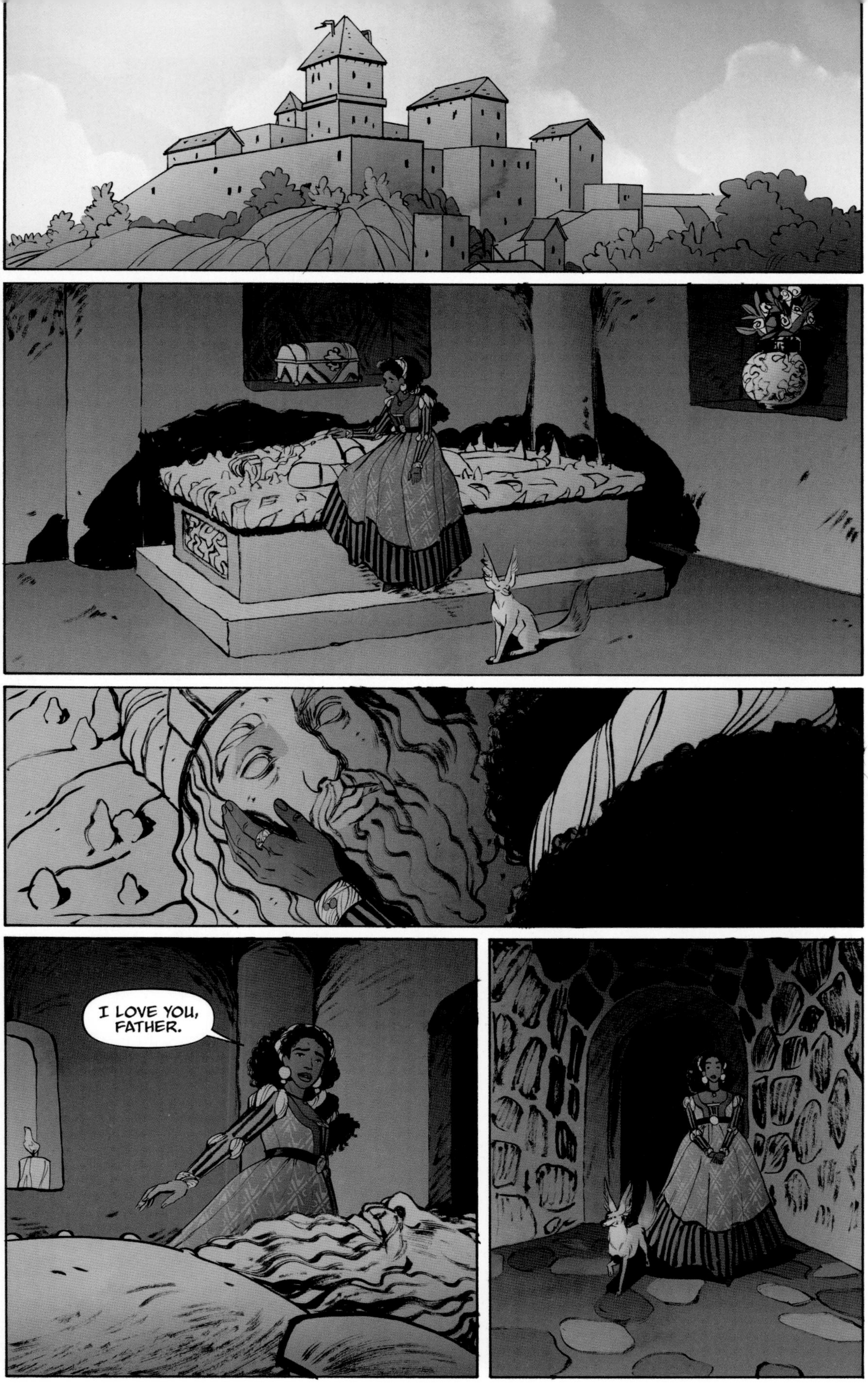
I LOVE YOU, FATHER.

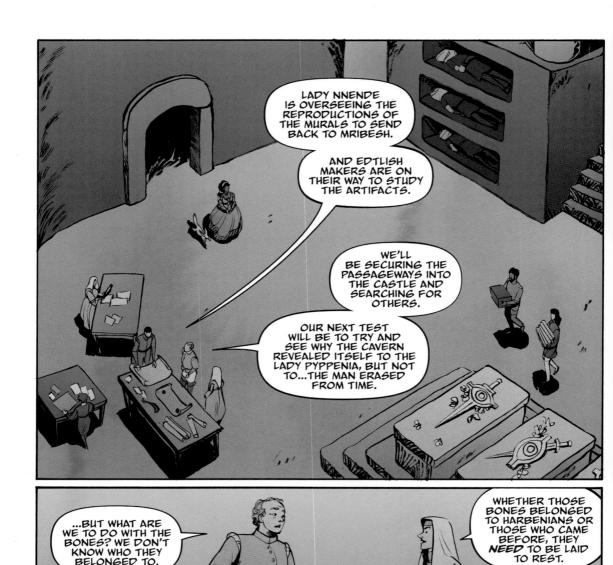

LADY NNENDE IS OVERSEEING THE REPRODUCTIONS OF THE MURALS TO SEND BACK TO MRIBESH.

AND EDTLISH MAKERS ARE ON THEIR WAY TO STUDY THE ARTIFACTS.

WE'LL BE SECURING THE PASSAGEWAYS INTO THE CASTLE AND SEARCHING FOR OTHERS.

OUR NEXT TEST WILL BE TO TRY AND SEE WHY THE CAVERN REVEALED ITSELF TO THE LADY PYPPENIA, BUT NOT TO...THE MAN ERASED FROM TIME.

...BUT WHAT ARE WE TO DO WITH THE BONES? WE DON'T KNOW WHO THEY BELONGED TO.

WHETHER THOSE BONES BELONGED TO HARBENIANS OR THOSE WHO CAME BEFORE, THEY **NEED** TO BE LAID TO REST.

TOSSED LIKE GARBAGE! WE **COULDN'T** HAVE TAKEN THE BODIES FROM THEIR RESTING PLACES! THAT ISN'T THE HARBENIAN WAY!

BUT WHEN DID OUR HARBENIAN WAYS BEGIN? THIS COULD HAVE HAPPENED A THOUSAND YEARS AGO.

HERE THE SLEEPLESS LIE NEVER TO WAKE AGAIN

YOU DON'T THINK WE NEED TO ENLIST AN AENITIAN TO RESEARCH WITH US, DO YOU?

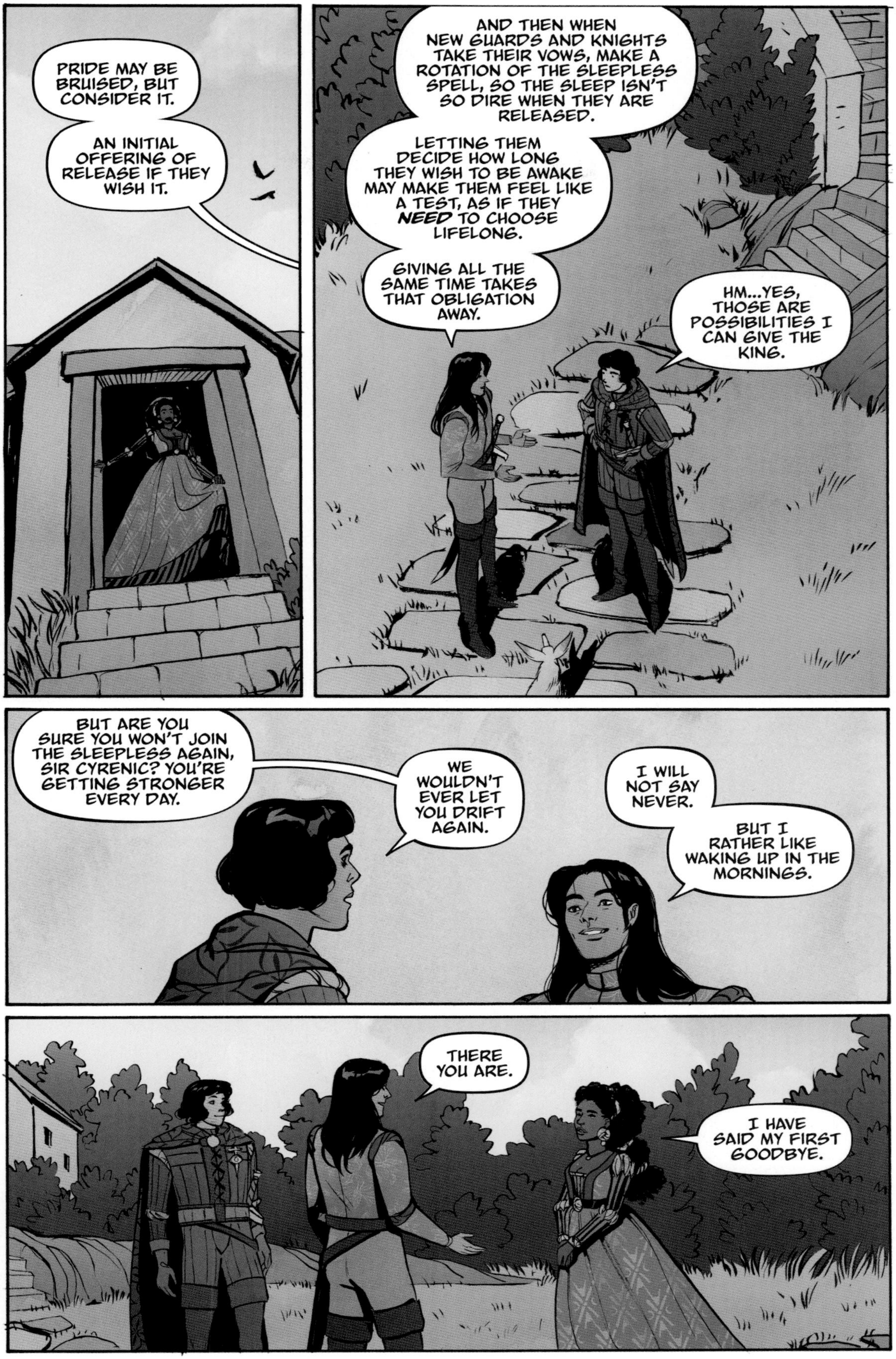
PRIDE MAY BE BRUISED, BUT CONSIDER IT.
AN INITIAL OFFERING OF RELEASE IF THEY WISH IT.
AND THEN WHEN NEW GUARDS AND KNIGHTS TAKE THEIR VOWS, MAKE A ROTATION OF THE SLEEPLESS SPELL, SO THE SLEEP ISN'T SO DIRE WHEN THEY ARE RELEASED.
LETTING THEM DECIDE HOW LONG THEY WISH TO BE AWAKE MAY MAKE THEM FEEL LIKE A TEST, AS IF THEY ***NEED*** TO CHOOSE LIFELONG.
GIVING ALL THE SAME TIME TAKES THAT OBLIGATION AWAY.
HM...YES, THOSE ARE POSSIBILITIES I CAN GIVE THE KING.
BUT ARE YOU SURE YOU WON'T JOIN THE SLEEPLESS AGAIN, SIR CYRENIC? YOU'RE GETTING STRONGER EVERY DAY.
WE WOULDN'T EVER LET YOU DRIFT AGAIN.
I WILL NOT SAY NEVER.
BUT I RATHER LIKE WAKING UP IN THE MORNINGS.
THERE YOU ARE.
I HAVE SAID MY FIRST GOODBYE.

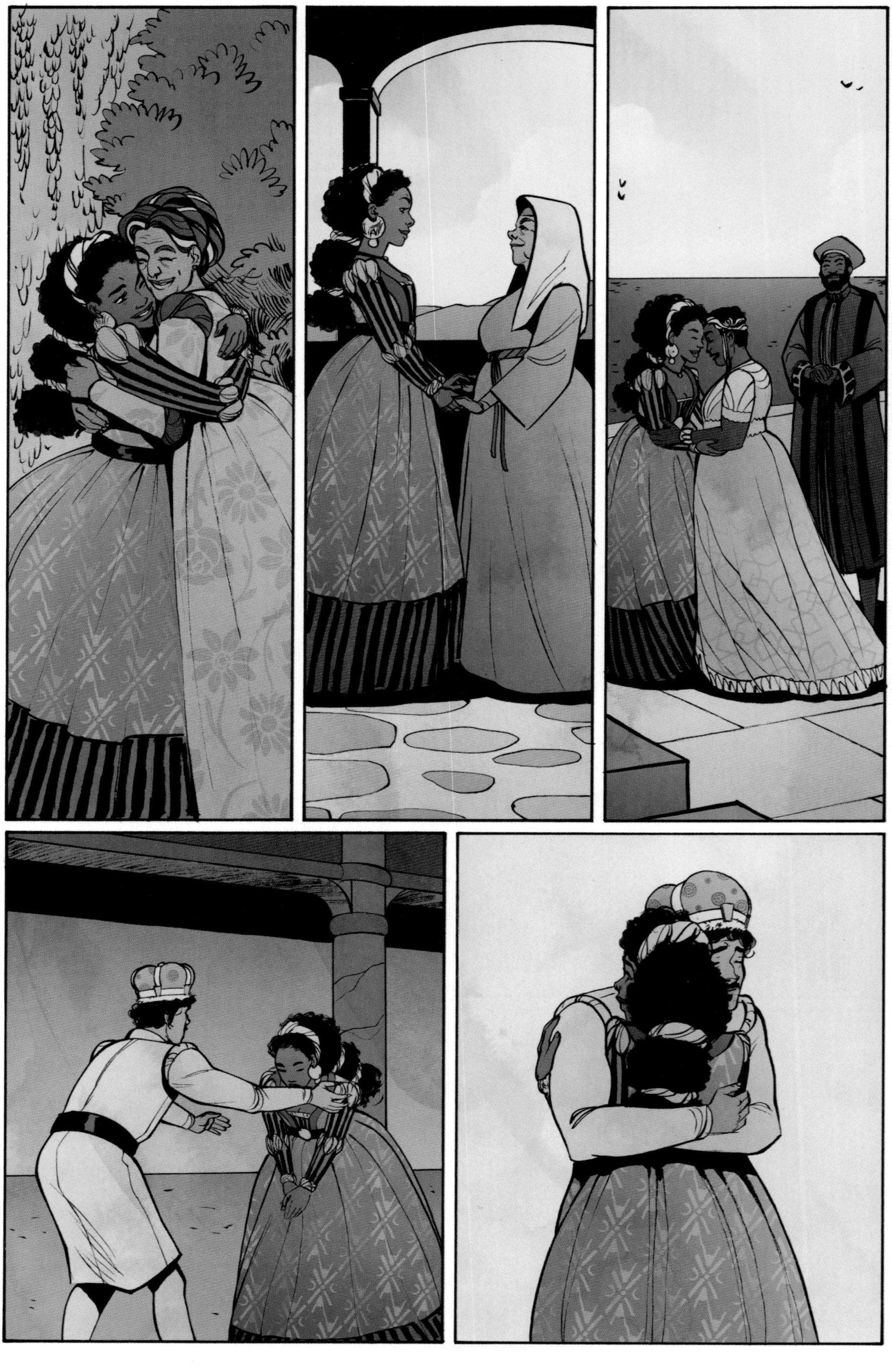

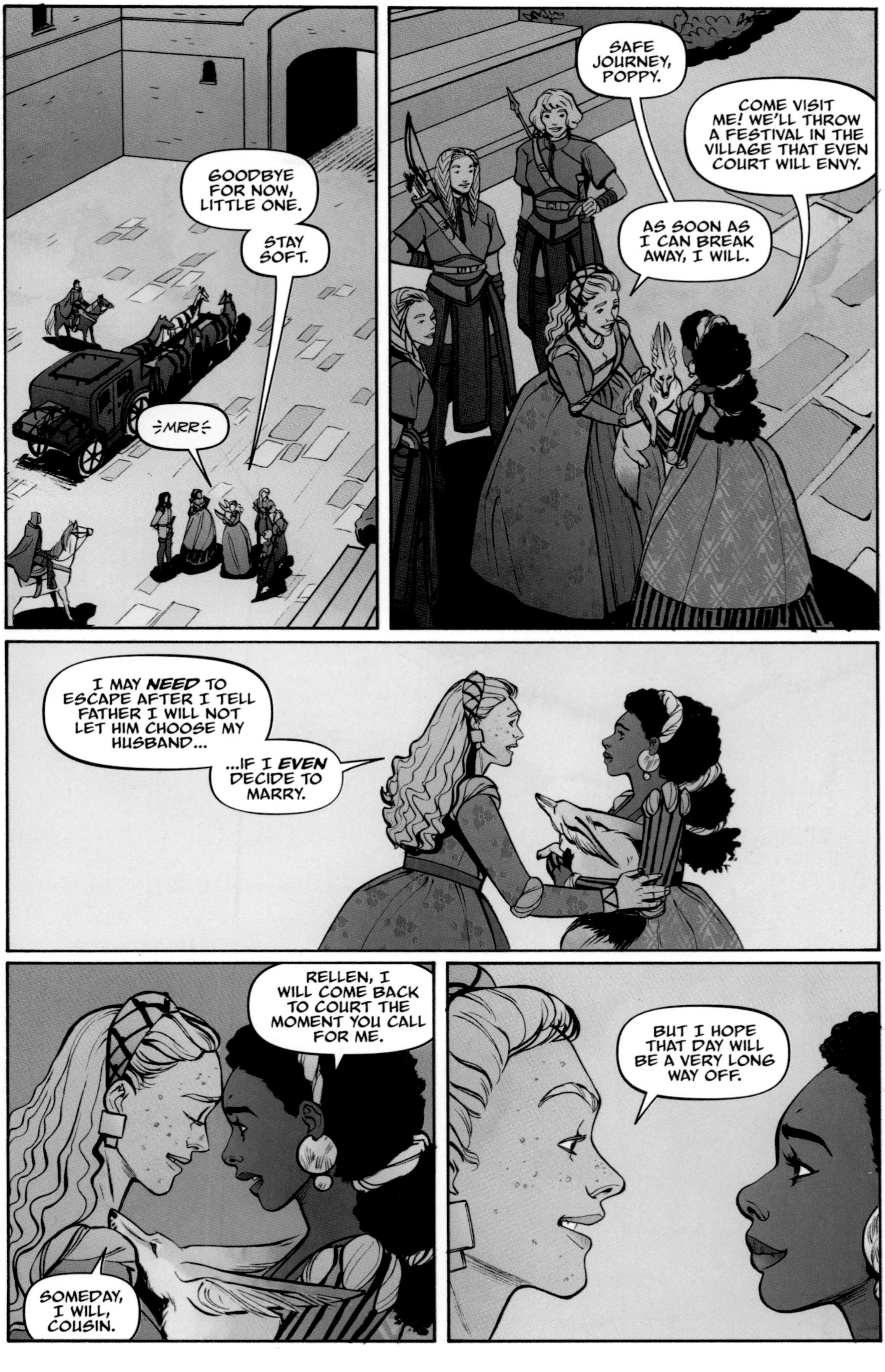
GOODBYE FOR NOW, LITTLE ONE.
STAY SOFT.
≈MRR≈
SAFE JOURNEY, POPPY.
COME VISIT ME! WE'LL THROW A FESTIVAL IN THE VILLAGE THAT EVEN COURT WILL ENVY.
AS SOON AS I CAN BREAK AWAY, I WILL.
I MAY *NEED* TO ESCAPE AFTER I TELL FATHER I WILL NOT LET HIM CHOOSE MY HUSBAND...
...IF I *EVEN* DECIDE TO MARRY.
RELLEN, I WILL COME BACK TO COURT THE MOMENT YOU CALL FOR ME.
SOMEDAY, I WILL, COUSIN.
BUT I HOPE THAT DAY WILL BE A VERY LONG WAY OFF.

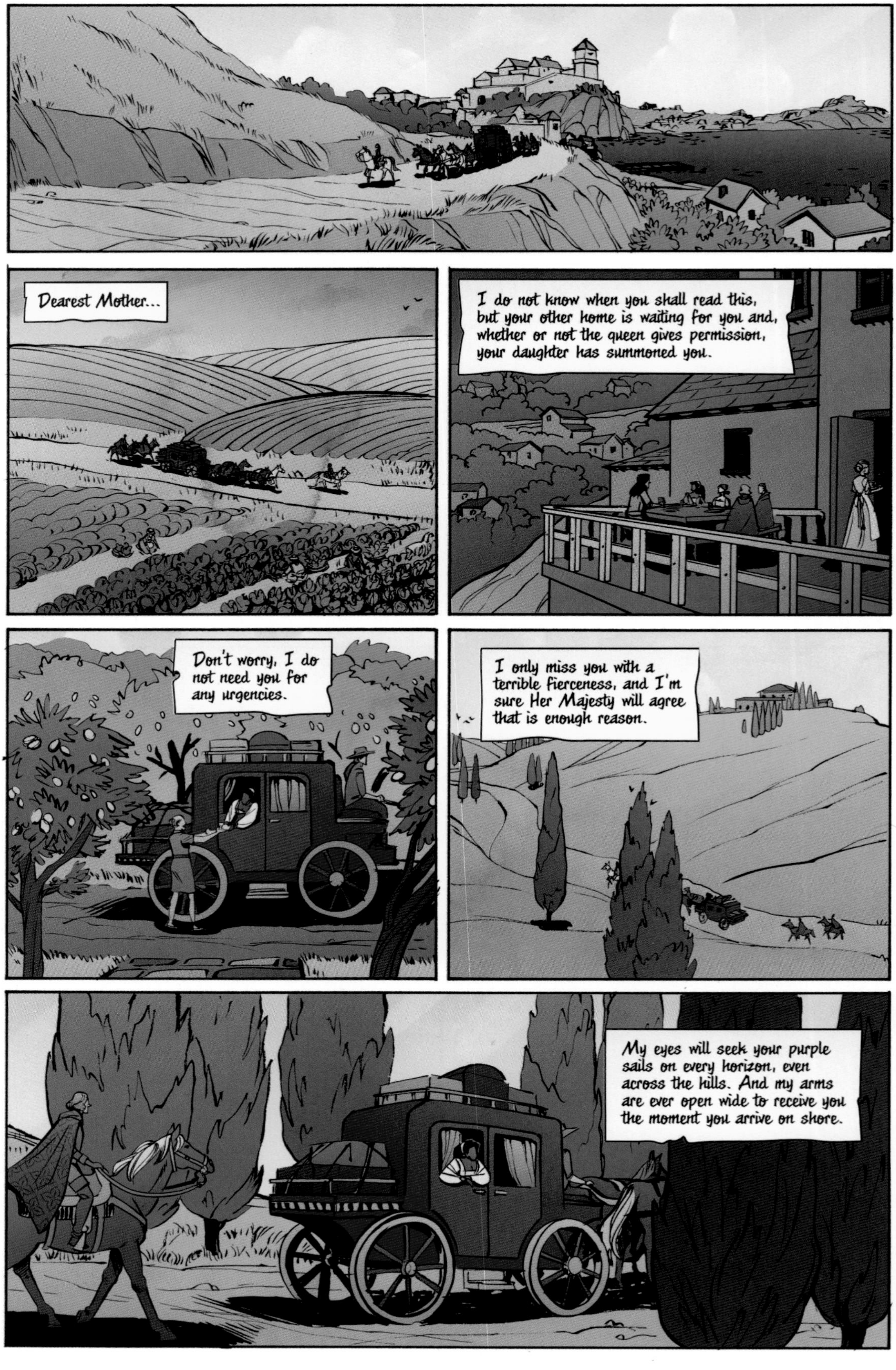
Dearest Mother...
I do not know when you shall read this, but your other home is waiting for you and, whether or not the queen gives permission, your daughter has summoned you.
Don't worry, I do not need you for any urgencies.
I only miss you with a terrible fierceness, and I'm sure Her Majesty will agree that is enough reason.
My eyes will seek your purple sails on every horizon, even across the hills. And my arms are ever open wide to receive you the moment you arrive on shore.

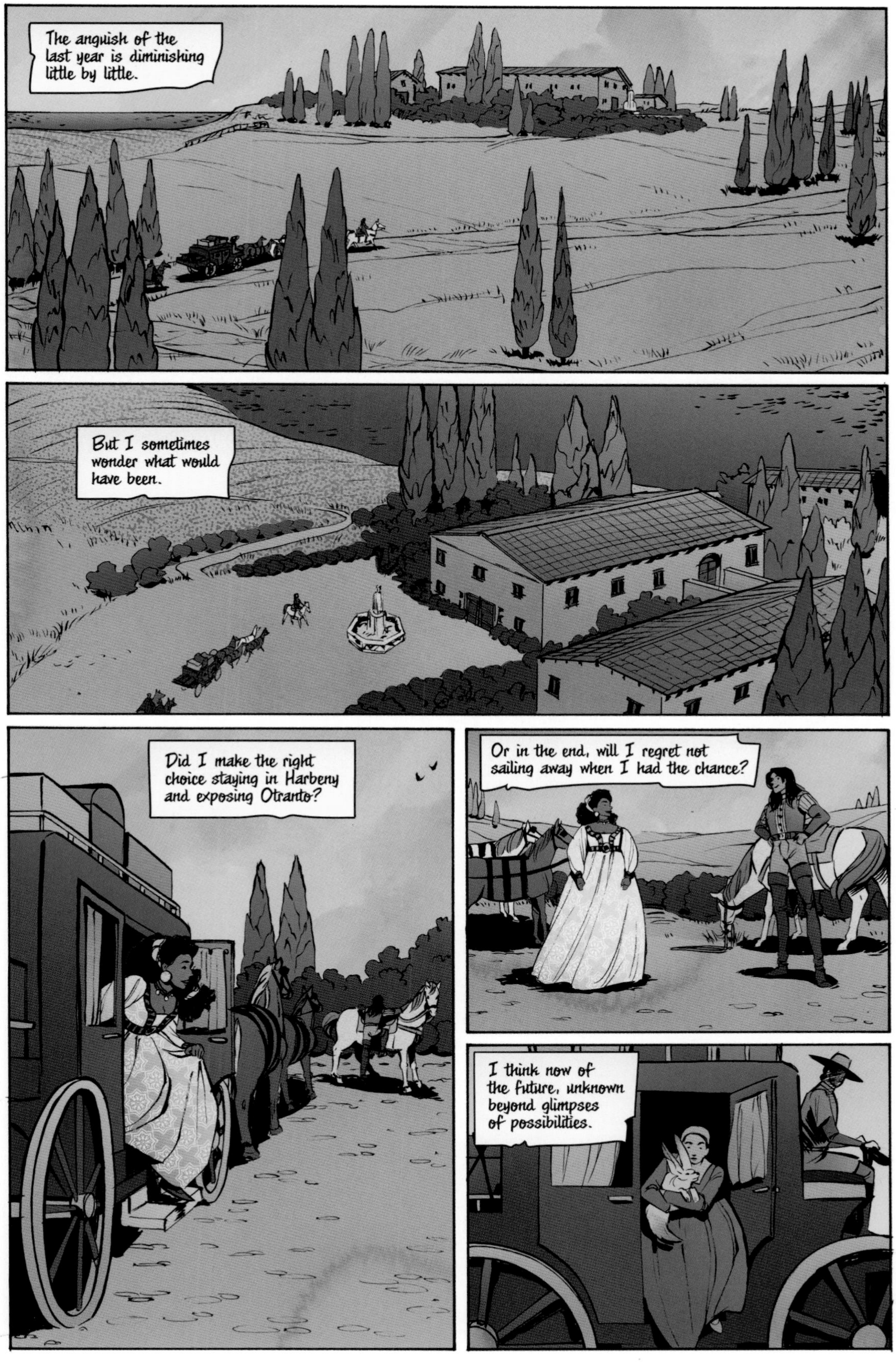
The anguish of the last year is diminishing little by little.
But I sometimes wonder what would have been.
Did I make the right choice staying in Harbeny and exposing Otranto?
Or in the end, will I regret not sailing away when I had the chance?
I think now of the future, unknown beyond glimpses of possibilities.

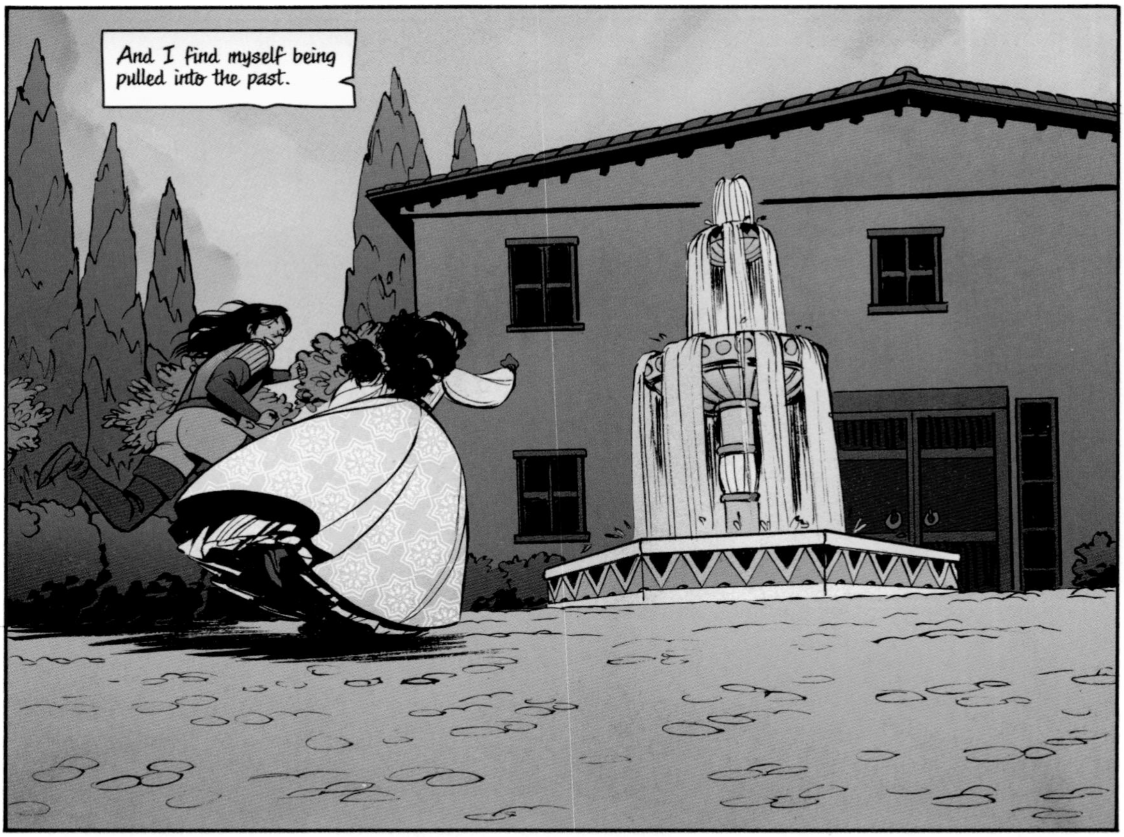
And I find myself being pulled into the past.

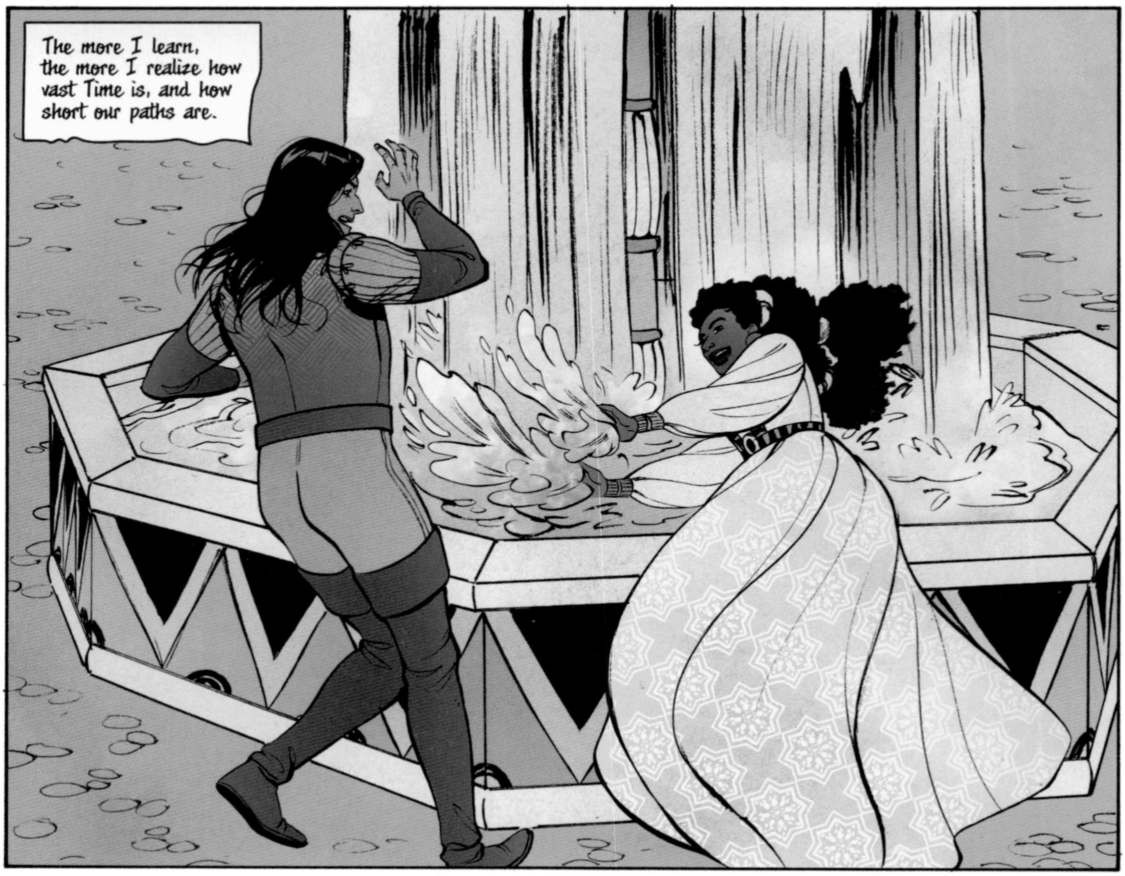
The more I learn, the more I realize how vast Time is, and how short our paths are.

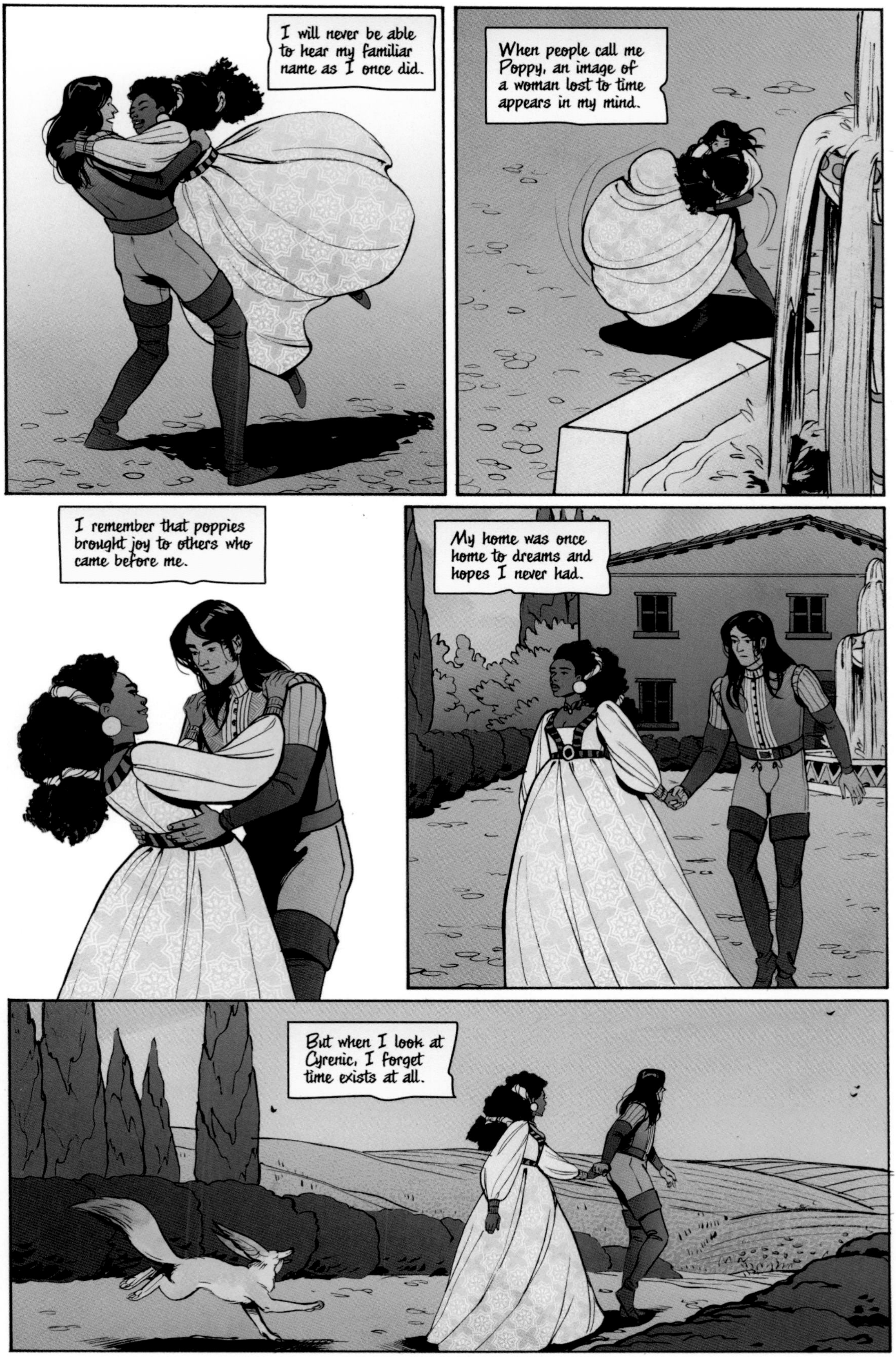
I will never be able to hear my familiar name as I once did.
When people call me Poppy, an image of a woman lost to time appears in my mind.
I remember that poppies brought joy to others who came before me.
My home was once home to dreams and hopes I never had.
But when I look at Cyrenic, I forget time exists at all.

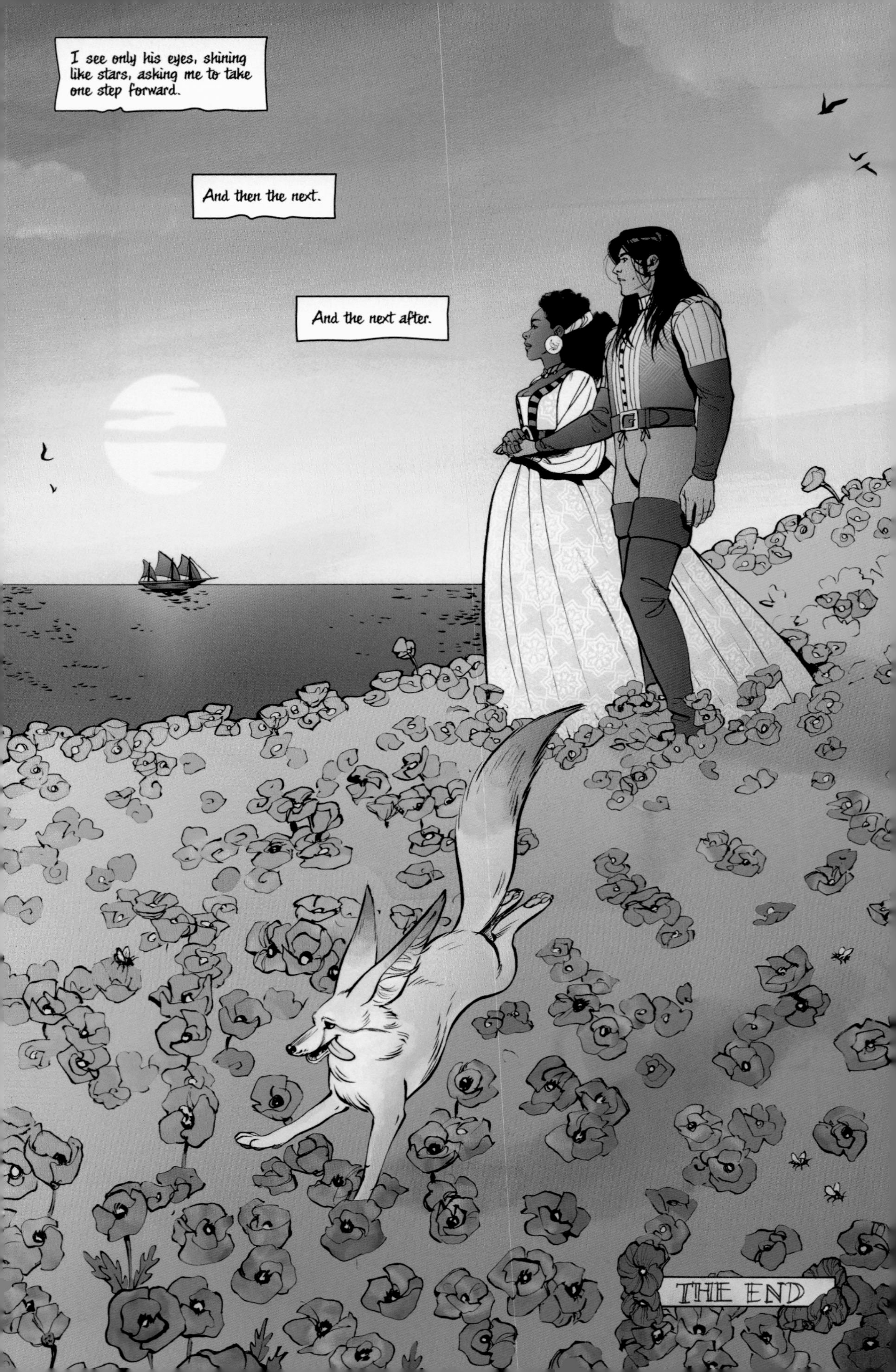
I see only his eyes, shining like stars, asking me to take one step forward.
And then the next.
And the next after.
THE END

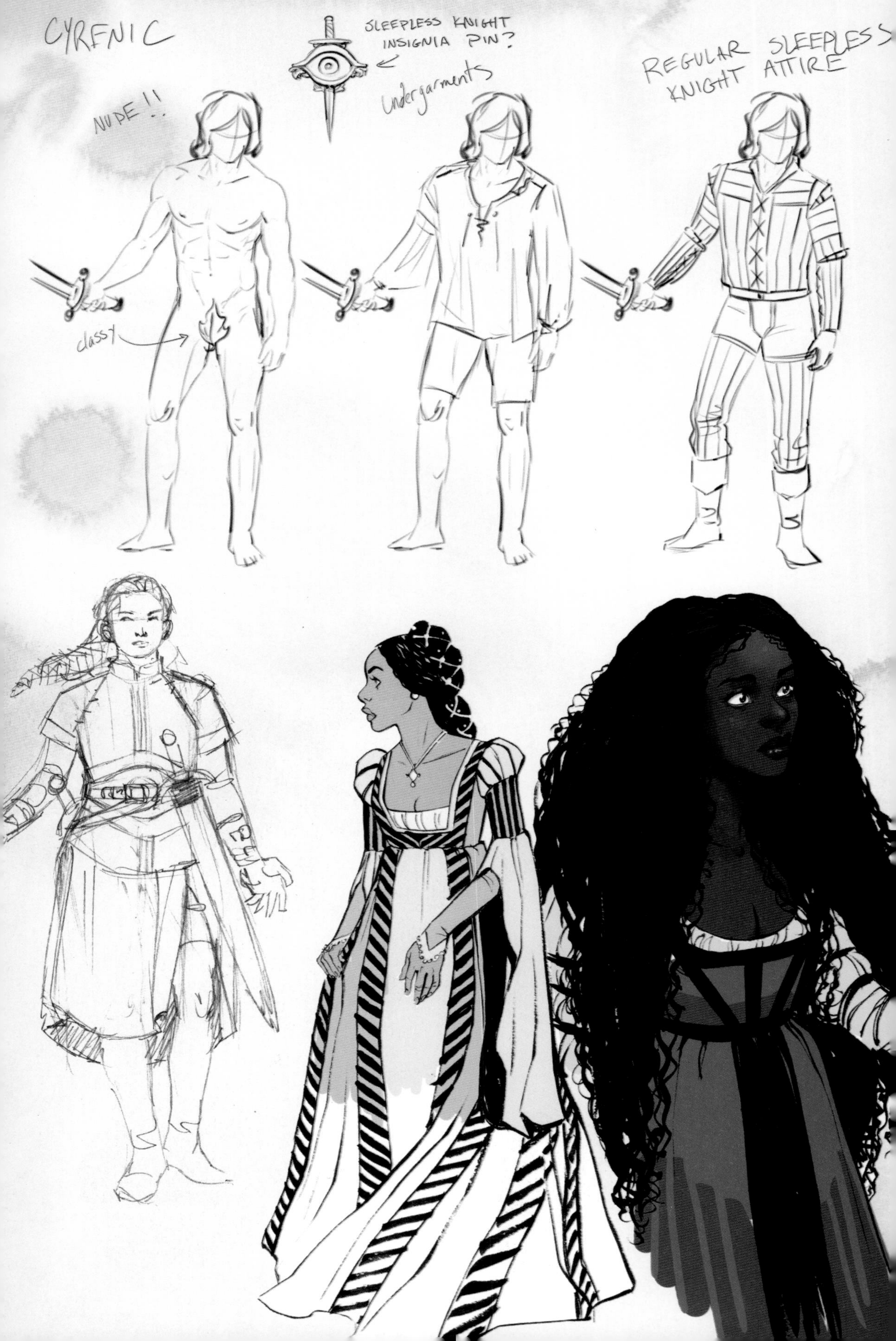
CYRENIC
SLEEPLESS KNIGHT INSIGNIA PIN?
Undergarments
REGULAR SLEEPLESS KNIGHT ATTIRE
NUDE!!
classy

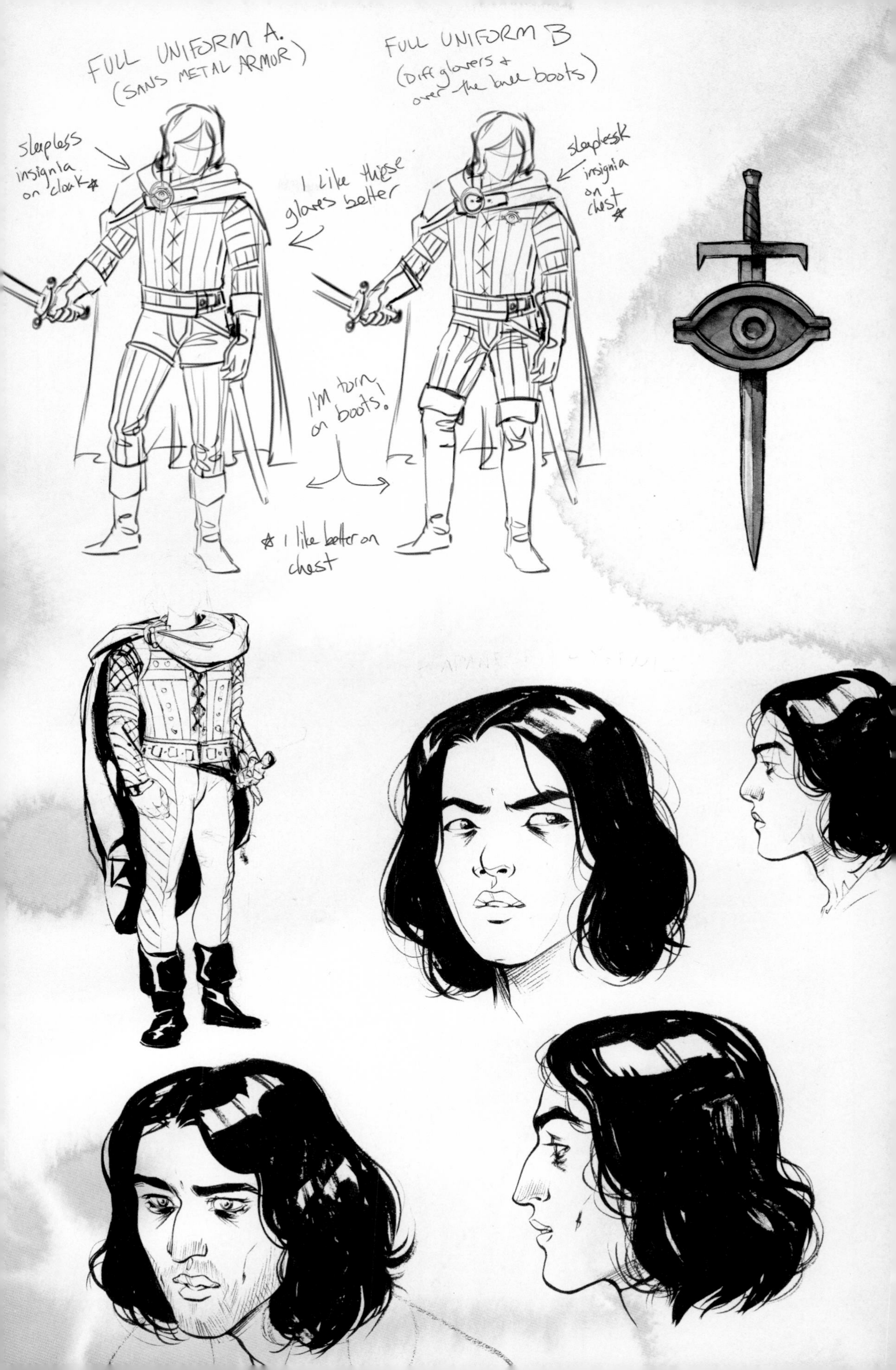
FULL UNIFORM A.
(SANS METAL ARMOR)
FULL UNIFORM B
(Diff glovers + over the knee boots)
sleepless insignia on cloak ✩
I like these gloves better
sleepless insignia on chest ✩
I'm torn on boots!
✩ I like better on chest

PROCESS

PAGE 6

Panel 1
Cyrenic rolls over on top of her.

1 Poppy: I didn't mean for you to come with me.
2 Poppy: I had a plan.
3 Cyrenic: I know you did.

Panel 2
They kiss passionately.

Panel 3
Cyrenic kisses Poppy's neck, his fingers on one of her earlobes.

4 Cyrenic: But I could never have left things the way I did.
5 Poppy: Y-you had every right to be angry at me.

Panel 4
They pant, their foreheads touching. Cyrenic regrets how things went, and a part of him feels guilt for the position Poppy is now in. Poppy doesn't judge him at all. She's just grateful they're together again.

6 Cyrenic: You had every right to release me.
7 Cyrenic: And now I am here, simply as Cyrenic who wishes to help you.
8 Cyrenic: Unless you don't want my help.
9 Poppy: I do. I always want you here.

Panel 5
Poppy looks worried.

10 Poppy: If only we had light.

Panel 6
The glow of a soft magical light surrounds them. Poppy and Cyrenic look surprised.

script

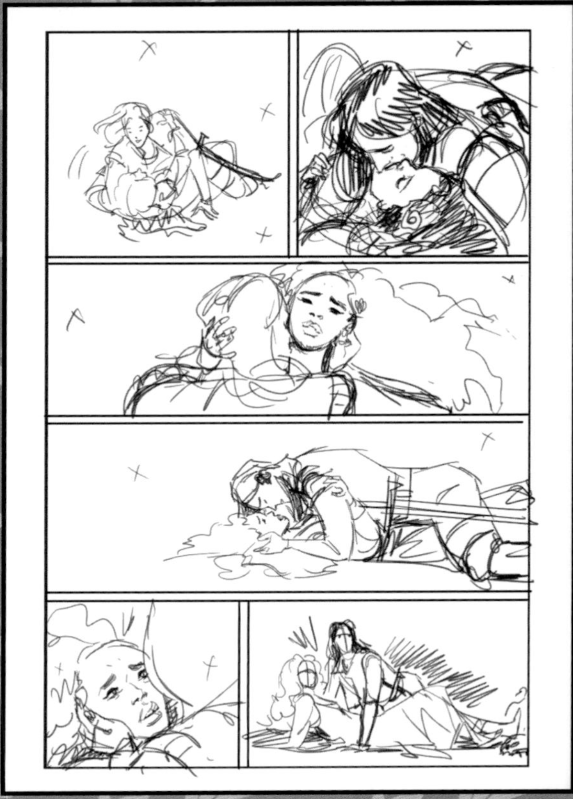

thumbnails

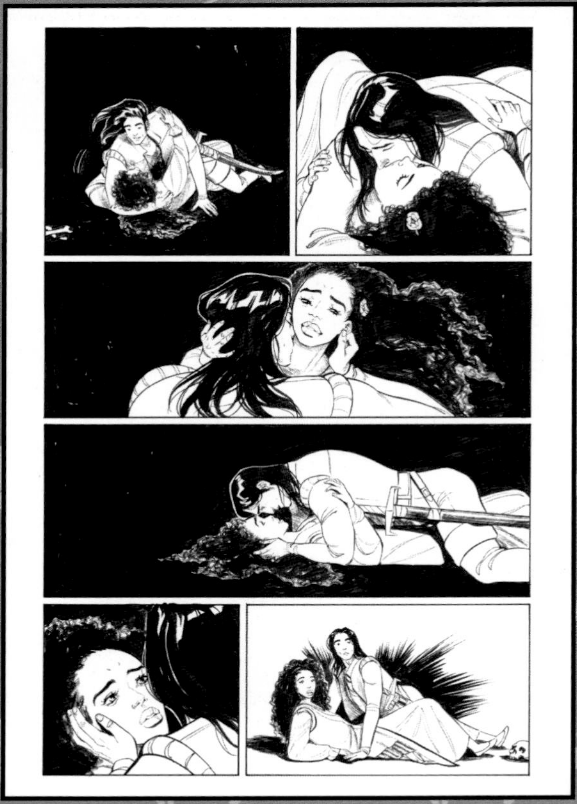

inks

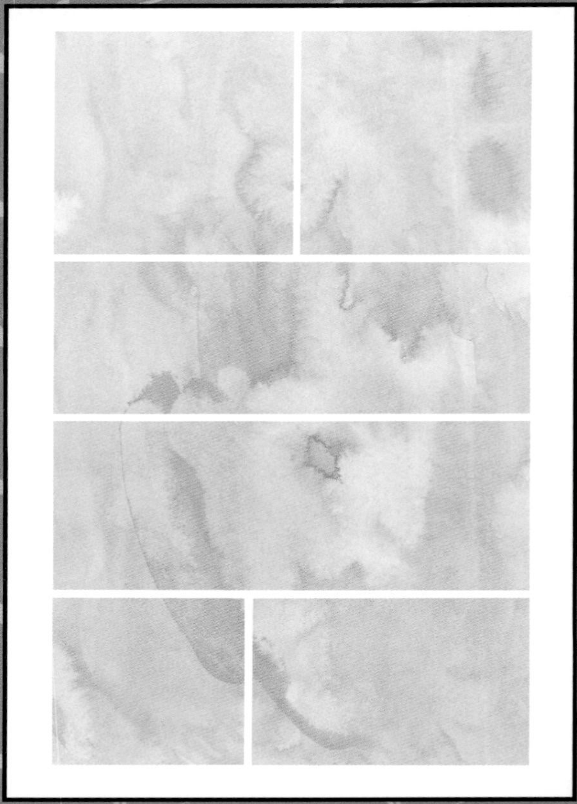

texture

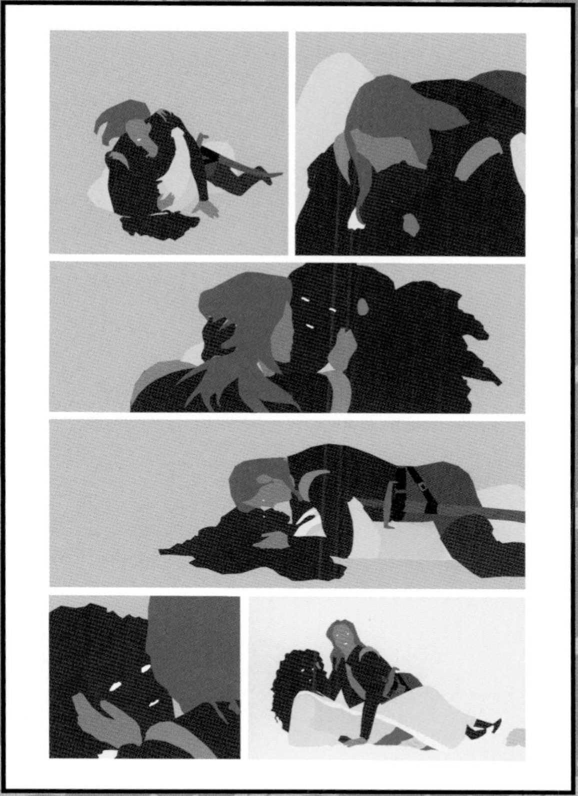

flats

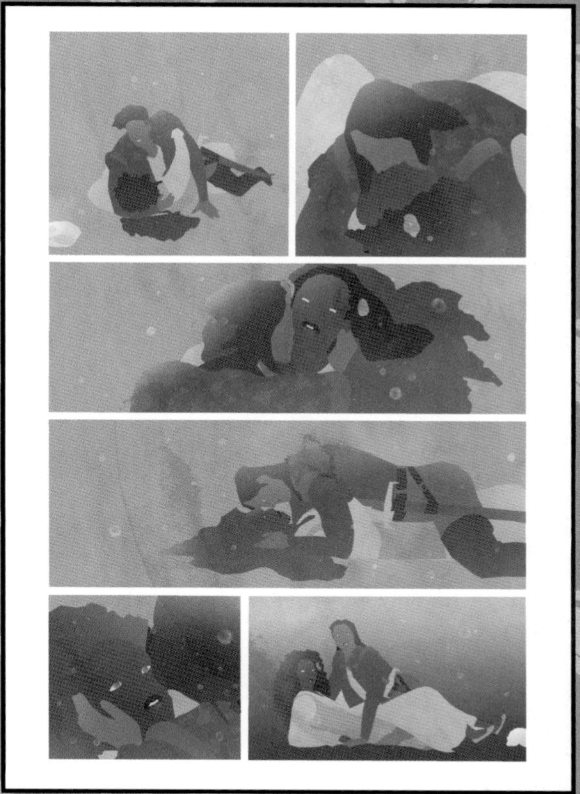

shading

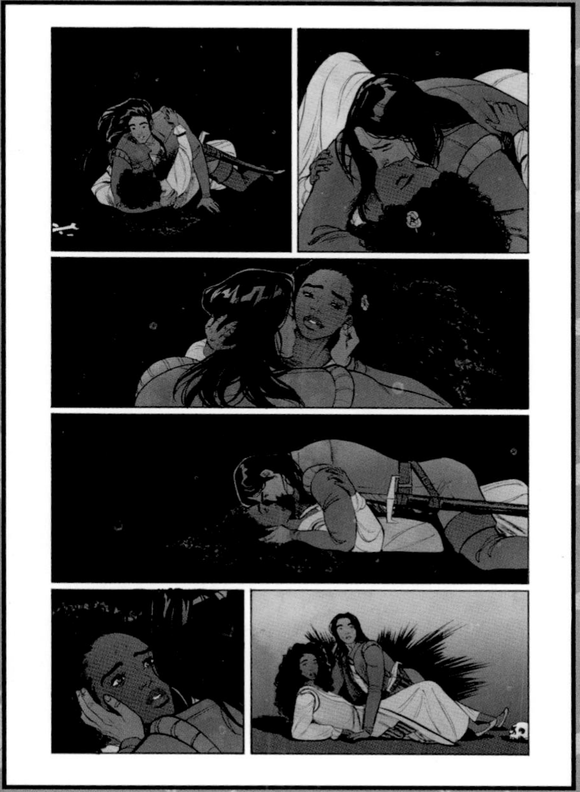

ink layer added

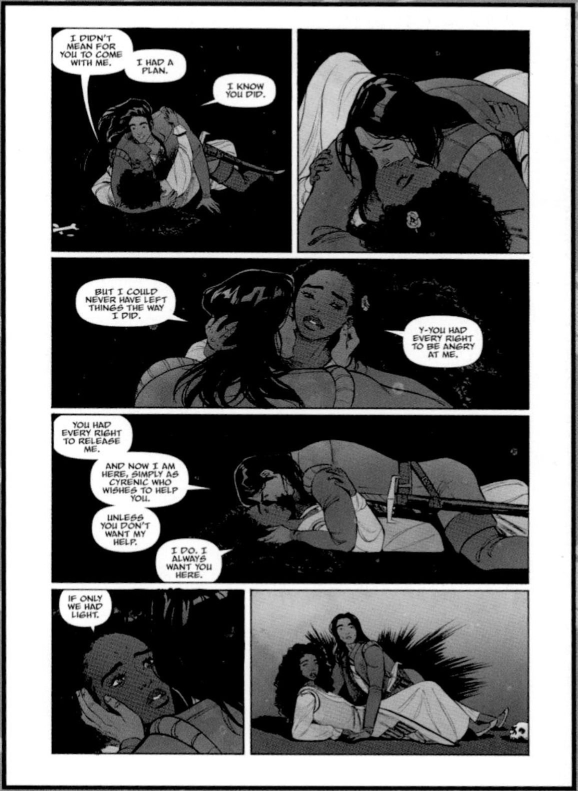

I DIDN'T MEAN FOR YOU TO COME WITH ME.
I HAD A PLAN.
I KNOW YOU DID.
BUT I COULD NEVER HAVE LEFT THINGS THE WAY I DID.
Y-YOU HAD EVERY RIGHT TO BE ANGRY AT ME.
YOU HAD EVERY RIGHT TO RELEASE ME.
AND NOW I AM HERE, SIMPLY AS CYRENIC WHO WISHES TO HELP YOU.
UNLESS YOU DON'T WANT MY HELP.
I DO. I ALWAYS WANT YOU HERE.
IF ONLY WE HAD LIGHT.

final page with lettering

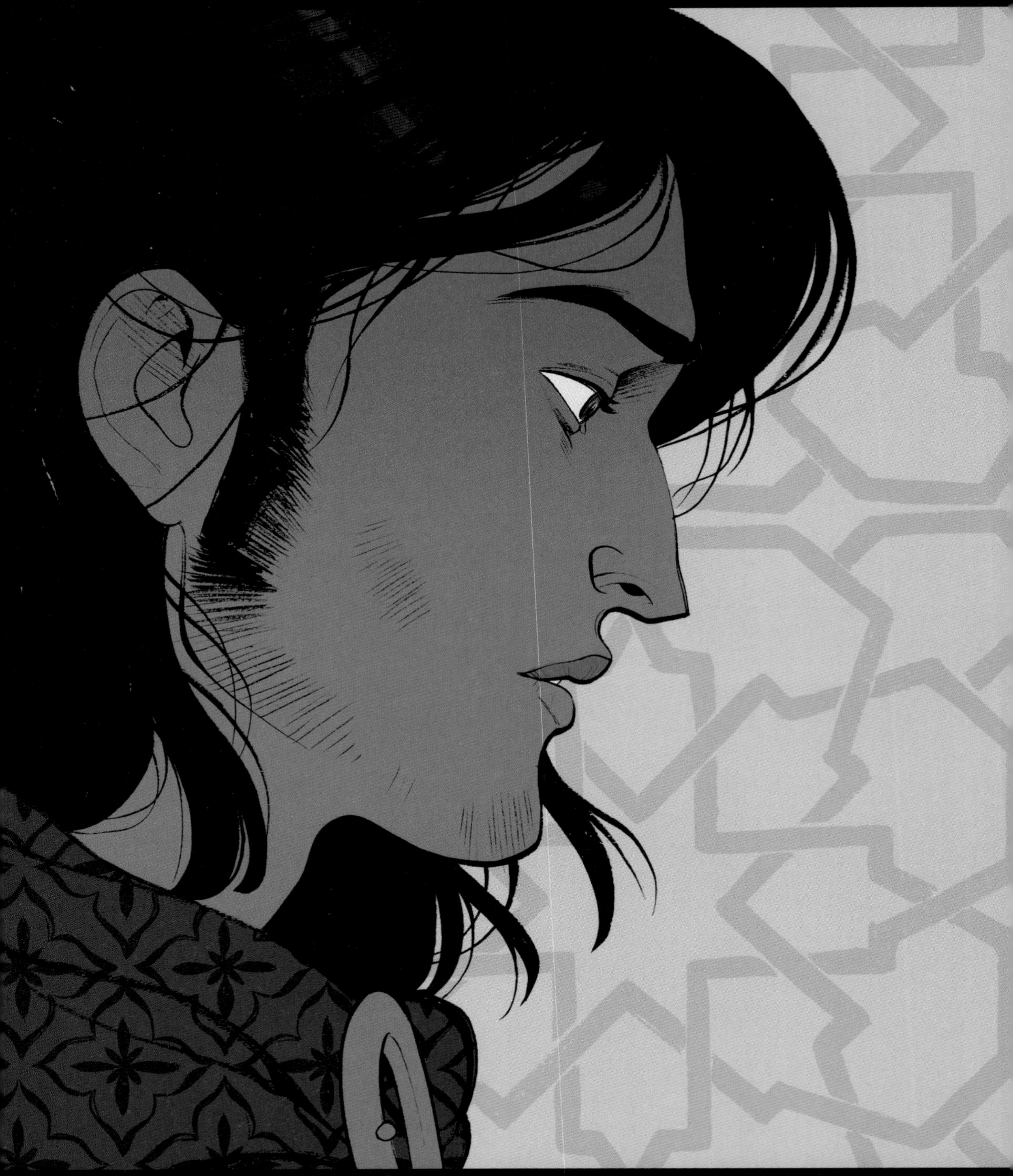

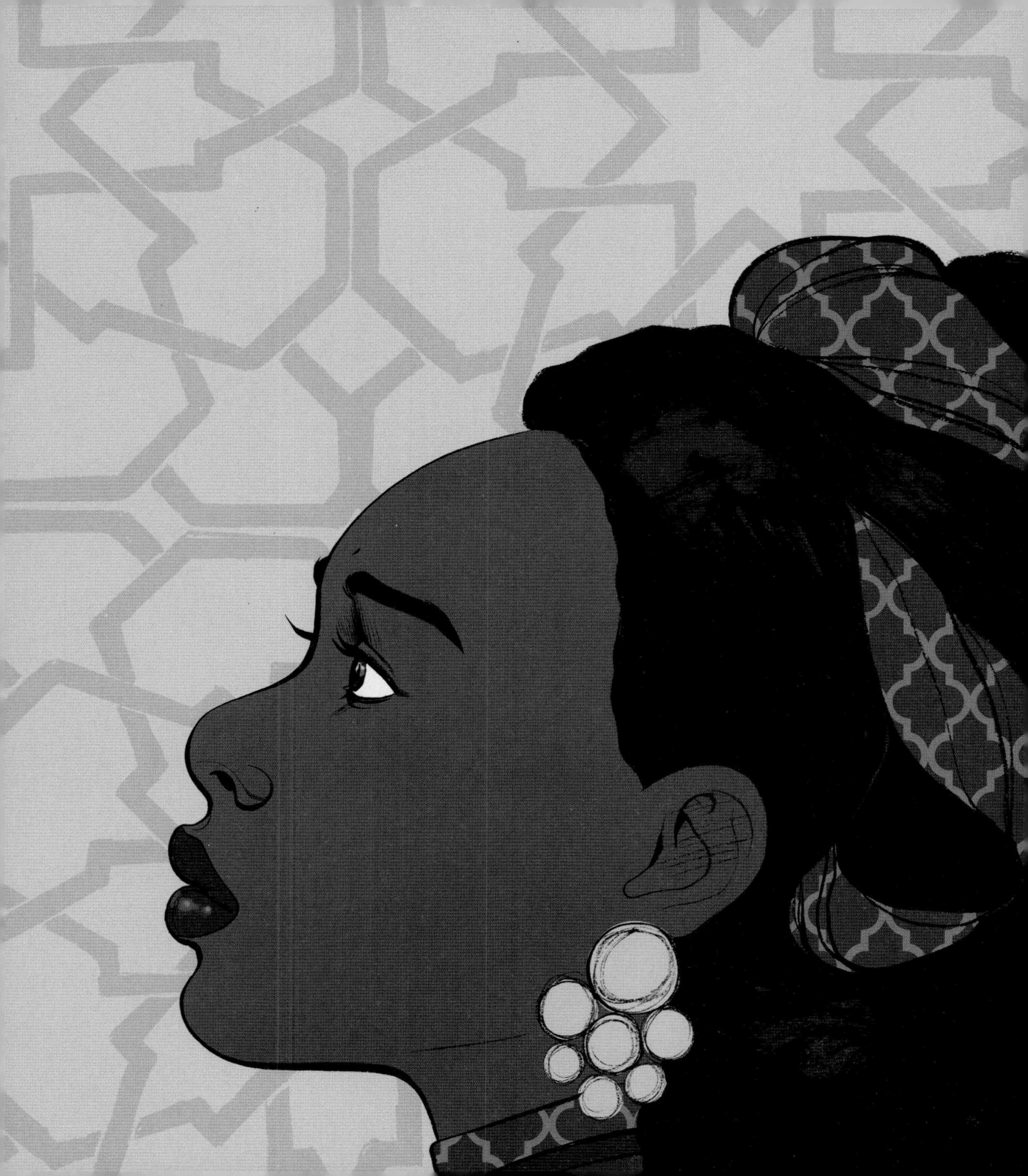

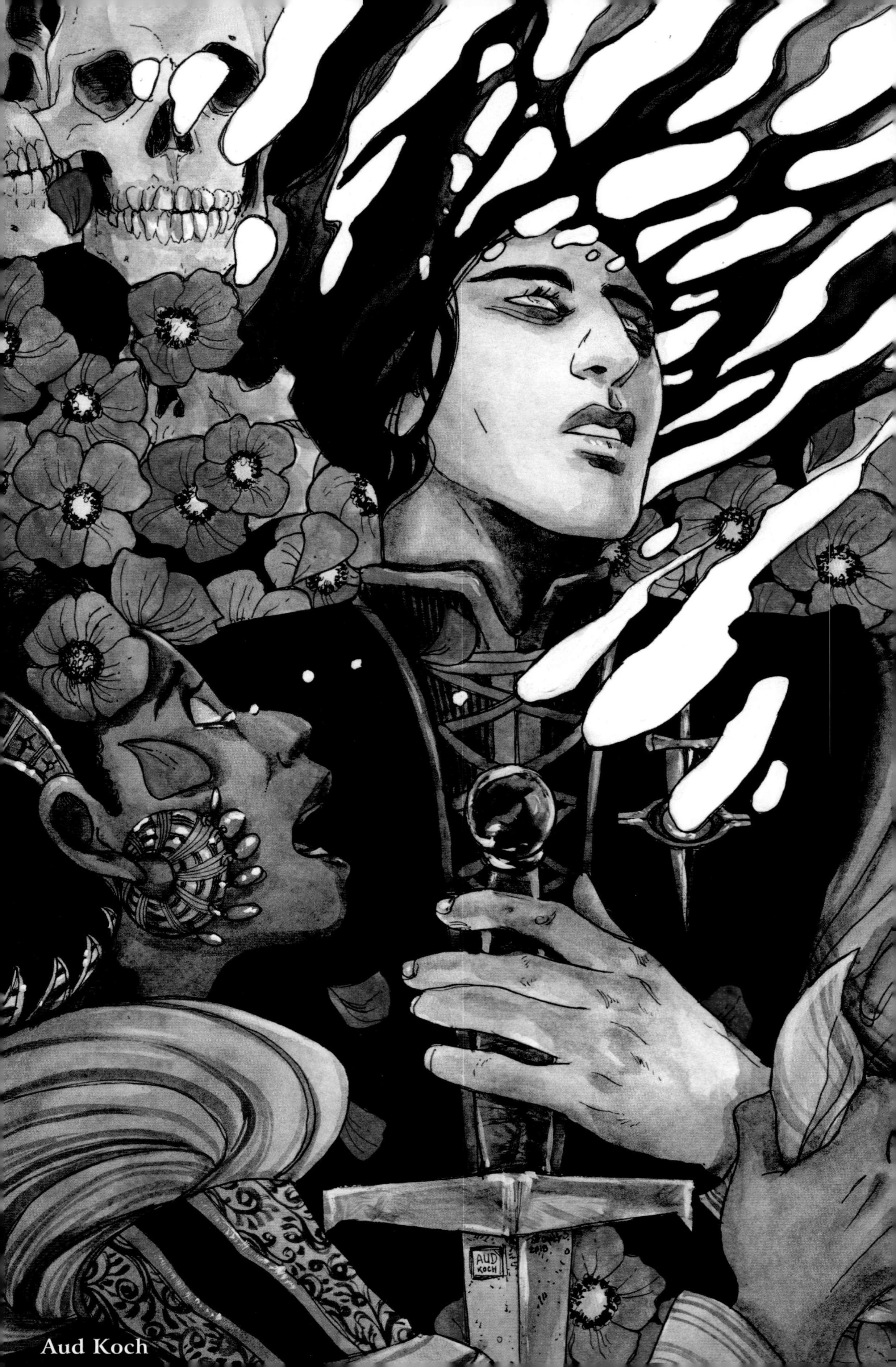
AUD
KOCH
Aud Koch

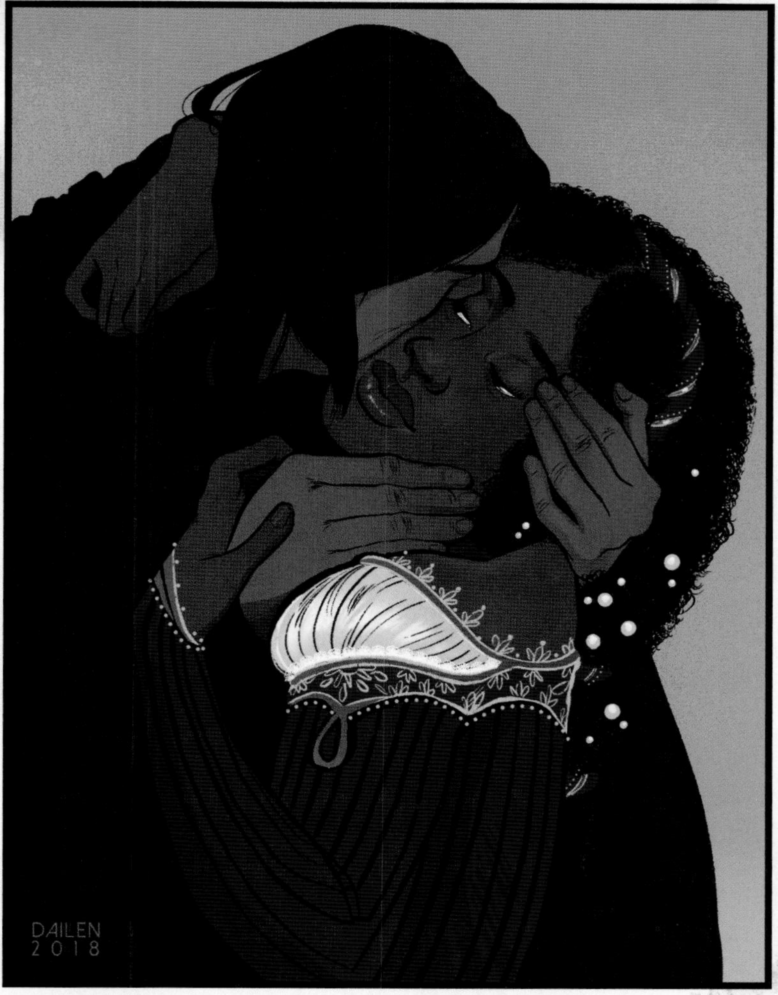
DAILEN
2018

Dailen Ogden

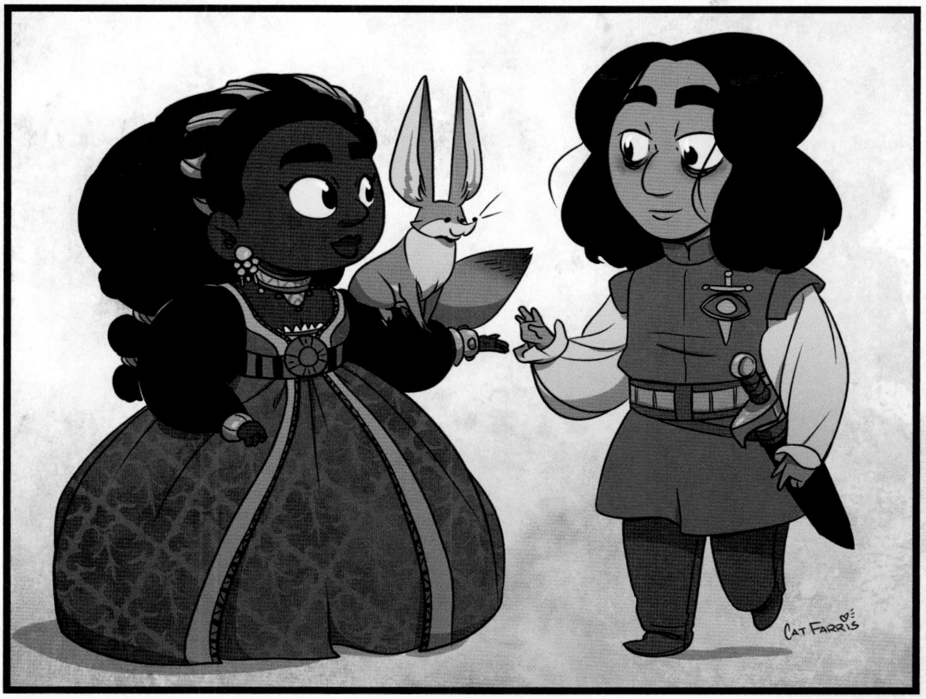
CAT FARRIS

Cat Farris

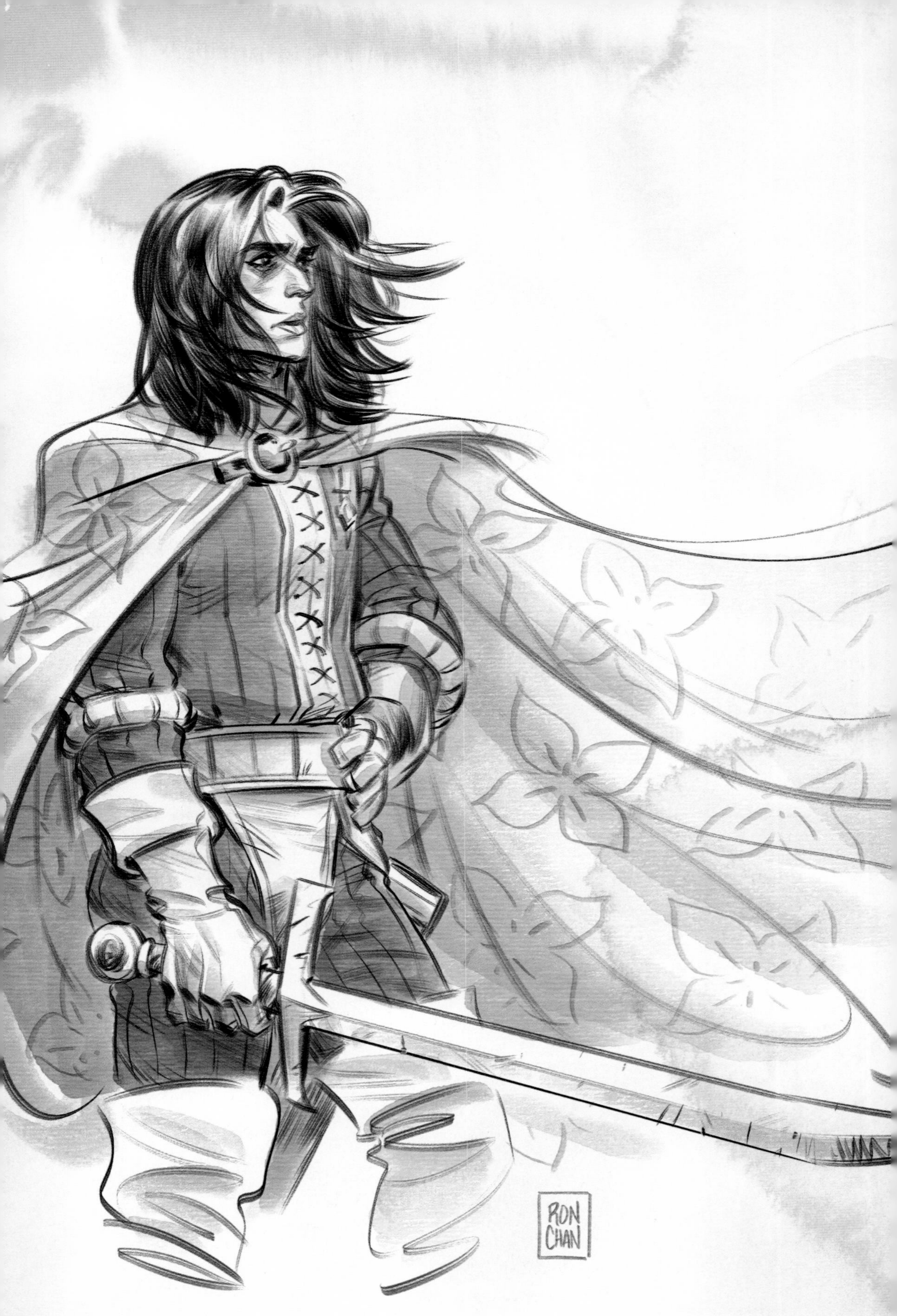
RON
CHAN

Ron Chan

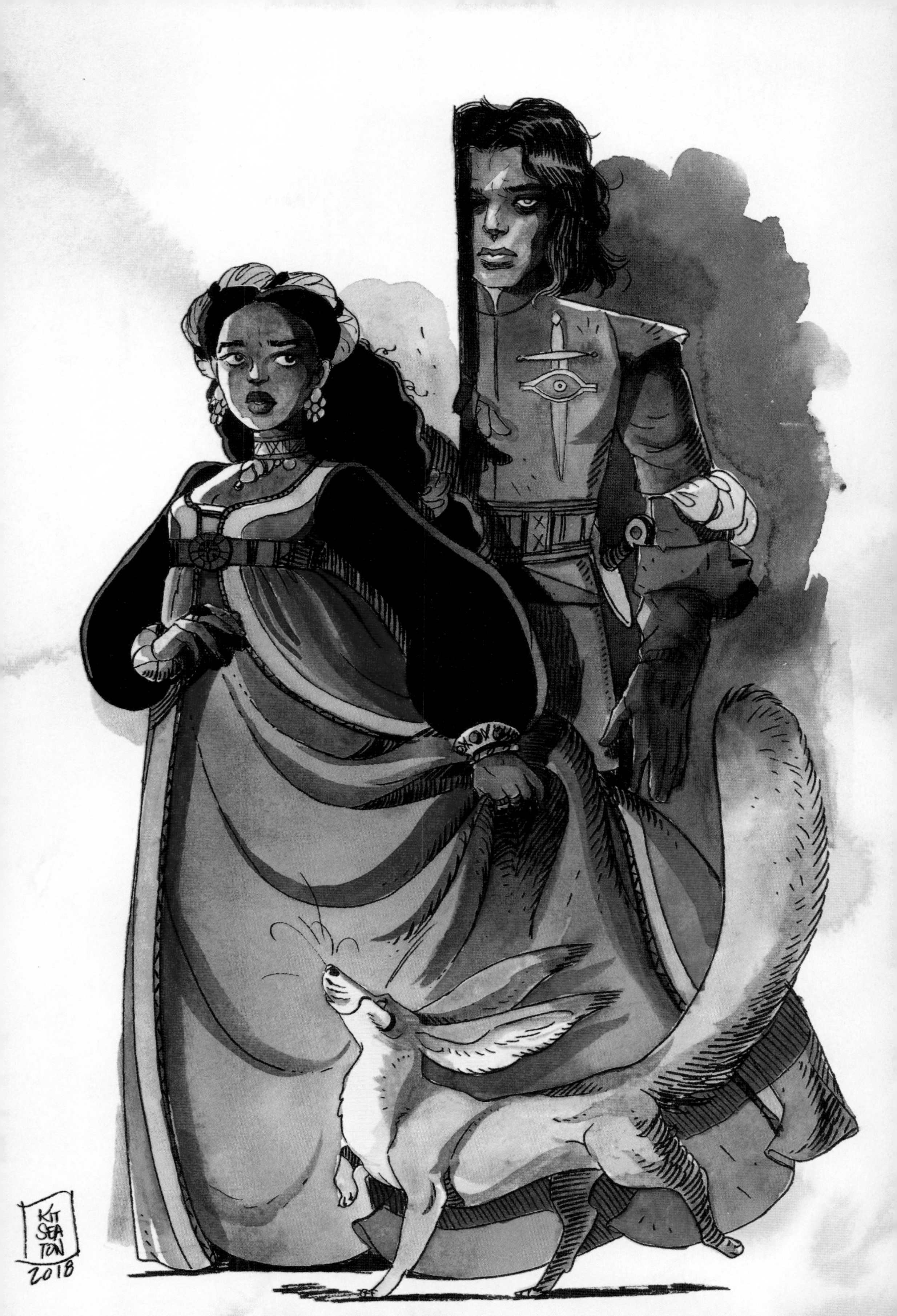
KIT
SEA
TON
2018

Kit Seaton

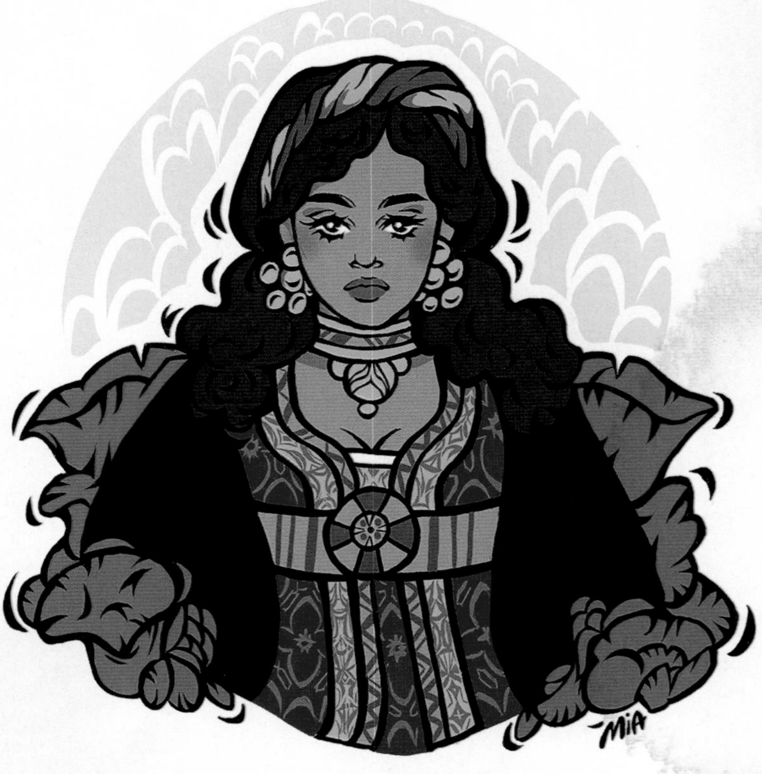
MIA

Mia Carnevale

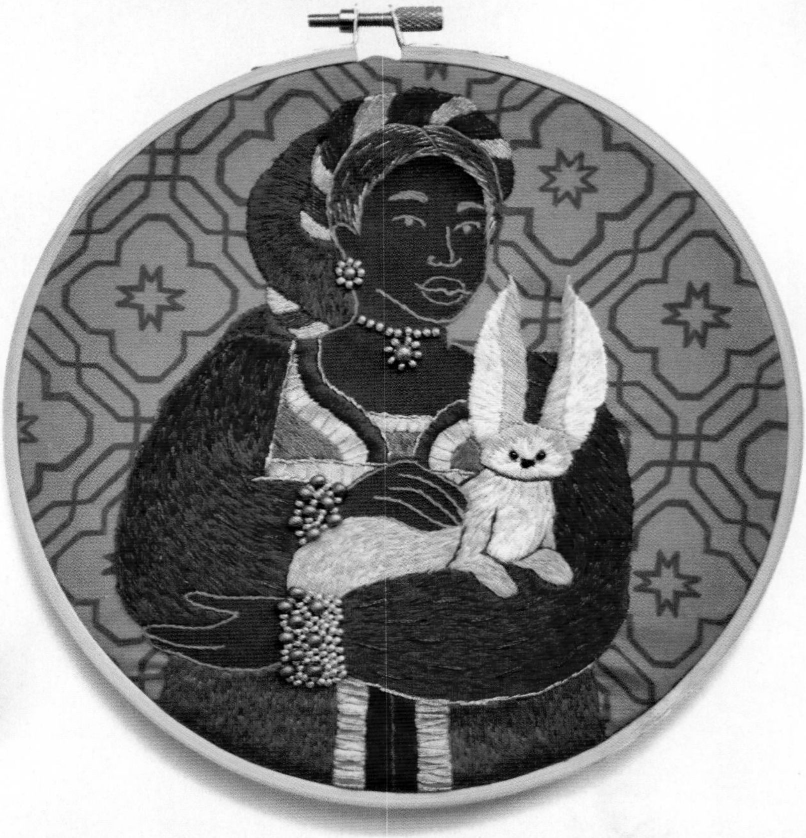

Erika Moen

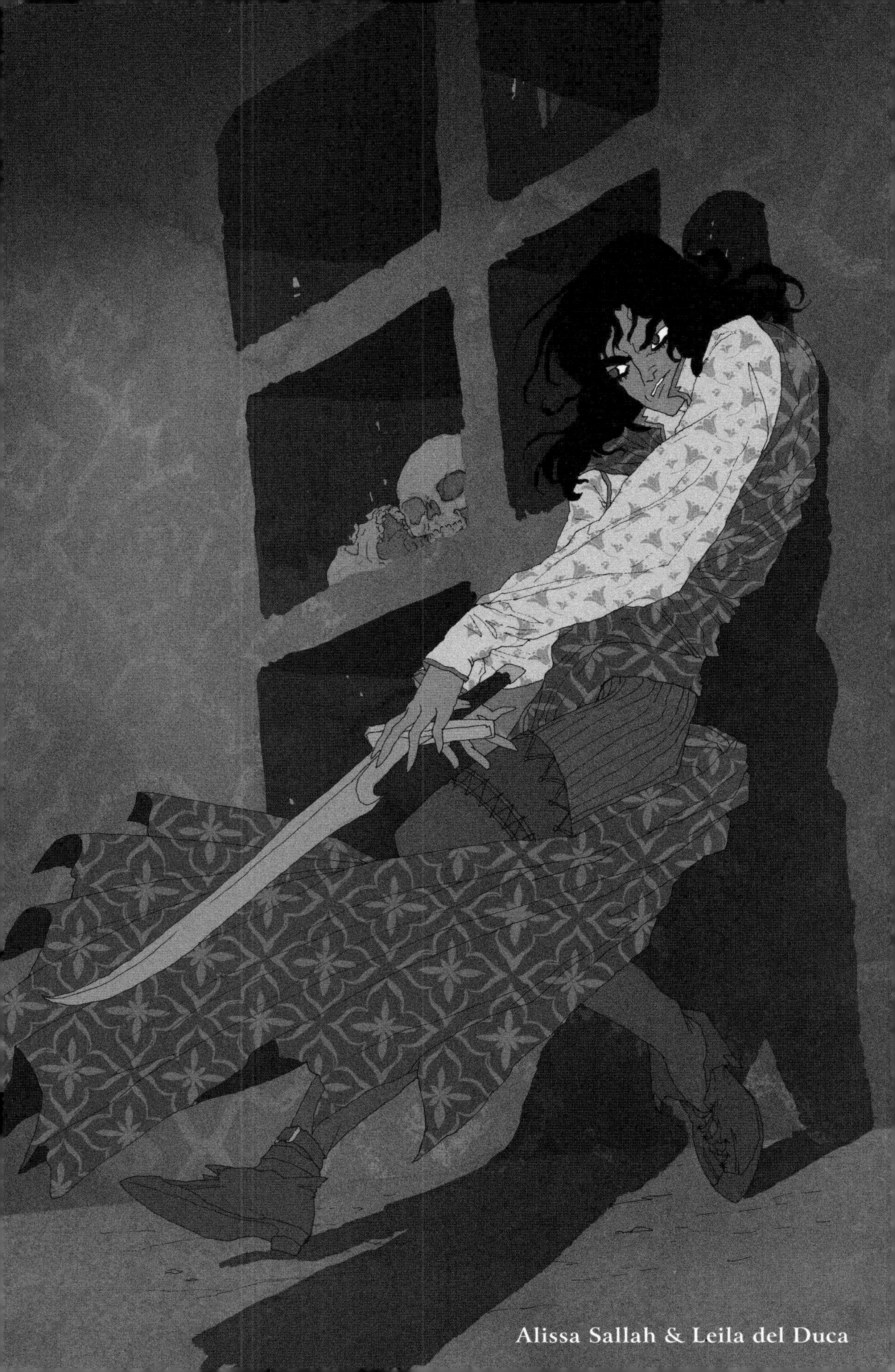

Alissa Sallah & Leila del Duca

CREATOR BIOS

SARAH VAUGHN is the co-creator of ETERNAL EMPIRE and ALEX + ADA (Image Comics) with Jonathan Luna, co-creator and writer of the Regency romance comic *Ruined* (Rosy Press) with Sarah Winifred Searle, and wrote *Deadman: Dark Mansion Of Forbidden Love* (DC Comics). She loves comics, history, fantasy, romance, drama, and fashion, in any and all combinations. Her pastimes have included making chainmail, knitting, and starting things without finishing them. Lately, she has added to the list accumulating historical costumes she only wears around the house, and rewriting bios that she never knows how to end. Her website is www.savivi.com.

LEILA DEL DUCA is a comic book artist and writer living in Portland, Oregon. She draws SLEEPLESS, SHUTTER and writes AFAR at Image Comics. Leila has drawn for titles such as THE WICKED + THE DIVINE, *Scarlet Witch*, *American Vampire*, and *The Pantheon Project*. In 2015 and 2016, Leila was nominated for the Russ Manning Promising Newcomer Award for her work on SHUTTER. Leila is part of a comic artist collective in downtown Portland called Helioscope, where she spends part of her work week. Her website is www.leiladelduca.net.

ALISSA SALLAH is a cartoonist dabbling in being a colorist and editor for SLEEPLESS. She has worked in various anthologies such as the *Spitball Comic Anthology*, *Bonfire Yearly Charity Anthology* (Shonen Trump, Black Water, Silk & Metal), and the BITCH PLANET TRIPLE FEATURE. She has also been featured in the *Yakuza 6 Song Of Life* artbook and spends a sizeable chunk of time/money cosplaying. Her website is www.alissasallah.com and you can find her on Twitter & Instagram as @sallataire.

Eisner and Harvey Award-nominated letterer DERON BENNETT knew early on that he wanted to work in comics. After receiving his B.F.A. from SCAD in 2002, Deron moved out to Los Angeles to pursue his career in sequential art. He quickly became a letterer and production artist with Tokyopop, but soon found himself returning to his hometown in New Jersey to raise a family. There, Deron founded his own lettering studio, AndWorld Design, and has been providing design and lettering services for a multitude of comic book publishers ever since. His body of work includes the critically acclaimed *Jim Henson's Tale Of Sand*, HACKTIVIST, and the enchanting SLEEPLESS. He has also written his own fantasy adventure in the form of QUIXOTE, which is currently being retooled for re-release. You can learn more about Deron by visiting his website www.andworlddesign.com or following @andworlddesign on Twitter.

GABE FISCHER was born and raised in Cleveland, Ohio. He moved to Portland, Oregon in 2015 to pursue a life of comics and guitar repair. He's been a flatter for three years now and is currently refining his color theory and rendering skills to become a professional colorist. A lover of cats, cars, and guitars, Gabe has a big heart and an even bigger beard.